Trembling, Debrah ... ...
ground, and stood before Beladus naked, in the greatest
of fear.

For a long time he studied her, marveling at the milk-
whiteness of her skin, smooth and without blemish. He
saw breasts that were still budding, with tiny pink nipples
surrounded by areolas that were so faint as to be almost
invisible; the breasts of a virgin. He reached out and
touched them lightly. "You will share my bed tonight.
Does this please you?"

She could not speak, nor control her emotions. There
was a moistness in her lovely dark eyes. Lifting up her
chin, he said, a trifle mockingly, "What, tears? That is
not very flattering to a man who offers you his love."

Beladus moved behind her, putting his arms around
her, cupping her breasts and molding them firmly. One
of his hands moved slowly down over her soft stomach
and found the junction of her creamy thighs, and the
fingers touched her lightly. He whispered in her ear: "I
can force you. By the authority of my position, or more
simply, because I am a man."

A tear fell on the hand that covered her breast, and
he raised it to his lips and touched it with his tongue.
"The salt of a beautiful woman's tears," he sighed, re-
leasing his hold and turning her to face him.

Suddenly, with a powerful gesture, he placed his hands
below her waist and pulled her in tightly to him. She
gasped as she felt the strength of his manhood throbbing
against her. He whispered fiercely, "I have women without number, women with skilled hands and lips that drip
with honey, and yet . . . the mere thought of you in
my arms hardens my muscles."

His flashing eyes bored into hers. "One day, Debrah,
I do not know when, nor how, I will make you mine.
With your consent, and with your pleasure. I swear it
to you on all the gods I believe in. . . ."

Other Pinnacle Books by Antoinette Beaudry:

Tropic of Desire
River of Desire

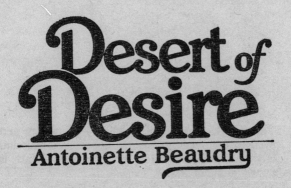

Desert of Desire

Antoinette Beaudry

PINNACLE BOOKS   LOS ANGELES

DESERT OF DESIRE

An original Pinnacle Books edition, published for the first time anywhere.

First printing, October 1980

ISBN: 0-523-40672-X

Cover illustration by John Solie

Printed in the United States of America

PINNACLE BOOKS, INC.
2029 Century Park East
Los Angeles, California 90067

1

The fierce heat of the day had gone, and the dusty plain below the olive grove had changed its color from yellow-gray to a fine red-gold as the shadows lengthened along the broken ground.

The bluff was more than two hundred cubits high, a dark green place of shade where the gnarled old trees had been planted—very long ago—quite close together.

Captain Beladus, his armor set aside now, was pacing slowly among them, wrapped in thought. He was thinking of the historic events that were shaping this strange land of the Israelites, a land of bigoted and self-righteous people who prattled all the time about their one God . . . His own beloved city of Tyre, perched on its little offshore island, was so far away, not only in distance, but in spirit, too!

His steps had taken him to the edge of the bluff, where the sentry was standing rigidly at attention and awaiting any orders; this was the commander, a man greatly to be respected.

Beladus was a tall, muscular man not yet thirty but with fifteen years of soldiering behind him; in the eastern Mediterranean, a young man grew up very quickly. His skin was nut-brown; his eyes were dark and flashing under finely arched brows, his auburn hair and beard tightly curled. He was a Phoenician, and therefore a Canaanite of Semitic stock whose forefathers had

1

come to these parts many centuries ago from Babylonia.

He put out a powerful arm and leaned against a tree, staring down into the valley they called Elah. A little to the west lay the great stone reservoirs and the little springs that were known as Solomon's pools. The waters there, too, were red-gold in the afternoon sun.

He spoke at last to the sentry, not deigning to look at him. "Your name, soldier?"

There was the slap of a hand against an iron breastplate, a salute. "Mirhapi, Commander." He was young and slender, and like so many of his people, a little effeminate. "Run to the camp, Mirhapi," Beladus said. "Send a slave to me with my chair and a goblet of wine. I will rest here for a while."

He heard no movement at all, and he stared at the rigid soldier in surprise. "You did not hear me, Mirhapi?" he asked.

The young man was very uncomfortable, and he said, stammering: "I may not leave my post, Commander. I am a sentry on duty."

"And your devotion to that duty," Beladus said drily, "commends you to me. Go now. My chair, and a goblet of wine."

The sentry still did not move; he was staring straight ahead with dark, unblinking eyes. "I may not, Lord," he said. "If it is your wish, I will raise my voice and call the sergeant of the guard. He is within earshot."

It was a game now, and Beladus tried to hide his smile. "Then give me your sword instead, that I may relieve you as sentry. And then you may do my bidding with no qualms."

Mirhapi, his eyes glazing over, said very quietly; "Nor may I surrender my sword, Commander."

"You choose not to obey me?"

Those blank eyes moved now, and held the captain's cold stare. There was alarm in them, but a kind of stubbornness as well. "I will obey you in all things, Lord,"

2

he said quickly, "and to the death. But I may not leave my post, nor surrender my sword."

The game had gone far enough. Beladus laughed softly. "Then raise your voice," he said, "and call whom you must."

Mirhapi turned and, cupping a hand to his mouth, called out: "Sergeant of the Guard! At once!" He stood rigidly to attention again, and in a moment the sergeant came running, with four archers behind him. He too snapped to attention when he saw the captain, and his voice was like a thunderclap: "Your servant, Lord!"

Beladus moved to the edge of the cliff and stared out across the vast panorama. To the left of the pools, the walled City of David was perched on its commanding hill. To the right, the valley of Elah wound its way through the rolling plains to the sea and the five city-states of the hated Philistines—Gaza, Ashkelon, Gath, Ashdod, and Ekron—which had remained unconquered by the Israelites.

These dreaded sea-faring warriors, of European stock, had come here from Greece, and before that, perhaps from as far north as Scandinavia, tall, blonde immigrants who still wore the Minoan plumes in their iron helmets. Compressed now between the sea and the inland armies of the Israelites, they were constantly bursting out of their confined lands to raid, murder, rape, and pillage.

The captain turned back and said, "My chair, Sergeant. I will sit here till darkness falls. Inform the officer of the day of my whereabouts. And send a slave girl with wine. Perhaps the girl who came to us recently, from Aramathea, I believe. I do not recall her name."

"The girl from Aramathea, Lord, is named Seria."

"Ah, yes, Seria. A dove, burned by the sun. Tell her to bring me wine and . . . the comfort of her idle Israelite chatter. I find myself depressed today, and there is nothing that drives dejection away faster than the foolish talk of a woman."

3

The sergeant saluted and turned away, but Beladus stopped him: "And Sergeant . . ."

"Sir!"

"The sentry here. His name is Mirhapi. I commend him to you as a soldier of merit. Go now."

The little entourage moved off, and Beladus strolled back to where the sentry stood by his tree. He said softly, "You are very young, Mirhapi."

Those strange Phoenician eyes were still staring straight ahead. "Not young, Lord. I am eighteen. And I have been in the army for eight years now."

Beladus raised his eyebrows. "Eight years? Are ten-year-old children now fighting our battles?"

"Not always as a soldier, Lord. On my tenth birthday, my father offered me to King Hiram's Guard as a runner, and I was accepted. At the age of twelve I was admitted to the Swordsman's School in Byblos, and at fourteen—I became a soldier."

"And can you perhaps read and write?"

Pleasure suffused the young man's face. "Both, Lord," he answered. "And if it will not sound arrogant, I wish to say that I do both with some skill."

"It is no arrogance; a man must always be proud of his capabilities. Present your sword for inspection, Mirhapi."

There was a soft sibilance as the weapon came from its sheath. Beladus examined its cutting edge minutely, and laid a finger on its point. He said: "The edge is excellent, but the point is not sharp enough, it needs attention."

"Yes, Lord."

"It must prick the skin of a man who touches it, with even the lightest pressure. When you are relieved of your duty here, you will spend two hours on it with the honing stone. Bring me the sword again at daybreak, and I will inspect it again."

"Your servant, Lord."

"Only a few years ago, Mirhapi, our swords were made of bronze or even of copper, and they would not

4

take an edge sharp enough even to open up a Philistine's throat. But the modern weapons of iron we have today must be cared for in modern fashion. You have leave coming to you, perhaps?"

"Two days, Lord, at the middle of the month."

"You will spend them sharpening the points of our lances. Tell the armory sergeant."

"Yes, Lord."

Two young men hurried up with the heavy cedar chair, richly upholstered in soft red cloth, and set it down at the edge of the bluff. Beladus looked at the slave girl who was with them, standing a little to one side, a wineskin in one hand and a beautiful goblet of cloudy blue glass in the other. She was very straight and slender, with a lithe, sunburned figure and long, untidy black hair that fell down over her naked shoulders. Like all the female slaves in the Phoenician camp, she wore only a kind of kilt, drawn up between her golden thighs and tucked into her leather belt like a loincloth. He said, remembering, "Ah, yes, Seria." He eased himself into the chair and stretched out his long legs. "I believe I have taken you to my bed on occasion."

"Yes, Lord. Three times."

"And I remember we talked once, and you told me something of your people's history." He laughed. "If, indeed, so backward a people can be said to have a history. Pour me wine, child, and sit at my feet."

She sat down on the sand beside him, slowly curling her long legs under her, a graceful, feline movement. He watched her as she balanced the goblet carefully, taking pleasure in the delicacy of her gestures. When she handed it to him, she cradled it in both hands, slim brown fingers curled around it. The sky above the valley was a brilliant gold, and the rocks below cast weird, unearthly shadows on the ground, a vista of incomparable beauty. He murmured, "Even as a man watches, the valley changes its form, its contours, every aspect as the shadows creep along it. It was down there that your

5

David fought with Goliath and killed him, did you know that?"

"Oh yes, Lord, I know it! A battle of the greatest importance to my people. There is not an Israelite alive who cannot take you to the very bank where it was fought."

"And I have never discovered why that unequal combat should be deserving of any place at all in your history."

"Because it *was* unequal, Lord," Seria answered swiftly. "A giant more than six cubits tall, a famous warrior-champion, heavily armored and helmeted and carrying a massive sword and a spear. And he was slain by a young man armed only with a stave and a sling."

He found her enthusiasm very pleasing, and he was happy to correct her. "I use the word 'unequal' designedly, child," he said, smiling. The sling, as you should surely know, is a long-range weapon and very deadly, as the Assyrians have proved in a thousand battles. It can hurl a stone as big as an onion for more than a hundred paces with unerring accuracy. And what use is a sword at a hundred paces? No, the only wonder of it is that Goliath accepted such an unequal duel. Its outcome could not have been otherwise. And still, the children of your people are taught that . . ."

He broke off and stared at the distant pools below. A young girl, dressed in a long gown and covered from head to foot with a goat-hair cloak called an *aba*, was moving toward one of the springs. The slave girl had followed his look, and seeing his interest, said quietly, "By her dress, Lord, a woman of Bethlehem. She goes to fetch water from the pools."

"To fetch water? No. She carries no jar. And the women fetch their water in the morning. I have watched them often. Ten, fifteen, twenty of them gathering there to gossip, chatting interminably, as women will when they should be working. She is very young, I think. She moves like a gazelle."

Hidden among the dense trees of the grove, they

6

watched as the young woman stood by the pool and stared around her as though to make sure she was unobserved. With slow, languid movements, she removed her long cloak and laid it on a boulder. She undid the drawstring at the top of her gown and let it slide down over her white shoulders, her breasts, her hips. She stepped out of it and laid it down with the *aba*, then moved naked into the water.

Beladus caught his breath. He watched as she crouched there and bathed herself. "Beautiful," he whispered, "truly a creature of great beauty. Her skin is like milk . . .

Seria laid her long fingers over her own breasts, bronzed by the constant sun to a deep copper. "The women among us who are free," she said quietly, "cover their bodies completely. The sun cannot scorch their breasts, as mine have been scorched."

"Yes, I have noticed . . . But I think I have never seen a more lovely woman, even in Tyre. Go to my tent, Seria, and send two men to bring her to me."

"Yes, Lord."

As she rose to her feet, he held out his goblet. "More wine before you go."

She poured the dark red wine for him, and set the skin down on the ground again. As she made her way among the trees, she looked back and saw that Beladus was still watching the young girl below.

She hurried off toward his tent.

The young woman by the pools was named Debrah, and she had indeed come from Bethlehem, a tiny village that lay below Jerusalem, less than an hour's walk down the steep stony hill.

After the stifling heat of the day, it was sometimes her custom to bathe her body when she passed this way alone. This hour of the evening was a very special time for her, a time when the glorious copper of the sun cast its last rays over the hilltops. It was a time when the air was still warm and fresh, when the only sounds that

7

came to her were the bleatings of distant sheep and goats and the occasional tinkling of the bells that some of them wore around their necks.

She was fifteen years old, the ward of a wealthy merchant of her village whose name was Uzzi ben Ezra, a man of some importance who owned more than two hundred goats and who dealt in hides as well as wine and olive oil from his own vineyards and groves. The family house in Bethlehem was a very good one, in some respects the envy of all his neighbors.

Debrah stretched her smooth, unblemished body in the shallow water and luxuriated for a while, thinking of the young man she was soon to marry . . . So many times they had lain side by side in the straw of the stables, each of them with probing fingers, exploring their bodies like innocent children, knowing that they could go just so far and no further. He was a very rough-and-ready young man named Joah, and he always wore skins, refusing even to use the cloak she had made for him from the homespun she wove on her loom. It did not occur to her that she did not love him particularly. This was a marriage that had long been arranged for her by her foster father; she was a woman and had no say in the matter. And she said to herself, daydreaming: "And he's really a very *nice* young man . . ."

She left the water and stood by its brink for a while, letting the breeze caress her slender limbs. As she began to dry herself on her *aba*, she saw the two young men approaching her, scrambling down the steep cliff that led to the high bluff above her. They were slaves from among her own people, she thought, judging by the clothes they wore. She hurriedly slipped her gown over her still-wet body and found that she was trembling at the shame of her discovery.

As they drew closer, she saw that one of them was indeed an Israelite, though she was not sure about the other. They wore short tunics of good cotton cloth, and even wore sandals, which was not the habit among slaves. They were smiling at her, perhaps amused by

8

her embarrassment, and one of them said politely: "Your pardon, Lady. My master wishes to speak with you. If you will come with us, please?"

"Your master?" Her voice was shaking, and the other boy said: "Our master, Lady, is Captain Beladus, a Phoenician. Please, you will come with us now."

She summoned up her courage and said, her voice faltering, "And if I choose not to?"

They were both laughing suddenly, like old friends enjoying a secret joke together. The older of the two said happily, "*Choose?* You are a woman, what choice have you? By the blood of Melqarth, no choice at all!"

"Then . . . if you will tell me what it is your master wishes with me?" She could not control her shaking now, nor keep the fear from her voice. She was aware that the Israelite, the younger of them, was no longer laughing but seemed unaccountably saddened. But he said drily, as though forcing a lightness he did not really feel, "I am not in my master's confidence, Lady. But if you ask that I *guess* what is in his mind . . . I can only assume that he wishes to take you to his bed. But you must not be afraid. He is a good man, and no harm will come to you."

She was biting down hard on the tip of her tongue, trying to drive the great fear away, knowing that she was lost now. She held his look and said, "You are one of us, I think."

"Yes, an Israelite from the tribe of Dan. My name is Nemuel, and I come from Aramah, where King Abimelech lived."

Debrah said sharply, "Abimelech was a monster! He murdered sixty-nine of his brothers to become king! Are you as evil a man as he was, that you wish to carry me off like a stolen goat to your master? I am not a goat, Nemuel of Dan, nor even a slave! I am the ward of Uzzi ben Ezra ben Hanamel ben Eliab of the tribe of Reuben! I am a woman of quality!"

"But still a woman—though a spirited one, I see! I have told you that my master is a good man and that no

9

harm will come to you if you do his bidding with good grace. Come!"

She was desperate now. "If I beg of you . . ."

He shook his head slowly. "No good will come of it. You must obey the captain's orders, as I must too."

"And have you no shame that you obey in such servility the orders of . . . a foreigner?"

"A foreigner?" He was smiling again now. "No, Lady, there is no shame. I was once a slave in the service of the great and wise Solomon himself, who sent me to Captain Beladus with instructions to serve him well, which I now do. Serving the captain, I serve your king and mine."

"And your friend, he is not one of us . . ." She was fighting desperately for time now, time for something—anything—to happen that might save her from the shame that was in store for her; perhaps the earth would open up and swallow them all . . .

The older boy, taller and slighter of build than Nemuel, said with a slight smile, "I am Hinnon, Lady, and I too once served a king, King Hiram of Tyre, who is the friend and ally of your King Solomon. So you see, Lady, that you are in excellent company. But I fear we are wasting time that is neither ours nor yours to waste. We will go now."

He took her by the arm in a firm and yet gentle grip, and she knew that further resistance would be futile; the earth had not opened up to receive them, nor had the heavens rained fire and brimstone down on them as it had so often done in past times of trouble. And in a little while, she was facing Captain Beladus in his tent. But in spite of her great terror, the overpowering sensation was one of absolute awe . . .

This was not a tent as she understood it, though it was made of black goat-hair like the tents of her people. (There were still many among the Israelites who considered themselves nomads and would have nothing to do with the squat mud houses that were springing up everywhere.) But there, the similarity ceased. It was

10

enormous, more than twenty paces long and half as much across, and it was lined with fine Egyptian cotton that had been dyed to a bright and very beautiful yellow; she wondered what recondite plants they had used for the dye. There was even a splendid carpet on the floor, so large that she could not imagine how many families must have been engaged in its manufacture! More than a dozen bronze lanterns were hung on the tent poles, and many smaller ones were on low tables everywhere. A slave girl was moving among them, lighting the wicks with a taper that seemed to be made of some kind of wax, and Debrah was conscious of the pleasing lemon scent of the burning oil. (In her own home, they used mutton fat, and the stench of it was abominable.)

And the couches! There were three of them, as well as several stout chairs, all made of the fine cedar that the Phoenicians were sending here from their mountains of Lebanon, with interwoven strapping of leather, all covered over with thrown sheep skins. But to her astonishment, there was not just a single layer of sparse skins as she was accustomed to. Instead, they were laid one on top of the other in great profusion, perhaps as many as six or eight or ten fleeces thick!

But in the center of all this sinful luxury, it was the presence of the officer who had sent for her so imperiously that held her attention, and she caught her breath as she looked at him.

He was, she thought, perhaps twenty-five or thirty years old, with startling, very dark eyes that were not at all fierce as she would have imagined, but instead very gentle and expressive. He was slim-waisted, with a very powerful chest and strong forearms and hands; his hair and beard were almost the color of cedar and tightly curled, with strange flecks glinting in them; had they been lightly touched . . . with *gold dust?* She could not credit it! He wore a beautiful robe of the softest purple cotton bound at the waist with a scarlet sash into which gold wire had been skillfully woven. His sandals,

11

too, were decorated with red and gold, and altogether he was a very imposing figure.

He was lounging comfortably in one of the chairs and eating grapes from a silver bowl at his elbow as she stood before him. He was smiling at her, not at all the monster she was expecting.

His voice was soft and conciliatory. "Your name, child?"

Her head was held high as she tried, very hard indeed and without much success, both to hide her fears and not to be overawed by the sumptuous surroundings. "My name, Lord, is Debrah."

"And do you know your age, Debrah?"

"Fifteen, I think, Lord. My father tells me that my mother began to carry me when King Solomon had been on the throne for five years."

"And your father is . . . ?"

"Uzzi ben Ezra, Lord, a merchant of Bethlehem. But he is not truly my father."

Beladus laughed. "It is the custom among your people," he said, "to talk in riddles, I know that. Uzzi the son of Ezra is your father, but he is also not your father."

"My true parents, Lord, are dead. They were killed in a Philistine raid when I was a child. They hid me under the straw in the stables and I . . . I escaped their knives. But my parents did not. Uzzi ben Ezra, a neighbor whom I now call father, found me and took me into his house. There was none other to care for me."

There was a sudden, even surprising, sadness in the captain's expressive eyes. "So great a pain, for one so young . . . Yes, the Philistines are a menace to all of us. No one is safe from them." The sorrow had gone as quickly as it appeared, replaced by that little half-smile. He said quietly, "Do you know why I sent for you, Debrah?"

She shuddered. "No, Lord. I cannot guess."

"I watched you bathing at Solomon's pools. I will

confess to you, I have rarely seen a woman more beautiful, even in Tyre. Take off your clothes."

She hesitated, and the tears came to her eyes. "Must I, Lord?"

He did not answer her. Trembling, she slipped the long *aba* off her head, and opened her gown and let it fall to her waist. The captain reached for a bunch of grapes and plucked at them, not taking his eyes from her. "No. Step out of it, girl."

"Your servant, Lord."

She let the gown fall to the ground, and stood before him naked and in the greatest fear.

For a long time, he studied her, marveling at the milk-whiteness of her skin, smooth and without blemish. He saw breasts that were quite small and still budding, yet prominent, firm and well-rounded, with tiny pink nipples surrounded with areolas that were so faint as to be almost invisible; the breasts of a virgin. Her waist was slight, the points of her hip bones well defined, and her thighs were pillars of alabaster. His eyes returned to hers and held them; the anguish there worried him. He rose to his feet, and she steeled herself to accept the touch of his hands. But instead, he began pacing slowly, before and behind her, and he seemed to be . . . was it *puzzled?*

The young slave who was lighting the lamps had finished her chores, and Beladus said sharply, "Leave us!"

The girl bowed and went out, dropping the flap of the tent behind her, and the captain stood close in front of Debrah and looked with admiration at her gently swelling breasts. He reached out and touched them very lightly, his fingertips playing with the nipples. He said, "You will share my bed this night, does that please you? It is my hope that it may."

She could not speak, nor control her emotions. There was a moistness in her lovely eyes. Lifting up her chin, he said, a trifle mockingly, "What, tears? That is not very flattering to a man who offers you his love."

13

She tried to find the words to answer him and could not. She found herself trying to avoid the sight of the big couch with its covering of fleeces more than a cubit deep, and she stared disconsolately at the carpet as he began his thoughtful pacing again, moving in and out of the periphery of her vision and not even looking at her now.

He said abruptly, "My name is Beladus, a name that is known and respected throughout the length and breadth of Phoenicia. I am an officer of King Hiram's Palace Guard, at present in the service of King Solomon. I am a man of wealth and of noble birth, entitled—as you see—to wear the royal purple. I am considered to be a sensitive and perhaps overly gentle man. I flatter myself that I am neither ugly nor old, that I am capable of bringing pleasure even to the somewhat jaded appetites of our Tyrian women . . ." He was frowning now, drawing his fine eyebrows together. "Yet when I tell you of the great honor I propose for you, I find you weeping. I do not believe they are tears of happiness. They puzzle me deeply. Somewhat to my own surprise, they even . . . distress me."

Her voice was a whisper. "Forgive me, Lord."

"Then tell me why it is that you weep, Debrah."

"I am a virgin, Lord."

Beladus said drily, "I would not have expected otherwise. But it is a great advantage to both of us . . ."

"Only to you, Lord . . ." Her voice was so low he could hardly hear it, but he said impatiently, "No, to you, too—any child should be glad to be made a woman. And in the span of my life, I have taken scores of virgins, without number. Not one of them, I assure you, has ever *wept*."

"And . . . I am betrothed, Lord."

"Ha! To some unschooled goatherd, no doubt!"

"Yes, Lord. He is both a goatherd and unschooled."

He was mocking her openly now. "But you love him . . ."

"Yes, Lord."

14

"And will marry him."

"Yes, Lord. And I must go to him a virgin still, it is the law."

"To the devil with your Israelite laws! Those of the Phoenicians are more accommodating! *Our* laws tell us: life is short, love where you may, for love is even better than war."

He was behind her now, and he moved in close and put his arms around her, cupping her breasts and molding them firmly. One of his hands moved slowly down over her soft stomach and found the junction of her thighs, and the fingers touched her lightly. He whispered in her ear, "I can force you. By the authority of my position, or more simply, because I am a man. I am sure that you know that."

She was fighting the rising passion in her body, a stirring at her loins under his caresses that brought her to the verge of helplessness.

She whispered: "Yes, Lord, I know it. I know that if you command me, I must obey."

"And while I enjoy the pleasures of your thighs, as white and pure as cream . . . If I look into your eyes, they will be red with your tears."

"Yes, Lord. Without a doubt."

A tear fell on the hand that covered her breast, and he raised it to his lips and touched it with his tongue, and he whispered: "The salt of a beautiful woman's tears . . ."

He moved away from her and began pacing again. And then, to her surprise, he picked up her gown and handed it to her, and said gruffly: "Cover yourself, child. You arouse me more than I can bear."

She heard her own gasp of relief. She slipped quickly into the gown and fastened it, then stared at him wide-eyed. "And may I go now, Lord?"

"No. I have not finished with you yet."

He sat down again on his chair and studied her once more. "Your father who is not your father. Uzzi the son

15

of Ezra, a merchant. Is he, like so many merchants, a selfish man?"

"I think not, Lord. He has always been very good to me. I have never gone without food in his house."

"If I were to make an arrangement with him?"

"He would not sell me, Lord, I am sure of it." If only she could tear herself away, now that she seemed to be safe! But the realization came upon her that she did not really want to.

Beladus was shrugging. "I find it hard to believe," he said offhandedly. "Is it the custom among the Israelites, as it is with my own people, for a concubine to be purchased from her parents?"

"Yes, Lord, it is the custom and the law. But my betrothed is his own son. And therefore, he would not sell me."

"Your betrothed! A fig for your betrothed! And his name?"

"Joah, Lord. "

"Well, then . . ." There was the mockery again! But there was a touch of restrained anger there, too, as though he were annoyed by a frustration he could not readily accept. He went on: "I can easily have this uncouth goatherd killed, and I can offer your father money . . . But then there would be more tears. I do not like to see a beautiful woman in tears because of me."

She held his look, a strange emotion was sweeping over her; she knew that it was not only relief, and this troubled her.

Beladus said slowly, "It is not customary for me to debate with a woman. If I need her, I take her. And why I have chosen not to force you, I cannot tell. An aberration, perhaps, that has come over me for reasons that are beyond my understanding. But I will say one thing more . . ."

His handsome, flashing eyes were boring into hers now. "One day, Debrah, I do not know when, nor how, I will make you mine. With your consent, and with

16

your pleasure. I swear it to you on all the gods I believe in." He laughed suddenly, showing his strong white teeth. "You know our gods, Debrah?"

"No, Lord. I know only the one true God, our own, whom we call Yahweh."

He waved a hand airily. "Oh, yes, I know all about *him*, a very primitive and puritanical deity indeed, not suited to the needs of a cultivated man. We have our Ba'al, and Astarte, and Melqarth, and a hundred others, all of them dedicated to our good fortune and to our enjoyment of the blessings they have showered upon us."

He rose to his feet and took her hands in his. "You may go now. But remember what I have sworn to you on our gods. Particularly on Astarte, who is the goddess of fertility. We will have many sons, Debrah."

The blood was mounting to her cheeks. He took her to the entrance to the tent and opened the flap. They stood there together in the friendly light of the moon, and Beladus said softly, "For the first time in my life, I have met with a woman I greatly desire and not taken to my bed. It is because I believe that in the course of time, your aquiescence will come, even your own strong desire that we lie together."

Suddenly, with a powerful gesture, he placed his hands below her waist at her back and pulled her in tightly to him. She gasped as she felt the strength of his manhood throbbing against her. He whispered fiercely, "I have women without number, women with skilled hands and lips that drip with honey, and yet . . . the mere thought of you in my arms hardens my muscles. Go now! While you still can!" He released her quickly, and she was ashamed of her own longing. "Then by your leave," she said hesitantly, "I will return to Bethlehem."

Beladus sighed. "Yes, to Bethlehem. There is a good moon, but if you wish it, I will send a slave or a soldier to accompany you to your home."

"No, Lord, though I thank you. It is not far."

17

"And will you do one thing for me?" His voice was a zephyr.

"Yes, Lord, if I may." She looked up into his somber eyes, and he smiled gently and said, "I wish to hear you speak my name."

She was trembling, with a different emotion now. She whispered, "*Beladus,* Lord . . .

"Debrah . . . Do not forget me."

"I will not, Lord."

He stood outside the dark mass of the tent and watched her moving slowly away, gliding among the moonshadows of the olive trees. He said to one of the guards, "Call Nemuel for me, and Seria. Send them both here at once."

The soldier saluted and hurried off, and in a moment the two slaves came running. The captain said to the young man, "She goes to her village, to Bethlehem. Follow her, Nemuel, at a distance, you understand? I wish to be assured that no harm comes to her; there are wolves abroad tonight. Do not show yourself, or let her be aware of your presence. And I wish to know where her house is."

"Your servant, Lord."

Seria was waiting, and he took her into the tent and said to her, "You will love me this night, Seria, as you have never loved me before."

He stood by the lamp while she removed his long purple robe and his embroidered loincloth, and crouched on her haunches while she carefully unlaced the straps of his sandals. When he lay back on the couch and sank into the deep soft warmth of its sheep skins, she took off her kilt and lay down beside him, her glistening body close against his, a soft and slender thigh thrown across his loins.

She ran a light fingertip over his aquiline face, tracing the fine arch of his eyebrows, the line of his cheek, the tight curls of his beard. She whispered, "I am never happier, Lord, than when I serve you . . ."

Her gentle hand, light as a peacock's feather, was

moving over the strong muscles of his chest, down across the taut stomach, seeking out his strength and finding great delight in it, caressing him, using those nimble fingers skillfully, as she had been taught. He buried his face in her breast, and pulled her hungrily to him, and plunged deeply into her. He held himself there for a long, long time, knowing that she found as much delight in him as he found in her; her gasping, when the relief came, was a great pleasure for him.

He slept for a while, still joined to her, and when he awoke again he took a corner of soft fleece and moved it back and forth across her breasts till the nipples hardened, and then loved her again and yet again. Her desperate response to his urgency surprised him, and moved him deeply too, and with a sense of shock he thought: is it possible that this sweet young slave girl, in her own way, is truly fond of me?

Sleep came to him at last. Dreaming, he was still conscious of the warmth of her limbs against his, and he murmured, over and over, "Debrah, Debrah, Debrah . . ."

But only half awake, he could hear her brittle voice, talking interminably as she always did, and phrases floated to him out of the limbo that surrounded him: "Gideon, yes, it was after the period of Joshua's invasion . . . he was the fifth of the judges . . . the struggle between the Desert and the Sown . . . of the tribe of Manasseh who was the son of Joseph . . ."

He shrieked, "Be silent, woman, and love me . . !"

Under her expert ministrations, he fell into deep sleep again.

2

Twice on her journey across the moonlit hills, Debrah was sure she had heard the soft sounds of stealthy movement behind her.

The first time, there was the faint slithering of gravel that could have been caused by a lost goat, perhaps; but if it was a goat, and it was lost, why was it not bleating?

A wolf, then? Or even a bear? She quickened her footsteps, her heart beating fast. And then, there was definitely the sound of lightly running feet, and for a moment she was sure that she was in terrible danger. She moved quickly to one side and hid among the dark boulders. She cowered on the ground and waited, and in a moment she saw the slight figure of Nemuel passing very close to her hiding place.

"A slave or a soldier to see you to your home," the fine captain had said, and she knew what was happening. The thought gave her great pleasure, but she waited for him to go on his way and thought of the handsome Beladus. He was so tall and straight and gracious! And of a refinement she had never seen before! And the luxury of his tent! She wanted to weep when she thought of all those soft sheepskins piled up in such abundance, and imagined herself sinking into them, feeling the warmth of the fleece at her naked back as he took her; she could still feel his hands at her breasts, burning her with a sense of her own desire.

There was no more sound from Nemuel, searching far ahead of her now, and she rose to her feet and went on her way. She could not drive the image of Captain Beladus from her mind, and as she climbed slowly on up the hill, she tried to remember all that her father had ever told her about these strange people, the Phoenicians.

Industrious and highly artistic, they had come to the Mediterranean coast centuries ago from what they called 'an eastern shore,' by which they meant Babylonia. They were Canaanites, and their language was very close to both Hebrew and Moabite, as well as to the Aramean of northern Syria; each in his own tongue could converse easily with the others in theirs. Now, they were friends and allies of the great Solomon, whose father David had first invited them to Israel from their coastal cities—Acre, Tyre, Sidon, Beirut, Byblos, Sarafand, and others—to build temples and palaces, and above all ships, as only the Phoenicians knew how to build them. They were constructing a great port and a fleet of ships at a place in the far south called Ezion-Geber, a port that would open up trade with Ophir and the distant Indies. The world's greatest trade route now ran from Europe to the city-states on the coast, on to Jerusalem, down the desert to the Reed Sea, that great lake that Moses had parted while leading their people out of Egypt, and on to the rich, mysterious East. And Solomon's tiny kingdom lay astride this great commercial highway.

But the angry Philistines, whom the Greeks called *Palaestines,* were at Israel's throat, as ever. And to protect the arduous convoys from Lebanon to the south and back—cedarwood, other building material, and artisans in one direction, with payment in oil, copper, and gold in the other—the two friendly kings had stationed troops along the route of march.

Captain Beladus, a noble of King Hiram's Palace Guard, was one of the soldiers posted along the trade

21

route. His assigned territory was the valley of Sorek, which spilled out of Philistia and ran almost all the way to Jerusalem itself, together with the valley of Elah to its south, and as far north as the twin towns of Beth Horon, which commanded the ancient road; these two towns lay half a day's march away and had been fortified by Solomon.

He had been posted here just a few weeks ago. He did not know it, but he was being exiled from Hiram's court because of his outspoken and very unsoldierly concern for the oppressed and the unloved. The creed of the nobility was: *Take what you want, and the peasants will pay for it.* And Beladus, though a soldier, was a gentle and scholarly man, and he did not approve.

The king had called him to audience, and had said to him, reclining on his cushioned marble couch: "I am sending you to Jerusalem, good Beladus, to help Solomon keep those damned Palaestines away from our convoys. We are sending our cedar by raft down the coast to Joppa, sometimes landing it on the beaches of the plain of Sharon, and this raises very little difficulty. But from there to Jerusalem it's two or three days of constant harassment, with raiders springing up from behind every rock. Worse, we're being attacked on the return journeys that bring us our payment. Why, in the last month alone, I've lost more than four talents of gold in olive oil, and I'm not prepared to accept such losses. They don't steal it, you know. They simply cut open the skins and let it all drain out into the sand, the finest pressed oil in the world! They're savages! Solomon will furnish you with quarters in the city if you can stand the stench of it—it's not a very civilized place. But if you can't, you have my permission to find a good defensive site outside the walls."

He had snorted contemptuously. "Ha! A city, they call it! A hard-working farmer could plough up the whole of it in twelve days! Why, Solomon himself won't live there; we're building his Temple and his Palace outside the walls."

It was an important assignment, and Beladus was quite unaware that Hiram was merely getting rid of him. The talk went on for more than an hour, and the king said: "Come, let us take a look at the charts the cartographers have prepared for me. They are not very accurate, of course; just what the simple Israelites call 'doing their humble best'."

They moved to the great map table that had been set out in Hiram's favorite room, bordered by tall marble columns, with a balcony that overlooked the blue sea. He stabbed at the map and said, "Here, there's no border between Palaestine and Israel, but if there were, the valley of Sorek would cut right through it. It's ideal country for raiders, and I learn there's a fearsome fighting man named Akish there somewhere, with a guerrilla band of some competence, two or three hundred strong."

"And how many men, Lord," Beladus asked, "will I have at my disposal?"

"You'll have three hundred of our best troops, perhaps a few more if and when they can be spared. I want these raids to stop, Beladus."

The captain said impetuously, "I will send you the head of this man Akish, Lord."

Hiram interrupted him brusquely. "No, I fear that you never will, for he's a formidable man. Never engage him in personal combat, or I'll lose a good commander and a dear friend." He sighed. "Has it ever occurred to you that even the Israelites are better soldiers than we are? And that the thrice-damned Palaestines are better still?"

"I will not agree," Beladus said. "But if it is true, there is a reason for it."

"Oh?" Hiram's bushy eyebrows shot up. "And what is that?"

"Ours, Lord, are the arts of peace. I would not wish it to be otherwise."

"And still," the king observed drily, "I do not wish

to learn of my good olive oil running to waste in the thirsty sand."

"It will cease, Lord, you have my promise."

"The troops will be at your disposal by morning. I want you to report to Solomon personally as soon as possible. Take a quinquereme to Joppa, and thence, the fastest horses you can find."

"Your servant, Lord."

"Give Solomon my compliments in the most fulsome terms you can devise. Above all, congratulate him on his recent marriage to that Egyptian whore, the daughter of Pharaoh Siamon. Say to him, in my words: 'A fine stroke of diplomacy, friend and brother, which can only add stature to the alliance'."

"I will do so, Lord."

"They say she's very beautiful, though her father's a nonentity. And how he's ever going to find the time or the energy to service her, only the gods can know."

"Perhaps Astarte knows," Beladus murmured, and the king dissolved in laughter. "Astarte knows!" he echoed. "Friend, I will miss you! I will confess that your philosophies sometimes disturb me, but I find your sense of humor refreshing."

Beladus was startled. "My philosophies, Lord?" he asked. But Hiram would not be drawn. "Go now," he said, "I will spend some time with my women. And perhaps after all you may send me the head of that terrible fellow Akish, if it pleases you."

Beladus bowed and withdrew, and King Hiram went back to his chamber and rang the little copper bell that would summon the master of the king's house. His name was Ardru, an old man bent with the weight of his years, his long beard white and flowing. He doubled up his old body and said, "Your pleasures, Lord?"

"Food, Ardru," the king said. "Good red meat, and wine, and some women."

"Immediately, Lord."

"There is a girl who was brought to us a few days

24

ago, from Sarafand. Very young, with strange grey eyes?"

"Her name, Lord, is Epipheset, a virgin still."

"Good. Inform her that if she does not arouse me, her head will be on the block in the morning."

"As you say, Lord."

"And two others. One a little older, the other a little more plump. I leave the selection to you, Ardru."

"Your confidence does me honor, Lord."

"And if you disappoint me—your head too on the block."

The old man backed out, and the king lay down on his couch to await the ministrations of his women. He was very pleased with the arrangements for Beladus, knowing that he had assured the safety of his convoys, and had at the same time rid himself of a man whose views were sometimes quite troubling.

And a week later, Beladus met with King Solomon.

Somewhat to his dismay, he had been handed over almost at once to the master of amenities, after a brief, though very friendly, exchange of courtesies. Solomon was gracious and apologetic, but he was in conference, it seemed, with some of his generals, who wanted to send the Israelite armies over the northern border on the banks of the Euphrates, even as far as Nineveh on the Tigris. The king would have none of it; there was trouble enough in his vassal states of Damascus and Edom.

Very quickly, Beladus's dismay was turning to consternation.

First of all, the minuscule size of Jerusalem astonished him. Hiram had spoken of ploughing up the whole of it in twelve days, one hard-working farmer . . . He had taken this to be an exaggeration, but it was indeed true. He soon found out that the area of the city was a mere thirteen yokes; and since a yoke among the Hebrews was the area a farmer could plough between sunup and sundown, Hiram's estimate was almost correct. A man could walk around its walls completely in seven or eight minutes.

And *this* was a city? The buildings were squat and ugly and made of mud as much as of stone. And the eight miserable rooms surrounded by their own tiny courtyard that had been allocated to the commander of the Phoenician troops and his officers, together with the twelve stables, scattered all over the place and now cleared of the horses that Solomon loved so dearly to make room for his men, were all a shock to him.

He went from room to room, and reached up to touch the ceilings, only a few inches above his head; the mud there, packed in between the palm-trunk rafters, crumbled at his touch. He said sarcastically, "It never rains in Jerusalem, I take it?"

"Oh, yes," the master said earnestly. "The hill on which this great city stands has some of the best rain in the whole of Israel." He added apologetically, "And as you are so quick to perceive, Lord, the filling is on occasion washed away. But we have slaves, as your people do, and the repairs are very quickly made."

Beladus said coldly, "I will not live in such humble quarters, nor will my men. I will make my own arrangements, slave."

"Not a slave, Lord," the master said swiftly. "The wise King Solomon gave me my freedom many years ago."

"Then, freedman, I will set up my tents outside your stinking village."

"Not a village, Lord, but a fine city."

"In Tyre, the meanest whores do not live in such squalor. And forgive me, freedman, if I misjudged your station. Your garments deceived me."

The master was not only a garrulous man; he suffered also from the arrogance that is the defense of primitive people against the more cultivated. He said slyly, "In Israel, Lord, the purple cloth means very little. It is by a man's intelligence that he is known."

"And you, no doubt, are a man of high intelligence."

"It is my belief, Lord, that I am."

"Then tell me, where do you defecate in Jerusalem? On the streets?"

The master laughed. "Of course, Lord! Where else? Would a man defecate inside his own house, like the goats that wander there?"

"And your water. I see no signs of a water supply."

"There is water in abundance, Lord. You will have observed the troughs everywhere. They are not only for the donkeys and the oxen! They are for men to drink from, and also, on occasion, for washing. There is no shortage of good water here."

"My men bathe daily," Beladus said, and the master's eyes lit up with great pleasure. "Daily!" he echoed. "A jest, Lord! And how well your lordship jests!"

"And there will be women with us too. It is required that they, too, bathe daily before they are perfumed."

Aha! It was time to put this proud foreigner in his place once and for all. "Permit me an observation, Lord," the master said with great glee. "If the women are to be *perfumed*, which I have learned is the custom among your people, then surely, Lord, they do not require bathing first! You see, Lord, the value of logic?" He added hastily, "From a very humble man, of course."

Beladus sighed, and reiterated, "I will make my own arrangements, freedman."

He stayed in Jerusalem for a few miserable days and sent out runners to scout locations. He learned, with great pleasure, that Solomon had placed a considerable number of slaves at his disposal, both male and female. Finally, a young Israelite scout reported to him of a suitable place for the Phoenician camp. His name was Zimri, a fiery-eyed young man of some twenty years.

"The bluff above Solomon's pools, Lord," he said. "There is an olive grove there where a whole army could conceal itself if need be. It lies only two hours' march to the southwest of the city walls, one hour from

27

the valley of Sorek where the great Samson lived, a little less from the valley of Elah where David, who was to become king over Israel, slew the Philistine giant Goliath . . ."

Beladus said wearily, "Enough of your damned Israelite history! I never saw a people so hypnotized by their damned heroes! Is the site defensible?"

"Defensible, Lord. I spoke with your Lieutenant Remposar and showed it to him. He approves."

"Then take me there," Beladus said. "And swear to me that on the way you will not talk to me of Samson, nor of David, nor of Saul, nor even of Delilah." He corrected himself at once. "No. You may talk to me of Delilah. I am told that she was a woman not only of great beauty, but of a certain quality."

"An evil woman, Lord," Zimri said. "A Philistine. But it is indeed said that she was very beautiful."

"Then you may tell me all you know of her as we go to Solomon's pools . . ."

And so, the goats'-hair city had come about. Beladus's own tent was set up in the center of the grove, and surrounding it were the eight less elaborate tents of his officers and his own personal bodyguard. Close by were the four tents of his servants, who numbered fourteen including the female slaves set aside for him. Beyond this circle were the semi-portable stables for the horses and the chariots, and beyond those were the tents of the soldiers. Sentries were mounted at every two hundred paces around the complex, and guards were stationed at the tops of the three goat paths that led up from the plain below.

It was indeed a defensible site. It overlooked both the valleys, and yet, because of its height and the sheer drop of its edge, any encampment there would be well hidden.

For the needs of Captain Beladus, it was perfect.

Debrah arrived at last at the house, with a waist-high mud wall enclosing the compound. And Joah was there, the easy-going young goatherd to whom she was be-trothed.

He was shutting up his flock for the night into its pens, kicking a reluctant rump here and there as the dogs barked out in mock savagery. (The true savagery would come later, when they were left to guard their charges.)

These were by no means the kind of dog that would, over the centuries, eventually become domesticated. They were, instead, the wild canines that had been used for hunting and for protection since the prehistoric times of the earliest cavemen. They were huge—some of them stood almost three feet at the shoulder—and a pair of them could outrun and bring down a lion or a bear with the greatest ease and rip it to pieces, hungrily devouring every shred. Their tempers were terrifyingly ferocious. They seemed to take a fiendish delight in killing for killing's own sake, and were almost always ungovernable save by their closest masters. When they were fed at all (they were kept permanently hungry to increase their malevolence), they were given only raw bones to sharpen the long yellow teeth and strengthen still more those slavering jaws. A prudent man would give these fearful brutes a very wide berth indeed.

One of them snarled as Debrah approached, even though she was a member of the family and known to it, and Joah picked up a rock and hurled it at the animal with an oath.

Joah was a cheerful young man of eighteen years, hairy, bearded, and dressed in skins so that he looked like a bundle of fur. He scorned the homespun cloth, even though Debrah wove it for him. He liked to say, happily, "And why should I wear *cloth*? In ten or twenty years cloth will become threadbare, but my skins will last forever . . ."

He was smiling broadly, pleased to see her at last, and he said, "Debrah! You are late I was worried about you!"

She perched on the edge of the watering trough, her

hands in her lap. "And why should you worry about me, Joah?"

"The sun went down an hour ago or more. Where were you?"

"Oh . . . wandering in the hills. The night is very pleasant, and I did not choose to hurry home."

"The hills are full of wolves tonight. And somewhere out there is a female bear, though I did not see it."

She wanted to laugh. "If you did not see it, then how do you know it is a female?"

He said calmly, "Because I killed the male, and the female will not be far away."

"You did *what*?"

He could not contain his elation. "Yes, a very big male. He must have stood more than eight cubits high when he rose up to threaten me. I put a slingshot to his head and stunned him, and when he fell I was on him at once with my knife, and I cut his throat. In no time at all I had skinned him, and I left the flesh there for the wolves to feed on. I brought the skin home. Come, I will show you."

He took her by the arm and dragged her to a corner of the yard, where the great skin was stretched out on pegs driven into the sand. He said happily, "Tomorrow, my mother will scrape it, and then she will chew on it for a week to soften it, perhaps longer, you know how she is about these things . . . And then, she will stitch me a fine new cloak from it. All the neighbors will see it and marvel, and they will say to each other: 'There goes Joah, who killed a bear with his sling.' I cannot wait for them to see my new cloak!" He embraced her at last, and said softly: "And now, tell me what you have done today. Was it a good day for you too?" He could be very tender sometimes.

"Well . . ." She thought about it for a while. "First, I fetched water and filled the trough and the jars. Then I went to Jarmuth with cheese and sold it for a good price, really, a very good price—Father will be pleased.

And then I stopped at the pools on the way home and bathed . . ."

She broke off, remembering. She said, her voice strained, "Did you know there is a foreign army camped on the bluff above them?"

There was sudden anger in his eyes. "Philistines? So close to Bethlehem?"

"No, they are Phoenicians, very many of them, in splendid tents under the trees, tents with . . . with carpets on their floors!"

He breathed a sigh of relief. "Ah, the Phoenicians, we have nothing to fear from them. They are our allies." He looked at her suspiciously. "But how do you know this, Debrah?"

She would not meet his eyes. "I met with a young slave," she said, "one of our own people. His name is Nemuel from the tribe of Dan. He told me of them." There was a faraway look on her face now, and she said dreamily, "He told me that they sleep on couches covered over with sheepskins, but not just a single skin as we use, very many of them, as much as a cubit thick. Nemuel told me . . ." Behind her back, her fingers were crossed so that the lie would not return and harm her.

Joah laughed. "What foolish talk!"

"And in their tents, they have tallows and rush lights burning, not just one but very many of them, so that the whole place is lit up at night, almost as if it were day . . ."

"Gossip!" he said scornfully, "the gossip of women at the wells! You should not listen to such nonsense!"

She was abashed. "Of course, Joah. Forgive me."

He was whistling up the watchdogs, and they came running, three huge and scraggy monsters with lean flanks and sour tempers. He tethered them in their appointed place to guard against any intruder, and said to Debrah roughly, "Come, I am hungry, it is time for you to bake bread."

"Yes, I, too, am hungry." Hand in hand, they went

31

into the house, where Debrah's foster mother Micah had already lit the fire among the small round boulders in the corner of the room.

It was a good house, the house of a wealthy man who liked to live well. It was built of mud bricks in the shape of a U, with the living area which was also used for sleeping, at the center. This main room was very large and spacious, nearly four paces across, but quite low; a man of medium size could raise a hand and touch the ceiling with ease. Most of the available space was taken up by the two beds (Debrah had reached the age of puberty long since, and slept on her own bed now.) They were made of skins stretched out on pegs driven into the packed-mud floor, a foot or so off the ground so that they could easily be swept free of the goat droppings that accumulated there. To one side, the table had already been spread out on the ground; it was a large hide with a drawstring around its borders so that it could also be used, when necessary, as a bag in which to carry all the family possessions.

On wooden pegs driven into the wall, plaited bags of wheat were hanging out of reach of the rats; Uzzi ben Ezra preferred his bread made from wheat instead of the more common and cheaper barley. There was a small wooden cupboard (an item of great luxury) in which the family eating bowls were stored, and a big red pottery jar of water stood in one corner with a wooden ladle for drinking laid on top. An assortment of small skins had been scattered about for seating.

Uzzi ben Ezra was sitting cross-legged on one of them, his day's work done, and he was deciding that he would do nothing any more today except sit and think, and perhaps not even think, and then sleep. He was watching his wife Micah, twenty years his junior at the age of forty, and wondering why she looked so old and haggard. She was crouched on her haunches in front of the fire on which she had set a large upturned earthenware bowl, fanning the embers.

Uzzi looked up as the children came in and said

sharply, "Debrah! I will not have you stay out so late, child! Once the sun is down, you will come home, always."

"Yes, forgive me, Father." She gave him a peck on his cheek and said: "I stopped at the pools to drink and to bathe myself."

"Ah, your bathing . . ." He sighed. "The good Lord, in his wisdom, gave you oils in your body, to keep your skin smooth and soft, as a woman's skin should be. It is not good to wash them away with so much bathing."

"Yes, Father. You are right, as always."

She crouched down and began mixing the flour and water, adding a little olive oil to the dough (another luxury!) and tossing it expertly into thin round sheets, dropping them onto the upturned bowl for baking. They ate together in silence, a good meal of freshly baked bread with cheese, followed by grapes, melon, and the bitter little figs from the sycamore trees.

And then, satiated with good food, Uzzi leaned back against the mud wall and began to regale them on his favorite subject—King Solomon's extravagance, and the astonishing scope of his harem diplomacy by which he allied himself with the families of women from among the Moabites, the Hittites, Amonites, Edomites, and very many others of the vassal states. He spoke of the sheer magnitude of the king's building projects, of the eighty thousand slaves and forced laborers working in the quarries, another thirty thousand cutting Hiram's cedars and hauling them here; of the king's personal household of more than five thousand men and women, including seven hundred wives and three hundred concubines; of the astonishing splendor of the court, where every drinking vessel was made of beaten gold.

He said, brooding over life's vast inequities, "I am a wealthy man, the wealthiest merchant in all of Bethlehem. But can I afford to drink from beaten gold? No! Like any other of his subjects, I must be satisfied with humble earthenware!" In a sudden rage, he hurled his

33

cup across the room, where it shattered against the wall.

Debrah silently picked up the pieces and threw them outside, and while her father sat in glowering silence she cleaned the dishes with sand and stored them away. Then the youngsters retired to the stable, where Joah slept and where the loom had been set up for the cloth that Debrah was weaving.

The stable, which housed the donkeys and a few of the very young goats, was one third of the U-shaped building (the other side was the store for grain, hides, and oil). Joah sank down into the hay and found a sweet straw to suck on. For a while he watched Debrah's skillful fingers flying with the bobbin, admiring the speed with which she worked. Then he said, grinning, "Leave your loom, and come and lie beside me. We will play for a while."

She raised her eyebrows and flashed her lovely eyes at him. She was smiling as she slowly shook her head, but her heart was beating faster. He clambered easily to his feet, and stood there with his hands on his hips for a moment, his bare feet wide-spread as he grinned at her. Then, with a sudden rush, he was on her. She screamed, very quietly so as not to disturb Uzzi or Micah, as he picked her up bodily and tossed her down in the hay. He fell on top of her to bury his face in her neck and nibble at her skin. She squealed her delight, and he rolled off her and thrust a leg over her slender waist, imprisoning her, resting a hand on her breast and cupping it.

She whispered, "Oh Joah . . ."

He slipped the hand under the linen of her gown and found the naked breast and pressed it with strong, coarse fingers. "The time for our marriage," he whispered, "will soon be on us."

"Yes, soon now." There was great excitement for her in his touch.

"It is so hard for me to wait."

"But we must. You know that we must."

"Yes, I know it. It is not easy."

34

"I *must* be a virgin when we marry. Think of the scandal if I were not!" A donkey brayed suddenly, and Joah picked up a stick and hurled it. "Quiet, you son of a donkey!"

Debrah giggled. "What else would he be a son of?"

He turned back to her and began caressing her again. She lay very still as he slowly pulled the long gown up over her knees, exposing her thighs. "A touch," he said, "a touch can do no harm."

She was trembling. "Very gently, then," she whispered.

He slid the gown up to her waist, and she opened her legs just a little to let him caress her, shuddering with the pleasure; his hands were rough, but his touch was light. His lips were close to her ear, "Sleep here with me tonight."

She was shocked. "Joah! How can I do that? What would Uzzi think? In Heaven's name!"

"I will touch you no more than this, all night long."

"No! I cannot!" She could feel the strength of his manhood pressing against her hip, his skin cloak wide open. She slipped a hand under his loincloth and grasped it tightly, and he eased his loins in gentle cadence with her movements. He tried to roll on top of her, but she whispered fiercely, "No, no, like this . . . !" and held him there. His movements increased, and his eyes glazed over as he strained and thrust beside her, and in a little while he gasped and rolled away from her, pulling the cloak down to hide himself. He was breathing heavily, catching his breath, and soon he began to laugh at his own foolishness. He propped himself up on his elbow and played with her hair. He bent down and rubbed his beard into her loins and bit her lightly, and said, mockingly, "Shame on you, woman! How can you display yourself to me, naked? Even though I love you dearly . . ."

"Oh Joah . . ."

He pulled her gown back into place, and said firmly,

35

"Tomorrow, I will go to Uzzi and demand that the wedding be at once."

She giggled. *"Demand?"*

"Well, ask him, then."

"And he will tell you what he always tells you—the time has been set, and we will wait."

"Yes." He sighed. "I fear you are right."

"It is only two months now."

"It is two months too long. A man can die of frustration."

"A woman, too . . ." She was planting little kisses over his face, and he said: "When the time comes, I will give you ten, fifteen, twenty sons . . ."

The image was before her eyes at once, of the tall and noble captain standing before her in his fine purple robe and saying quietly (and with such assurance!), "We will have many sons, Debrah . . ."

Her mind was deeply troubled. She knelt beside her betrothed, her hands in her lap, and said softly, "I will go to my bed now. Sleep, Joah. Sleep well."

"And you too, my love. Till another day comes."

Later in the night, she awoke in her bed and found the old Micah crouched beside her in the darkness, holding her hand and whispering: "Debrah? Are you all right, child?"

She was startled. "Yes, yes, I am well . . ."

Micah said: "A dream? A bad dream, perhaps?"

"No, my dreams were good dreams. Why?" "They were whispering together, fearful of waking Uzzi.

"You were calling out in your sleep," the old woman said. "A name, I think, a very strange name. It sounded like . . . *Beladus?*"

Debrah shivered. She turned over onto her side and drew her knees up to her chin. "Go back to sleep, Mother," she whispered. "All is well with me. Go back to sleep."

She slipped a hand between her warm thighs, and lay awake for a long time, thinking about the captain. And when the morning came, she was unaccountably sad.

All night long she had dreamed of Beladus; and she wondered if she would ever see him again.

In the Phoenician camp, at about the same hour, Beladus dismissed the slave girl Seria and sent for his personal aide, a young man from Tyre who enjoyed the rank of brevet-lieutenant. His name was Remposar, and his father was related to one of Beladus's wives. A bright and cheerful youth hardly out of his teens, he strode into the tent and saluted. "You sent for me, Captain, and I came."

"A logical sequence of events," Beladus said drily. He was strapping on his iron breastplate, and Remposar hurried to assist him, pulling the straps tight and making sure that the vital areas were well protected.

The captain said, "I ride to Beth Horon this morning, Remposar. The garrison there refuses to leave the safety of its walls, and our northern flank is unprotected."

"Of course it is," Remposar said cheerfully. "Beth Horon is garrisoned by Israelites. Why should they venture out to fight when honest Phoenicians can be persuaded to do that for them? They are not fools, the Israelites."

"But venture out they must now. We have a convoy moving north, two thousand slaves carrying gold, ivory, and olive oil, and they are very vulnerable. If the Philistines find them . . . But there is a matter which affects you personally." He grimaced as the sharp edge of the armor cut into his side, and said, "No, not so tight. I need more freedom in my right arm."

As Remposar adjusted the straps, Beladus said abruptly, "I want you to join that convoy. I am sending you on a mission to Tyre."

"To Tyre?" There was great delight in those youthful eyes. "My home, as it is yours."

"When you reach Joppa, take the fastest boat you can find. In Tyre, seek out my half-brother Juntus. You know him, I believe?"

37

"Indeed I know him. His sister Breha is married to my first cousin Shukrit. He is a man of astounding quality."

"A comment, Remposar, that reflects well on your own judgment. Ask him to find me three or four concubines of merit, and bring them here for me as fast as you can."

"Of course." But Remposar was abashed. He said uncomfortably, "You took Seria to bed this night. If she did not satisfy you, I will have her flogged."

"No, she satisfied me. Indeed, I am quite satiated with her love. But these foolish Israelite women talk too much! Can you imagine, at the moment of climax, a lecture on one of their damned heroes named . . . Gideon, I think it was. In the moment of my personal ecstasy, lost, you will understand, in the kind of delirium that can be brought on only by silken thighs like those . . . can you imagine being told that this great hero told his troops, thirty-two thousand of them, that those who were fearful of an impending battle were free to return to their homes? And that twenty-two thousand of them promptly did just that? She was lying under me while I thrust into her, and saying: 'Oh, what a great hero Gideon was . . . !' I was driven to distraction!"

Remposar laughed. "Then better I have her stripped and flogged a little in front of the assembled women, a lesson to all of them."

Beladus sighed. "No, let her not be punished. I'm really quite fond of her, and her mouth does indeed drip with honey. No, say nothing of this to Seria. But in the name of Astarte, bring me some Tyrian women to comfort me! But examine them well yourself, Remposar—they must be women of quality. My brother is a man of excellent taste, but I do not want him to foist off onto me any women he himself has tired of. Seek out one, if you will, by the name of . . ." He broke off, trying to remember. "Shortly before we came here, at the launching of the new ships, there was a woman at the reception in whom I found the greatest pleasure.

38

Her breasts were the shape of pears, her hair was un-fashionably long, and her thighs were the color of milk that has been left to stand overnight and has turned to cream. And her lips . . ." He sighed. "Oh, how I long for our Tyrian women! Her name was . . . Adruspah, I think, or Adrisel . . ."

Remposar was smiling broadly. "Not Adruspah, nor even Adrisel, Beladus. Her name is Adruphet. She is my sister."

"Your sister?" The captain's eyes were wide with de-light. "Splendid! Then you will find her easily . . ."

"Of course! And she will be as pleased as I am."

"Good, good."

"And if I leave now for Tyre, and you for Beth Ho-ron, shall we ride together as far as Gideon or Beeroth, so that my sword may be at your side? Akish is out raiding, they tell me."

"Oh? You have heard . . . what?"

Remposar shrugged. "Only rumors, stories the mer-chants tell when they deliver our supplies."

"Sometimes, they can be believed."

"They say that Akish has more than five hundred men now, that he hides out in the valley of Sorek some-where with more than a hundred horses and a score of chariots."

"It may well be," Beladus answered. "Sorek could hide ten times that number. Yes, we will ride together. And if we see five hundred Philistines . . . well, we shall have to ride very, very fast. But our inland horses are better than theirs. Theirs are only fast on flat sand."

In less than an hour, they were riding hard together over the gray stone hills, empty of any vegetation save a few scattered clumps of gray-green scrub.

When the sun was very high, they halted on the crest of a sharp rise and looked down on a long column of men moving slowly along the defile, so far down that it seemed like a colony of ants on the move. There were two thousand slaves there, each with a shoulder pack or a skin of oil on his back. A group of horsemen led the

39

way, and there were a dozen other riders, Phoenicians all of them, thinly spaced and galloping along the flanks. Beladus scanned the hills and saw other scouts posted; one of them was less that a thousand double paces down the slope, staring up at them, and when he recognized the captain's purple robe he raised his lance in a salute.

"You leave me here, Remposar," Beladus said. "Ride down to them, while I proceed to Beth Horon. And when you reach Tyre . . ." He broke off, sighing. "I have always known Tyre to be the most beautiful city in the world, and at this great distance, it seems even more lovely. I would give my soul for the briefest sight of that island, with the blue sea all around it, the water lapping at its walls . . . But it is not to be. Be on your way, my good friend. And a safe journey to you."

"To you too, Beladus, friend and commander."

They clasped their forearms briefly, and the young brevet-lieutenant cantered easily down the steep hill to join the convoy.

Beladus sat his impatient horse for a while, thinking of his home, and of his four wives, women of great distinction who could charm him with their wit as well as delight him with their bodies. He thought of the other women who were dear to him, of the lovely young girl with the pear-shaped breasts whose name he had forgotten again; was it . . . Adruphet?

But in his imaginings, one vision would not leave him, would not join the parade as they all disappeared, but instead superimposed itself on all of them with a burning insistence. It was the image of a slight and downcast young woman of fifteen, frightened and anguished, standing in his tent with her gown, a bundle of coarsely woven cotton, lying at her feet as he callously examined her naked body and found perfect excitement in it.

He felt again the touch of her resilient young breasts under which her heart was pounding furiously, saw

40

once again the tears streaming silently down her face, tasted again the salt of them on the tip of his tongue . . . He remembered her large and lustrous eyes, like the eyes of a young gazelle that has been wounded by the hunter's spear, eyes in which a natural sense of obedience to his authority was struggling with an equally natural reluctance to accept such a cruel fate . . .

A wounded gazelle—*exactly!* he was thinking.

And then, he said aloud: "But she whispered my name, 'Beladus.' And there was no more of hurt in her eyes, there was instead . . . what was it? Could it have been an understanding of my need for her? Perhaps even a kind of . . . sympathy? Or of tenderness?"

He swung his mount around to the left, dug in his sandaled heels, and headed for the twin cities of Beth Horon.

Into the teeth of the wind, he shouted at the top of his voice, "Debrah . . ! One day . . !"

3

The camp of the notorious Philistine guerrilla Akish was skillfully concealed in a deep, narrow gorge not far from the tiny village of Zorah. Scarcely wide enough in parts for a chariot to pass through, the gorge wound its tortuous way among the jagged, red-gray rocks. One of the smaller chasms that led from it fell sharply down to a large crater, obliquely sheltered by the cliffs that towered over it, shielding it from the sun. Three great stone cisterns stood here, centuries old and now dry and dusty, though a very small spring flowed nearby.

Caves were scattered all around this hollow, most of them joined by tunnels like a monstrous rabbit warren, and it was in these caves that the Philistine raiders were camped. The horses and the chariots were kept under an overhang of granite, so that even a hawk would have had difficulty in spotting them. There were no tents at all; all the men, even Akish himself, were housed in caves.

The camp was so well hidden that even the five families in Zorah, hardly fifteen minutes' walk away beyond the steep cliff, were unaware of its existence. Even at night, when the Israelites would not leave the safety of their homes, the cooking fires were kept small and concealed among boulders. A shepherd could well wander into this enemy quarter without even guessing that there were Philistines all around him (though quite recently, one such shepherd, searching here for a missing goat, had indeed spotted the chariots; he had quickly been killed).

Today, Akish was out scouring the hills for meat for his men, accompanied by his chief lieutenant, Efruzendis, and seven mounted archers. He rode in his chariot, taking the reins himself, with his rear-guard archer riding behind him, ready with bow and shield.

Akish was a big, permanently angry man of forty years, red-bearded and beetle-browed, his fair skin burned by the desert winds to a rich red-gold. He wore a short hair tunic decorated with a frieze of red cloth, very heavy iron armored breast and back plates, and an iron helmet with a large red plume in it after the Minoan style of his forebears. A broad iron sword hung in a leather sheath at his belt, and he carried a shield, also made of iron, a cubit and a half across. The leather strappings of his sandals were bound around bulging calf muscles, and protective links of iron ran down his immensely powerful thighs.

He was a professional soldier from a long line of fighting champions. His father Sinrusa had been a famous warrior, and his grandfather before him was more famous still—he was the great Goliath.

The small commando group was riding along the ridge that overlooked Sorek, riding quite slowly as they stared out over the plain below them. Akish said to Efruzendis, "We need grain for the horses too, Lieutenant. Tomorrow at dawn, take a dozen men to Beth Shemesh and raid the granary there. Load up a few carts, carts drawn by bullocks that we can slaughter."

Efruzendis answered, "It shall be done." He was a short, stocky man with pale gray eyes and fair hair curled up under his helmet, a happy youth whose only delight was in fighting, a work in which he was greatly skilled.

A scout was riding in from his advance position. He reined in savagely and shouted, "A herd of goats below us, Lord!"

Akish leaned on the reins and brought the chariot horses to a prancing halt. "Where, soldier?"

The man pointed. "On the plain to the left, Commander. Fifty goats by my quick count, a single shepherd, a woman, and three dogs with them."

"Good. And a way down to the plain?"

"No track, Lord, but the hill ahead of us is less steep."

"Guide us, then!"

The scout swung his mount around, and they galloped to where the hill sloped gently down, and looked across a panorama that rolled all the way to the sea twenty miles away. Akish fancied he could even see the glittering white stones of his home city there, the beautiful Ashdod where the swan-necked boats lay at anchor, but it was only a mirage.

But closer, less than a thousand double paces distant, the goats, small black specks against the yellow sand, were searching for pasture. A youth dressed in skins was wandering barefoot in the broad, shallow stream, and the *aba*-clad figure crouched there, Akish was sure, was a woman, though her back was turned and he could not see her clearly. The Philistine leader turned his head and saw that his men were forming a half-circle behind him, waiting for his orders. He raised his arm and gave the signal that meant *forward*.

Behind him, the rear-guard archer aboard the chariot put aside his bow and threw his weight onto the twin wooden bars that applied pressure to the iron rims of the wheels. The horses were stumbling over the steep and broken ground, angered by the sudden shift of the chariot's weight. Akish said furiously, "Harder on the brakes, soldier, or you'll turn us over!"

Slowly, the group moved down the steep hill.

The goatherd was Joah.

On this day-long excursion into the beautiful valley, he had brought his betrothed and much-loved Debrah with him, though it had not been easy to arrange. His

44

father Uzzi had said to him, "There is a merchant in Beth Shemesh, Joah, by the name of Gabbai, a good man even though he is not of our tribe, but a Kenite, as Jael was who killed Sisera. I have sold him forty-eight good goats, though for a very bad price. He drives a hard bargain as all the Kenites do. Take them to him, my son, and when you select them be very sure that none of them is with kid, the price is low enough as it is."

"There are seven that have the mange, Father."

"No. I will not cheat him. I am an honest man. Besides which, he will examine them all most carefully before he pays you—he is a Kenite, I told you that, have you no sense at all? If you leave before sunup, you will be home again before it is dark. Take three of the dogs with you."

"And with your permission, Father," Joah said, "I will take Debrah too."

"There is no reason," Uzzi said mildly, "to take Debrah away from her work."

"I will help her to carry the water up before we leave; it will be done more guickly."

"No. No man in my house will demean himself by carrying water."

"Then she can fill the trough again this evening, so that when the morning comes, it will already be full. It is really very simple, Father." Joah was shuffling his broad feet; he was quite unaccustomed to arguing with this stubborn old man.

Uzzi sighed. "For more years that I care to count, the trough has been filled in the morning. I see no need to change so well-established a custom. No."

Joah was grinning again. "As you wish, Father," he said. "Then since we talk of Debrah now, allow me to ask you instead, will you change the time of our marriage? To days from now instead of months?"

Uzzi held his look for a moment, then turned away and muttered, "Do not pester me about the marriage, boy. It will be at the time I have selected, the time for which the neighbors are already preparing. Any change would be unseemly. It might even cause unhappy conclusions to be drawn, a marriage in such unseemly haste . . . quite unfounded conclusions, I hope."

"Of course, Father. It shall be as you wish. You know of my devotion to you in all things."

"And you may take her with you tomorrow, provided the trough is filled this evening. I cannot send Micah to do this any more. Your mother is too old to climb the hill with water on her hip."

"It shall be done, Father." Happily, he went off to find Debrah and tell her the good news. They had set out at first light for Beth Shemesh.

They had wandered slowly with the goats over the parched and arid sand as the well-trained dogs herded the animals to whatever scrub there might be to eat along the way. Now, they had come to the stream that meandered through the valley of Sorek, and there was good grass growing on its banks, with wild flowers in abundance; it was a very pleasant place indeed.

Joah was walking barefoot in the stream, his eyes cast down to stare at the water as he searched out just the right pebbles for his sling, filling his leather pouch as he found them.

For a good slingsman, just any stone would not do at all. They all had to be of identical size for consistency of aim, all perfectly round and smooth for true flight, all of equal density so that a large stone would be the same weight as a smaller one.

The pebbles were good here, and very plentiful, and he had found more than a dozen of them to replenish his dwindling supply. Examining them all very carefully, discarding those that were not exactly right, he said, laughing, "We must come to this place again, Debrah, and I will bring a large bag to carry stones home in. I can find enough shot here for my sling to last a year or more, beautiful stones . . . !"

She was sitting on the bank and making a chain of wild flowers to hang around his neck, splitting the stems open with her thumbnail and stringing them all together, tiny red and yellow daisies. The dogs were trotting around the small herd and making sure that none of them strayed too far, their little short barks signals that the goats well understood. But now Sasu, the big black dog with the yellow splotches on his monstrous chest, was growling angrily. Joah swung around in alarm, squinting against the sun. The other dogs were barking furiously now.

To his horror, he saw a line of mounted men urging their horses carefully down the slope, a chariot in the center of them. And he knew that they meant dire trouble.

His heart was beating fast as he stared at them. There was no possible way of escape. Behind them, the land was flat and hard-packed all the way to Bethlehem; could they hope to outrun horsemen?

Debrah, too, was staring at them in shock. Their helmets and armor, to say nothing of their sheer size, proclaimed them to be the dreaded Philistines. And in her terrified mind a picture was forming, a picture out of a past she had tried for so long to forget . . .

In that picture, her young mother was running with her to the stables as her father tried to barricade the door of the house. There was the rough feeling of stifling straw, and she could hear her mother's shrill whisper: *they are Philistines, child, do not make a sound, do not move, and perhaps they will not find you.* She could not breathe under the straw, and then it was dark as the stable door slammed. She could hear the trampling of horses' hooves, and terrified screams; she lay still and shivered in fear. The light streamed in again, and a giant of a man was standing in the open doorway, silhouetted against the beams of the sun that poured in and fell across her hiding place. Dressed in heavy armor and a plumed helmet and carrying a sword, he walked quickly past her. There was a shout from the compound, and the giant turned and ran out and she never saw him again. She waited a long time in silence.

47

At last the neighbor women found her and scurried back with her into the house, trying to shield from her eyes the sight of the four bloodied bodies in the court-yard that she knew were her parents and her two broth-ers . . . She remembered it all so clearly!

And there on the hill now, were seven of these fear-some giants, led by the chariot with scythes at its wheels, breaking into a gallop and bearing down on them fast. She heard Joah's voice, surprisingly calm, "Do not be afraid, Debrah, I am with you. If we must die . . . then it will be that we die together."

It was only his voice that was calm, a deadly kind of calm that he was forcing upon himself for her sake. Two thoughts were coursing through his young mind, and even though he knew that they would both be killed now, he could not drive the foolish distractions away. . . . An obligation had been bred into him since childhood, one that he instinctively knew to be correct—that his first responsibility in the face of any danger was to his goats, come what may. And yet, his love was with him now, so perhaps his first duty was to her? Deep inside him, he knew that he could protect neither the one nor the other, but his unschooled mind was tortured with helpless confusion.

Debrah whispered, "Philistines . . . We are lost, Joah!"

He had stepped out of the water and was winding his sling around his head, waiting for the first of them to come within carefully calculated range. An arrow swished past her head with a terrifying sound, and an-other buried itself in the ground at her feet. She heard the sharp crack of the sling as Joah let go, and the strange hissing noise the pebble made as it flew at great speed through the air. She saw the stone smash into the forehead of the leading rider in the charge; as he fell, she heard his scream as the iron forepiece of his helmet embeded itself into his skull.

A great roar of anger rose from their attackers, who drove their mounts furiously on. The arrows were flying fast around them now, and as Joah wound up his sling for a second strike she felt, with very little pain, the sudden slicing of a honed arrowhead across the front of her thigh. She fell to the ground in shock at the warm feeling of the blood that ran down her leg, and Joah fell close beside her; she saw, in terror, that an arrow had gone deep into his side, just above the hip. He had dropped his sling, a dazed look in his eyes. She was sure that he had been killed, and she threw herself, screaming, on top of him. The enemy was all around them now, the horses prancing wildly, the thick dust of the furious charge almost smothering them. She rolled to one side as the wheel of the chariot almost crushed her. She saw to her horror that one of the soldiers was dragging Joah by his long hair into a sitting position and spitting into his face. She saw him pull a long dagger from his belt and raise it high, heard their leader shout, a voice of livid rage: "No! He shall not die so easily . . . !"

The soldiers had dismounted, and for the first time she saw that the dogs were dead; the big black beast Sasu had four shafts sticking from his body. She was clutching at Joah with both hands. His eyes were closed, but he was still breathing. The red-bearded man from the chariot put out a foot and thrust her away, and when she reached again for Joah he kicked her savagely in the stomach, sending her writhing back to the ground. She could not believe the fury in his face as he roared, "He killed one of my men—a goatherd! He will die at my hand, at no one else's, when I am ready."

He was standing above her now as she gasped for breath, staring down on her. The fine yellow dust was shrouding him, seeming to make him even bigger than he was. He growled, "Set her on her feet."

Hands gripped her as she tried to suck in great gulps of air and could not, and then a whip-cord forearm wrapped around her throat from behind, another tucked under her upper arms and holding them securely as she struggled. The commander reached out with his huge hands and seized the neck of her gown; he ripped the heavy homespun open as though it had been made of the flimsiest cotton. He stared at her naked torso for a long time, then reached out and took both her breasts in his hands, crushing them cruelly. He thrust a hand down under the torn gown and gripped her between the thighs, clutching hard, and said quietly, "A dove, an Israelite dove. The gods are good to me today."

He turned away from her and strode to where Joah lay on the grass at the brink of the stream, one arm, unmoving in the water. Akish lashed out at him furiously with a foot, and shouted, "Efruzendis!"

"Sir!" Efruzendis came running, and Akish said brusquely, "Three men, Lieutenant, to round up the goats and drive them to the camp." He kicked out at Joah again and said, "A rope around this damned Israelite's ankle, the other end to the saddle of the man who was killed. His name . . . ?"

"Sisik, Lord, one of the new recruits. Is it your wish that we bury him?"

"No," Akish said coldy. "A Philistine who dies at the hand of an uncouth goatherd is not deserving of burial. Take his armor and his weapons and leave him here for the jackals to find. Jackals, too, need meat."

"It shall be done, Lord." Efruzendis's greedy eyes were on Debrah. She still hung in the brawny grasp of a soldier. Her gown was open almost to her thighs, and he was wondering if the commander would give her to him when he himself had finished with her. He licked his lips and said hoarsely, "And the woman, Lord?"

"Tie her, to the same horse. Facing backwards so that she may watch as we drag him."

"At your command, Lord."

Akish stared up at the hilltop they had come from. The blinking midday sun was high in the sky now, where a solitary hawk wheeled, a tiny dark speck against the blue. "We return to the camp at once," he said. "I do not like this valley, I do not like the dust we have made."

50

And then, as though echoing his fears, the long, drawn-out note of a trumpet sounded from the hills behind them. Akish turned quickly, and stared across the rising ground on the other side of the stream.

A long line of horsemen was moving on the crest of the ridge, twenty-five or thirty of them, armed with lances, swords, and bows. And it was indeed the high column of dust that had brought them here; in these dry deserts, it was always a telltale sign that betrayed the presence of galloping riders.

Akish swore, and shouted, "Line of battle!"

Debrah fell to the ground, moaning as the strong arms left her, and she crawled to Joah, lying there still and silent and with the life draining out of him. Desperate in hysteria and shock, on the edge of unconsciousness, she could not even begin to think what was happening now. She gave the distant horsemen no more than a glance; she knew only that the poor, bewildered young Joah who had been her close companion since childhood, was lying there unconscious, an arrow protruding from his side and his cloak stained with his blood. She knelt beside him, sobbing, draping their bodies with her *aba*, ignoring her own blood that was streaming down her thigh. She closed her eyes and prayed as she had never prayed before, slipping in and out of consciousness.

Akish growled, watching the Phoenicians on the ridge, "What devil's chance brings them this way?"

But it was not chance alone.

This morning, a column of slaves had left the city with ingots of gold for shipment to Tyre. They were taking the southern route, by way of the Wells of Keren and Abu Gosh and on to Gezer. Captain Beladus, on his return from Beth Horon, had ridden out with thirty men to protect the convoy's southern flank.

As he rode above the ruins of Jarmuth, a scout had come racing in, shouting: "Horsemen, Lord, two hills away, I think, on our right."

51

Beladus raised his arm for a halt. "How many horse-men, soldier?" he asked.

"I do not yet know, Lord, I saw only their dust. But now that you are warned, with your permission I will discover that at once."

"Do so. We will be close behind you." The scout rode off, and Beladus turned the column into line and climbed the first of the hills, and when he saw the dust beyond the second they rode toward it, riding faster now but still not fast enough to betray their presence with their own dust. The archers were already stringing their bows (on the march, only one man in five rode with a strung bow). The swordsmen had drawn their iron swords; the lancers had readied their blades.

The scout cantered back and reported to the com-mander. "A handful of men, sir, no more, and a single chariot. Two- or three-score goats, and two Israelites, I think, bundled up in their cloaks on the ground and not moving. Perhaps they are the goatherds, and they both may be dead."

"A foraging party, then. Philistines?"

"Philistines."

"Very well. At the rear of the column you will find Lieutenant Rekam. Send him to me."

The scout rode back as Beladus took the column to the top of the hill and along its ridge, turning in the saddle to look down on the enemy below them, one fiercely bearded and heavily armored man standing by his chariot with six archers and their horses. And at the edge of the stream, what he took to be an *aba*-shrouded woman crouching over the body of a man dressed in heavy skins, neither of them moving. Fifty goats or so—and three dead dogs.

Rekam came cantering up, and Beladus halted the column and said to him idly, "Only seven men, Rekam. And why would so few men send up so much dust?"

"It could be, Lord, that they were riding very hard."

"What, to round up goats? No, they would have been riding at the walk."

"Unless it was sent up deliberately?"

"Perhaps. To draw us into a trap?"

"With a hundred or more men," Rekam said lightly, "waiting beyond the hill for us to ride into it. A degree of circumspection is needed, Lord." Rekam was only twenty-three years old, but already a battle-hardened veteran of six years' service. He was tall and very thin, and awkward in the articulation of his limbs. He said, laughing, "But the easiest way to find out if that is true, Lord . . . is to charge them."

"Beware of chariots, Rekam."

"Indeed, Lord, I have learned to do so." The chariots of the Philistines, like those of the Assyrians and the Israelites, were fitted with sharp knives at the hubs of the wheels; driven through the ranks of the enemy, they could quickly cause havoc.

Beladus told the young lieutenant, who was nominally in command of the troop, "Follow me down, Rekam, in line of battle twenty paces behind me. They are waiting for us to move, so we will oblige them."

They walked their horses slowly down the incline to within two hundred paces of the stream at the bottom, and Beladus raised his hand again for the halt. The Philistines had not moved; they stood with their horses like rocks on a wide front, each man fifty paces from his neighbor, the chariot in the center.

A sudden thought came to Beladus, and he turned and signaled Rekam, and when his lieutenant rode up he spoke quietly. "There are few full beards among the Philistines, Rekam. And a *red* beard? Could this be the famous Akish himself?"

Rekam was alarmed. "It could be, Lord Beladus. From what I have heard of him—yes, this could be Akish. If so . . . great care at all times, Captain, I beg of you."

"But unless it is indeed a trap, he is hopelessly outnumbered."

"Which means, that he will challenge you to personal combat. You *must* refuse him!"

53

"Refuse him?" Beladus sighed. "Yes, perhaps I should, though it will not gratify my sense of honor to do so. But first, I will find out if he is indeed the notorious Akish. Return to your men."

Rekam rode back to his position, and for a moment the two opposing groups faced each other on opposite sides of the valley, each of them pondering the possibilities:

For Beladus: *is it indeed a trap?* And for Akish: *is our fame so great that he is afraid to attack us?*

And then, almost simultaneously, the two commanders rode down for the mandatory confrontation.

It was a scheme of combat set down thousands of years ago, perhaps hundreds of thousands. Indeed, a fanciful man might imagine even more ancient, atavistic origins. Had not the apes, when first they came down from their trees, developed an instinct for the bluff, beating their chests and shrieking out their fury at one another? Over the centuries, it had all become very formalized, a kind of vaunting over an enemy that said: touch me if you dare . . .

The two captains, Phoenician and Philistine, were only fifty paces apart now, on either side of the stream that marked a kind of tacit boundary, each waiting for the other to begin the long rigmarole, just as their fathers and their grandfathers before them had played this deadly game.

Beladus shouted at last, "A Philistine, I see! By all that's unholy, Philistine, did your father, if you knew him, give you a name?"

Akish shouted back, mockingly, "By the gods! I hear the voice of a child, Phoenician, coming from the bearded mouth of a girl! My name is Akish! Tremble at the sound of it!"

Beladus laughed. "And why should I tremble at the name Akrish?" It was a pun. In Aramaic, *Akish* meant lion, but *Akrish* meant panderer. It was the first of many blows, and the Philistine's temper was already rising. "Not Akrish," he snarled, "but Akish! And your

54

name? If the whore who was your mother ever gave you one!"

"My name is Beladus, a captain of King Hiram's court in Tyre! And in Tyre, Akrish, the cubicles in which we defecate are better than the houses in your Gath and Ashkelon!"

Akish was moving his chariot now, driving slowly up and down the left bank of the stream and turning it expertly to show how adept he was, hoping that the captain might be awed by the sunlight glinting on those fearful wheelblades. For his part, Beladus was wheeling his horse up and down the right bank. Behind the challengers, the opposing forces held their positions, six Philistines on the one bank, thirty Phoenicians on the other.

"When my slaves wish to amuse me," Akish shouted, "they tell me that your people cut off their children's foreskins Are you circumcised, pig?"

"Yes! As you soon will be when you feel the edge of my sword!"

"And what is a sword doing in the hands of a woman? Put a stop to your babbling, and come to my arms! I will love you as I have never loved a woman before!"

The Philistines were a coarse and hardy race, the Phoenicians delicate and perhaps effeminate. Beladus shouted, angrier now, "A curse on the donkey that loved your leprous mother and spawned a creature like you!"

"Come forward and fight, Phoenician, if you have the stomach for it! We will fight in personal combat to decide this conflict!"

"Why should I soil my good sword with the blood of a mangy Philistine jackal? Better I send my dogs after you!"

"A dog cannot kill a lion!"

"I spit on you instead!"

Akish screamed, "I will rub your woman's face in my excrement before I cut off your head!"

55

They were like angry children snarling at each other, each raising the other's temper—and his own—to lethal heights.

The shrouded bundle at the edge of the stream was stirring, and Beladus looked at it curiously. He heard the quiet moaning that was coming from under it. Moaning? Or could it have been, perhaps, the muttered prayers, rising and falling, of a woman recovering from a sort of trance? Below her were the wide-spread legs of a thick-set man dressed in skins. Beladus turned back to Akish and said scornfully, "Why should I fight you, Philistine camel dung? I see that you have already done your fighting for the day, against what—a goatherd and a woman? Worthy enemies for you! How could you fight against an honorable *soldier?*"

He did not hear the furious reply . . .

The bundle on the ground had turned and raised its head. And he found himself staring into the beautiful eyes, ravaged now by grief and terror, of the young girl he had been dreaming of ever since their first, exciting meeting. His own dark eyes were wide with sudden shock, and hers were boring into his, unfocused and filled with anguish. For a brief moment of incomprehension, their looks held. And then, Debrah screamed the one word: "*Beladus . . .*"

Her long, drawn-out shriek echoed through the hills: "*Bel-aaa-dus!*"

Beladus raised himself in the saddle and spun around. All the niceties of formal battle were gone from his mind now. He drew his sword and raised it high, shouting, "Rekam! To me . . . !"

He spurred his horse over the stream and charged his hateful opponent, his sword held level and aimed at barrel chest. He tickled the reins expertly, and jumped the horse over the long scythe as he lowered his point below the level of the heavy iron breastplate. Akish swung his shield and deflected it, yanking furiously on the reins. He drove at great speed toward Beladus as the Phoenician swung quickly round. The chariot's rear

56

archer was poised, and as the horse leaped nimbly over the knife again he loosed off a shaft and sent it through its throat. Mortally wounded, the horse screamed and fell. Beladus leaped to his feet as the archer dropped his bow and swung the big wood and wicker shield into place, catching three arrows on it as Rekam and his men came charging in. Akish drove furiously at their line, which scattered to avoid the scythes, and then, he was gone.

There was scarcely a moment of fast, furious fighting. Efruzendis was the first to die, two arrows close together in his chest, another in his neck. And when it was all over, all of the Philistines, save their commander, lay dead or wounded. Two of the Phoenicians went from one to another, making sure that none of them lived.

Beladus was crouched over Debrah's recumbent form, and she whispered urgently, gasping, "No, I am not badly hurt. But Joah . . ."

"Ah yes, your unschooled goatherd . . ."

He was very calm and controlled now, though strange and perhaps unwanted thoughts were disturbing him. He examined Joah's wound, and fingered the arrow there lightly. It had entered the side an inch or two below the rib cage and had been stopped by the bones of the spine. Joah opened his eyes, veiled with pain and shock. He looked at the purple robes and whispered, "I am not . . . not worthy . . . of your attentions, Lord."

"Be quiet, boy," Beladus said. "You are hurt and I will help you." He looked up at Rekam. "We have no medic with us, I think?"

Rekam shook his head. "No, Lord. But I know what has to be done."

"Then do it, Rekam."

Debrah's tortured eyes were on the lieutenant as he dropped to one knee, her face very drawn and pale. He moved the arrow a little. Joah screamed, and Rekam said contentedly, "If he can scream, he will live." He

57

looked kindly at Debrah. "Do not fear, girl. He will live." He took the leather pouch from Joah's waist, emptied out the pebbles and filled it with sand. When it was just the right weight, he swung it for a moment to test its value, and then raised it high and brought it down very hard on the back of Joah's skull. At Debrah's gasp he smiled and said cheerfully, "There is no better anaesthetic, better even than copius draughts of wine. You might like to turn your face away from what I must do now."

She would not. She watched as Rekam took the shaft in a strong hand and pulled it carefully to one side to free it from the spine. He murmured, "The range was very great, or the bone would not have stopped it. Even heavy armor will not stop a well-sent arrow." He pushed on it slowly till the point began to come out at the back; Debrah moaned as she saw the sharp blade, heavily barbed, break through the skin. Once it was completely clear, Rekam took hold of it and with one sharp pull, drew the shaft from his body. Debrah caught her breath, and Beladus took her by the shoulders, his heart melting for her. "If the gods are generous," he said, "the boy will live."

She could not hold back the tears. "Yes, I am sure of it. Yahweh will not let him die so miserably."

He said drily, "I have more faith in my own surgeon. And your own wound, Debrah . . ."

"It is nothing, Lord."

"Nonetheless, it must be attended to—you are losing too much blood." It was staining her gown, and he made her lie down on the ground and pulled the hem up to her loins. The arrow had passed across the front of her left thigh, cutting into it very high up, and the blood was pumping there in little rhythmic beats with the pounding of her heart. He said, smiling, "You are very lucky, Debrah. Half a span to one side would have crippled you for life, and a half-span higher . . . there would have been no procreative life left in your loins at all. That is a calamity that I myself would not wish to

58

face." He tore a strip of purple cloth from his gown and bound her thigh with it. "We will take you both to my camp now. Your own wound is slight, but your young man—he needs the care of my surgeon, which is far better than anything he will find in Bethlehem, or even in Jerusalem."

Debrah hesitated, knowing that he was right. Her gown was still open at the front and she was aware of his eyes on her. But there was no offense in them at all, and he was even smiling. "But what we shall do with your goats," he said, "I really do not know."

Rekam was padding Joah's wound with strips of cotton from his own gown, and calling for one of the men to bring a horse and unsaddle it. She told Beladus how the goats had been sold to the Beth Shemesh merchant named Gabbai, and he listened gravely, knowing that there was comfort for her in talk of simple matters, the relief of letting the words just tumble out. When she faltered and turned her tear-stained eyes to Joah's unconscious form, he prompted her quietly, trying to tear her attention away as the men picked the young boy up and draped him over the back of the horse.

When she had finished her tale, he nodded. "Then I will send some men with the goats to your merchant. And a runner, also, to your house in Bethlehem to tell your father what has happened, to assure him that you are both in good hands."

He turned to Rekam. "Three men, for the goats, to a man named Gabbai in Beth Shemesh. And one of the scouts to the house of Uzzi ben Ezra in Bethlehem to inform him of what has happened. Pay him my compliments, tell him his son and his daughter will be at my camp and that he should not be anxious for their welfare. Tell him also that if he wishes to visit them there, he will be well received, as an honored guest should be. Explain to him, Rekam. You know what has to be said."

"Of course."

Beladus looked toward the east, to where Akish had

fled. He said thoughtfully, "Send also two good scouts to follow the tracks of that chariot before they are lost on the wind. Let them ride with great caution, ready to withdraw at the first sign of danger. I do not want men uselessly killed in the name of valor; they are more useful to me alive."

Rekam nodded vigorously. "Yes, it will be good to know where those vermin hide themselves." He moved off to give the orders.

Beladus took Debrah by the hands and helped her to her feet, and when he put an arm around her and her own around his shoulder, she protested weakly, "No, I can walk, though I thank you . . ." He smiled and held her the tighter. "Come. You will ride behind me."

He mounted the horse that was brought for him, and with the help of a man who came running with cupped hands to form a stirrup, swung her up behind him. "Your arms," he said gently, "put them around my waist and hold me tightly. It will be easier for you."

The men were forming up behind him. He looked over the battlefield for a moment and said tightly: "I am sorry that Akish escaped, but there will be other occasions. Sorry too, for a good horse that lies there dead . . ."

Some of the men had been detailed to remain behind and collect the valuable weapons and armor, and the rest of them, with Beladus at their head, began the slow walk home.

For a long time, Debrah could not tear her eyes away from Joah, lying across the led horse, motionless and silent and seeming dead. But soon, the exhaustions of the day's events quite overcame her. And with her arms about his waist as he had told her, she let her drooping head fall to rest lightly on his shoulder and closed her eyes, still moist with tears. She knew that in spite of Beladus's protestations, Joah was dying.

Soon, the sleep of utter fatigue came over her, and she did not wake again until they reached the bluff.

4

The hooves of the chariot's horses thundered from side to side of the gorge as Akish lashed their steaming, foam-flecked flanks. Their nostrils were flaring, their eyes wide with an anger that seemed a reflection of his own.

He pulled back savagely on the reins as they reached the stables, so that they reared up and pawed at the air with their forelegs, two fierce and spirited animals that had been driven too hard for too long. The rear archer hung his shield on the side rail and plucked the arrows from it for future use; the Phoenician arrows were very good, exquisite works of martial art.

Akish jumped to the ground. They were in the deepest part of the gorge here, under the shadow of the great gray rock that towered above them. The opposite wall of the gorge was less sheer, scattered with precariously poised boulders, interpersed with patches of scrub in which a few goats sought food. He shouted, "Orderly!" and when a soldier came running he said, "Find Lieutenant Tarson for me, at once. And have them set beer on my table. I've ridden hard these past hours."

The orderly pointed. Lieutenant Tarson, a short, barrel-chested man in his forties, was hurrying to his commander. He had been born in the same city-state as Akish, the town of Ashdod, which lay between Gaza

61

and Joppa, and they had grown up as firm friends together, bound in a kind of blood brotherhood by their mutual hatred of the Israelites. He was carrying his shield and his drawn sword, looking back at the entrance to the gorge.

Akish said to him sourly, "Put up your weapon, Tarson, the fighting is over."

"You descended on us like all the devils of hell," Tarson said. "I was convinced that half the Israelite army was at your heels." The men above them had caught the sense of danger and were coming out of their caves, their weapons ready. Akish waved a furious arm at them and shouted, "There is no alarm!"

"Efruzendis and the others?" Tarson asked, sheathing his sword. "They are not with you?"

"They are all dead, Tarson. Thirty or forty Phoenicians found us in Sorek, and cut us to pieces."

Tarson shrugged. But his eyes were on fire at the thought of blood. "I am grateful, at least, that you escaped."

"I may have been followed. Come with me to my quarters."

They climbed up the unstable rocks together and made their way along the ledge to the big cave and went inside. Its floor had been hewn roughly flat many centuries ago; there was a smoke-blackened hearth of equal antiquity, with a few small niches cut into the soft limestone wall above it for storing food. A long table of cedar planks, which had been set up with cedar benches, was covered with rolled up parchment maps, eating bowls of clay, and some drinking vessels for beer, skillfully fashioned with strainers below their rims to trap the barley husks and pieces of fomenting bread. To one side was a crude bed made of wood and improperly cured skins that smelled strongly and had been stitched where they were cracked.

A young Israelite slave, a slim and sullen youth of fourteen years or so, was pouring beer. He had been taken in a raid on the village of Akekah some months past, and it had been the guerrilla leader's whim to paint his face like the face of an Ashkelon whore; there was blue *kohl* around his eyes, and his lips and cheeks were stained with carmine worked from safflower plants. Akish glowered at him and said, "Is there meat?"

"There is meat, master, for the officers."

"Bring some, then, with bread, cheese, and honey."

The slave withdrew, and Akish unrolled one of the parchment maps and spread it out on the table. He leaned over it, his arms heavily muscled and sunburned. "There is a decision to be made," he said. "If it is true that I was followed, then either we must leave this place at once or add to our fortifications. What do you think, Tarson?"

"We'll find nowhere more secure than this gorge," Tarson said promptly. "A few men on either side of the entrance can hold it against an army. Not even chariots can force their way in here."

"I drove in at speed, and I was deep in the heart of the gorge before anyone knew I was here."

"No. The sentries saw you and gave the alarm. You yourself had to cancel it, you remember."

"From above us, an enemy can roll boulders down on the chariots. We cannot afford to lose them, Tarson."

The chariots had been imported from Egypt at enormous cost—six hundred shekels of silver or forty of gold for each of them. They were built like those of the Assyrians, with eight-spoked wooden wheels bound in iron joined by a wooden axle on which the basket rode directly, unsprung and open at the back so that the combatant could easily jump down when need be. There was no seat, and usually room for only two men, one of whom would be the driver and the other the rear archer or swordsman, though the leather reins were made long enough so that they could be wound around the driver's waist to allow him use of both hands for his weapons. Along the waist-high guard at the front were

63

four, five, or more quivers for arrows (always kept well filled), the driving pole ran between the two horses, fastened to their necks by wooden yokes. They could be raced at high speed over fairly flat ground, but were easily impeded by rocks or gulleys. It was the custom for the charioteers to bind ropes around their waists and fasten them to the rails, to save them from being thrown out by the heavy bouncing.

"The stables are well protected," Tarson said, "but let us build a dike around it."

"Yes. Perhaps we should have done that before." Akish drank from his beaker and spat out the husks that eluded the strainer. "Very well, we stay where we are. And tomorrow, find me a man who is skilled with maps, a man who knows well how to draw a chart from what he sees with his own eyes."

"Grenik, without a doubt," Tarson said. "Grenik is a skilled cartographer who studied at the school in Gaza."

"Good, Grenik, then. Have him wear Israelite robes to hide his sword and dagger, let him carry no other weapons. Send him to Solomon's pools, have him study well the hill that rises above them, where the Phoenicians are camped. I want every possible approach to that bluff put down on parchment for study. Every goat track, every outcrop of rock that might give us cover, even every shadow on the ground. It is time we took that camp of theirs away from them."

"It is impregnable, Akish."

"We have always believed that. Perhaps we were wrong. Let us find out." They stood at the entrance to the cave together, and drank their beer, watching the men and the women at work down below them. Some were filling skins with water from the spring and carrying them to the brewmaster for his huge clay vats in which the barley was fomenting. Some were honing their swords, some grooming the horses. The camp women were baking bread and washing clothes.

For the women here, conditions were very different

from those their sisters enjoyed in the Phoenician camp, though in each case they were mostly Israelite girls. There on the bluff they were serving cultured men who were Israel's allies, while here they were prisoners captured in raids by men to whom cruelty was natural. There, they lived in great comfort and could have their freedom at the allotted time, while here they lived like animals and were closely guarded. There, the aspect of their lives was an enviable one, while here—it was hateful. So here, they did those things for which they had been brought here, but they did them sullenly, unsmiling, without spirit.

Akish glared down at the women and spat. "Cattle!" He went with Tarson back into the recesses of the cave as the painted slave boy returned with the food, a great copper tray of goat's meat, cheese, and a bowl of honey, and they sat down to eat and drink together. "Also tomorrow," Akish said, "send two good men to the west, one to Gath and one to Ashkelon. Have them find me more recruits, a hundred and fifty in all."

Tarson tore at the tough meat with broken yellow teeth. "There is, of course," he murmured, "the question of gold to pay them with."

"They will share in the booty, as all the others do."

"A new recruit, to be tempted, must see gold with his own eyes, the easiest way to convince him of the good fortune awaiting him. And yet, if we give the two men their own share to take with them, or part of ours . . . I fear we will never see them again."

Akish sighed. "Yes, you are right." He thought about it for a while, and said at last, "Very well, they will go first to Gath, where my father is, before they move on to Ashkelon. I will prepare a letter for them to take, and my father will provide them with a few shekels of gold to show to a very greedy populace." He was laughing suddenly, pleased by memories. "You remember my father Sinrusa, Tarson?"

"Of course!" Tarson, too, was remembering. "There

65

is a *man!* It's ten years or more since I last saw him. How is he, Akish?"

"Far better than a man of his age is expected to be. Still selling his ships at exhorbitant prices to anyone who will buy them. Yes, a fine man . . ."

"I remember the day," Tarson said dreamily, "when you had a quite insufferable toothache, and you were crying like a baby, though we were both—what was it?—six years old?"

"Less, I am sure, if I was crying. But I remember it well—it's burned into my childhood memories. You were sitting on his knee, I recall, when I came weeping into the room. It was the room with the white pillars that overlooked the sea. He picked me up, I remember, and looked into my mouth and could not find the bad tooth . . . So he took a bronze hammer and a copper rod and knocked out three of them for me! And he cured me!" He sighed. "Yes, a truly great man, greater even than his father Goliath."

"Yes," Tarson said quietly, "Goliath's son was a greater warrior than his father. And Sinrusa's son is greater still, Akish. The legend does not die . . ."

Akish was brooding over his defeat. "A legend!" he echoed. "And still . . . I was defeated today! Thirty Phoenicians to our seven, and I was forced to run!" He slammed a fist onto the table. "It's my *pride* that's been offended! I can take a sword cut as well as anyone, I've done it many times! But this? It's not easy to stomach, Tarson! And it was a woman who called for the charge, I heard her!"

Tarson was startled. "A *woman?* Fighting in the ranks of the Phoenicians? You know how they worship their women, Akish, it cannot be!"

"No, not fighting." Debrah's image was still heavy on him. "She was a simple shepherdess. But she looked up at their captain, and she called him clearly by name, and he screamed like a maniac for the charge, which was instantly carried out."

"A *shepherdess* . . . ?"

"A shepherdess and a dove. A woman of remarkable beauty, dressed in rags like all the damned Israelites. Little more than a child, but her breasts were full and very hard, and pointed. I touched them, and they drove me to perdition. Had it not been for the troops, I would have taken her there and then, and I nearly did. But I saw Efruzendis leering at her and licking his lips, and I knew that if I spread her legs there on the ground I'd be obliged to give her to him out of common decency. I didn't want to do that. I wanted to keep her for myself, for days, perhaps even weeks! It's been a heavy day for me, Tarson."

Tarson raised his beaker. "Then drink, Akish," he said. "With enough beer in a man's belly, the world fast becomes a better place to suffer in."

Akish drank, and glowered at the empty vessel, and then refilled it. "You know the village of Zorah?"

"I know it. Not far from here. Four or five miserable families, no more."

"As soon as the moon rises, you and I will take three men and ride to Zorah. And we will put every man, woman, and child there to the sword. What do you say, Tarson?"

The lieutenant's eyes were on fire. "I will be beside you, brother," he said. "And mine will be the second sword to strike off an Israelite head."

They raised their mugs and drank to the venture. And when the pale silver glow in the dark sky told them the moon was on the rise, they set out together and forced their horses up the nearly vertical track that led to the top of the mountain, with three soldiers in line behind them. The three men, Tranei, Pilkro, and Laskir, were all spoiling for a fight and were all very young indeed; the oldest of them, Laskir, was sixteen. They moved down on the other side of the rise till they saw the tiny cluster of mud huts down there among a few palms; they were very humble houses, but in the light of the moon they had assumed a very great beauty.

67

Akish said coldly, "There is arrogance even in their serenity. We will need fire. Has someone a tinder?"

Tarson answered him. "A good flint in my pouch, Akish, and an iron to strike it with."

"A flare, then."

The three well-trained young soldiers dismounted and brought dry grass and thorn twigs. Tarson crouched over them and struck his flint, repeatedly, dropping them on the grasses and blowing on them. He was very skilled at this, and it seldom took him more than three or four minutes to produce a flame. The grasses flared at last, and he held a thorn branch to them until it, too, was burning well.

And then the Philistines, whom the Greeks (and King Hiram, too) called Palaestines, rode slowly down on the Israelite hamlet.

They slipped off their horses at the first of the huts, and Laskir tossed the flare onto its roof. The dried fronds caught fire at once, and were quickly raging. And now, they waited, but only for a few moments.

The first of the villagers to run out of the hovel was a screaming woman, and Akish cut her down at once with his sword. They burst through the door and killed the seven bewildered people awakening there, and then the flames spread from house to house as the occupants, wailing their terror, came streaming out. The five Philistines moved among them, using their swords with murderous efficiency on man, woman, and child. Pilkro was tearing flaming fronds from the low roofs and throwing them onto others, spreading the flames faster.

But the raid was not entirely without its difficulties for Akish. By the purest of chances, a young Israelite soldier was visiting his family here. He was a very angry and volatile young man of eighteen years named Hamul, and he was filled with an undying hatred of the Philistines, who had killed two of his brothers in other raids. At the first sounds of alarm, he had leaped naked from his bed and snatched up his sword. He wielded it like a madman, and before Tarson sliced open his chest

68

from shoulder to stomach, he had killed both Laskir and Tranei.

In fifteen minutes or less, the raid was over. Akish found a child, perhaps two years old, hidden under a pile of skins. Laughing, he took him by the ankle and tossed him high in the air, and caught him on his sword as he shouted: "Death to all of Israel, in perpetuity!"

He found it difficult to leave the embers of his triumph. He began picking up dead bodies and tossing them into the flames, but soon, even his venom had dissipated. He sprang on his horse and shouted, "We go now!"

With Tarson and Pilkro behind him, he spurred his horse and rode back, very fast, to his hidden camp. The loss of two men bothered him not in the least, and there was a fierce jubilation clutching at his heart.

Akish had recovered his pride.

But in that other camp above the pools, there was little jubilation.

Even among the slaves, the word had been passed around: *the commander is deeply distressed*. They gathered in little groups and whispered secretly together, watching the soldiers for any easing of the anxiety in their eyes that might mean that the crisis had passed. It was as though some terrible calamity had befallen the camp, and they could not understand its importance; all they knew was that it was centered on Remposar's comfortable little tent, which in his absence had been put at the disposal of a wounded peasant and the young girl who was with him. Why, they wondered, should peasants be treated with such solicitude? It made no sense at all.

Joah lay silent and motionless on one of those luxurious beds that had so excited Debrah's attention, while she crouched on the carpet beside him and held his cold hand. Sometimes it seemed to twitch—the only sign of life he gave.

The surgeon had taken a great deal of blood from an

opened vein in his leg, fastening the incision with a silver pin and binding it with cloth that had been dyed the requisite shade of red, a color that was very important if the wound were to heel properly.

Seria opened the flap of the tent and whispered, "Your father, mistress." Debrah rose quickly to her feet and ran to Uzzi, throwing her arms around his wrinkled neck and letting the tears flow freely now. He was still panting, his breath coming in labored gasps after his hard climb up the steep goat track, stumbling to keep up with the officer who had brought him the news of this terrible calamity.

He held her tightly, staring over her shoulder at the unconscious body of his son, bathed in the yellow glow of the candles. "How is he, Debrah child?" he asked quietly. Her head was rolling from side to side. "He is dying, Father," she whispered. "I know that he is dying."

His ancient body was shaking. "And you? They told me that you had been wounded too."

"My wound is nothing. But Joah . . ."

The surgeon was still there, sitting by the bed and looking at them quizzically, smiling. He was a very fat, stubby man with a trace of a hunched back, dressed in a light brown robe gathered at his enormous waist with a red and gold woven cord; his pudgy hands were clasped over his belly. He said, "No, girl, he will not die, you have my promise on it. In a few hours, I will take more blood from him, and again a few hours later if need be. And you will see—in a week he will be chasing his goats again all over the hills, as whole as he ever was. He is young and strong, and in excellent condition. The human body, child, is a creation of great resilience. And what is an arrow in the side? A trifle, no more than a trifle! He will recover."

As though suddenly conscious of the pain in Uzzi's eyes, he left his chair and waddled toward them. "And you, old man," he said, "you are the girl's father?"

Uzzi nodded, his eyes wide, his long white beard bobbing. "Her father, Captain, and not her father, and the boy's father, too. And will you tell me truly, he will live?"

The surgeon wondered briefly why it was that the Israelites took so much delight in equivocation: *her father but not her father* . . . He brushed it aside and answered him, "He will live. And I am no captain, sir, but merely a humble lieutenant-surgeon. My name is Felada, sir, a doctor of extended medical training from the Academy in Sidon, lately in the honorable service of the great King Hiram of Tyre, and now serving Captain Beladus in like capacity."

"An honor, Lieutenant," the old man mumbled, "that my son is in such good hands." He detached himself from Debrah's embrace and sank to his knees beside Joah. He whispered, "His flesh was never so white." He could not comprehend that awful immobility in a young man, so dear to him, who was always so full of life.

"That is because," Felada said didactically, "there is little blood left in him now. It is the blood, sir, that works the evil in a wounded man. We have to remove it, just the right amount, you understand, with skillful incisions. That is what I am doing."

Uzzi clutched at that limp hand and pressed it to his cheek. He was sobbing unashamedly now, the tears streaming down his tired old face and into his beard. He looked at Felada. "Forgive an old man his weaknesses, sir. This is my only son, and it is hard to see him so close to death." He sighed. "After thirty-five years of marriage, to three wives . . ." He added hastily: "Only one at a time, I fear—I am a poor man, a simple merchant. But after all those years, this is the only son I have."

The surgeon nodded wisely. "That, too, is a question of the blood." Uzzi shook his head. "No, Lieutenant, once there were others, three more children. Two of them, young boys, were killed in a Philistine raid, and then, some years later . . . a girl, only a child, carried

71

off to who can tell what fate? It is a heavy load for an old heart to bear."

"You have my sympathy, sir," Felada said, "and my word that this last of your sons will soon be the joy of your estimable house again. He will once again be laughing, and chasing after the girls of your village, and siring for you a great number of grandchildren to bring you happiness in your old age. And your village, I believe, is Bethlehem. You have come from there now?"

"Yes, from Bethlehem. My good wife Micah is awaiting my return there, but . . ." The tears were coming again. "I cannot bring myself to leave my son."

"Then you must stay. May I send you food?"

"You are kind, sir, but no. I will feed on my sorrow."

The surgeon was not a perceptive man, but he sensed their need to be alone, and he said quietly, "Then with your permission, sir, I will leave you for a while." He bowed stiffly to Debrah. (She was only a girl, and a peasant girl at that, but Beladus had shown great interest in her, and Felada reasoned that a little deference might not come amiss.) "Should the young man recover in my absence, there is a guard at the tent who will summon me, I will come instantly. By your leave, then?"

He left them alone together, and Uzzi rose and stared down at his son. "Tell me, child," he said, "how it came about. The officer who brought me the sad news spoke of a battle with the Philistines."

She sat on the sheepskin bed beside Joah and took that cold hand in hers. "A patrol of them, six or seven men led by a terrible red-bearded warrior riding in a chariot. They were after the goats, I think. They found us by the creek in Sorek, below the village of Zanoah, and rode down on us, and there was murder, and worse, in their evil hearts. Joah was selecting stones for his sling when death broke in. Alone, he fought them."

"He *fought* them? One, against so many? Ah good, my son indeed . . ."

"He killed one of them with his sling."

"Good, good!"

"And then he fell, an arrow in his side. I suffered a shaft in my thigh, but it was a cut only, and I have forgotten it already. But Joah was hurt grievously; the head of the arrow was deep in his belly. They would have killed us both, but then . . . Beladus appeared."

"Beladus?"

"A captain of Phoenicians. This is his camp."

"Ah, yes, the officer spoke of him. Go on, child."

"Captain Beladus came, with many horsemen, and they killed almost all of the Philistines . . ."

"Good, good . . ."

"Only their commander escaped in his chariot. And Beladus saved us both. He gave orders for Joah to be carried here, and I came with him. He also sent men to deliver the goats to Gabbai the Kenite in Beth Shemesh."

"Yes, yes, I was informed that this had been done. His name is Beladus? A strange name indeed."

"Beladus, yes. A good man, Father, even though he is not one of our people."

"And if he saved your lives, and my goats, then I must find him and humble myself before him."

A strong and vibrant voice came to them from the yellow-flamed obscurity of the tent. "It will not be necessary, sir."

They turned and saw Beladus there at the entrance. He had discarded his armor, and was dressed in his purple robe, fastened at the waist with a gold cord, and latticed sandals, his head bare, a fine and imposing figure of a man. He let the flap of the tent fall and, advancing toward them, said gravely, "I am Beladus, sir, commander of the Phoenician troops in this area. And you, I am sure, are Uzzi, the son of Ezra, father to this unfortunate boy, and father also to Debrah, with whose well-being I am deeply concerned. I welcome you to my camp."

Uzzi was bowing almost to the ground. Before, there

73

had been too much grief weighing on him, but now he was slowly becoming aware of the magnificence of his surroundings. A tent with a fine carpet on its floor! With not one, but many tallows flaring! And the bed on which his poor son was lying, at least a cubit deep in sheepskins! He had never before seen such prodigal luxury. And now, a tall, straight, and dignified man whose very presence—to say nothing of his robe!—proclaimed him to be a noble of very high birth! He said, "Yes, lord, I am Uzzi ben Ezra. I offer you my humblest thanks for what you have done for my family."

"They are not needed, sir, though I thank you for them."

"When I think of what would have happened had you not come to their rescue, with the skill and the bravery for which the Phoenicians are so well known, I cannot still the beating of my heart."

"You do us too much honor, sir," Beladus said, smiling. "I fear that our people are not as well known for their martial abilities as you are kind enough to suggest. Ours are the peaceful arts, though we are sometimes obliged to fight to preserve them."

The old man was weeping again. He said plaintively, "Your surgeon, Lord, tells me that my son will live. Are you, Lord, of like opinion?"

Beladus raised his eyebrows and sighed. "My surgeon, sir," he said, "is a man of perhaps unappetizing aspect. None the less, his reputation as a man of medicine is very high, and on medical matters I would never presume to argue with him. As for myself, I have seen men survive far worse wounds than that which was inflicted on your son. And yes, I have seen them die of lesser ones. It is always in the lap of the gods."

"Then I will pray to the one and only God, Yahweh, that he might be spared."

"Whoever our gods might be," the captain said, "our destinies are in their hands. They are often good hands."

He reached out and took Debrah by the shoulders and held her at arm's length, looking deeply into her troubled eyes, wide and staring. He said softly, "And you, Debrah? This is a cruel and painful time for you. Have you the strength to bear it?"

"Yes, Lord. I am a woman, and very young, but I am not weak. I will wait in patience for . . . for whatever will happen now."

"And your own wound? It was not severe, but neither was it slight."

"The surgeon closed if for me with three silver pins."

"It is painful for you?"

"I think only of Joah. And I too will pray to Yahweh."

"If you must . . ." He took her hands and held them tightly, and he said, very deliberately, "I will say this in the presence of your father, who is worthy of my respect because he *is* your father. Since that first glorious evening when I saw you bathing, I have set my heart on your well-being. I will do all that is in my power, and more, to see that your betrothed lives and brings you the happiness that I wish for you."

Debrah, alarmed, was conscious that Uzzi's interest had been distracted from the drained shell that lay on the bed. She whispered, "I am grateful for your concern, Lord, though I am not worthy of it."

"My happiness lies only in your own. You will stay with him tonight?"

"If we may, Lord."

"Then I will send you beds. You must sleep, Debrah. You must not pass the time in weeping."

"I know, Lord, that it will not help. It will not be easy."

"I am sure of it. A woman who does not weep when she must . . . is not a woman."

"It is our destiny to weep. We all have bitter tears to shed for those we love."

"I would not wish it to be otherwise. Eyes that cannot weep reflect a heart that cannot bleed."

75

Abruptly, as though aware of the old man's questioning eyes, he dropped her hands and turned to Uzzi. "You are welcome to stay in my camp for as long as need be, Uzzi ben Ezra. I will send you bread and meat and salt so that you will not go hungry here. There will be beds for you both to sleep on, and if in the night your son's condition should change, I ask that you send for me at once, regardless of the hour. The sentry at the tent has his instructions. I bid you both good night."

He strode out of the tent, and Debrah looked at her foster father with great trepidation; words had been spoken that troubled her deeply. Uzzi was still staring at Joah's unconscious body, but his thoughts were elsewhere, on a new calamity. He said at last, very quietly: "A man of high quality, the captain."

"Yes."

"He saw you *bathing?*"

Her heart was beating fast. She could not lie to her father, whatever he might ask her. "Yes, Father. He saw me while I was bathing at Soloman's pools."

"And you were naked?"

"Yes, Father."

"Since which *glorious* night, he has set his heart on your well-being."

She said steadily, "He is a good man, Father."

"And on this . . . *glorious* occasion, when he saw you in a state of such immodesty, you spoke with him?"

"Yes."

"In this camp?"

"Yes."

"But you told me nothing of this."

"No." Her lips were tight. "I was afraid that you would not understand that . . . that no harm was done."

There was a long silence, and then: "You came here to him?"

"He sent for me, and I came. I could not refuse."

"And he took you to his bed?"

"No, he did not."

76

"He saw you bathing, naked. He sent for you and you went to him. And yet . . . he did not violate you. I find it very hard to believe, Debrah, child."

"It is the truth, Father."

Her eyes, very wide and quite dry now, were on his, and he was trembling with a deep emotion. He said slowly, "In the presence of your betrothed, who is close to death, you can lie to me? Is it because you believe that you must?"

"It is not a lie, Father. I have never lied to you."

He tried desperately to read the thoughts that he was sure were being hidden from him, and he could not. He said, searching her soul, "Will you swear it to me?"

"On all that I hold most sacred, I will swear it."

Silence again, and then: "He did not touch you?"

"He touched me. He did not take me."

"He touched you . . . where?"

"My breasts."

"And between your thighs?"

"Yes."

"And still . . . he did not take you?"

"No, he did not. I wept, and pleaded with him, and he let me go."

He could not take his eyes from hers; there was agony here, an even deeper distress. "It is very hard for a father to believe, child," he said. "His hands explored your body . . . Were you clothed?"

"No. At his command, I had dropped my gown."

"And he did not take you instantly to his bed?"

"No."

"But his hands . . . ?"

"Yes, on my breasts, and even between my thighs. I told him that I am a virgin, that I wished to remain so. I told him, too, that I am betrothed to Joah, your son."

"And he accepted this so easily?"

"I do not believe that it was easy for him. But he accepted it."

Uzzi's tired old eyes, shrouded in pain, were on his son again. He said heavily, "I am old, Debrah, and

aware that times are changing, manners are changing
. . . I still cannot believe that I have raised a monster
at my own hearth who will lie to me."

She began to speak, but he raised a hand to silence
her, and said, "Do you remember your true parents,
child?"

The question startled her. "Yes, of course, you know
that I cherish my memories of them! I remember the
sight of my father, sword in hand and ready to die to
protect his family. Most of all, I remember my mother
thrusting me under the straw when the Philistines came
raiding. I remember the great fear in her eyes, and I
knew that it was for me, her child."

"Will you swear to me on their blood that what you
have told me is true?"

"I swear it on their blood," Debrah said steadily.
"And on their souls, too."

It was a strange comfort to him in this moment of
deep distress. Weeping, he took her into his arms and
embraced her. He was about to answer her, to tell her
of the great load that had dropped from his frail shoulders, when a terrifying sound came from the deep bed,
a long, drawn-out sound, part moan, part scream of anguish. And Joah opened his dark, glazed eyes and
screamed out the one word: *"Debrah . . . !"*

And then, Joah was dead.

They knelt together for a long, long time beside the
bed, weeping and praying together in their solitude. Beladus came at last in answer to their summons, together
with the surgeon, and the tragedy was heavy on all of
them. The old man swayed back and forth, seeking an
elusive comfort in prayer, while Beladus took Debrah
tightly in his arms and tried to still her tears.

He said gently, "My heart, too, is bleeding, Debrah.
Your pain is mine."

"He was . . . he was full of life, Lord! And
now . . ."

"Yes, now he is gone. You must be strong, Debrah."

"Strong? It is a word, no more."

"It is more than a word. It is a creed to live by."

"Yes, a creed to live by." She brushed a tear from her cheek. "Shall we ever see the end of these hated Philistines?"

"Perhaps, one distant day. Not in our lifetime, nor that of our children."

"It is hard to live with death all around us."

"But we must. And if I could comfort you . . . I am not inarticulate, Debrah, but I know that now, words cannot help you. You must face the future with whatever courage you can find. And I do not believe that you are lacking in courage."

"He was so young, so very young . . ."

"He is gone, Debrah. You must face it."

"Yes."

"I know very little of your laws, but I understand that the body must be quickly interred, that there are certain rituals to be observed."

"Yes."

"Then you must go now. I will arange for a litter, and for men to carry it back to Bethlehem." He took her hands and said gently, "We, too, have a ritual. When a lone soldier dies with honor, in battle, a trumpet is sounded. It brings little comfort to the dead, but perhaps it brings . . . a certain strength to the living who loved him. Go now, with my blessing. My sorrow goes with you too, for when you weep, my own eyes are filled with tears that are yours."

The body was wrapped in a shroud of white linen, and two slaves bore it away on a litter. Nemuel and Hinnon supported the broken old man who stumbled along beside it, and Seria held Debrah's arm and tried to find words of comfort for her as the little column wound its slow and pain-filled way down the goat track to the pools and on over the rocky hill that led to Bethlehem.

The sun was rising, casting a glorious golden light on the air, gilding the sand, and the hills, and the jagged outcroppings of yellow stone. The tinkling of little copper bells told of distant goats, and somewhere a dog was barking.

And then, another sound came to them from the top of the bluff where the camp of Captain Beladus and his Phoenician troops was sheltered among the dark shadows of the olive trees. It was a sad and mournful sound, a tremulous three-note dirge blown on a single trumpet. It was the burial call for a soldier who has died honorably, and alone, in battle.

Debrah heard it, and wept.

5

For all the villagers, it was a time of mourning.

Joah had been well liked in Bethlehem, but more important, Uzzi ben Ezra's wealth and stature demanded the presence of every professional mourner who could be summoned. They came in droves, their hair and their beards shaved off, dressed in the coarse sack-cloth garments, their arms and faces disfigured with dust and ashes; the more enthusiastic among them even lacerated themselves as they went through the ritual weeping and wailing and gnashing of teeth. The dead youth was placed in the newly dug grave in the family compound alongside his grandfather, his two young brothers who had been killed in childhood, and others of his clan. The symbolic artifacts required by custom were laid there with him—four small pottery lamps, copper replicas of a sword and two daggers, three miniature cooking vessels, a bracelet of beaten copper, and a tiny model horse executed in olive wood. At the last minute Debrah, restraining her grief, placed Joah's leather sling and three good pebbles in with the body.

After the funeral feast, a crowded, boisterous, somewhat drunken affair, Uzzi called Micah and Debrah to him for the final prayers. And then Joah, who had been gathered to his forefathers and was no more, was by a deliberate effort of will thrust into the limbo of their memories. Death was too much a part of Israelite life, and this was the turning of a page in the family history, like so many other pages in times gone by; life now was for the living.

And slowly, as the days and the weeks went by, family life in the household of Uzzi ben Ezra grew into a different form, but still much the same as it had always been. A new goatherd was hired, a twelve-year-old boy named Misham who was not as skilled as Joah had been in finding pasture for his charges, but who, because he was not family, could be driven a great deal harder. He was terrified of the dogs, which regarded him as an intruder, and he was bitten four times in the first week of his employ; the first time, before Uzzi rescued him, he had nearly been killed.

But for the rest—time passed, and life went on.

One month after Joah's death (the moon in precisely the same remembered phase), an exciting day dawned for Captain Beladus. It was a day he had long been planning.

He stood with Rekam and watched the morning parade. It was being inspected by the officer of the day, a lieutenant named Anipal. He was walking down the line of the men as they held their drawn swords out, laid across the heavy bronze bracelets of their left forearms, and he was testing every third one of them for sharpness with the nail of his thumb. Anipal was a man of middle age who walked with a very pronounced limp. As a young man, he had been on a mission from King Hiram to Soloman's father David, and quite by happenstance had found himself involved in the Battle of Ephraim Forest, where he had seen the fiery Joab plunge three angry darts into the trapped body of his cousin Absalom who was hanging by his hair, tangled in an oak tree (his mule having run out from under him). And in that battle, he had taken the copper head of a lance in his thigh, a wound so severe that it had severed almost half of the muscles. He could no longer ride or fight, but he was greatly respected and feared.

Beladus said, "I will ride into Bethlehem unarmed—it is more fitting. With ten soldiers and five slaves."

They had argued the matter of weapons before, and Rekam sighed; his commander was a very stubborn man. "Unarmed," he echoed. "And if the Philistines are out raiding?"

"I am sure they are," Beladus said mildly. "But they will be riding hard for Gezer, or perhaps Lydda, where my men will be waiting to receive them."

"Let us hope that this is true."

"There is a convoy of cloth from Tyre, a very rich one, destined for Solomon's court. I am told that it is valued at a quite incredible five talents of gold, a prodigal gift from the king to the ladies of his harem. Like the Pharaohs, from whom he learned the fine art of hedonism, Solomon has learned the great delights of luxury, even if his people are groaning under the burden of supporting it. Akish, without a doubt, will know of it, and will attack it. That is why I have sent nearly two-thirds of our force to await him."

Rekam sighed. "And so, we have only a score of men left to guard the camp."

"I will return by midday. And we ride out . . . unarmed. I do not wish to cause alarm in the hearts of the good people of Bethlehem."

Rekam shrugged. "It is your decision, Commander. And have you heard the news from Ashkelon?"

Beladus frowned. "From Ashkelon? No."

"Our spies there say Akish is recruiting more men."

"It will not be easy for him. The life of a guerrilla is a hard one."

"He has sent two men there, and they are spending a great deal of gold in the taverns, buying the services of the highest-priced whores in the city with reckless abandon, showing no regard at all for the value of money. Sooner or later, a great many dockside ruffians will be asking themselves the question: how is it that these guerrillas have so much money to lavish on their pleasures? When they find the answer to that question, many of these wretches will join him."

"Perhaps. But our troops are well trained and disciplined. Dockside scum who fight only for money will be no match for them."

"That is true."

The ten men Beladus had detailed were riding up, with the five slaves and the pack horse, and Beladus leaped to his own saddle and said, laughing, "Do not worry about Akish, Rekam—he will be far away! We will see neither hide nor hair of the Philistines!"

He was wrong on one count; Akish knew nothing of the rich convoy, and was skulking still in his hideout, wondering where he might strike next (and drunk with too much beer, thinking of the young shepherdess who had been stolen from him; the touch of her budding breasts still burned his coarse hands). And on the other count—he was only partly right.

They saw no Philistines when they left the bluff. But a single Philistine saw *them* . . .

They rode slowly past a man dressed in a long brown robe of goats' hair, a thin, heavily bearded man with shrewd and searching eyes who watched them carefully, bowing as they rode by him. One of the Phoenician soldiers called out, "A good day to you, Israelite!" He would not answer (his Gaza accent might have betrayed him), but contented himself with bowing more deeply than ever. And when they had gone, he sat down on a rock and produced a stylus, black ink, and papyrus from under his cloak, and began sketching the approaches to the bluff, marking down every track, bush, gully, rock, and even—as Akish had told him—every shadow.

His name was Grenik, a cartographer from the Philistine city of Gaza.

The Phoenicians moved on, and soon they entered the little village of Bethlehem.

Here, until their arrival, it had been just another ordinary day. In their timbered shelters, the potters were hard at work, spinning their heavy stone wheel with their feet as they molded the clay for jugs, bowls, beakers, and other vessels. Some of them were treading the clay, pounding their feet into great mounds of wet mud. At other tables, very young and naked children, learning the trade, were slowly turning the wheels of the master potters, who fashioned the more intricate jars. The huge clay ovens nearby were being fired by apprentices, and the floors were so thickly littered with with their products that a man had to pick his way among them with the greatest care. The potters, wearing loincloths of red, blue, yellow, or brown, traded their wares at the smaller huts of the dyers.

At the local dye house, other skilled craftsmen were at work, dipping their threads into deep stone vats, rinsing them with water and pressing out the excess dye (to be used again) in heavy olive-wood presses. The dyers were coloring their threads now instead of the finished cloth; multi-colored garments, introduced by a more sophisticated Phoenician culture, were becoming fashionable among the wealthier Israelite women; primitive as they were, they were quick to learn.

It was an ordinary Bethlehem day. The women were down at the wells, gathering into little cliques for the exchange of gossip. Sometimes, they would stay there for an hour or more, while their husbands and sons and mules all waited impatiently for the troughs to be refilled. The four narrow streets of the village, crowded with the early-morning activity, reverberated with the noise of their shouted greetings to one another.

Now, a magnificent entourage was moving along the straight street that ran through the center of the village. There were more than a dozen men on horseback, dressed in brilliant scarlet, yellow, or blue tunics, with magnificent sandals strapped to their feet by leather bindings that reached nearly to their knees. They were led by a tall, slender, bearded man of impressive nobility, dressed in purple. It was apparent that they were not soldiers, for none of them carried arms.

Above them, on the flat roofs of the single-story houses and on the balconies of those that boasted two floors, little groups of excited people were gathering to watch them. And here, as on the street below, there were excited whispers:

"They are Phoenicians, you can tell by their raiment . . .

"Did you ever see a more handsome commander . . . ?

"They come to bring trouble. Why else would they be here . . . ?

"But they carry no weapons . . .

"Such splendid clothes . . . even the slaves are well dressed . . ."

On the street, the throng was crowding against the walls of the houses to give them passage, staring in wide-eyed amazement, some of them very frightened because this was something out of the ordinary and could therefore bode no good at all. A bent and bowed old man was hobbling on a long staff, moving as fast as he was able to get out of their way. The commander raised his arm for the column to halt and called to him pleasantly, "By your leave, sir?"

The old man stared, and looked over his shoulder to see who was really being addressed. A beggar, he had not been called "sir" since the death of his last child. His face was dark and wrinkled, his beard long and grey. He said hesitantly, "Lord?"

Beladus had seen the fear on many of their faces, and he wanted to put them all at their ease. He said amiably, "There is a merchant here named Uzzi ben Ezra. If you would tell me, sir, where I might find him?"

He knew where the house was. On that memorable night, Nemuel had lost Debrah in the darkness, but he had found her again and had duly reported back to his captain as ordered. But to Beladus, it seemed necessary to explain his peaceful presence here.

86

The old man pointed, not sure he was doing the right thing. "There, Lord," he said. "You turn toward the sun where the hill begins." He was shaking with fear, and Beladus, seeing the worry in the anxious old eyes, said gently, "Do not be afraid, old man. I come as a friend. You can see that we carry no weapons. We carry only gifts for Uzzi the son of Ezra, whom we hold in high esteem." He hesitated. "And by your aspect, sir, you are a beggar, I think?"

The old man nodded vigorously. "A beggar, Lord. For a man of my frailty, there is no other way to earn a day's bread."

"A gift, then, will not be amiss, I think. A man should not suffer because of his great age." He fumbled in the pouch at his side and found a small bar of silver, a shekel, and tossed it to him. The beggar was not so frail that he could not recognize worth when he saw it. He caught the shekel expertly and stared at it in shock—its value was more than he could beg in a year or more.

Beladus looked back at the halted column and signaled, and as the slow walk of the horses began again, the old beggar bent down to a child beside him, took him by the ear, and whispered urgently, "Run, boy, to the house of Uzzi ben Ezra. Tell him that strangers have come here to kill him . . ." They were not Philistines, he was almost sure; or were they? In any event, dressed in such finery as they were, they were patently not Israelites, and therefore, they were enemies.

The child, dressed in a rag, his eyes wide and frightened, ran off, scuttling expertly under the horses' hooves as they threaded their way carefully among the mules and the donkey carts that crowded the narrow street; he was sure that the most dreadful calamity was about to fall on his little village, and he could not still the beating of his child's heart.

Soon the horsemen arrived at Uzzi's compound, the brilliant colors of their robes and accoutrements bright against the drab grays of the mud and the stonework. A slave slipped from the saddle to open the heavy timbered gate, and they wheeled their mounts in and lined up in orderly array to await their commander's orders. The neighbors—men, women, and children—were already lined up at the walls, staring.

Uzzi, forewarned, was at the door of his house, his frightened wife Micah beside him. He whispered to her impatiently, "Why are you frightened, woman? This nobleman is my friend. You think a merchant has no friends among the nobility? He comes, without a doubt, to trade with me. It is apparant that my good reputation for fair dealing has reached his ears at last. So cease your trembling! And smile!"

He said, fawning, "My Lord Beladus, you honor my humble home. A modest house of indifferent quality, but yours to use as you desire."

Beladus was sizing him up. What before had been a broken old man in the depths of understandable grief was now a merchant, and he had come prepared. He slipped lithely off his mount and went to Uzzi, stopping the requisite three paces from him. "It is my hope, sir, that this is not an intrusion upon your serenity?"

"No intrusion, Lord," Uzzi answered. "Indeed, it is not only a great honor for me, but a matter of great interest as well."

The low wall of the compound was lined with eager, staring faces. Uzzi gestured at them and said deprecatingly, "Forgive the ill manners of my neighbors, Lord. They are not accustomed to the magnificence you present to their avid gaze. The splendor of your robes—I have seldom seen such finely spun cloth! The very magnificence of your external majesty, down to the quality of the leather with which your company's sandals are made." He coughed. "Well, not the leather, perhaps, but the rest . . . Yes, Lord, a splendid sight for the poor people of this miserable village."

Amused, Beladus said, "Not our leather, sir?"

Uzzi was bowing deeply again. "The most excellent leather, Lord, I should not have spoken so precipitately.

It is simply that the hides I personally hold in my warehouse are of considerably higher quality, but . . . so be it. Indeed, why should a man worry about what he wears on his feet, even though it be a poor complement to the very high quality of his robes? An idle thought, Lord, and I crave your pardon for it. It should never have passed my lips."

"Then we will talk of hides and leather," Beladus said, "but on a later occasion. For the moment, there are more important matters for discussion. I bring you, sir, gifts that I hope you will accept as small tokens of my admiration, which is great."

"*Gifts*, Lord?" Uzzi was startled, and a little worried too; customers did not bring gifts. "And why should I be so deserving, Lord?"

"A man of quality," Beladus said, "visiting for the first time the house of another man of quality, should bring presents. It is so written in our code of conduct, as it is in yours." He called out, "Nemuel! The presents!'

"Sir!"

The slave Nemuel dismounted, ran to the pack horse and led it forward, and began the ceremony of the laying out of presents. And as he placed them on the hard earth of the courtyard, Captain Beladus called them out in accordance with the strict protocol that had been laid out centuries ago by the Phoenician branch of the Semites.

He intoned, almost nonchalantly, "One bale of white cotton cloth from Egypt, the finest ever woven. Thirty cubits of that same cloth dyed to scarlet, immaculately and without blemish, sufficient for three gowns for a man or four for a woman. Five skins of wine from Tyre, pressed from the grapes that grow near Sidon. There are none better in the world. Four shekels of gold in a single bar, and twelve of silver in four bars . . ."

Uzzi's eyes were goggling, and poor Micah was ready to swoon.

But it was not finished. Beladus went on: "The gold

and the silver to be worked at your desire into household vessels or ornaments to beautify the women who share your bed. A polished cedar statuette of King Hiram of Tyre, executed by a craftsman of high repute in Sidon, and another in ivory, carved in Egypt . . ." Conscious of the gasps from around the walls, he continued: "A copy in papyrus from Byblos of the plans we drew for King Solomon's palace, now being completed. It is my hope, Uzzi ben Ezra, that you will graciously accept these slight tokens of my respect and esteem."

Slight tokens? Uzzi could not credit the great wealth that was being spread out before him. His eyes were wide with wonder, his heart beating fast in bewilderment. But his native shrewdness was not impaired. He said carefully, "Your generosity, Lord, exceeds even the wonder of your personal magnificence."

"And I am pleased," Beladus said, "that you accept them with such good grace. If you could spare me, sir, a little of your time? There are matters we should speak of. Matters of great moment to both of us."

"Ah, you honor me, Lord! Then perhaps we should go to the roof? As you see, I have a fine shelter there." He turned to Micah and said, blustering, "Why do you stand there like a donkey, woman? Go into the house and bake bread for our guest! Can you not see that he is hungry? And bring salt."

Micah scurried into the house, relieved that she had been dismissed. Uzzi led the captain up the stone steps to the roof, stumbling as he always did over his gown, turning back and bowing repeatedly. "I am a poor man, Lord," he said, "as you can well see, struggling to keep body and soul together in a land that takes our very skins in taxes." He added quickly, "A joke, Lord. I deal in skins . . . But a good shelter on a man's rooftop is a very small luxury."

The arbor was made of woven palm fronds supported on sticks of olive wood, open on all sides and screening out the burning rays of the sun. It was a gath-

90

ering place for the family in the evenings when the heat of the day and the smoke from the cooking fire had made the room downstairs intolerable. Half a dozen small stools had been set out with a few sitting-skins, and there was a porous jar of water with a ladle on it. "Be seated, Lord," Uzzi said, "we have stools . . . And tell me how it is that I may serve you. If it is a matter of supply for your troops, permit me to say that there is no merchant in the whole of Bethlehem who has finer grain or oil or honey or hides. Nor indeed, who enjoys a better reputation for fair dealing. Not the lowest prices, of course, for I learned long since that quality costs money. Cheap and shoddy merchandise, I have none of it, Lord Beladus. And I am convinced that a man of your nobility would not want it."

To one side of them, the gray hill rose steeply, topped by the wall of the city. Far beyond it they could see the great stone edifice, nearly sixty feet high— Solomon's Temple, built from dressed limestone blocks, many of them as much as eighteen cubits long, that had been dragged here from the quarries by slaves and piled upon each other with meticulous precision. They had been perfectly formed at the quarries themselves, so that the sound of hammer and chisel should not be heard within the temple area. To the other side, the land rolled down to the pools and the beginnings of the valley of Elah, a wonderful panorama stretching all the way to the land of the hated Philistines. The early-morning air was cool, and from up here, the sounds of the street were muted.

Beladus said quietly, "I did not come to speak of commerce, Uzzi ben Ezra, though I will be happy to entertain your suggestions later. I came to speak to you of Debrah, your ward."

Ah, Debrah . . . !

Uzzi wondered why he had not known it at once! The memory came flooding back to him of their close embrace. *Your pain is mine*, the captain had said, and *my happiness lies only in yours*. Talk, he had thought,

91

simple flattery from a sophisticated man to an innocent young girl. But now? All this pomp and ceremony? And the gifts! He could not contain his excitement, nor did he quite know how to confront this frank approach. He said, searching for time in which to think, "A fine young girl, Lord, to bring great pleasure to a frail old heart like mine."

"To my heart too," Beladus said. "Has she recovered yet from the death of her betrothed?"

"None of us, Lord, will ever recover. He was a fine young man. Though life must go on, of course."

"Of course. You have been searching, no doubt, for another husband for her?"

"It is not so much a question of searching, Lord," Uzzi said craftily, "as of choosing among those who are anxious to wed her. There is one young man, for example, whose father owns eight hundred olive trees in Azekah in the valley of Elah. Eight hundred trees! Such wealth gives a man cause to think deeply when the welfare of his only daughter is at stake. He has offered me forty homers of grain and fifteen bales of unprocessed flax for her, together with twelve donkeys." He sighed. "That is a very substantial offer indeed, one that has caused us all to gasp in astonishment." (It was not true. The offer was fifteen homers of grain, four bales of flax, and no donkeys at all. It was still a very good price indeed.)

Beladus asked, "She is not here today?"

"At this hour of the morning, she goes to the pools to fetch water. She is a very dutiful daughter."

"I am sure of it."

"And the best housekeeper in the whole of Bethlehem! She puts not only honey, but raisins in the bread she bakes. And the cotton she looms! Exquisite, Lord! And in cleaning out the stables, there is no one to match her. And of course, her great beauty cannot entirely be ignored. A virgin, of course . . ."

Beladus felt the panegyric might go on for ever, and he raised a hand and said, "Her beauty is beyond dispute, passing all others, and she has a sweetness of temperament which endears her to me greatly, a delicacy of both form and mind that I find enchanting. But she has other qualities that may not be as apparent to her father as they are to . . . dare I say a friend? I have seen a light in her glorious eyes that speaks of a hidden strength unusual in one so young, a promise of fullness far beyond her years."

"A weak and untried young girl," Uzzi murmured deprecatingly, knowing that the time had come for a little subtlety. Beladus shook his head vigorously. "No!" he tried. "Untried, perhaps, but not weak! I have known many women, Uzzi ben Ezra, and I flatter myself that I have an instinct for understanding them. And in your lovely Debrah, I saw at once what might not be recognizable to those less discerning—a sure potential for the kind of authority that few women, young or old, are blessed with. It even confused me when I first became aware of it. Even though, I believe, there have been many women of consequence among your people."

"Oh, yes indeed!" Uzzi nodded wisely. "There was Bathsheba, who was wise enough to gain a promise from her husband King David that the great Solomon would succeed him instead of the eldest son Adonijah, whom Solomon felt constrained to put to death . . . There was Ruth, who was the mother of Obed, who was the father of Jesse, who was the father of David . . . yes, a great woman indeed . . . And Jael, of course, who drove a tent peg through the head of the evil commander Sisera of the Canaanites . . . yes, I would call her a woman of consequence. And we must not forget the great Deborah herself, Debrah's namesake of course, who raised an army of ten thousand men and delivered us from the yoke of King Jabin of Hazor . . ."

"So many of them," Beladus said hastily, interrupting the old man's history lesson. "And it is this quality, my dear friend, that I have found in her. A woman indeed who could lead an army, and at the same time . . .

soft, and gentle, and warm-hearted. And very, very lovely. I will confess that I cannot sleep at night for thinking of her. And it is my belief that she remembers me with some affection."

The old man sighed, wondering how he could turn these elusive benefits to his best advantage. He said at last, very casually, "It is true, Lord, that her remembrance of you is not without its attendant pleasures. My wife Micah tells me that Debrah has, on occasion, cried out your name in her sleep, though this, of course `. . .`"

"She calls out my name?" There was a fire in the captain's eyes now.

"It means little, Lord. At her tender age, all young girls suffer from . . . from certain physical weaknesses which are sometimes reflected quite shamefully in their dreams. I know that you mean well for her, and I speak now, not disrespectfully as it might seem. Indeed, disrespect is very far from my mind, as it should be! I can say what I must because I am an old man, and devoted to her well-being too. It would bring a certain unhappiness on me were I to sell her into concubinage, as so many good fathers do with their daughters." Daringly, he added, "Especially, perhaps, to a foreigner. A nobleman of high quality whom we all admire and greatly respect, but nonetheless, a foreigner." He was wondering what form Beladus's anger would take, and how he might counter it.

But to his surprise, the captain was smiling broadly; this was the kind of talk he understood, and he was good at it. He said amiably, "It is not concubinage I have in mind, but a higher state."

Uzzi stared, quite unbelieving. "But you are not suggesting, Lord, the possibility of . . . of *marriage?*"

"That is precisely what I am suggesting. A slight difference in rank and honor, but one that should not be ignored entirely."

"*Marriage?* To an Israelite woman?"

"And why not, pray?"

Uzzi swallowed hard. "I find it . . . surprising,

94

Lord. I know very little of your people, but I have heard it said that your own women are . . . may I say *different* from ours. More refined in all things, more . . . advanced in their wifely duties. I have been given to understand, as they pertain to, ah, the physical comfort of a Phoenician husband. Skilled in certain aspects of those duties upon which it would be unseemly for me to dwell."

"If you mean," Beladus said calmly, "that our Tyrian women are whores, I will debate the point with you . . ."

"No, Lord!" Uzzi said hastily, "not whores! But I have heard tell that they are beautiful and very, ah, adept in those matters. Whereas Debrah has had no preparation in this direction whatsoever . . ."

Beladus smiled. "She can be taught. There is a hidden passion in her eyes which leads me to believe she will learn quickly. Provided that she is obedient, as I already know her to be."

"Er, yes." Uzzi hesitated. "You have other wives, Lord, no doubt?"

Beladus shrugged. "Only in Tyre, not here."

"And if I were to agree to such a startling course, you would take her there?"

"Not immediately. And the future . . ." He gestured. "It is in the lap of the gods. And as for my being a foreigner, you must know that there is a great deal of intermarrying between our two peoples now. Even your great and wise Solomon—very few of his countless wives are Israelite women. He openly encourages mixed marriages with all of your neighboring peoples, if only because they help cement the alliances which are so dear to him. His wisdom is legendary, Uzzi, and he knows that peace among nations begins in the mixing of their blood, not with treaties that can so easily be broken. I believe that your great king himself would bless you if you were to give Debrah to me."

They were fencing with each other now, and Uzzi was crafty enough to know that Beladus, too, was a very shrewd man, and was offering him an argument to be pursued to its logical and profitable conclusion. He already knew its outcome; but advantage could always be increased, this was the code he lived by. He contrived to look as downcast as possible and said, "The king would bless me? Ah, if only that were true, Lord!"

"Believe me," Baladus said earnestly. "It would greatly elevate you in his esteem, which I am sure is already high."

"And if only that were true, too! Alas, he has never even heard my name . . ."

Ah, so that was the little extra profit! Well then . . . ! Beladus said easily, "He has heard *mine*. I have even met with him, and he was gracious enough to find pleasure in my presence. And Solomon, as you know, maintains a very open court. There is not one of his subjects who may not approach him. Shipowners, horse-breeders, builders, merchants, peasants . . . Indeed," he said drily, "even prostitutes haggling over owner-ship of a baby, as we have all heard in such great and often-told detail. His court is open to anyone."

The talk was proceeding in exactly the right direc-tion! Uzzi said, feigning surprise, "Are you suggesting, Lord, that I should go to Solomon and ask his blessing on this transaction? I would never make so bold!"

"Then we will go to him together." The captain was playing his role well too, always a step ahead, in his de-vious Phoenician mind, of Uzzi's wiles. "We will ask his advice together. I have his ear."

"Ah," Uzzi said wistfully, "to have the ear of King Solomon himself! It could make a humble merchant burst with pride."

"It could also," Beladus said calmly, "make him very, very rich."

Uzzi fingered his beard. "Yes, perhaps it could," he murmured. "Though the thought had not occurred to me before you were pleased to mention it."

"No, I am sure it had not. Then are we agreed? That

if between us we can obtain King Solomon's blessing on such a union, your daughter Debrah will be mine?"

"As a wife, Lord? Not as a mere concubine?"

"As almost my only wife. My word that she will be my favorite, for many years to come."

Uzzi had won his battle, and to great advantage. He still did not want to appear too eager; there were other matters to think of. He fiddled with his long beard again, frowning darkly as Beladus, already knowing what the answer would be, composed himself and waited. He said at last, raising a finger, "Agreed then, Lord, provided of course that suitable terms can be arranged between us. We must not forget that she is a young woman of great merit, that she has also a great . . . potential, not weak and untried as she may seem to a casual observer. I have noticed that hidden strength in her many times, though perhaps you have not."

"Of course," Beladus said gravely. "Suitable terms will be arranged. I will send an emissary to you to discuss the matter. Livestock, cloth, skins, oil, gold . . . whatever may be your pleasure."

Gold? Uzzi's eyes gleamed. He said offhandedly, "My warehouses are already bursting with merchandise I find it hard to dispose of, but gold . . . Yes, I would say gold is perhaps the most suitable form of exchange. Yes, I would say gold."

"Then I will have my emissary speak only in terms of minas of gold."

Uzzi stared. *"Minas?"* he echoed. "You mean, no doubt, *shekels?"*

"No, my dearest friend. I am a wealthy man, and I mean *minas*."

It was very hard for Uzzi to recover his senses; they were reeling. A mina was fifty shekels, and even a shekel or two in gold was almost more than he could imagine. He was already wondering where he could hide such vast wealth. Perhaps if he were to dig a hole in the sand under his own bed? Stealthily, in the night? He composed himself by a strong effort of will, and

97

said, trembling but trying to hide his excitement, "Then if you will so honor me, we will drink wine on it together." He went to the top of the steps and shouted down, "Micah! Where are you, woman! Where is the bread? Where is the salt? And bring wine!"

Her voice was a whimper. "I am coming, husband, coming now, it is ready . . ."

Uzzi turned back to his guest and said apologetically, "She is old, and therefore slow. Perhaps it is time for me to purchase another wife or two, much younger. If Debrah is to leave me, who will do all the work that must be done? Yes indeed, two very young wives. I would have done this long ago, but I am, as you see, a very poor man."

"But rich, dear friend, in the qualities that make a man admirable."

"Ah . . . How gracious of you to notice, and to remark on it."

The bread that Micah brought was still hot on its clay platter and very good; she had added oil and honey to the dough to show what fine taste her husband had. And the skin of the wine was fine and new, bulging like the body of the young goat it had once been.

"The bread is made from wheat, not barley," Uzzi said proudly. "A little quirk of mine. I feel it would be dishonorable to offer so distinguished a guest bread made from barley such as the peasants eat."

Beladus made a little half-bow. "You are very gracious," he said. "I have seldom seen such refinement, even in Tyre."

"Oh surely you exaggerate, Lord!" Uzzi said, delighted, and Beladus shook his head. "Not in the slightest, I assure you."

They broke the cake of salt ceremoniously over the bread as Micah hovered and filled their cups for them, and ate and chatted like old friends. When he had eaten his fill, Beladus belched loudly to show his appreciation and went over to the edge of the roof to look down on the distant slope. Some of the women in their *abas* were moving up the path in a single line, carrying their huge jars of water on their hips; Debrah was not among them.

"And now," he said, "I must regrettably leave you. I have been away from my duties too long, seduced by your splendid hospitality, for which I thank you."

"If you must, Lord." Uzzi could hardly wait to go and examine the magnificent gifts. "The honor of this visit, and of the arrangement we have almost completed, will long remain with me."

"And if, indeed, you have good skins in your warehouses, perhaps you would send a man to my camp with a few donkeyloads. We are always in need of good leather."

"Your servant, Lord."

"No more servant, nor Lord," Beladus said cheerfully, clinching the matter. "From now on, a simple 'Captain' will suffice. Or even . . . Beladus."

He ran down the steps and leaped on his horse, and the column followed him out through the crowd that had gathered there, along the narrow, noisy street and out of the village. And as he had hoped, he saw Debrah struggling up the hill with her heavy load among a score of other women. He reined in his horse and called out, laughing, "Greetings to you, Debrah, on this wonderful morning!"

Her heart was beating fast as she answered him, "And to you too, Lord Beladus!"

The eyes of all the women were on him, a fine and striking figure on a prancing horse that tossed its mane back and rose up impatiently on its hind legs. Even the soldiers and the slaves looked cheerful and good-humored, as though something marvelous were happening. She, too, was laughing, caught by the infectious pleasure on the captain's face. "And what is it, Lord," she caled out, "that brings you to Bethlehem? An honor for our humble village . . ."

"Your father will tell you, Debrah! Hurry home, child, he has news for you! Excellent news that will make you, I dare hope, as happy as it has made me! So run! As fast as a gazelle! Good news should not wait in the telling!"

He did not wait for a reply. He dug in his heels and raced off, turning in the saddle to wave at her as she stood there, staring after him in utter bewilderment. He shouted again, "Run home, child! Fast as you can!"

Debrah gasped, and one of the women said, her dark eyes wide and puzzled, "Good news for you, Debrah? What can it be? And who is he?"

Debrah recovered. She dropped to her knee and twisted her lithe young body around to lower the heavy jar to the ground; when she ran on up the hill, tears of happiness were streaming down her face. Aware of their consternation, neighbor women and friends all of them, she turned and shouted back to them, her young breast rising and falling fast in her excitement, "I know what the news is! I know . . . !"

She turned and ran on to Bethlehem, not stopping till she raced into the compound and saw her father Uzzi doing a little dance of the purest delight. The neighbors were all gathering around her, laughing and clapping her on the back, trying to embrace her as she ran to her father and threw her arms around his neck. Micah was there, weeping copiously, and Debrah said breathlessly: "I know, I know . . . He wants me for a concubine . . ."

Uzzi could not hold back his great pride. "Not a concubine," he said. "A *wife*."

Her hands went to her cheeks, and she stared at him, speechless.

6

The great day arrived at last.

King Solomon sat on his imposing throne, which was decorated with a frieze depicting the musicians and dancing girls of his court, each of its seven steps guarded by miniature ivory lions, and flanked by two larger lions, sculpted from ivory and solid gold and extravagantly winged. It had been crafted by Phoenician artisans (this kind of artistry was far beyond the capabilities of the Israelites) from sandalwood, inlaid with ivory, gold, and precious stones.

Solomon wore a long, short-sleeved robe of fine white cotton, half-covered with a blue mantle fringed in red, the blue and white band at his waist decorated with gold wire. A plaited gold strap around his forehead controlled his thick black hair, and his square-cut beard was neatly trimmed and curled. His leather sandals were studded with ivory and bound in gold cord. He leaned forward, a long gold staff in his hand, to study a fine red stallion that was prancing on the polished stone floor on its tether, held by two slaves who could not fully control it. It was frightened, not only by the blare of the music, but also by the crowd that had assembled here.

This was the Hall of Judgment in the palace, a huge and very beautiful room, its high ceiling supported by pillars painted in blue, brown, and gray, with overlays of beaten gold. The main entrance, high and wide and doorless, led to the paved courtyard outside, and was flanked by magnificent murals showing the king's favorite horses, his chariots, and his troops advancing into battle. A dozen or more of his favorite concubines reclined on divans scattered around the hall, not so much because they might be needed, but merely because it was their privilege to listen to the great king's wisdom. Four guards, carrying spears and heavily embossed shields of solid gold, were posted at the sides of the throne, beside which a scribe crouched at a low table with his jar of ink and a reed stylus. A very old, white-bearded man, the sage, rocked slowly back and forth on his heels in a corner. There were nearly a hundred people here all told, and a young slave was elbowing his way to the king, bearing a gold cup of wine on a gold tray. The noise of the horse's screams, together with the sound of the drums and the trumpets, was excruciating.

It was a splendid animal, well over sixteen spans high, with a powerful neck and chest and a very long and full tail; its hocks were banded in white, and its eyes were very large and angry.

Horses, even more than women, were the king's great love; and he was very knowledgeable about them.

The groom who had brought him here, a wiry man with a pock-marked face, was dressed in Egyptian robes. The king, hardly able to tear his eyes away from the stallion, said to him, "Your name, fellow?"

The Egyptian bowed. "My name, Most High and Mighty, is Anusis, and I am equerry to the Pharaoh, from his stables in Alexandria."

"The horse is what, three years old? A trifle more?"

"Three and a half, Most High."

"And how many colts has he sired?"

"Four. They are in the stables in Alexandria, worthy animals all of them."

"And the price you are asking for the stallion?"

"Three hundred and fifty shekels of silver, Most High and Mighty."

"That is more than double the price I pay for my finest chariot horse, Anusis."

The equerry was smiling. He had seen the fiery light in Solomon's eyes when the horse had been brought in, and he knew that price did not matter now. "But this horse," he said, "will never feel the yoke of a chariot! Would you send your strongest warrior to kill flies? No, he will sire many splendid horses for you, and when you ride him, he will carry you with the speed of the wind across the desert. And he is as sure-footed as he is fast."

"Yes, he prances on polished stone and has not once lost his balance. Three hundred and fifty then. And I will pay you two hundred each for those four colts. Send the stallion to my stables in Megiddo at once, and deliver the colts there as soon as you can."

"At your command, Most High and Mighty." The equerry bowed and led the prize horse out. Solomon said to the scribe, "And now, whom have we now?"

The scribe, who was making a mark with his stylus against the entry *a stallion from Egypt*, said: "A Phoenician captain, Lord, whose name is Beladus, together with a merchant of Bethlehem named Uzzi ben Ezra and his foster daughter Debrah."

"A matter of concerning what?"

"I do not know, Lord, it has not been stated."

The king was frowning. "Beladus? Do I not know that name?"

"In command, Lord, of the Phoenician convoy guards."

Solomon's face lit up. "Ah, yes, I remember. A soldier in whom I am greatly interested. There is a scroll on him—send for it." The king kept the most meticulous records—sometimes very secret—on all those who served him in high rank. The scribe summoned a slave and sent him off to the archives. Solomon said, "I will see them."

He sipped the wine the slave boy at his elbow was offering him as the trumpets blared again and the reception-master called out, in a stentorian voice: "Captain Beladus of Tyre. Uzzi ben Ezra of Bethlehem, a merchant from the tribe of Reuben. Debrah bat Uzzi ben Ezra, also of Bethlehem and his foster daughter."

Beladus swept into the room and strode to the embroidered carpet at the foot of the throne. He dropped to one knee, bowed his head, and said clearly, "I am Beladus of Tyre, Most High and Mighty, a Phoenician, and your devoted servant." Behind him, Uzzi and Debrah dropped down too, and held their peace; they were lesser beings here.

"Rise, Beladus," the king said, and the captain rose to his feet and put his strong hands on his hips and waited; he could not, by strict protocol, state his case till he was invited to do so. Uzzi and Debrah remained on their knees, and Solomon ignored them completely (though he wondered why this pretty young child had chosen to appear before him in a such a strange dress.)

"I remember you well, Beladus," Solomon said amiably. "For a few regrettably brief moments you brought me pleasure on a day that was not a happy one for me. The quarters I set aside for you, they are satisfactory, I trust?"

"They were splendid quarters, Most High," Beladus said carefully. "But on more mature reflection it occurred to me that I could serve you better if I were to establish a camp further to the west, to inhibit any surprise attack by the Philistines should they dare to approach Jerusalem itself. With this thought in mind, I have set up a camp above the pools, from which point of vantage I can not only send out my patrols more easily, but also serve as an outpost to guard against such attack."

Solomon *knew*. He sighed and said, "I, too, found it wiser to build my quarters outside the walls. Jerusalem is sadly lacking in the civilized amenities. And I am

104

grateful that my personal safety is so dear to you. Are you comfortably installed there?"

"Not as comfortably, Most High," Beladus said smoothly, "as we would have been in the splendid houses your Greatness was pleased to set aside for us. But for a simple soldier . . . a camp of tentage is adequate."

"Good. Then before we hear your suit, Beladus, let us find out who you are. Scribe . . . !"

The Scribe rose to his feet and unrolled the scroll brought by the slaves. He cleared his throat noisily and read: "Captain Beladus of the House of Tirgan, a nobleman of Tyre, lately a commander of King Hiram's Palace Guard and exiled by that exalted monarch to Jerusalem . . ."

Exiled? Beladus could feel the blood draining from his face. But he held his peace. Watching him, Solomon held up his hand to silence the scribe and said gently, "I see, Beladus, that you did not know of your exile. Will you tell me the reason for it?"

But before Beladus could find the angry words, the scribe coughed and said apologetically, "It is written here, Lord."

"Then read on."

". . . exiled by that exalted monarch to Jerusalem for his outspoken opinions concerning what he has been pleased to call, on numerous occasions, 'the sad and unjustified condition of the oppressed peoples of Israel who are left to suffer, almost unaided, the depredations of the Palaestines who call themselves Philistines, with none to offer them the military assistance they must have if they are to survive as a nation.' King Hiram has seen fit to provide only military escorts that bring him payment for his services, and therefore, these sentiments have not found favor in his eyes. Beladus was born in Tyre, of noble family, some thirty years ago. He is known as a scholar of repute, a soldier of undoubted courage, and as a man of good will . . ."

105

The king waved a hand again. "Enough," he said, "I will hear no more."

The scribe rolled up the parchment. The king, smiling slightly now, looked at the white-faced Beladus and said quietly, "It seems to me, my friend, and you must tell me if I am wrong, that the facts of your exile were not known to you."

The captain said steadily, "It was not known to me, Lord, and I will confess that it comes as a great shock. It does not diminish my loyalty to my king."

"Well spoken, Beladus. Hiram, as you well know, is our friend and brother. But I know him to be a hard and ruthless man, as a king must be if he is to rule. There is no disgrace, Beladus, in the circumstances of your exile. Indeed, they please me greatly."

Now, at last, he looked at Debrah, who still knelt there beside her father, wondering if permission to rise would ever come. She wore a very simple gown that she had made from the fine Egyptian cotton that Beladus had brought. It was bound very tightly at her narrow waist, high under the breasts, and Uzzi had made her cut almost a whole span away from the neckline, saying angrily when she protested, "No! You cannot appear before the king looking like a peasant! You are the daughter of a man of quality, never forget that! And the king must know it at once!"

Solomon said casually, "Debrah bat Uzzi and Uzzi ben Ezra, you may rise."

They regained their feet, and Debrah searched for her father's hand and found it, seeking courage. But Uzzi was clutching hers for the same reason; his eyes were almost goggling. There was so much splendor here! There was more gold around him than he would ever have thought to see in a lifetime! And in spite of the great number of people, there was the persuasive scent of sandalwood on the air instead of the sour stench of goats and donkeys that pervaded his own house. And the clothes that everyone wore! Even the slaves were dressed magnificently! And the concubines

106

lounging everywhere, half-naked, with gowns of such flimsy stuff that he could see their breasts and even their thighs! He could never have imagined such decadence, and he was thinking: so this is why we are so heavily taxed!

It was common knowledge throughout Israel that Solomon, wise only in limited aspects of his complex personality, had readily agreed to Hiram's first-stated price for the building of this magnificient palace, not even bothering to haggle with him. The Phoenician king had demanded, and had been promised, no less than one hundred and twenty talents of gold, more than *three tons*. (Solomon was never able to find this huge fee, and was forced to hand over, in part payment, a strip of land in Galilee together with its twenty villages.) The cost of the earlier and smaller temple had already impoverished the humble taxpayers of the land; the fee had been seven thousand tons of wheat and 185 gallons of olive oil per year, for each of the seven years the building was to take. All this as well as hundreds of thousands of copper bars for building the port and the ships at Ezion-Geber! Uzzi wanted to weep when he thought of it.

But now, Solomon was studying Debrah intently. He saw a slender, fragile young woman hardly out of her childhood but with wise, somber eyes of a deep intelligence and even pride, shining eyes that held his look unflinchingly. Her long dark hair, he was sure, had recently been washed, perhaps even with some kind of crude soap, and was shining very nicely indeed. The skin of her shoulders was white as the snows of Hiram's Lebanon. He wondered about the strange gown she wore, of very good cotton indeed, without even the all-covering *aba* to conceal the smooth contours of a delectable body that was beginning to arouse him intolerably, even though he had been well-served this past night by two Edomite women and a very supple Moabite girl. The gown seemed to cling, poorly cut as it was, to very desirable hips and thighs, to a very narrow waist, and to

107

breasts that he found enticing in the extreme. Her hands were clasped together, her head tilted back a little as she waited for him to speak.

He wondered what her connection could be with Beladus; she had borne his child, no doubt, and her crafty-looking father was come to ask him to order recompense . . . He saw that the eyes of the assembled crowd were on him, conscious perhaps of his interest in her and wondering where it might lead. He turned his gaze back to Beladus, sighed, and said, "Well, you came to seek my help, good friend. Let me hear what you have to say."

"A simple matter, Lord," Beladus said. "I wish to take Debrah, daughter to Uzzi ben Ezra, as my wife."

"A simple matter indeed," Solomon said, shrugging. "Buy her."

"Her father, Lord, is concerned that such a union might not meet with your approval."

The king was frowning now; he was very quick to anger. "And why should he be concerned?" he asked. "A very good marriage, obviously, from his point of view. Does he suggest that a captain of Phoenicians is not good enough for his peasant daughter? Lovely though she may be? Have you not offered a price for her?"

"I have, Most High. In gold."

"*Gold?* For a *woman*?"

"Yes, Lord. I am prepared to pay a very high price."

"And still . . . he refuses?"

"He does not refuse, Lord. He merely seeks your approval."

"Gold, you say. Silver would be sufficient! I have women among my concubines who were purchased with donkeys, which they sometimes resemble. What is it that makes this girl worth *gold*?"

Beladus said quietly, "A quickening of the heart, Lord, when I see her."

Solomon was highly amused. " 'A quickening of the

108

heart'—I like the sentiment. And what is it in her that so moves you?"

"A quality, Lord," Beladus said, "that I cannot easily define. The heart does not always listen to reason."

"The heart, indeed, does not. But the mind should." He turned his dark and questing eyes on Uzzi. "Then tell me, merchant," he said, "why it is that you do not readily accept the noble captain's very generous offer, with hands reaching out for gain, in the manner of merchants?"

The old man could not control his shaking, though he tried desperately to do so. He was utterly convinced now that some awful calamity was about to overtake him. Was this a *confrontation*? He stammered, "It seemed to me, Lord, that is to say, Most High and Mighty, that . . . that such an alliance, since . . . since the noble captain is . . . is a foreigner, might not find favor in your eyes. Your *august* eyes."

"And why should it not? Look over the women you see here. Most of them are concubines, but some of them, I am sure, are my wives. You will find few Israelites among them. Friendship between nations, Uzzi ben Ezra, is cemented in beds, and with commerce."

"Yes, High and Mighty, yes. And I am honored to receive the benefit of your great wisdom."

"And the girl. Has she been consulted?"

His eyes were staring. "No, Lord, of course not! Humble as I am, I would not so demean myself!"

"Then let us hear what she herself has to say about this dreadful misalliance." Those dark eyes, highly amused now, were probing Debrah's. "Come forward, child."

"Your servant, Lord." Debrah stepped beside Beladus and waited, her eyes cast down. Solomon said sharply, "Look at me, girl, when I talk to you!"

"Your pardon, Lord." She raised her eyes and looked at him, recognizing an aspect of truly awesome power, a regal demeanor that could not be denied; it

109

was in his look, his bearing, and most of all in his enormous self-assurance. But she was not afraid; Beladus was with her.

The king said mockingly, "And when you look upon this handsome young captain, do you feel that quickening of the heart too?"

"Yes, Lord, I do."

"And in your loins, a stirring?"

"Yes, Lord." It was a whisper, and the king said, "Speak up, child! I wish to hear your voice!"

She said clearly, "There is a stirring in my loins too, Lord."

"A great desire to lie with him? To feel him between your thighs?"

"Yes, Lord, a great desire to bear his children, who will be sons."

"Ha! I detect there a passion which is not common among our Israelite women. It is an admirable quality. Or does it mask a shrewd merchant intelligence which prompts a desire for a wealthy marriage?"

"No, Lord, it does not. Were Beladus a peasant, as I am, I would love him as much."

There was a slight touch at her side, and then Beladus's hand was in hers, gripping it firmly. Solomon said drily, "Would you have me believe that Beladus's high position means nothing to you?"

"The honor means a great deal to me, Lord," Debrah said quietly. "But not as much as my love for him, and my wish to serve him as a wife should."

The king turned to his sage, who was no longer rocking to and fro but listening attentively now. "What do you think, Jachin?" he asked. "Does this young girl speak the truth? Her father is a merchant, and therefore venal, as all merchants are. Has his daughter learned from him? Is she merely seeking to better her condition? Is she trading her great physical beauty like so much commerce?"

The sage was silent for a moment. He never liked to answer his king's questions too quickly, preferring to

110

gaze out into space for a moment as though weighing the proposition very carefully. He rose unsteadily to his feet at last, and struck a posture he felt might indicate his deep concern for the question, and said: "You have chosen the apt phrase, lord: 'great physical beauty.' For she is, as these old eyes observe, a creature of exquisite loveliness. Let us then analyze the implications of this one indisputable fact. The first question we must ask ourselves is: is she herself aware of her own beauty? And to answer that question, I will propose another; does an eagle know that it can fly, does a lion know its own strength?"

"Well said indeed," Solomon murmured, wondering if he really should have given this old fool the opportunity to talk. "Go on, Jachin," he said. "Show me that the confidence I have in you is not misplaced."

Jachin bowed deeply and nearly fell. He recovered his balance and said, "The eagle and the lion both know their talents, and put them to good use. Is this young woman putting *her* blessing to use? That is the question we must ask ourselves. As the eagle swoops down on the hare, as the lion stalks the jackal, is this young woman casting her eyes on the wealth and position of the noble Phoenician captain?"

Beladus said amiably, "I am neither hare nor jackal, scribe," and Solomon silenced him with a look.

Jachin went on. "It may well be that she is. If so, then this marriage can result only in disaster. But"—he raised a didactic finger—"there is an alternative, Lord. You yourself have been pleased to notice the suppleness of her limbs, the grace with which she moves; the fire in her eyes shines like the precious stone of Ezion-Geber when the rain has dropped on it . . ."

"In all my years on the throne," Solomon said, amused, "it has never rained in Ezion-Geber."

"No, Lord." Jachin was bowing again. "A whimsical fancy, Most High, no more than a fancy." He raised a finger again. "But from the pinnacle of wisdom that my great age has brought me, I will enunciate that alternative. She has excited your interest, Lord, so therefore, take her yourself. Deny the marriage, and bring her to your own harem with all the others. Provided, of course, that she is a virgin indeed, which can quickly be established. This, Lord, is my considered opinion."

Having said his piece, he sat down again on his haunches and continued his rocking.

There was a look on the king's face of half-hidden amusement. He said softly, "I sometimes think, Jachin, that you have outlived your usefulness and that I should put you out to pasture with my older horses. But there are also times when you astonish me anew, and this is one of them."

He turned back to Debrah. "You are truly a virgin, child?"

"I am, Lord."

"No man has ever lain with you?"

"No, Lord. I am intact."

"Good. I am pleased." He looked around the vast room at the crowd of expectant courtiers, all hanging on his words, and he called out, "Where is Captain Libni?"

A voice came from the courtyard beyond the entrance, "I am here, Great Lord, to do your bidding!"

A young officer came running in, surely no more that twenty-two years old, tall and heavily-built with an unruly shock of black hair under his helmet. His skin was swarthy, his eyes very large and dark but unsympathetic. The heavy muscles on his arms rippled as he moved, like those of a lion on the prowl. He was dressed in a lightly armored tunic of heavy brown cloth, a sword at one side of his belt, a dagger in the other. He made a deep obeisance before the king, and Solomon said, "Rise, Libni, and give me the benefit of your wisdom, which I know to be very great in these matters."

"You do me honor, Lord."

"And it is not undeserved, I believe. Indeed, I am told that there is scarcely a woman in the whole of Jerusalem whom you have not taken to your bed."

"Only those, Lord," the young man said slyly, "who can excite my natural passions."

"Then tell me," Solomon said, "what you think of this young woman. Jachin suggests that she would be a worthy addition to my harem. I am told that you judge women as expertly as I judge horses. So give me your opinion of her. You may speak freely, and without fear."

Those hard eyes turned to Debrah, and they were gleaming. He said blandly, "She seems worthy, Lord."

"*Seems?* A trifling word, Libni, it means little."

"Then I will indeed speak freely, Lord. She is fair, with dove's eyes that have a hidden depth in them, a mouth that should be sweet to savor, a commendable straightness to her limbs, and a bearing, which is very important, like that of a young lioness resting. Her skin is white, her elbows are well-formed, her thighs are like the pillars of your temple, which are cast in bronze, and no less beautiful."

He moved to her quickly, the pounce of a wildcat, and put his hands at her waist, the fingers and the thumbs touching each other. "A waist a man can embrace with his spread hands—it is good, it suggests a delectable suppleness, which is also important."

The hands moved quickly to her head, tilting it back as her angry eyes burned into his. He ran his fingers through her hair and whispered, "Her hair is like the finest silk, and the eyes again . . . there is *spirit* in them, Lord! This is good or not good, depending upon the occasion." They slipped down and held her breasts, molding them, and he said, "Twin mounds of excellence, Lord, quite small, but firm and very resilient to the touch."

She cast an anguished look at Beladus and saw the restrained fury on his face. Then a hand slipped under her gown and felt her naked flesh. "With tiny nipples," Libni said, "that might well drive a man to the very heights of passion. There is no horse in your stables,

113

Lord, that can bring you more pleasure than this woman in your bed."

But now, there was a powerful grip on Libni's shoulder, crushing the bone, and she heard Bedalus's quietly savage voice, a hiss: "Take your hands from her, fellow!"

The hand did not move. It remained there, cupping, the hard fingers digging into her tender flesh, and the rasping voice said, "My hand from her? No. And I will discover now, for my king and yours, whether or not she is a virgin."

There was that terrible martial sound of an iron sword being quickly drawn from its scabbard, and Beladus stood there, his naked weapon in his hand, ready for combat. There was a shout: "He is armed . . . before the king . . . !" and it seemed that the huge room was instantly filled with running soldiers, their spears leveled and awaiting only the order to strike.

But Solomon had risen from his throne, a hand raised high in the air, and at the silent command all movement stopped. A dozen of the guards had formed a circle around the two captains, and Beladus had instinctively put his back to one of the pillars. He shouted, his eyes on fire, "Give me your permission, Most High and Mighty, and I will kill this man!"

Libni faced him, half-crouched, his hands at his side. Not taking his eyes from his adversary, he said, "I, too, Lord, crave your permission to draw my dagger. I will slice off this Phoenician's head and cast it out for the jackals to feed on!"

Solomon lowered his arm and took his seat again on the throne. He said wearily, "There will be no blood shed in my Judgment Hall—it is a place of wise deliberation, not of violence. Put up your sword, Beladus. It is not needed here."

But Beladus could not be calmed so easily. He said furiously, "The woman is *mine*, Lord! And this offensive offal has dared to lay hands on her in my presence! A liberty he would not be rash enough to presume

114

had you yourself not been here to say: 'put up your sword, Beladus.' As I do now." There was the sibilant sound again, slower now, of the sword sliding back into its sheath.

"She is not yet yours, Beladus," the king said with a sigh. "This is still a question we are pondering. And are you aware of the penalty for drawing a sword in the presence of the king?"

"No, Lord, I am not. Whatever it may be, I will face it. Though I crave your pardon. A moment of excitation brought on by a cause I believe to be just."

"That quickening of the heart again?"

"Yes, Lord."

"The penalty, Beladus, is death."

Beladus did not hesitate. "If you take her from me, Lord," he said, "then my life means nothing. I accept your judgment."

"In the name of all your multitudinous gods, Beladus," the king said, exasperated, "calm yourself! The judgment, under our law, is at the discretion of the king, and I choose not to exercise it. Your head will not roll at my command. But this passion leads you to defy me? It must be very great indeed."

"Not to defy you, Lord. My loyalty to the great Solomon is as strong as it is to the great Hiram, my master."

"Nonetheless, you are prepared, it seems, to fight with Libni here, third in command of my Palace Guard, a warrior of great repute who has slain no less than six Philistines in personal combat and countless others in open battle? A champion who could have killed Goliath himself?"

"If need be," Beladus said evenly, "I will fight with him, Lord. Though his death would not serve you well, no doubt."

"Ha! And you accuse *us* of arrogance!" The king reached again for his golden goblet of wine and said, "There will be no dueling. Leave us, Libni."

Captain Libni hesitated; his anger was still very hard on him. But he made his obeisance and stalked out.

115

Solomon said languidly, "Scribe, write that Captain Bel adus drew a sword in my presence and that I am pleased to forgive him his rashness."

"It is already written, Lord."

"And we will return to the matter in hand." The guards around Beladus had not moved, nor had they raised their leveled spears. The king roared: "Stand back! Away with you all!"

They fell back at his command, and the concubines who had risen to their feet at this startling interruption in their boredom were draping themselves on their divans again. Uzzi was shuffling his feet and plucking nervously at his beard, trying to thrust from his mind the awful thought of the fighting that had so nearly come about and concentrate instead on the great king's apparent thoughts . . . His daughter, a *royal concubine!* Surely no greater honor could accrue to him! But—he paled at the thought—had not the great king said, *have women among my concubines who were purchased with donkeys?* He was in an agony of indecision.

Debrah felt very uncertain now, staring at Solomon and trying to gauge his temper; but no one could ever do that . . .

This was an aloof, distant, even intellectual figure who had inherited none of the boisterous militancy of his father David (though the early years of his reign had been marked by ruthless violence and murder). But he was still a man whose volatile mind was a closed book even to his closest associates.

Now, without a doubt, he was in good humor. He turned to Beladus and said: "Your loyalty, you have affirmed, is as strong to me as it is to Hiram?"

"As strong, Lord," Beladus answered.

"Then control your Phoenician impatience, Beladus and do not speak now." His somber eyes moved to Uzzi. "And you, Uzzi ben Ezra. I see that you are already counting, in your merchant mind, the shekels might pay for your daughter."

"No, Lord, no!" Uzzi said hastily. "I was not count-

116

ing shekels or . . . or minas, Most High, but merely thinking of the very great honor you do me if you take her. An honor that, like a large and precious ruby, is beyond price."

The king's eyes were on Debrah again, and his voice was very soft and comforting. "It seems, child," he said, "that my words might well be with you now. The suggestion has been made that I take you into my harem, and I will confess that is is an idea that intrigues me. You have been offered marriage to a man of wealth and nobility, but I offer you, instead, concubinage to the mightiest king in the world today, a man whose wealth and nobility far exceed that of the man you claim to love. Your duties, after the first few nights, would be minimal. You would live in great luxury and refinement, as my women will tell you. And the position carries with it great personal dignity and advantage, as well as profit to your father, who would be on my doorstep every week selling me something . . ."

Debrah cast a look at Uzzi and saw the eagerness in his eyes. But when she looked at Beladus, she could not fathom the expression there at all. He was angry, yes; but his mood had changed completely, and his eyes were darting from her to Solomon and back again . . . There was a searching look in them, as though he were trying to solve a problem that vexed him sorely.

The king was saying, "I can, of course, command this, and you will obey. But it is my whim to make the choice . . . yours."

Debrah was startled. "*Mine,* Lord?"

"Yours. If you decide to marry this military commander, you will lead a very trying existence that will be imposed upon you by the exigencies of constant warfare, always in dread that one day his head might be catapulted into your camp by a particularly savage enemy, a defiant gesture that would herald your own death too. Have you thought of these things, child? Are you even capable of thinking of them?"

Debrah said steadily, "I have, Lord, and I am."

117

"The daughter of a venal merchant, capable of such speculation?"

"My father, Lord, is indeed a merchant, but he is not venal."

"You dare to argue with me?"

"Only in defense of my father, Lord. It is a daughter's duty."

Solomon was greatly surprised. "Well," he said. "Beladus, you are contemplating marriage with a vixen! With a child-woman whose tenderness is quite deceptive! This is not the pliant and submissive child she seems to be!"

"I do not require submission in a wife, Great Lord," Beladus said. "It is not the custom among my people. I know that she will obey me in all things, as she should. I too have seen that the bud is ready to burst into flower, and I welcome it."

"A resolute woman, Beladus! One who dares to lecture her King on a daughter's duty! It bodes ill for you."

"I am informed," Beladus said blandly, "that your own God called the Israelites a stiff-necked people."

"You are a heathen, Beladus," Solomon said, equally bland. "Do not throw Yahweh's wisdom in our teeth."

"Your pardon, Lord."

The king turned back to Debrah. "So, child," he said, "the choice is yours."

Her lustrous eyes were still holding his, a challenge between them. "But how can I *choose*, Great Lord?" she said. "I am a woman, it is not easy to assume such unaccustomed responsibility."

"Assume it, Debrah, because I so order you."

"Forgive me, Lord. I find it very strange."

Solomon was smiling benignly, and there was even a quiet chuckle. "Do not try and peer into my mind," he said. "For reasons of my own, which I will not enumerate, the choice is yours, and yours alone."

She heard Uzzi's desperate whisper: "A royal concubine, Debrah! Accept, accept . . . !"

Beladus's hand was in hers again, and there was something in that touch . . . She turned to look at him and saw that all the anger had gone, and in its place was a look in those mesmerizing eyes that she could not understand at all; it was a look of panic.

She could not know it, but he had heard Uzzi's hoarse whisper and was wondering, in alarm: would her devotion to this stupid and greedy old man who was her father, at this crucial moment, lead her to her destruction? Would she, a dutiful daughter as she had proved herself to be, meekly say: *I accept your offer, Lord,* and so seal her own doom, and his?

Beladus understood exactly the game that Solomon was playing with her; in this kind of deviousness the Phoenicians were far more adept than the Israelites, even more that Solomon himself, to whom scheming was second nature. But he was not at all sure that Debrah was aware of the danger here; Uzzi, certainly, was blissfully ignorant of it. He wanted to speak, but he knew that now, he must remain silent. He clutched her hand more tightly and held his piece.

His heart was pounding as he looked at Debrah, and he was astonished to see that there was a look in her eyes that challenged the king. There was a look of . . . what was it? They were flashing with anger, and scorn, and even mockery.

She said, very quietly, "Then as you command, Most High and Mighty King, I will make that choice. I am Debrah bat Uzzi ben Ezra of the tribe of Reuben. And if I come to you, Lord, it will be as a slave, serving a mighty king who can command her to perform any service that might whet his appetite, to obey whatever whim takes his fancy. Yes! If you order me to lie back and spread my thighs for you, I cannot refuse, and I am sure that as Captain Libni said, my mouth is sweet to savor. If you wish, Lord, to kiss the breasts of a statue, to suckle on a statue's nipples, to lie between a statue's legs, parted in abject obedience . . . yes, I will lie with you. But there will be no love, Lord, because my heart, from which all love flows, will be elsewhere. There will be only resignation, Lord, a duty to my king, whom God preserve for all eternity to enjoy the great love and respect his people have for him. You said the choice is mine, Lord."

"It is yours, child. I said it." His eyes were gleaming.

"Then I make it, Most High and Mighty. Though I am aware of the great honor you do me, it is for Beladus."

The king was almost laughing. "A life of great danger, fraught with potential tragedy, instead of the luxury I offer you?"

"Yes, Lord. If Beladus wants me, I will be his."

"So be it then. Scribe, write down our wise decision."

Solomon was looking at Beladus now, a shrewd understanding in his eyes. "I see a great relief reflected on your face, Beladus," he said. "And yet . . . it is not what it might seem to be. Will you tell me the reason for it?"

"I was aware, Lord," Beladus said calmly, "that had Debrah accepted your offer, and thereby proved herself to be nothing more than the scheming woman you thought her to be, you would have had her exiled, perhaps to the desert of the Negeb to carry stones and water. Had she not chosen wisely, moved by the dictates of her heart . . . I shudder to think what would have happened to her."

"No," Solomon said deliberately. "Had she chosen wrongly, I would have taken her to my bed, and in the morning I would have had her head struck off. There are enough of schemers in Israel, men and women alike."

"She is no schemer, Lord, but a woman of good heart."

"Yes, I am convinced of it now. And she loves you dearly, Beladus."

"I believe it to be true, Lord."

"Then take her, Beladus, and with my blessing," the

120

king said quietly. "And know how fortunate you are. I have wives and concubines without number, and yet . . . I have to ask myself, have I ever truly known the *love* of a woman? I think not. They remember my love more than wine, they know that my fruit is sweet to their taste. But when they look on Solomon . . . they see only a king."

"No, Lord," Beladus said. "They see a *man*. A wise, great, and compassionate man."

"Perhaps, though I think not. You are a good friend, Beladus, and your words, true or not, are a comfort to me." He turned his eyes on Uzzi, and they were glazed and distant now. "You have heard my decision, Uzzi ben Ezra. Give your daughter to this noble Phoenician, and may your tribe prosper."

Uzzi was shaking with very mixed emotions. He bowed deeply and said, "And if I have found favor in your eyes, Most High?"

"You have found favor. It will go well with you. Go now. And you, Beladus, my blessings on you. Bring me your first-born, that I may bless him too."

"I will do so, Lord."

Beladus put an arm around his beloved Debrah and led her away from the king; Uzzi hobbled out after them. Solomon said to the scribe, "Is there more business? I am weary."

"The case of Shashak of the tribe of Benjamin, Lord, who was robbed of fourteen cors of oil."

"Tomorrow."

"That of Hadar of Edom, whose daughter Jerioth was seduced by a neighbor named Oholiab of the tribe of Dan."

"Tomorrow, too."

"Your servant, Lord, as ever."

"I go to my quarters now. Send to me Rehab, or Elisheba, and two other women."

"It shall be done."

The king rose, and the trumpets blared, and as he

strode across the great room to the door that led to his sleeping quarters, he raised his arms high and shouted, "Enough! Your trumpets are bursting my eardrums!"

They fell silent.

7

Debrah had returned with her father to Bethlehem, still trembling with excitement and expectation. She sat cross-legged on the floor by his bed and commiserated with him in his pain; doing a little dance as he recounted the astounding events at the audience, poor Uzzi had fallen and twisted his ankle. But he was still dancing mentally, and not even the discomfort could detract from his great satisfaction.

And in his camp, Beladus too felt that his heart was bursting with pleasure, though he was a trifle uncertain now of how next to proceed. As Nemuel was serving him his evening meal in the flare-lit area outside his tent, he said, "Send for Zimri, Nemuel. I must speak with him."

"At once, Lord."

The young boy put down the flagon of wine he was pouring from and hurried off. When the fiery-eyed scout came and saluted, Beladus, chewing on a roasted lamb's rib, said, "The great Solomon, whom I have added cause to love now, gave you to me as a scout, Zimri, and you have always performed your duties in a fashion I can only describe as excellent."

"I am grateful, Lord, that you find the king's trust in me not unwarranted."

"But now, I need a different service from you. Sit

with me, Zimri, and eat from the dish. The meat is good."

Zimri was startled. "*Sit* with you, Lord? Indeed, I dare not."

"I command it. I command you also to eat your fill, so that your liver may be as satisfied as mine is."

The young scout moved a chair to the heavy cedarwood table and hesitantly took a rib from the platter. "Eat," Beladus said, "and know, Zimri, that this day I have taken an Israelite woman to wife."

The boyish face was wreathed in smiles. "Yes, Lord, it is known throughout the camp. In the soldier's mess, they are drinking wine in your honor. Some of them have seen the Lady Debrah, and know her to be of great quality."

"Then drink to my good fortune too, Zimri. Nemuel! A cup for Zimri, no longer a scout, but a sergeant of scouts."

Zimri's heart was beating fast. He took the cup that Nemuel poured for him, and rose to his feet and said formally: "Then I drink, Lord, to your continued happiness and that of the Lady Debrah. May you have sons without number."

"As, Zimri, I am sure I will. Now, I know something of the ways of your people, but insufficient. This is a mixed marriage, differing customs, differing laws. Though we are both descended from the same Semitic stock, your people and mine have drifted apart over the centuries. I am anxious not to offend Uzzi ben Ezra through my ignorance of your religious laws. Today, I think I became betrothed. So, how long must I wait before I can claim the Lady Debrah as my bride? Days, weeks, months? I must know what is expected of me, Zimri, so that I may behave correctly. How long?"

"No time at all, Lord," Zimari said happily. "There is no formal waiting between bethrothal and marriage." He shrugged. "Except on those occasions when a man is not eager for his bride."

"Ah . . . the eagerness is there, Zimri."

"I am sure of it, Lord. There is only the matter of the recompense now."

"Then I may take her as soon as the purchase price is paid, and still give no offense?"

"Not a *purchase price*, Lord," Zimri said gently. "Among my people, it is regarded as recompense to a father for the loss of his daughter."

"Of course, and very rightly so. Then how soon, without unseemly haste, may I send my emissary to discuss that . . . recompense?"

"At once, Lord. May I say without disrespect that Uzzi will not sleep now till he sees your emissary on his doorstep."

"And no ceremony? No damned priest to officiate?"

"None, Lord. With us, marriage is a legal, not a religious state. Once the recompense is negotiated, it should be paid at once, together with the presents you have allocated for your bride, which normally take the form of jewelry, as much or as little as you desire. By custom, Uzzi is expected to provide a dowry, which might take the form of two or three personal maids, who must be virgin in case you should require them too, as is your right."

"And then?"

"You go to Uzzi's house, Lord, accompanied by your closest friends and admirers, where he will receive you accompanied by his. You return here with your bride, and all of the friends of both parties, for a feast which should not last less than a week."

"A week!" Beladus echoed, dismayed, and Zimri nodded. "No less, Lord, for a nobleman of your stature. Indeed, a fortnight would be more fitting." He added slyly, "And in this feasting period, it is the law that you be absolved from all military service."

"Well," Beladus said tartly, "I hope Akish realizes that too . . . And the emissary should be a man of rank, no doubt?"

"Yes, Lord. Of lesser rank than your own, and known to be a friend. Lieutenant Remposar, who is your friend and aide, would be ideal, but since he is in Tyre searching for concubines for you, perhaps it should be Lieutenant Rekam, also known to be a close friend."

"Good. Then Rekam it shall be. Send him to me, Zimri. I am impatient for my new bride. Tell Seria to come to my bed when the moon sets. I am greatly aroused tonight."

"Your devoted servant, Lord." He gulped down the rest of his wine and rose to his feet. "And I thank you, Lord," he said diffidently, "for the trust you have placed in me."

"It is well deserved, Zimri."

"And for the promotion, Lord."

"That too is deserved. Tell the officer of the day that it is my command. Go now."

Zimri withdrew, and Beladus went to the edge of the bluff and looked down on the great moonlit plain spread out below him. The night was cool, and the stars were bright. Rekam came to him, and Beladus slipped an arm over his shoulder and said, "Good friend, you will do me a great service now. Tomorrow at dawn you ride to Bethlehem. Find Uzzi ben Ezra and negotiate with him a price . . ." He broke off, remembering, and said, laughing, "No, not a price, but a recompense! Negotiate a recompense for his daughter Debrah. Take with you five minas of gold from my store. Offer him three, let him raise you to four, or to five if need be. Let him understand the value I place on his daughter."

"A high value indeed," Rekam murmured, and Beladus shrugged. "There is almost half a talent of gold in my coffers. I would willingly give all of it. There is also the matter of jewelry for my bride, so let us go to my tent and see what I have."

As they walked slowly back to the tent together, Beladus said: "And it seems we must hold a feast, to last for a week or more . . ."

"A *week?*"

Beladus sighed. "They are strange people, the Israelites. They live in abject poverty because of their taxes

126

to pay for Solomon's love of a kind of luxury that can only be called oriental. It has drained them, impoverished them all. And still, when the occasion demands it, as this does, they burst out into a kind of extravagance that you and I, perhaps, are accustomed to as part of our daily lives. This, too, I will leave in your good hands. Tomorrow, also, send a courrier to King Hiram to inform him that his most loyal and devoted servant Beladus of the House of Tirgan has taken an Israelite wife, and hopes with all his heart that this furtherance of the alliance will find favor in his eyes."

"It shall be done."

They entered the tent, and Beladus dragged a heavy coffer from under his bed and unlocked it. He took out a pendant of lapis lazuli on a fine gold chain and held it up to the flickering light of the lamps. "This, without a doubt. It was my grandmother's, Rekam, carved in Egypt, I believe." He found an ivory bracelet, very broad but no thicker than parchment and intricately carved with gazelles and flowers. "Also from Egypt, and very old . . ." A ring, then, fashioned from iron in delicately woven straps, with no trace of rust on it even after two hundred years. "Ah . . . this marriage ring has been handed down in my family for more than six generations." He took out a belt made of tiny ivory plaques inlaid with gold, so fragile that it seemed it might break if the wearer even breathed, each alternating square and circle carved with elephants, lions, bears, and wolves. "From the land of Ophir," Beladus said.

There was a necklace of green jasper and another of red, a beautiful blue pendant of gold-mounted turquoise, a silver chain threaded though twenty-four miniscule cylinders of hematite, each of them finely carved many hundreds of years ago by the Hittites in their famous Smyrna workshops. And finally, another pendant, a black opal combining the iridescence of a dew drop with the blackness of a dark night, in which all the colors of the rainbow shimmered as it was turned in the hand, a smothered mass of living flames; its chain was made of alternating links of silver and gold, each of them so minute that a man could not imagine how it had been made. It was a work of unbelievable artistry.

"This," Beladus said, cradling the masterpiece in his hands, "is what she will wear when we ride here together."

He laid the selected pieces aside, and Rekam said wryly, "You are spending half your fortune on her," but Beladus laughed and clapped him on the back. "Only a small part of it. And I do not spend it on a mere woman, Rekam, but on a lifetime of great happiness. She is a jewel among women herself."

"And my wishes for your happiness, with those of every man in the camp, are with you."

"I thank you, Rekam, my friend. And we will have a feast that our guests will never forget! Lamb, goat, and find an ox for slaughter too. Onions both raw and cooked, cheese from Bethlehem itself, with cucumbers, leeks, and garlic. Strong flavorings, Rekam, let them not be sparing with the coriander and black cumin. With beans and lentils, and a few dozen skewers filled with plump locusts. Have the woman Keturah bake the bread, hers is the best in the camp. Then, melons, grapes, and raisins. Figs too—not the figs of the sycamore, you understand, but the true figs which the Israelites seldom taste. Send runners out to find them, and if you have to raid into the land of the Philistines for them . . ." He laughed. "Then bring dates too. All the officers will attend the feast, but only one or two at a time, after which they will all return to their duties and make sure that in spite of our riotous celebrations we are well defended. To drink . . . milk in abundance, the juice of pomegranates, and a dozen or so skins of good wine. See to it, Rekam."

They were both delighted with the thought of it, and Rekam said happily, "They will feast as they have never feasted before—it is a worthy occasion!"

"Good. It is in your hands now." They went out of

the tent together and looked up at the vast canopy of the dark blue sky, and Beladus said quietly, "There are more stars out tonight than there have been this past week. It augurs well."

"Yes, a fine night, a night for love."

"A night for love . . . The moon will be setting soon, and then Seria will come to me." He hesitated. "I have been wondering, Rekam, if I should give Seria her freedom. What do you think?"

"I cannot answer you, Beladus," Rekam said, "since I do not know what she means to you."

"She means . . . satisfaction."

Rekam shrugged. "So does every other slave girl."

"Yes, but I have a certain fondness for her, even though she talks so much."

"Then free her if it is your wish. It may be that her time for freedom is close at hand, in any case. Has she mentioned the matter to you?"

"No. Nor do I know what you mean by 'her time of freedom.' "

"Under Hebrew law," Rekam said, "the term of servitude for a slave is six years, and she served Solomon, I believe, for some years before she came to us."

"Oh. I did not know this."

"On the advent of the seventh year, a slave must be set free, unless you choose to nail her ear to the doorpost to signify your desire for a continuance of her servitude—"

"To do *what?*"

"Nail her ear to the doorpost," Rekam repeated. "You have to lead her to the door, and there pierce the lobe of her ear to signify that she is still your slave. But it can only be done with her consent. If she insists upon her freedom, and wishes to return to the hovel in which she lives, it is her right." He laughed. "It is purely symbolic. But it is their law."

"A barbaric custom!"

"Yes, but they *are* barbarians. Seria's time must surely be hard on her now, so unless you wish to take

129

an awl and drive it through her earlobe . . ." He shrugged. "Let events take their own course, Beladus. In my opinion, Seria will *never* choose freedom. What, to fend for herself, unsupported by some rough peasant she might marry, to live in squalor for the rest of her life? No, she is not so foolish."

Beladus sighed. "Well, perhaps you are right. And I thank you for the benefit of your advice. I will leave you now, the moon is setting."

"Good night, Beladus."

"Good night. Tomorrow to Bethlehem to assure my everlasting happiness."

"To Bethlehem."

Beladus went back into his tent, stripped off his armor and his robe, and lay down naked on his back, sunk deeply into the warm caress of a dozen layers of sheepskin.

When Seria came, she wet her thumb and forefinger, and snuffed all but one of the seven burning tallows, the one that was nearest the bed and cast his strong muscles into marvelous chiaroscuro. She slipped out of her loin cloth and sank to her knees beside the bed at his waist, resting her head on his taut stomach and letting her long hair drape across his loins, placing it just so with delicate fingers.

She whispered, running her hands over his body, "I never saw a more handsome man, Lord. No broader chest, nor shoulders . . . Never a more muscular stomach, nor stronger thighs." Her fingertips were moving with the lightness of a peacock's feather, and he groaned at her touch, raising his loins to meet it. She whispered, "And in what fashion may I please you first, Lord?"

He could hardly catch his breath. "Tonight," he said, "my thoughts are far away. Tonight . . . as you see fit, Seria, I am in your hands."

"Then close your eyes, Lord, and dream of that other woman, as I love you."

She kissed him for a while, covering his body with

her kisses. When he began to gasp, she climbed onto the bed and straddled him, and took his hands and placed them on her full breasts, luxuriating in his instinctive molding of them, the hard fingers digging deeply into soft and resilient flesh. Her hands were on him, finding the way, and she whispered, "In all his glory, Lord, our great Joshua could not have been more powerful. And truly, he was one of our greatest heroes." She lowered herself on him. "Do you know, Lord, about Joshua?"

"Ah . . . !"

"He took Jericho, you know. For seven days he marched with his men around the city walls—"

Beladus shouted, "Be silent, woman! Love me and be silent!"

"Yes, Lord, of course, at your command." She bent her supple body down, placing a hand on each side of his head, and brushed her nipples against his lips, and she knew, when he began to suckle on them hungrily, that all was well again. "Yes, Lord," she muttered, "I will be silent and love you." He raised and lowered himself against her very fervently, deeply enclosed within her; and when at last the climax came, he lay quite still and let the urgent need for sleep overtake him.

Seria looked at the grapes on the table beside the bed and wondered if she could reach them without losing him. She decided that she could not, and so she lowered her head onto his brawny chest and slept too. But before she fell asleep completely, she murmured, "He truly was a great hero, Joshua."

The cartographer Grenik had completed his assignment.

Dressed now in the short brown tunic the Philistines favored, he sat for a while in the shade of the particular clump of bushes that he had made his home in the hidden gorge of the Philistine camp, and worked on the four separate sheets of papyrus that contained his sketches, annotating them carefully and making sure that they could easily be understood by anyone not as skilled as he in map reading.

And when at last he was satisfied with his work, he hailed a passing slave. "Girl! The commander is in his headquarters?" She was an Israelite woman, unkempt and sullen, and she said angrily, "No. Akish is with the other animals."

"Watch your tongue, woman!" He took a handful of her hair and struck her across the face, his dark eyes narrowed and searching hers. "I ask you again," he said savagely. "Where is the commander?"

She wondered for a moment if she might defy him, but she knew him to be a violent and brutal man, like the rest of them. "He is with the horses."

"My name."

"He is with the horses, Grenik."

He thrust her away from him, and when she fell he drove a sandaled foot into her side and growled, "Thank your miserable God that my temper is good today, or I'd run a sword through you." He pulled off her kilt and ripped it in two, tossing the pieces contemptuously aside, and stepped over her recumbent form and went to the stables. She waited till he had gone before she spat in the dust where his shadow had passed, then climbed to her feet and went about her business.

Akish was watching the smith as he hammered a new rim onto one of the chariot wheels, and the air was filled with the acrid smell of burning wood as he drove it home. He said angrily, "Tighter, it must be tighter! If I lose a rim, I lose a wheel, and I lose a battle . . ." He turned at Grenik's approach and said, "Well?"

Grenik saluted. "I have maps for you, Lord, as you commanded. Four maps, one for each side of the bluff where the Phoenicians have their camp. Only two of them will interest you. Those of the south and the east."

"The others?"

"On the north and the west, the cliffs cannot be

132

climbed. Indeed, on the east it would not be easy. But on the south . . ."

"Show me."

He took the maps and sat down on a rock, poring over them at great length. He discarded three of them at last, and studied the fourth very carefully. "One hundred cubits to the top?"

"Not less than ninety, not more than a hundred and ten."

"The sentries, you saw their sentries?"

"By day, the top of the cliff is lightly patroled, and indeed, that is all it needs. Two or three men can watch the whole of the plain on all sides. At night, they are stronger. I counted thirty men patroling the edge of the cliff."

"And at its base? Patrols, too?"

"A few men only, but constantly encircling the bluff."

"And we have never known their strength, which changes constantly."

It was the opportunity Grenik had been waiting for. He said softly: "I am only a simple soldier, Commander, but . . ." He hesitated, and Akish said, "Go on, Grenik. I will listen to a mule if it talks sense."

"I do not think, Commander," Grenik said, "that the bluff can be attacked except when they are at their weakest. And as you say, their strength changes constantly. If, however, we could learn of a time when most of them are elsewhere, on their incessant patrols . . . The merchants of Bethlehem visit the camp almost daily, bringing them their supplies of grain and oil."

"Those merchants," Akish said with heavy sarcasm, "are Israelites themselves. They are not likely to send us news when we need it."

"No, Lord. There is, however, one way to hear what the merchants have to say, and to profit by it."

Akish stared at him. He was suddenly aware that this was a shrewd and ambitious man who spoke well and carefully. *From the school in Gaza,* Tarson had said,

133

and he remembered that all of the pupils there were youths of good education; he wondered what this devious man was driving at. "I am listening still," he said, and Grenik went on: "If I could be detached from my camp duties, Commander, I could go to Bethlehem and listen to the talk of the merchants in the marketplace. I am sure they must discuss the Phoenicians among themselves at great length, and then . . ."

But Akish interrupted him angrily. "A Phoenician can pass among the Israelites as one of them, Grenik, but you think a Philistine can? You think we look as they do? You are a fool, Grenik! In the space of a day, your head would be on a pole for the peasants to spit at!"

Grenik was smiling gently. "I think not, Lord," he said. "There are many Philistine slaves in Bethlehem, soldiers taken in battle and sold to those same merchants. I would dress as a slave, and be merely one among many, with a story that I would invent . . . searching for a new master, perhaps, after my own had died, not wishing to escape and return to my own people for fear of more military service. Such would be the tale that I would tell as I search for a new master. And I would listen to the gossip of traders, the idle chatter of women, the tidings of other slaves. I would endeavor to separate the false from the true, and in time, I would bring you news that might be of inestimable value. It is *listening*, Lord, that brings information about those who are our enemies. I would wear a loincloth like the other slaves, and carry no weapons, not even a dagger. My only weapons would be my wits, and my desire to serve you."

"A spy!" Akish said. "A spy in Bethlehem itself! It is indeed an advantage to be greatly desired." He paced slowly back and forth for a while, and he realized that he was dealing with a man of very unusual intellect, a man capable of *thinking* . . . He said, laughing suddenly: "A lieutenant of the Philistine armies in the loincloth of a slave? It is a very intriguing idea, Grenik."

134

"A *lieutenant*?" Grenik's voice was hushed, and Akish answered him abruptly, "Go then to Bethlehem as a slave. I see great profit from such work there. And if the profit is great enough, yes, you will be a lieutenant on your return, with all the advantages that accrue to an officer's status."

Grenik was not the kind of man who could fawn. He said casually, "A great honor, Lord. You will not regret it. You have my word."

But Akish had other thoughts on his mind now. He said slowly, "There was a brief battle, Grenik, in the valley of Sorek, a battle which to our shame we lost. You heard of it, no doubt?"

"I heard of it, Lord."

"And what did you hear, Grenik?"

What dared he say now? He did not want to give the impression that the question required much thought. He shrugged, saying, "I heard that our force was greatly outnumbered and annihilated."

"You heard other things too? Concerning a woman?"

He was conscious of a tight, restrained anger in Akish, and he answered carefully: "I heard, Lord Akish, that there was an Israelite woman there, who called the enemy into battle."

"I do not even know her name, Grenik. But the image of her . . . I saw her breasts and my hands were on them, breasts to drive a man mad! I determined to take her to my bed, and I am still so determined! I cannot sleep for thinking of her!" He was shouting now. "She governs my dreams! I have set my heart on her and I will not rest until I have her!"

Oh, the prospect of that officer status! It was coming more and more within his grasp! Grenik said quietly, "Perhaps I can bring her to you, Commander. I will ask questions of other slaves, and when I find out who she is . . ." He shrugged. "It is not hard to abduct a woman from her house. I will steal a horse and throw her over its back and bring her to you."

135

Akish said tightly, "Go, Grenik! Go to Bethlehem *now*."

And so, the shrewd and erudite Grenik began his short career as a spy. In the morning, he put away his weapons and his leather sandals and his tunic, wrapped a loincloth around his waist, and left the camp as soon as the sun came up over the mountain. And by the time it was overhead, he was in Bethlehem, unchallenged.

The marketplace was a place of frenetic activity. Groups of women were crouched over little heaps in the sand of raisins, grapes, melons, pomegranates, gourds, and olives. Some of the piles were very small indeed, reflecting the great poverty there; one poor woman sat on her heels over a single melon, all she had to sell that day. They crouched there in their *abas*, with delicate fingers weaving, their lustrous, worried eyes probing every passerby who might be interested in their wares. Potters squatted by their red clay jars, calling out their wares: "A single shekel for the largest of my jars, no more, a single shekel . . ."

The dyers were out in force, more dignified (their trade was the highest on the social scale) and proud of the transformation they had wrought with simple linen. Merchant and buyer in their section of the marketplace were both served by their slaves, like a second line of argument as the haggling went on:

"The latest color, mistress, a dye from Sidon, no less . . ."

"But the dyeing is imperfect . . ."

"No, Lady, perfection itself, no streaks, no pale patches, examine it carefully."

"My slave will examine it carefully . . ."

"Your pardon, Lady . . ."

"And four shekels a cubit? No, never!"

"Three and a half then, the threads dyed individually before weaving, a new color from Tyre."

(The dyer's slave, a brawny young man with yellow-stained hands, and the lady's slave, a bare-breasted

Moabite girl, were crouched at their feet together, whispering furiously over the quality of the cloth.)

"No. I would not pay even three shekels for work of such inferior quality."

"Three shekels, then. But at that greatly debased price, I cannot sell you less than fourteen cubits."

"I need thirty. At two and a half."

"Thirty cubits then, for eighty-five shekels, a price that will ruin me. But if you tell your friends, Lady, when they admire it, that you were lucky enough to find it in my little workshop, nowhere else? The most exquisite color, Lady, the dye comes from Egypt and is very expensive."

"From Egypt? You said Sidon."

"Yes, Lady, Sidon. A slip of the tongue."

"My house is on the narrow street, the one with the fig tree in the courtyard. Deliver it to me there. But one span less than thirty cubits, one half-span even, and you will not be paid."

"Your servant, Lady. It shall be done, and speedily."

But now, a hand shot out from nowhere and gripped the dyer by the shoulder, and a deep, resonant voice said pleasantly, "You cheat the lady, merchant! Eighty-five shekels? No! She will pay only sixty, a fair price. Or I set fire to your store, and tomorrow . . . you will have nothing to sell."

The dyer's eyes were wide with astonishment; it was an affront! But there was something in this aggressive young man that frightened him. "Seventy shekels, then," he said, stammering.

It was Grenik, and he was not a man to trifle with. "Sixty-five, then," he said, "and no more! Or tonight, your miserable workshop will be burned to the ground. You are a thief to charge such prices! And why? Because you see a lady of such regal quality?"

The merchant's eyes were on the loincloth. A *slave*? And a Philistine slave at that! Daring to talk this way to a respectable dyer? But he knew the Philistines well, knew that the threat was not an empty one. He nodded furiously. "Agreed, then, sixty-five . . ."

Grenik said: "And for this price, you will deliver thirty-five cubits, the extra five to remind you of your thievery."

The dyer did not know how to answer this slave who spoke with such assurance, and, in truth, resembled a fighting man; all he could do was nod stupidly.

The Israelite woman was staring at him curiously. He was young, and lean, and very virile-looking, perhaps even handsome. And the impertinence of his speech! She said coldly, "A Philistine slave, I think?"

Grenik bowed. "From Gaza, Lady. Taken in battle with the brave Israelites and sold to a merchant of Beth-Arabah. His name was Jeriel ben Sheal."

"*Was?*"

"As we came to Bethlehem to buy donkeys, Lady, he died. The way was hard for him. He was very old. And so, I search for a new master. Or mistress."

She held his searching eyes. "If your master died, then you are free to return to your own people—it is the law."

"I do not wish to, Lady. If I return to Gaza, I will be called again to military service. I prefer bondage with the Israelites, who have been good to me. So now, I search for a new home—in some desperation, I would add, for I am hungry."

"And your name?"

"Grenik, Lady."

"You are strong, I see . . ." She looked him up and down, taking in the tight, well-muscled chest, the taut stomach. She reached out and felt his biceps. "Yes, very strong. Are—are you also willing and obedient?"

"In all things, Lady."

"I have need of more slaves in my household. But they must be well disciplined."

"Discipline comes easily to me, Lady. I know that my duty is to serve, in any way I can."

"Then I offer you a renewal of the bondage you

138

spoke of. You will be housed, fed well, and cared for. In return, you will provide me with all the accepted duties of a slave."

"You honor me, Lady. I will serve you well, in gratitude."

"I am the Lady Reumah. My house is on the narrow street. Ask, and you will find it." She said to the girl crouched at her feet: "Come. We go now to the cheese market."

She looked at Grenik again. "You will be content in my service. I have seven slaves, and two of them are Philistines, so you will make friends. But you will do all that I demand of you, or I will have you whipped."

"All that you demand," he said, "and more."

She turned on her heel and swept imperiously away. She was a tall, statuesque woman of strong sensuality, no longer young but straight and firm-bodied, full in the breast and narrow at the hips. She was dark, with very commanding eyes that reflected authority. Her husband, a money lender, had died some four years since, and in the absence of sons (she was sterile) she had taken over his huge fortune. She was a woman of formidable and demanding appetite.

For three nights, she drained Grenik almost of his life's blood. She whipped him herself, frequently, on one pretext or another, and once had him tied down, his body monstrously bent back over a rail, while she impaled herself on him and tore at his bare stomach with raking nails. Once, she had him lashed to a ladder and spent the long night crouched on her knees beside him, working him to frenzy after frenzy. She was quite insatiable.

And on the fourth day of his servitude, Grenik made his move. In the few hours of his relative freedom he had talked with the two other Philistine slaves, both of whom suffered these indignities and more, and he knew whom he could trust and whom he could not.

One of them was a boy named Heskar, hardly more than fourteen years old and cursed with a twisted leg and a club foot. They were eating their evening meal together in the stable among the donkeys, a good meal of bread and pomegranates; in spite of her other many weaknesses, the Lady Reumah was not ungenerous when it came to feeding those who served her. Heskar, a very cheerful youth in spite of his deformity, said, spitting out seeds, "Well, Grenik my friend, do you find our mistress demanding?"

Grenik laughed. He liked this outgoing youth. "In a few weeks," he said, "she'd grind a man down to nothing. But I am strong. Though to tell the truth, I'd rather have that pretty little maid of hers in my arms."

"Ha! Stay away from her maid, Grenik, or she'll flay you alive!"

"So that's the way it is . . . I should have known it."

"Of course. The close touch of warm flesh, man or woman, it's the same to her. She spent some time in Tyre, I'm given to understand, and learned a trick or two from those damned Phoenicians. Like the butter she pours down your throat to make you hard again quickly."

"Yes . . ." Grenik filled the pocket of a flat loaf with pomegranate seeds, tore it it two, and handed half to his friend. "And speaking of the Phoenicians," he said, "I heard a story in the marketplace of a fight between our people and theirs, out in the valley of Sorek, in which an Israelite woman was commanding the Phoenician army. Can it be true?"

"A story," Heskar said happily, "which has become much exaggerated in the telling." He went to the trough and scooped the scum away from the top of the water there, and filled the wooden ladle, sipping as he spoke. "It was a young girl who lives nearby. Her name is Debrah, of the Uzzi ben Ezrah family. Her father is a merchant here, very rich. It is true that she was captured by a guerrilla captain named Akish . . . You have heard of him, perhaps?"

"No, I think not . . ."

"A fearsome fighting man of ours who lives out in the hills somewhere, he came across her driving goats in Sorek. But before he could have his way with her—she's very beautiful you understand—a strong force of Phoenicians rode by. And it seems that she called to their leader, speaking his name, Beladus. There was a skirmish, and all of our people were killed, save only Akish himself and his rear archer, who escaped in a chariot. It is a famous tale, Grenik, that has been told many, many times, each time with a little more embellishment."

"And this Debrah," Grenik said carefully, "she lives nearby, you say?"

"The house at the foot of the hill with the shelter on its roof. But you have not heard the best part of the story, which is true. You want water?"

"Yes, I will drink. I ate cheese today, and there was too much of salt and coriander in it."

"Our mistress likes the food to be well spiced, to make the blood boil when she takes her slaves to her bed."

He handed the ladle to Grenik and said, "Beladus, I saw him once. He came here with an unarmed retinue, and I will tell you, friend, he is a very imposing man. He is tall, and very good-looking, and he rides a horse as though he were born on the back of one."

"Or in a stable."

"No! A man of very noble blood, he wears the royal purple of Tyre. Yes, a rich noble and a poor peasant girl. It is the stuff that romance is made of!"

"You mean he came here to see *her?*"

"Not only to see her, Grenik." Heskar paused dramatically. "But to marry her!"

"*Marry* her!" Grenik was aware that his mouth was open, and he snapped it shut. "And has he . . . has he taken her to his camp?"

"The whole village knows that he comes for her tomorrow. A great deal of wealth has changed hands, and yes . . . tomorrow is the day."

141

Outside, there was the loud rattling of chains as the guard, locking up the slaves for the night, fastened the stable door shut. Grenik heard the heavy bolts being thrown with the sound of finality, and there was great alarm on him. He said urgently: "Had you told me this an hour ago, minutes ago even . . . !"

Heskar stared at him with bewilderment, and Grenik went on, speaking very quietly now. "Tell me, Heskar, there must be another way out of the stables. Where?" He was peering up into the darkness of the timbered roof. "Under the eaves, perhaps? A space large enough for a determined man to crawl through?"

Heskar was alarmed. "You mean . . . to escape? But why?"

"I must leave here at once, Heskar, tonight! Tomorrow will be too late!"

"But you cannot leave! You are a slave, not a freedman!"

"I *must*, and at once! There is urgent work I must do!"

"Are you mad? A slave on the streets at night? After dark? A Philistine slave, what's more! They will take you and kill you—it is the law!"

"Nonetheless, I must leave this place at once!"

Heskar was greatly alarmed now; he had found a certain fondness for his compatriot. "Grenik," he said, urging, "there is no other way out! And if there were, then it would lead to your death, you must know that! Only by the door, which is chained now, and even so . . ."

"Then I will wait," Grenik said, interrupting him, "and when the Lady Reumah sends for me, as no doubt she will again soon, I will elude the guard and run."

Heskar was whispering furiously, frightened now by the incipient disaster. "Run?" he asked scornfully. "Can you run faster than a thrown spear? The gate to the compound is chained at night too.

"I will climb over it!"

"And the dogs are loose now! If the guard does not

142

kill you, the dogs will! You have seen the lady's dogs—they can bring a bear down with ease . . . And there are seven of them!"

"Yes, the dogs . . ."

Grenik sank down on his pallet again and put his head in his hands. "I had not reckoned with the dogs."

Heskar crouched beside him and put an affectionate arm over his shoulder. "Forget this foolishness, Grenik," he whispered. "You must stay here now, you are one of us, a slave."

"Yes, a slave. Though when she sends for me . . . Who knows?"

He was thinking: *a whole night or a whole day to reach the gorge where Akish is waiting for just this kind of news, and I will be late because of a pack of dogs* . . . He said desperately, "Help me, Heskar! I *must* leave here, and at once!"

"You cannot! Not until sunup, when they unbar the stable door and confine the dogs. Then, and not before, Grenik my friend, you can do what you feel you must."

Grenik nodded slowly, deeply distressed. He had once seen a man torn to pieces by dogs; he had not forgotten the sight of it, nor the screams, and he shuddered. "So much to gain," he whispered, "and so much to lose . . ."

The guard came for him shortly before midnight and escorted him through the pack of snarling, vicious dogs that snapped angrily at his heels to the Lady Reumah's chamber, where he was tied down securely for her pleasures. All night long, she ravaged him. When, from time to time, she slept, he struggled furiously with his bonds but could not free himself. And it was not until the sun had risen that he was released and sent to bring oil from the marketplace.

Once clear of the compound, he began the long, hard run back to the gorge in the valley of Sorek.

8

Almost all of the village was there to await Beladus's arrival. Uzzi had not been able to keep the secret, as he had determined to do, of the huge amount paid out for the recompense. Micah, not privy to the negotiations, had asked him fearfully, "Will you tell me, husband, how much has been paid?" And he answered angrily, "It is none of your business, woman! All you need to know is that I am satisfied." But the jubilation was exploding within him, and as she turned away to fetch wood for the fire, he whispered fiercely, "Five minas of gold, Micah, a veritable fortune."

She could only gasp, and he said excitedly, "Come, I will show you, you will be privileged to see it." He took her up to the roof and removed the heavy bars from the big water jar that was their hiding place, and whispered, "Five of them, Micah!"

Now, he could contain himself no longer. He ran to the edge of the roof, stumbling over his gown, then lifted up his arms and called out: "People of Bethlehem! Let it be known that the recompense for my ward Debrah is almost beyond counting! And that he comes tomorrow to claim his bride!"

There was a sniffling sound behind him, and when he turned he was astonished to find his wife in tears. He said, bewildered, "But . . . why are you crying, woman? You have a truly wealthy husband now! It is a great day for all of us!"

She gestured helplessly at the robe she wore, holding up its torn hem, and whispered at last, "Then if I could have a new robe, husband . . . ?"

"A new robe?" he asked, frowning. "But why? Your robe has lasted for twenty years and will well last another twenty!"

"But it is . . . torn and patched . . ." She could not restrain her weeping.

"So repair it, then! What, now that your husband is rich, you cannot sew?" But he relented quickly and embraced her, and he said gently, "Very well, you may make yourself a new gown with some of the linen the captain brought me. I was going to sell it, of course, but I will hold some of it back for you. There, you see what a generous husband you have." He turned back to watch for Beladus.

Almost all the two hundred families of the village had given up their work to witness this momentous occasion. Every balcony, every rooftop was crowded. One house, indeed, had collapsed from the weight of the people on its roof. And when the little column appeared a great shout went up: "He comes . . . !"

Beladus, astride a fine roan stallion, was in the lead, wearing his favorite purple robe, his hair bound up with thick bands of gold wire. The trappings of the horse were of bronze, copper, and beaten gold, with inserts of carved ivory; the troops wore scarlet, blue, and yellow plumes in their helmets. Zimri was riding beside him, knowing that his mission now was to impart courage, and Rekam rode on his other side.

Uzzi was waiting, with forty-two of his friends and neighbors lined up, and by protocol Beladus spoke the first words of the ritual. "I am Beladus of the House of Tirgan, and I come to claim Debrah bat Uzzi ben Ezra as my bride. Bring her forth, that she may meet her husband-to-be."

145

Uzzi called out: "And I am Uzzi ben Ezra of the tribe of Reuben, and these are my friends and admirers. Jael of Bethlehem, Rechab of Bethlehem, Jonah of Bethlehem, Jarib of Bethlehem, Bakbuk of Bethlehem, Piha, who has come from Gibeon . . ." It went on and on and on, and Beladus whispered to Zimri, "But the bride, Zimri, when does she appear?"

"Soon, Lord. Be patient."

"I am patient."

Uzzi droned on, and when the introductions were all finished, he called out: "And now . . . come forth, Debrah."

She was waiting in the building, attended by the three virgins Uzzi had purchased as the dowry. She wore a simple gown that she had made over many nights of tallow-lit labor, fashioned from cotton that she had woven on her loom, decorated in honor of the occasion with soft tassels of brown wool stitched around all its hems. A white veil covered her face, and around her neck was the fiery black opal on its gold and silver chain, shining now, it seemed to her, with more iridescence than ever.

She was trembling, and at the sound of the call she found she could not move. Terrified, she looked back at one of the young girls. "Now?" she whispered.

"Now, Debrah."

"I am frightened, Shulah."

"You must not be. Come, it is bad luck to keep him waiting."

The girls ranged themselves beside her, dressed in white, their hands and faces freshly scrubbed, three very young children who knew that one day, perhaps, this kind of excitement might be theirs too.

She stepped out into the sunlight and looked at the crowd. Beladus, leaning forward on his horse, was staring at her, and a murmur ran through the crowd; she was *radiant*.

Beladus caught his breath as she moved toward him, her lustrous eyes cast down. She was sublime, ethereal,

146

a dream come to life. The dress clung like a skin to that desirable young body, and a shaft of sunlight caught the sheen of her hair. He thought he had never seen a vision more lovely. She stopped the requisite five paces from him and raised her head now. The great delight in his eyes gave her courage. Well coached, she said, "I am Debrah bat Uzzi ben Ezra, and I come to you as your bride, Beladus, to serve you as a wife should."

He was almost bubbling over. He turned quickly to Zimri and whispered, "I may dismount now and approach her?"

"You may, Lord."

"And embrace her too?"

"It is customary, Lord. But with restraint."

Beladus slipped from the saddle and went to her. He put his powerful hands on her shoulders and said softly, "Debrah, the most beautiful among women, a dove and a gazelle . . . If you could only know, my love, of the great happiness I feel."

"If it equals mine, Lord, it is very great."

"From the first moment I saw you . . ."

His eyes were laughing now, and she found his good humor infectious; she could not help smiling at the memory of that quite terrifying day. "When first you refused me," he whispered, "I knew that one day, somehow, the gods would bring us together again. And now, they have answered my prayers."

"My heart is beating so fast . . ."

He pulled her close to his body, and as he put his arms tightly around her, he heard Zimri's whisper: "With restraint, Lord . . ." He kissed her on both cheeks and whispered huskily, "How can I restrain myself . . . ?" He heard a murmur in the crowd and tore his eyes away from his beloved to see the musicians streaming out of the stable with their instruments, and he knew, with great relief, that it was the signal for the procession to begin. There were two women with hand drums; a young man with a sistrum, a harp-shaped frame of olive wood through which thick metal bars

147

were loosely threaded so that they would rattle pleasantly when shaken; an Assyrian harp with twelve double strings to be played by a woman; two pairs of copper loud-cymbals and four pairs of the high-sounding cymbals; a metal trumpet; and two double oboes.

The Israelites were renowned for their music, particularly in the use of percussion instruments, and they still thought consciously of music as possessing a strange quality that would appease demons they no longer believed in.

Zimri whispered, "The invitation, Lord . . ."

"Ah yes, the invitation . . ." Beladus stood at Debrah's side, holding her hand, and called out: "Uzzi ben Ezra! In honor of this notable occasion, I invite you, together with your friends and admirers, to join me in a feast, to take place at my camp immediately."

There was a shout of approval and much handclapping. Slaves were coming from the stables, dragging out the donkeys and cursing them roundly when they shied away from the great crowd there. In a few minutes, the column was on its way.

Debrah rode with Beladus, behind him with her arms around his waist, all the others following with the musicians out on their flanks, dancing as they played. When they came at last to the bluff, Beladus saw all his troops lined up on the edge of the cliff in full armor, their swords and lances raised high as they shouted out their welcome. A trumpet sounded, adding to the cacophony of the musicians. The soldiers were still cheering as the procession wound its precarious way up the goat tracks to the summit.

Eyeing the men speculatively, Beladus was pleased by their splendor and military bearing, but he was appalled to see how few there were of them. He murmured to Rekam, "Thirty men? No more?"

"No more, Beladus. Five others on various sentry duties, a total of thirty-five men under arms."

"The patrol from Beth-Horon?"

"It has not yet returned. A runner came in with news

of an attack on a convoy to the east of Gezer. The Beth-Horon force has gone to its assistance."

"Akish again?"

"I think not. Akish will not raid so far to the north."

"And they will return when?"

Rekam shrugged. "As soon as the battle is over. There is only a small force of Philistines, it seems. Once they have been driven off, our patrol has been ordered to hurry back at all speed."

"And meanwhile, we eat and drink and make merry, with thirty-five men to guard the camp."

Rekam smiled. "The danger, Beladus, must not be allowed to interfere with your celebrations, and I will see that it does not. By tomorrow, or the next day, Lieutenant Hasorar will be here, with his Beth Horon force, a hundred and ten strong. Very soon now, Lieutenant Laris returns from Jarmuth with forty more, we will be strong again. And now . . . I have set up a special tent in the center of our grove for the guests, and the food is ready."

"Good. Send the men back to their duties, Rekam, and thank them for this demonstration of their affection—it has pleased me greatly. Each man is to be given a silver shekel, a small token of my gratitude." He raised his voice: "Zimri! Take our guests to the feasting place."

"Your servant, Lord."

"And Zimri . . . must I join the guests at once if I am not to offend?"

Zimri's eyes were twinkling. "It sometimes happens, Lord, that a groom is detained for a while, perhaps showing his bride her new quarters."

"Ah . . . 'a *while*' being how long, Zimri?"

"An hour or two, or even more, would not be amiss, Lord. Rekam will be there as your representative. And by the end of the first hour or less, most of them will be so filled with good wine that they will not care who is there, even if they know it."

"Then stay by Rekam, Zimri. See that all custom is

observed, and I will join the celebrations shortly." His hand was on Debrah's arm, and he could feel her trembling as he led her to his own tent. The guard there sprang to attention at his approach, a very young and somewhat delicate youth, and Beladus said to him happily, "Ah, Mirhapi, is it not?"

"Mirhapi, Lord, adding his good wishes for you and your lady on this happy day."

"I thank you, Mirhapi. And for the next little while, should the Philistines come calling, or the armies of Aram-Damascus, of Gad or Moab, of Ammon, Edom, or even Egypt . . . should ten thousand horsemen led by five hundred chariots attack us . . . I will not be disturbed. See to it, Mirhapi."

He let the flap fall in front of the startled sentry, and shepherded his bride into the tent. And now, all the necessary restraint that Zimri had urged on him in the name of protocol was quite gone. He threw his arms around Debrah, and his eager hands explored her welcoming body, molding her young breasts as he buried his face in her neck.

"My love," he whispered, "how long I have waited for this moment!"

"And I too, Beladus, my love, my husband . . ."

"My nights have been sleepless for thinking of you . . ."

"And since that day you called to me, remember?— *'run, child, your father has news for you'*—I have lived in an agony of hope." She laughed. "I ran so hard! Leaving my jar of water for someone else to carry home for me, which was very wicked, and poor Uzzi threw his arms around me and could not even speak!"

"And since that happy day, I have sadly neglected my duties, and thought of nothing but this moment."

His hands were at her hips, gently removing the white gown. He eased it up over her naked body, his fingertips lightly touching her sides, and pulled it over her head. He took the hanging opal and fingered it be-

150

tween her budding white breasts. "On fire," he whispered, "as I am."

He picked her up and laid her down on the bed, and she felt the soft warmth of the deep sheepskins enveloping her nakedness, and she could not believe that such sensual luxury existed. She stretched out her long, slender limbs as he stripped off his robe, loincloth, and sandals. When he, too, was naked, a tall, muscular figure towering above her, slim and powerfully built, his flashing dark eyes filled with desire for her, she reached out and touched him, feeling the instant hardening. "My love," she whispered. "I, too, am on fire. You must quench it for me now." The emotion was very strong in her now, a craving for him that was quite overwhelming her. In his fine robes he was a very impressive figure, but naked, she thought he was godlike! There was a symmetry to his limbs that she could not admire enough; his muscles were taut and supple, his skin the light brown of almonds, but shining as though it had been oiled. He moved with a very feline grace, like a desert lion, and she could not believe that a man's body could be so beautiful. She wanted this long moment of admiration to last forever, and when he smiled at her, her heart melted. "I never saw a more lovely woman," he said, looking down on her with shining eyes, eyes that were filled not only with longing, but also with a great tenderness that must surely be unusual, she thought, in a man so strong.

His hands were reaching down to her, one of them straying from one pink nipple to the other, just the lightest touch of fingertips, the other at the junction of her thighs, lighter still, the touch of a butterfly's wing. She clutched at his manhood feverishly, seeking to draw him closer, and he lay down beside her and kissed her full on the lips, and then her neck, her shoulders, her breasts, lingering on the rounded undersides and running his tongue over her nipples. He eased himself on top of her as she pulled at him, holding that strong, pulsating shaft with both hands and guiding him, gasping at the touch of it. Tremors were running through her now, and she could not wait, but thrust herself up to meet her own probing, taking her hands quickly away as he entered her so that he could fill her completely, throwing her arms around him and holding him tightly. She bit her lip in silence at the sudden, sharp stab of pain, and then wrapped her long legs around him to drive him even deeper into her; his strong arms were around her, crushing her fiercely. The pains were shooting through her still with the strength of him, but there was great relief for her too as she flooded incessantly with all of her pent-up desires. Little choking sounds rose up in her throat, and she raked at his back with her nails, drawing blood.

For a long, long time he stayed joined with her, and time and time again he began that thrusting, sometimes gently and sometimes fiercely, as though he could not restrain his passion. She could not count the spasms that came to her and left her exhausted, only to come back, again and again and again.

At last, he was satiated, and he was very, very gentle with her. He touched her lips with his fingers and whispered, "No other love . . . Henceforth, there will be very few women in my life. Are you happy, my dove?"

"So happy . . . there are no words."

"Tonight, we will love each other again, many times. I will teach you the ways of my people, too."

"I will learn, gladly," she said, greatly surprised by her own daring. "I have heard something of them. From the women, at the wells."

He laughed. "So *that* is what all your interminable gossip is about! And in the joy we have found in each other, fear that we have perhaps been away from our guests too long, what do you think?"

"Time cannot be too long when we are together."

"I know it. And yet . . . a respite?"

"Yes, we must return to them."

"Till tonight," he said fiercely, "when we love each other again. And night after night, forever."

152

They found, when they joined the others, that the feast was a great success. The musicians were playing again, and Uzzi had taken far too much of the good Tyrian wine and was dancing a little jig in the center of the tent to show his happiness; Rekam was coming and going, making his inspections of the camp and returning to pay the expected compliments to the guests and eat a piece of meat, sip a little wine with them . . . The slaves were filling and refilling the platters with lamb, goats' meat and even beef, which the Israelites were devouring eagerly. It was not their habit to eat meat save on very rare occasions, and then only sparingly, because a sheep or a goat or especially an ox could be more profitably kept for other purposes; they ate them only when the beasts died of old age. But now, the meat was being replenished as fast as they could eat it, and the consensus among them all was that this was a very good feast indeed. And they would not sleep until the drowsiness, brought on by too much wine, overtook most of them soon after the sun came up.

Some, now, would rest, while others went on feasting. There much gossip exchanged, a great number of compliments passed back and forth, and always, the sound of the music.

That same sun, well past its zenith now, was shining on Akish's camp, finding its way down into the gorge, where Grenik stood shame-facedly before his angry commander. He knew that he had failed in his duty, and knew also what the inevitable consequence had to be. If only he had felt safe enough, back there in Bethlehem, to speak out a single day earlier! There would have been time for what had to be done!

Akish said furiously, "And he has taken this woman to his camp *today?*"

"Today, Lord, to my shame."

"With fifty men, I could have ambushed them as they rode to the camp!"

"I know it, Lord Akish. I have failed you."

"You could not have brought me this news last night? Last night! It would have been time enough."

"I was locked in a stable, Lord . . ."

"And you could not escape?"

"There were guards, and dogs. A guard can be killed, but no man can outrun the dogs. At midnight, the lady of the house sent for me to comfort her . . ."

"Ha! You spend your time fornicating, while news such as this must be brought to me at once? Thrashing around in a young girl's bed while I await information that only you can bring me?"

"Not a young girl, Lord, but of middle age, and with no pleasure for me at all. I was tied down while she satisfied herself on me all night long. And there were the dogs, seven in number . . ."

"Eight in number, Grenik. For you are one of them. A dog."

"Yes, Lord. I am a dog, and unworthy to live in your service."

Akish stood with powerful legs wide-spread, a giant of a man in a fury of frustration. He said coldly, "It is the truth. I await only your death."

Grenik said quietly, "I die, Lord Akish, devoted to you."

He was wearing his full uniform, with the armored breastplate and the leather leg guards and the plumed helmet. He drew his sword and, placing the bronze handle in the sand, he put a foot on the guard to drive it home. He took the point in both hands and eased it carefully under the lower edge of the breastplate. He said quietly, "I salute you, Commander."

He thrust his body forward and fell on the sharp sword. And when, at last, the thrashing and the screams were finished, Akish shouted, "Slaves! To me!" Two Israelites came running and stared down at the now-still body. Akish said, "Take this carrion out of the camp and throw it to the jackals. And send Tarson to me."

They turned the dead body over and pulled the sword from it, then dragged it away, hiding their elation

154

that another of the hated Philistines was no more. Akish went to his cave, and when Tarson came to him he said, "Drink beer with me, Tarson. I am in need of company, and we must talk."

Tarson's eyes were alight with curiosity. He had seen the slaves bearing Grenik's body away, but he chose not to raise the subject. Instead, smiling broadly, he said, "I am honored to know that you seek the company of those you know to be your friends."

The sad, attentive slave with the painted face was pouring their drinks. He said fearfully, certain that he was going to be whipped, "The beer is not good today, Lord—there is too much bread in it."

"No matter. Beer is beer."

The slave breathed a sigh of relief, and the two men took their beakers and stood at the mouth of the cave, watching the women down there at work, washing tunics and loincloths in the stream, pounding them with stones, though with great care not to destroy the fibres; a garment of any kind, representing weeks of hard work at the loom, was an article of immense value, to be zealously treasured.

Akish said somberly, "I see only women, Tarson. Where are our soldiers?"

"The troops, Akish, are doing what we all came here to do. They are raiding. Thirty hard by Gezer, seventy at Timnah, forty-two at Gibbethon, and some eighty-five at Baalah. In the camp now, there are less than seventy men, half of them recovering from wounds."

"I need a show of great force," Akish said. "Two hundred, perhaps as many as three hundred men. The recruits from Gath and Ashkelon, when may we expect them?"

"Not for some days yet," the lieutenant replied. "I learn from the runners that more than two hundred are gathered there. But it will be a week before they arrive."

"So, today, instantly, send out runners to bring in all

155

of our troops. As soon as they ride in, we mount an attack on the Phoenician camp."

Worried, Tarson said, "It may be possible to take that bluff, I do not know. But we will lose half our men and more in the process. Is it an objective worth so high a cost?"

Akish, his breath was coming fast now, his eyes on fire, answered, "Yes! If, at the end of that battle, only you and I, and Beladus and his new wife are alive, it will be worth the cost!"

Tarson was angry. A barley kernel from the beer had lodged itself in a decayed tooth, and try as he might with the tip of his tongue, he could not dislodge it. The pain destroyed his innate sense of caution, and he said: "Beladus and his . . . *new wife?* Are you still under the spell of that Israelite whore? Forget her, Akish!"

Unable to control his sudden rage, Akish shot out a strong left arm, seized his lieutenant by the throat, and smashed a powerful fist into his face, shouting furiously, "Send out the runners, *Sergeant!*"

Tarson picked himself up and tried to muster as much dignity as he could, but how could a man assert his dignity with blood pumping out of a broken nose? He said stiffly, "My devotion to you, Akish, is exceeded by no man's . . ."

"Send out your runners! Now!"

The lieutenant (or was he truly a sergeant now?) staggered away to give the orders. And as the day and the night drifted by, the outlying patrols came in, answering their urgent summons, wondering what it was all about. The new recruits began arriving, too, many of them riding their own horses, a welcome addition.

In a very few days, Akish had more than three hundred troops at his disposal. His last command to them, before they wrapped themselves up in their cloaks and lay down in their caves to sleep, was a triumphant: "Tomorrow, at sunrise, we slaughter the Phoenicians of that devil Beladus! Man, woman, and child, we put them all to the sword, save only Captain

156

Beladus himself and his woman, who will be brought to me still living! I am your commander, and this is my order!"

The men slept, dreaming of events to come and waiting for the sun to rise.

When the first pale streaks of the dawn appeared over the dark silhouette of Jerusalem, Beladus lay wide awake in his bed. Debrah, her comforting back to him, was asleep, and he was holding himself within her, thrusting very gently back and forth in the tight confines of her warmth, moving very slightly and rhythmically as he loved her.

Hearing urgent whispers outside the tent, he withdrew himself from her, rose from the bed, and put on his gown. He found Rekam outside. "What is it, Rekam?"

Rekam's badly articulated legs were troubling him in the early-morning cold, and he shuffled his feet awkwardly. He said, his voice very low, "The Philistines, Beladus. They are all around us, three or four hundred of them perhaps. A very large force on the south, a few patrols on the other sides of the bluff."

Beladus looked at the eastern sky; it was streaked with red. He said quickly, "Send three men on fast horses to circle the bluff at its base and report back at once."

"I have done so, Beladus. I sent Zimri there with a patrol an hour ago, when the sentries first reported them."

"Their total strength?"

"Three hundred, perhaps as many as five hundred men."

"And ours?"

Rekam said grimly, "Thirty-five effectives. If we arm the servants and the slaves, twice that number."

Beladus said lightly, "Then it is a matter of personal combat, is it not?"

Rekam said, alarmed, "No! Beladus! You cannot

157

fight Akish in personal combat! He is a champion of great renown, a grandson of Goliath himself!"

"Then what? Shall I send thirty-five men to their deaths against ten times that number? No, it cannot be. Their lives are in my hands, Rekam. I will not so easily betray men who trust me."

"But Beladus, my dearest friend! You cannot defeat so very formidable a warrior!"

"If I do not fight him personally, then he will throw a force against us that we cannot hope to defeat."

"No, Beladus, no . . . !" Rekam was almost wailing, and Beladus said quietly, "He cannot know how weak we are, and we must not disclose this weakness to him and so give him courage for what he has come to do. And will you do me a service, Rekam?"

"Of course, dear friend! Anything!"

"It will not be easy for you, I know. I will ride down there with very few men, and I will see what the gods have ordained for us. And while I am gone, I ask you to stay with the Lady Debrah, close by her side."

"Of course, of course, you have my promise!"

"And if I do not return, if you see the Philistines mounting an attack that cannot be stopped . . . As soon as they begin to climb the bluff and you see that we cannot hold them . . . then, you will drive your dagger into the Lady Debrah's heart. I will not have her fall into the hands of this evil man for a fate far worse than a quick and honorable death. Will you do this for me, Rekam?"

All the fight had gone out of him, a very brilliant young man whose whole life was bound up in warfare. But *this*? He stammered, "B-Beladus! I cannot do this thing!"

"You can. You must. Will you accept that she lie beneath him while she weeps for my death, as he takes her in whatever crude fashion he may desire?"

"No, dear friend, I will not accept that."

"Then you must kill her for me. A swift and painless strike to her heart. And if, as she dies, she whispers my name, as well she might, then . . . when they kill you, Rekam, shout at the top of your voice before you die, the single word: *Debrah!* Then, in the heaven of our God Melqarth, I will hear you and know that all is well. I have your promise, friend?"

Ashamed of the tears streaming down his face, Rekam nodded. "Then it shall be as you wish, Beladus. No longer friend, but brother in deep sorrow." He threw his arms around Beladus and embraced him.

"Nothing of this, then, to anyone else. Go and prepare the men. Tell them . . . tell them I will do what I can, the battle is not yet lost. I am a Phoenician, and therefore not without cunning—perhaps I can still save the day. If not, Astarte will welcome all of us to the skies, with young virgins for every officer and soldier alike. She is a goddess who greatly loves men who die honorably. As for our guests . . . they are still feasting on our meat and wine. Do not let them know what is happening till they must. It is easier for a man to die drunk than sober. Go now. Prepare the men for what is ahead of them."

The two good friends embraced briefly, and when Rekam had gone about his orders, Beladus went back into the tent and found Debrah sitting up among the fleeces of the bed, wide-eyed and apprehensive. But Beladus smiled down at her, and the fear vanished. She said, hesitantly: "You left me so quickly. I was afraid . . ."

The smile broadened. "Afraid? But for what? There is nothing to fear."

"I heard whispering. I heard the dreaded word 'Philistines.' "

"Oh, that!" He shrugged. "There is indeed a detachment of Philistines below us. I must parley with them." He laughed. "Two or three times every month, they come to my camp to hurl insults at me, and I hurl insults back at them. A very childish game, but part of the life we lead. But do not be frightened, Debrah, my love. While I am gone, Rekam will be close beside you.

159

He has his orders. There will be no danger for you, nor for anyone else in my camp. I will not permit it. And now, help me on with my armor. This is Nemuel's duty, but . . . were you to do it instead, it would please me greatly."

"Of course, dear husband." She slipped his breastplate over his shoulders, and as she laced it into place, he murmured: "Ah, yes, just so, what do I need with Nemuel?" He embraced her and strode out of the tent.

Rekam was there, with twelve men lined up on horseback and waiting for him, and he said clearly, "No. Three men will suffice. Sergeant Zimri of the scouts, and two others."

"As you say, Beladus." Rekam was certain he would never see Beladus again, and his heart was very heavy. The three men detached themselves from the waiting patrol, and together, they rode slowly down the track to meet with the massed Philistines.

Akish was riding in his chariot up and down, a hundred yards in front of the first line of his horsemen. Beladus approached to within two hundred yards of him, signaled his men to halt, and rode on to fifty paces.

Akish shouted, "Welcome to your beheading, Phoenician pig! I have heard that the swine urinate on your food before you eat, is it true?"

Bedalus returned the insult. "And I am told that the Philistines will not allow their children to be circumcised in case, perchance, the wrong piece be thrown away!"

"I am told that there is no greater delight for a Phoenician than copulating with a donkey!"

"And I hear that you copulate with your mother, because the donkeys refuse you!"

Furious, Akish shouted, "How can you talk of mothers, Phoenician, when yours was a syphilitic mule mated with one of the ugly camels that have lately been brought into your land and mine?"

Beladus laughed. "But I do not come to trade insults

with you. I come to tell you that if you are not gone from this place within the hour, four hundred and seventy men will come charging down from the bluff that is our home, and cut you to pieces!"

Four hundred and seventy men? It was not customary to lie about such matters. Could it be possible? A commander, faced with two hundred men, when he himself had only a hundred, was expected to taunt, *I come with a hundred men against twice that number, and we will destroy you!* It was a very important part of formal military behavior; how else could battles be fought? But this was a Phoenician, and therefore a man who would not hesitate to lie to serve his purpose. And would he have ridden down only three men if he were not sure of his superiority? Was there a great force there under the olive trees waiting for the order to ride down and charge?

Akish was uncertain now. Trying to hide his uneasiness, he shouted, "Four hundred and seventy men, you say? No man who is circumcised ever tells the truth!"

"Not counting my reserve, *Akrish!*"

A reserve, too? Akish, greatly alarmed now, shouted: "And yet, you ride down with three women in attendance!"

"To show the contempt I have for your paltry force, savage!"

"I do not believe you, whoremonger!"

"What do I care whether you believe me or not? Advance your animals, Akrish, those miserable carrion you call soldiers, and you will see! The jackals . . . No! The jackals will not devour you—they are revolted, as we all are, by unclean flesh!"

Near five hundred men? And yet, he could not be sure! He shouted furiously, "You lie, Phoenician fornicator!"

"And why should I lie? We are stronger than you are! See, I turn my back on you!"

It was the ultimate insult. Beladus turned his horse around and commanded the others to do the same, and for a moment the four of them sat their horses with their backs turned to the enemy. (Zimri was in shock, sure that he would die now.) Beladus shouted mockingly, "You see? Four shafts now from your archers, and four of your enemies will lie dead at your feet! And it will be a signal! Four hundred and seventy men will ride down on you, and not one of you will remain alive! We will be rid of you for ever!"

Akish did not move. Tarson cantered up to him, and he was glad now that he had relented and allowed this able young man to keep his rank. He turned and said, "Well? Is it a lie, or not?"

Tarson hesitated. "I do not know," he said at last. "It may well be. It may well *not* be. But you did not come, I think, for Beladus alone." He was still smarting from their earlier exchange. "You came for his woman."

"Yes, his woman. Half a victory is better than no victory at all, is it not?"

"If we are to continue our work, it is." Tarson did not like this confrontation at all, mounted as it was on insufficient intelligence. He said urgently, "The woman, Akish! She may mean less to him than you believe . . ."

Akish changed his tactics. He shouted, his voice harsh and scornful, "Turn about and face me, Beladus, if you have the courage! I did not come for your head, not this time. I have come for your woman. A small price to pay for your life!"

Beladus was in shock. For Debrah? He remembered that sad day when he had come upon them, remembered her gown ripped apart . . . The thoughts were tumbling over in his mind as he slewed his mount around to face the enemy again. Glad of his example, his escort followed suit. For a moment he did not speak, his devious brain at furious work. He said at last, "My woman? What woman? I have fifty women in my camp, Philistine!" He knew what he had to do now, and the plans were racing through his head.

"The woman from Bethlehem," Akish said, "whom

162

you stole from me. I am told that you have taken her to wife. Her name—Debrah."

Beladus laughed. "To *wife?*" he said. "Are you mad, Akish? Why should I take an Israelite woman to wife? Am I a fool?"

"As a concubine, then?"

"Yes, as a concubine, no more than that." He said scornfully, "I took her for one night, and I have finished with her! If you want her, Akish, I give her to you freely, that there may be peace between us! She means nothing to me!"

Akish could not hide his astonishment. He said, unbelieving, "You give her to me?"

"Freely, that we may live in peace together!"

Akish was still not convinced, and Beladus said, "So much of blood—even Philistine blood—to be shed for so slight a cause? This is not the stuff battles are made of, Akish! We will fight again another day, over more worthy matters!"

A shrewd and devious man, he thought of the thirty-five devoted troops waiting to be killed; he thought of the men riding in fast now from Beth Horon, the men from Jarmuth . . . He knew that it was all a question of time, and he thought fiercely, *Time, time, I need time! And how may I escape from this trap I have set for myself?*

He called out, "I need a few hours with her first!"

"No! Send her to me now!"

"A few hours, Akish! For my satisfaction, and yours!"

"Mine? How?"

"I must speak with her first. If I do not, she will go to your bed like any other of your Israelite slaves, submitting to you in sullen anger only! Is that what you want? Or do you want her to be taken willingly, as willingly as I give her to you?"

"She will never come to me willingly!"

"She will! If you give me time to persuade her!"

163

"And how will you do that?"

"I am a Phoenician, Akish! I know the value of words! I will tell her of the advantages that will be hers if she pleases you. And if she is to continue to please you . . . you must not be harsh with her, Akish!"

"You tell me how to treat a woman?"

"Yes! I tell you! We Phoenicians have a way with words, and we have a way with women, as you must know! Treat her with gentleness if you can find it in your heart, and you will see the great advantages that accrue to you! Learn from me, Philistine! A woman is not a goat, to be taken for relief without pleasure! There is great delight in a woman's thighs if she is well treated!"

Akish was perplexed now. Studying the confused look on his face, Tarson said quietly, "He is right, Akish, he is right! The Phoenicians are known for the pleasures they extract from their women."

"Very well." Akish shouted, "And you give her to me freely?"

"I give her to you!"

"So be it, then. Tell her that I am a man of gentle persuasion who will treat her well! Tell her, too, that I am *demanding* in my pleasures!"

"As every man should be! Before the sun sets, I will ride down here with her."

"Before the sun sets, then. We wait."

Akish could not hide the sense of a very great and easy victory nor hide his gloating, as Beladus spoke, his horse prancing wildly. "I will sound the standdown, and your miserable force will no longer be in danger of annihilation. Zimri! The horn!"

Zimri was deeply disturbed by what he had heard, and could not find any understanding of what was in his captain's mind. But he was well disciplined, and he raised the ram's horn to his lips and blew a long, piercing note. Beladus said amiably, "Four hundred and seventy men are sheathing their swords, Akish. There is peace. And with that single trumpet note, we have saved the lives of all of your men, and yes—I will admit it—a handful of mine, too."

"For today, Phoenician. There will be other days."

Beladus wheeled his horse and signaled his escort. They rode at a steady canter to the top of the bluff, and to safety.

For the moment, at least.

9

As a Phoenician, Captain Beladus was above all an astute and resourceful man. It was by their wits, not their military strength, that the Phoenicians had built their great trading empire.

He was also a kind and gentle man, and what he had to do now caused him not a little concern. He took Rekam to his tent and found Debrah there, pale and drawn. She ran across the carpeted floor to him and flung her arms around his neck, breathing, "My husband . . . I was so frightened for you!"

He held her lovingly, wondering if she should hear what he had to say, and decided that he would have no secrets from the bride he loved so dearly. "Sit down," he said, "and listen while I discuss certain matters with my friend and lieutenant."

He turned to Rekam. "Send the guard for Zimri. I have great faith in this young man, and I feel he thinks I have today betrayed a great trust. And Seria, too, with wine for all of us."

"Of course . . ." Rekam gave the order, and as Debrah sat quietly and waited, Beladus said slowly, "There are three hundred Philistines or more drawn up down there. Our strength is thirty-five. Should they attack us, we cannot hope to hold them. Every one of my men, the women here, too, would all be killed. I will not allow it. But Akish, it seems, did not come here to destroy us,

166

though that is what he will do unless I find a way to hold him off until we are stronger." He paused. "He came here for Debrah."

She gasped. Her face was whiter than ever, but before she could speak, Beladus said swiftly, "My mind is not so clouded by my rapture that I cannot think how to outwit this evil man! You will not leave my protection. I have searched my mind, and I have found a solution. It is not one that pleases me greatly, but desperate conditions require desperate measures."

Zimri and Seria entered, and Beladus said to them, "Come, sit down and listen to what I must say. But first of all, the wedding feast —I need news of it."

"It goes well, Lord," Zimri answered. "They have all eaten and drunk very heavily. Though I fear they will quickly recover their sobriety if . . ." He hesitated, wondering how far he dared go. "If it be my painful duty, Lord, to tell them that the bride is to be given to the enemy, even to save so many lives."

"Your concern does you credit, Zimri," Beladus said. "But have no fear, such is not my intention."

Debrah breathed, "But . . . if it will save your life, Beladus, and that of so many good men . . . then I will go to him."

"No!" It was a shout of anger. "You will not!"

He swallowed at a gulp the wine that Seria had poured for him, and said, more quietly now, "There is another answer to this vexing problem." He turned to Rekam. "How many Israelite women are there in the camp now? Twenty? Thirty, perhaps?"

"Ah, yes . . ." The light was dawning on the lieutenant. "Twenty-six, I think," he said.

"And how many of them were professional prostitutes when they came to us?"

Rekam shrugged. "Half of them, perhaps. It is not an easy question to answer. Most of them were concubines sent to us by King Solomon. The distinction between a prostitute and a concubine who has served, over the years, a score of men for personal gain . . . It is not

167

easy to define. But there are many who can play the part you are thinking of."

"Some, perhaps, of the Lady Debrah's age and slender build? With the same young budding breasts?"

"Several."

Seria said clearly, "If I may speak, Lord?" He nodded, and she went on. "I know what is in your mind, Lord, and there is a woman here by the name of Helah. She is an Israelite, a professional prostitute from Jerusalem, which was once called Urusalim before our great King David, who was Solomon's father by Bathsheba, captured it from the Jebusites who had taken it from King Abdi Khiba who was a vassal of Egypt . . ."

"Seria!" Beladus said desperately. "Spare me! There are matters of greater moment now!"

She was abashed. "Yes, Lord. Well, Helah is much of the Lady Debrah's age, her breasts are small, her body very slender, her legs quite straight. This is the woman you need, Lord."

Debrah said, anguished, "No! No, Beladus! I cannot allow another woman to be placed in such danger!"

"The danger is slight," Beladus said. "I planted in Akish's mind the idea that a woman well treated is a woman who can please him better. And Akish is not so blind a man that he will not learn from those he knows are his betters in such matters. Until he tires of her, he will not be harsh with her I am sure of it. And in a very few days my reinforcements will be here. We will at once mount an attack on his camp, and bring the woman Helah back to the comfort and contentment she has known here. A few days only, to gain the time we need. Send her to me, Seria."

In his mind, there was little thought of any impropriety in what he was doing. Indeed, it seemed a facile solution to the problem. The duties of a female slave were clearly defined by ancient custom; they were to draw water, cut firewood, carry loads—and to give their bodies to whomever might require them. They were *women*—on the accepted scale of values only ten or fifteen times the worth of a goat, and just as easily bought, sold, or simply replaced. And this, moreover, was a position that had endured for thousands of years and was acceptable to them.

But Zimri said slowly, "The girl Helah, Lord, I know her well . . ."

"You have taken her to your bed, Zimri?"

"Oh yes, Lord, many times. But it is not of this that I wish to speak. With your permission, of course."

"Go on, then."

"She was taken to Solomon's court," Zimri said, "as a child of perhaps nine years. One of the king's men was gored by an ox belonging to Helah's father, and he died. By law, there was the matter of compensation, set down as twelve donkeys or forty goats. But her father was a poor man and could not pay, so the king was graciously pleased to accept the lesser compensation of his daughter Helah instead. It was seven years ago, Lord."

"Then she has the right to her freedom. Why has she not asked for it."

Zimri said quietly, "Because, Lord, she will not leave your service. It is her wish. Some time ago, when she passed a night with me, we spoke of this, and she said to me, quite fiercely—and you know, I think, how fierce our Israelite women can sometimes be—'I will not leave my beloved Captain Beladus, ever!' Her exact words, Lord."

Beladus was pacing now, wrapped in thought and frowning. "Helah," he said, musing. "Do I know her, Zimri? Have I ever taken her to my bed?"

"Twice, I think, Lord. Though you may not remember her. She talks very little."

"Ah, what a blessing in a woman."

He turned. Seria was ushering a young girl into the tent, dressed as she was herself in a simple loincloth, barefoot and bare-breasted. She said simply, "This is Helah, Lord, and we are both your servants, to do your bidding always."

169

He stared at her; the hard, up-pointed breasts, the slender waist, the long and quite slim legs hardly bowed at all by too-early labor in the fields. Her dark hair was very long, straggling over her shoulders. She was much the same height as Debrah, with the same finely arched eyebrows that were rare in the Israelite women, and only a little darker. Her eyes, too, were huge and lustrous and filled with a fire far beyond her years. The look in her eyes told him Seria had already informed her why she had been summoned; it was not a look of fear, but of excitement. But he could not recall ever having seen her before.

He said, smiling, "I believe that I have loved you on occasion, Helah?"

"Yes, Lord. Three times." Her voice was sweet and melodious.

"Three times? It must mean that you pleased me greatly."

"I will always try to please you, Lord."

"And how much has Seria told you of this game that we play?"

Helah said evenly, "That I must go to the Philistine Akish, and call myself the Lady Debrah, and submit to him, to save the lives of everyone in this camp, where I have found so much great happiness."

"Not *must*," Helah. I will not *demand* it of you."

From the depths of her anguish, Debrah wailed, "No, no, Beladus, please! You must not send this child to such an evil man . . ." Helah said swiftly, smiling, "I am not a child, Lady. I was made a woman very many years ago. And over those years, I have lain with harsher men than this Akish can be." She said scornfully, "I am strong, I have no fear of him at all! There is only one thing I fear, and that is . . ." She turned to Beladus and whispered, "I greatly fear that I am not as beautiful as the Lady Debrah. I fear that he may not be tricked so easily."

"You are a dove," Beladus said, "and more beauty, if needed, will come through artifice. Akish is a simple

170

and uncultured Philistine. He will expect to receive a young Israelite girl dressed in an *aba*, with unwashed hair and bare feet, as he saw her, briefly, before. Instead, he will receive a woman who has recently become the property of a Phoenician noble, and there will be a transformation in her the like of which he will not be able to imagine. That untidy hair will have been washed and curled and piled on top of her head, bound with bands of colored stones, a few enticing ringlets hanging down over her shoulders. He will see a woman dressed in a splendid gown of fine cotton, with leather sandals on her feet laced with gold thread. She will be bejeweled like the lady he imagines her to be, with rings and bracelets and pendants to bedazzle him, to blind him, even! When he sees you, he will only gasp at the splendor in which a simple Israelite girl is bedecked when she is taken by a Phoenician nobleman! Under all that magnificence, he will scarcely see the woman till he takes you to his bed. And then, you will not love him expertly as befits your trade, but hesitantly and with feigned reluctance, playing a part as you have never done before. But . . ." He broke off and took her by the shoulders, speaking gently, "I say again, Helah, I will not command you. You may refuse me if you wish. There will be no shame."

To his astonishment, Helah threw herself to the ground before him and kissed his feet. He said urgently, "Rise, Helah, rise!" She knelt by him and threw her arms around his waist and pressed her cheek to his loins. He was conscious of Debrah's eyes on him, of the half-smile on Seria's face, of Rekam's sardonic look. He said again: "Rise, Helah," and pulled her to her feet. Her eyes were brimming over with tears, and they cut him to the quick. He said gently, "You must not weep, Helah. You can tell me, *no, I will not do what you ask.*"

She shook her head vehemently. "They are tears of joy, Lord, that I can serve you as no other woman can."

"Two or three days only, Helah," Beladus said. "And then, when my troops return from Beth Horon, we will descend on Akish like angry lions and bring you home. The jewels you wear, and they will be considerable, will be yours when you return to us."

He turned to Seria. "Take her," he said. "Dress her in the fashion of our Phoenician women, braid her hair, wash and perfume her body with oil of lavender, myrrh, spikenard, and almonds. *Drench* her in perfume! Let the scents on her overwhelm the smell of his horses! When she says: 'I am Debrah, Lord', he *must* believe her. Unguents on her face, antimony at her eyes, let her eyes look like pearls in their shells, red at her lips and her cheeks, a woman to be greatly enjoyed . . . Take her, Seria! Bring her back to me a Phoenician lady of quality."

Seria said quietly, "It shall be as you wish, Lord." She was quite taken up with this game. "And it will be easy for me—we Israelites are adept at deception. In an hour, you will not recognize her."

She went out with Helah, and Beladus turned to Zimri, his new counselor. "What do you think, Zimri? Shall we succeed in this endeavor?"

Zimri nodded. "Yes, Lord, I think we will. It is my belief too that for a few days, at least, there will be little danger for her."

"Rekam?"

"Yes, I believe the problem has been well solved. If she can can play this game successfully for the first few minutes of their encounter, then she can play it long enough for us to gain the time we need."

Beladus fell into a brooding silence for a moment, and Debrah searched out the anxiety in his eyes. He said at last, "I had expected a certain difficulty in convincing her . I still do not understand why she agreed so readily. Did I force her? I hope that I did not."

Debrah said clearly, "Helah is in love with you, Beladus."

Astonished, he stared at her. "In love with me?" he

172

echoed. "How can she be in love with me. She is a slave girl!"

"A woman, still . . ."

Zimri was smiling. "My Lord Beladus," he said, "there is not one woman in the camp who is not *desperately* in love with you. And Helah . . . yes, above all of them. She believes that the sun shines only on your command, and she would lay down her life for you. This is why she will never demand her freedom, as is her right."

Beladus, unaware of his own great personal appeal, was quite dumbfounded.

And a little more than an hour later, Helah was brought to him for his approval. He caught his breath. The clothes, the cosmetics on her face, the elaborate coiffure with its wide bands of semi-precious stones, the lapis-lazuli pendant and the cornelian at her forehead . . . The fine robe of yellow cotton, the gold and blue band at her narrow waist and the splendid sandals interwoven with gold thread, the rings and bracelets of gold, silver and ivory—all these things proclaimed her to be a woman of distinction.

"Beautiful," Beladus whispered, "beautiful, perfect, and . . . desirable, too. I would strip off your robe and take you myself, but that my wife has left me drained. Come. If you are ready, we will ride down and meet with Akish." He hesitated. "Two, perhaps three nights with him, no more."

"For as long," Helah whispered, "as I can serve you, Lord. And do not fear for me. For very many years now, I have been a woman, and I have accepted men more brutal than this Akish. Even if there is pain . . . Sometimes, pain translates itself into a strange kind of pleasure, very easily."

"You are wise beyond your years, Helah. I have heard that this is true sometimes, with some women, though I have never understood how it can be so."

"A strong man, Lord, can be a delight to a woman, however harsh he may be. There is no fear."

173

"And I am glad of it. You do me a great service, Helah, that will not go unrewarded."

He went to Debrah and took her in his arms and held her tightly. "I leave you now, my dove," he said, "for a short while only. I love you so much, my dearest."

"My love . . . But my heart is close to breaking. For Helah." But she saw the good humor on Helah's face, a mischievous look in her eyes, and she was comforted.

He broke away from her and took Helah by the arm. "Come then, the time for confrontation is upon us. Rekam! We ride with you, Zimri, and one other man, an escort of three, only."

The evening was on them as they walked their horses slowly down the bluff, the shadows lengthening. The Philistine army was there, no longer lined up and waiting but squatting on the hard sand in small groups. Some of them had made fires and were cooking the evening meal as they waited—the whole slope of the slight hill was dotted with them, colorful bands of men in armor that reflected the rays of the sun. At a shouted command, they sprang to their horses and took up their battle positions.

The Phoenicians cantered across the valley and reined in when they reached the stream. They could see the astonishment on Akish's face as he stared at them, and they fancied they could hear the sharp intake of his breath as he looked at Helah. She was riding in front of Beladus in the saddle, and his strong arm was around her, his hand cupping her breast; he could feel her heartbeat, and he whispered, "Do not be frightened, child."

"I have no fear, Lord," she whispered. And then: "He is a very handsome man . . ."

Akish dismounted and strode to the stream, standing like the stump of a tree growing out of its bank. His eyes were gleaming, his voice hoarse. "I expected a simple peasant girl in a robe of coarse goat's hair, and

174

you bring me instead—a dream! What have you done with her, Phoenician?"

Beladus shrugged. "I have dressed her the way we dress our own women, Akish. I have groomed her, perfumed her, that you may see the way we treat them. She will serve you as you serve her, no better, no worse. With love if you are gentle with her, with sullen dispassion if you are harsh—the choice is yours! Learn from me, skilled in these things, that delicacy in a woman is to be treasured, it brings great reward! Ill-treat her, and she will be worth no more to you than the goats you are accustomed to! I have explained to her that she is to treat you equally well, measure for measure."

He dismounted and helped Helah from the saddle. He spoke loudly: "Go to him, Debrah, and serve him well."

"I am your servant, Lord, to follow your command." To his surprise, she reached up with both hands and pulled down his head, kissing him firmly on the lips. And then she stepped daintily over the stream to the other side. Akish's eyes had not left her for a moment, and they were wide with wonder. "Debrah," he said, and again, a whisper: "Debrah . . ." He could not control the fierce longing for her.

To Beladus's great satisfaction, Helah raised her head and tilted it back a little, saying clearly, "I am Debrah, Lord Akish, to serve you as I have been commanded by my late master Beladus."

Suddenly, Akish scooped her up in his massive arms and stood there triumphantly, shouting fiercely, "Trumpeter! Sound the retreat! We return to the camp at speed!"

The thin, incisive note of the horn sounded, and the men began riding their horses into position, four long lines of them in column. Akish, with the slave girl in his arms, strode to where his horse was chomping the grasses. He set her down and swung heavily into the saddle, then pulled her up after him and set her at his thighs, slipping a hand over her shoulder to fondle that

175

hard, swelling breast. He spurred the horse around and shouted to Beladus, "The next time I come, Phoenician, it will be for your head! But today . . . today I have a better prize! I am satisfied!"

Beladus shouted back, "Fairwell, sweet Debrah! Perhaps one day we may meet again, who knows?"

He watched them crest the rise until they had disappeared from his sight as the folds in the land swallowed them up. He turned to Zimri and said quietly, "Sergeant of scouts, follow them. I want you to spy out the defenses of their camp. I want to know with certainty how strong they are now, and tomorrow, and the days that follow tomorrow. Akish and his men have military duties far afield, as we ourselves do. This means that their camp, like ours, will sometimes be undermanned. Today, Akish caught us in a position of great weakness, and this is what I wish to do with him. Watch for their comings and goings. Take one man with you, and keep me informed constantly."

"Then . . . if I may take Nemuel, Lord?"

"Nemuel? Nemuel is not a scout, not even a soldier! He is a slave!"

"Nonetheless, Lord, he is a good horseman and is familiar with the mountains."

"Very well, then. Remember that if you are discovered, it will mean your life. And I cannot afford to lose you, Zimri."

"I will be careful, Lord. They will not discover us."

The young scout rode off, and Beladus turned to Rekam. "Well, good friend? Akish has been well deceived, I think."

"He has been deceived," Rekam said promptly. "I watched his eyes as Helah went to him, and they were filled with . . . with awe. There is no other word to describe the passion I saw in his eyes. Oh yes, he has been well deceived, and all is as it should be."

They rode slowly to the olive grove in the gathering dusk, and when they reached the top of the bluff, the brash and impetuous young Remposar was there to meet them. He slapped at his breastplate in a salute, and said, grinning broadly, "Lord Beladus, I cannot tell you how glad I am to come to you from the fleshpots of Tyre."

"Remposar! I had almost forgotten your mission!"

The young brevet-lieutenant was crestfallen. "I had hoped, Lord, that it was a mission of some importance."

"And so it was, Remposar! Come, come with me into my tent and tell me of your adventures." He turned to Rekam. "Let me know when word comes from Beth Horon."

Rekam nodded and left them. Beladus put a friendly arm over his aide's shoulder and went inside with him. At once, Debrah ran to him and embraced him. "Helah?" she whispered.

He held her tightly, caressing her. "Helah has been accepted," he said, "and is on her way to the Philistine camp in the company of a man she thinks of as handsome. You need have no fear for her. Akish is in awe of her. It has all worked very well and we have stolen some time from . . . from time itself."

"And yet . . . there is a feeling of guilt on me."

"There must not be," he said, very gently. "For many years, Helah has been a prostitute and therefore accustomed to even the most demanding of men. She will share his bed for a few nights, and then . . . We will bring her home and reward her well for the breathing space she has given us."

He broke away from her and said happily, "And this, my dove, is Brevet-Lieutenant Remposar, my personal aide, who has been on a mission for me to Tyre." He smiled at the young man. "My new wife, Remposar, the Lady Debrah. You will serve her with the zeal and affection you have always given me."

"Of course, Lord Beladus! And with the greatest pleasure."

"And Seria, where is Seria?"

She rose like a ghost from a dark corner of the vast

tent where she had been crouched. "Here, Lord," she said, "beside you as always, when you require it."

"Then pour wine for us, Seria. Sit down, Remposar, and tell me about Tyre. Is it still as beautiful?"

Remposar sighed. "When a man steps out of his boat and sets foot once again on that glorious island . . . the sea breezes, heavy with the scent of jasmine, tell him that he is once again in the most beautiful city on earth."

"And you spoke with the king?"

"At great length. He is pleased with the work you are doing here, and he ordered me to give you a message in his own words: 'Tell our brother and our son Beladus that he stands high in our estimation, for since his arrival in the land of the Israelites, we have not lost a single convoy. Tell him that he may now wear, at such times as he sees fit, the yellow sash that proclaims him to be a confidant of the king.' "

Beladus's handsome eyes were on fire. "The yellow sash?" he echoed, and Remposar answered him gravely, "Indeed, Lord, the king handed it to me with his own hands, and I have brought it for you."

The yellow sash! It was the highest of all honors, and Beladus was glowing with pride. "And Juntus?" he asked, "you spoke with my half-brother Juntus too?"

"Indeed, Lord. He entertained me at dinner one night, a gracious and generous man."

"And his health, Remposar?"

The young man hesitated. He said at last, sighing, "He seems a little older, Lord, than when I last knew him. My second cousin Shukrit who is married to his sister Breaha tells me that too much good wine, too much copulation, have made him old before his time. But he is happy, of that I am sure."

"And happiness is better than youth, is it not?"

"A man can live to be sixty if he chooses to live in abstinence and misery, like a peasant. A bright tallow burns faster than a small flame. And he found me women for you, as you requested, five of them. They

178

are in the women's quarters when you wish to inspect them."

Beladus said clearly, "Send them back to Tyre, Remposar, on the next safe convoy to Joppa."

The young boy was startled. "Send them back? I do not understand, Lord!"

"Yes, it is perhaps hard to understand, but I do not have need of them now. I have found in the Lady Debrah a kind of . . . a complete satisfaction of all my desires."

"But Lord!" Remposar was bewildered. "A man of quality can not be satisfied with the services of one woman alone—it is unheard of!"

"Yes," Beladus admitted, "it is not a common philosophy. Nonetheless, it is mine now. I am content with my new wife, and I will have no other women, save Seria here on occasion and perhaps Helah when she returns to us. But no others, Remposar. Send them home."

Remposar murmured, "One of those ladies, Lord, is my sister Adruphet."

"Ah, I remember her well, and with great affection! Her breasts are small, like half-formed pears, the color of old ivory and almost as hard. She always perfumed herself with myrrh, and to this day, whenever I smell that scent, I think of the lovely Asdupah."

"Not Asdupah, Lord. My sister's name is Adruphet."

"Yes, of course. But let us be fair, send her back, too."

"It may be, Lord," Remposar said, "that they would all prefer to remain here. There would be disgrace in being sent home so quickly."

"Ah, yes, of course. Then give them their choice. They may return if they wish, or they may stay. But let them understand that I myself cannot serve them. The other officers, yes, as they desire. But my own heart is elsewhere." He thought for a moment and added, "Perhaps Asdrupah on occasion, but only rarely."

Remposar said mechanically: "Adruphet, Lord."

"Yes, of course. Leave us now, Remposar. I wish to be alone with my wife."

Remposar bowed and left. Seria set the wine down close to the bed and whispered, "May your night be a good night, Lord." She began to move to the entrance, but Beladus said, "No, stay with us, Seria. I am very tired tonight, and you may be needed."

"As you command, Lord."

"Undress me."

She took off the armored breastplate and hung it in its place on one of the tent poles, then stripped off his purple robe, the undershirt and the loincloth, and dropped to her knees to unlace his sandals. She reached out to touch him and found that he was hard and strong, and she whispered, "Not as tired, Lord, as you say . . ."

He saw that Debrah had removed her gown and set it aside; she sank down into the fleeces, awaiting his love, not entirely unaware of the fire in Seria's eyes. He stretched his naked, muscular body beside hers, raising himself up on one elbow the better to admire those slender white limbs, so smooth and soft to his gentle touch! He was exhausted after the worrisome events of the day, and there was great comfort in her, a relief from all the anxieties that had been weighing on him so heavily. Cradled in her arms, he felt that he could put aside the responsibilities of command. He kissed her small breasts and stroked the inside of her thighs. Her hand grasped him eagerly, seeking to pull him on top of her, but he whispered, "No. Lie still, raise your knee . . ." He eased himself below her, holding her supple body to him, and thrust himself deeply into her, driving himself back and forth rhythmically. She felt his throbbing and delighted in it, and she gasped as the mutual climax came and she knew that in the whole of the land there could not be a happier woman. He whispered, "You must clutch at me now, with muscles you have never used before."

180

He fell asleep at last, still savoring the warmth of her, and she lay awake beside him, holding him tightly and trying to obey his command; she found it very strange, but rewarding. Then the drowsiness overtook her and she slept. She was only half-awake when he erupted in her again, but she heard his murmur in her ear, "Not even the gods can know of these delights . . . My heart is bursting with love for you . . ." He held himself within her as she lay cupped in his loins, and they slept together like children in each other's arms.

Seria woke him shortly before dawn with the light touch of a hand at his wrist. He was instantly alert, and he saw that Debrah was deep in sleep. He raised his eyebrows in a question, and Seria whispered, "It is Rekam, Lord. He is outside the tent."

He nodded, and his voice was very low. "A cloth, then, for my waist."

She brought him a scarlet kilt and wrapped it around him, and he went outside to find his lieutenant. The night was cool, and the breezes played over his naked torso. Rekam said, "A runner has come from Beth Horon, Beladus. I thought you would wish to be informed at once."

"And rightly so. The troops there, are they on their way south?"

"Yes, they are. But they have met with a raiding party of Philistines in the hills to the east of Aijalon and are driving them off."

Beladus said sharply, "Aijalon? Does this mean that Akish is raiding so far north?"

"They are not Akish's men. The runner reports that three prisoners were taken, and before they were slain they said they had come from Ekron."

"Their strength?"

"One hundred and seventy men, eight chariots. They are fleeing to the northeast, in the direction of Gezer. Lieutenant Hasorar is pursuing them."

"Let him not lead his patrol too deeply into Philistine territory. He is a good soldier, but sometimes rash."

181

"He will not do that; he is no fool. But it means that the return of our troops will be delayed, perhaps for as much as three days."

Beladus thought of Helah, and was deeply anxious. Rekam went on: "Meanwhile, Nemuel is here from the Philistine camp, and awaiting your orders."

A shadow detached itself from under the olive trees, the young slave who had gone with Zimri. Beladus said quietly, "Well, Nemuel? The news of the Philistines?" The sounds of the feast were still coming to them, the high-sounding cymbals ringing out as the guests danced in blissful ignorance of the dangers surrounding them.

"We have found a cave, Lord," Nemuel answered, "hardly more than a cleft in the rocks above their stables. There, we can see, and remain unseen. No moonbeams reach the gorge, and it is very dark there, but there are a great number of fires, which indicate a strong force. Zimri tried to climb down to the camp itself, but the dogs gave warning and he was forced to return. They have very many dogs."

Beladus said, worried, "No, he must not try and enter the camp, but perhaps in the light of day he can estimate their numbers. Above all, I wish to know if a sizeable body of men rides out—remind him of this. Go now."

Nemuel bowed and hurried off. Beladus turned to Rekam and said tightly, "More of our own force, and less of theirs . . . I am deeply concerned about Helah, Rekam. Every hour that passes increases her danger."

"Helah," Rekam murmured, "is perhaps more adept than you give her credit for. She is the kind of young woman—there are many of them among the Israelites—who can take her destiny into her own sure hands and mold it as she sees fit. Only in Israel will you find this, perhaps. They do not allow fate to take them where they must go; they go there of their own volition."

"I hope you are right," Beladus said with a sigh. "Good night, Rekam."

182

"Good night, Beladus."

The commander returned to his tent, and saw in a dark corner the two pinpoints that were the whites of Seria's eyes as she stared at him, a feline animal crouched there. She was lying curled up on the carpet, and as she began to rise he whispered: "No, Seria, rest . . ."

He stood by the bed for a moment and looked at the sleeping white body of his lovely bride, cast in a pale yellow glow. He saw that in his absence Seria had trimmed the tallow candle. He dropped the kilt to the floor as he stood there, and the slave girl moved quickly in the pale glimmer and picked it up, to fold it and place it where it belonged. She came back to him, and reached down and held him, and whispered, "Now, indeed, you are tired, Lord. If I may revive you?"

Beladus nodded. "A moment or two then, of your comfort, til I am strong again."

"Your servant, Lord." She dropped to her knees before him, and worked skillfully as she had been trained. In a little while he tapped with his fingers on her cheek to dismiss her and lay down beside his bride. Seria went back to her corner and folded her long legs beneath her, rolling over on her side and slipping her hand between her own thighs as she thought of her beautiful captain. He saw her eyes close, and he turned his attention back to Debrah.

Very carefully, not wanting to awaken her, he pressed himself against her, a hand at her breast, a thigh gently placed across hers. He fancied that in her sleep she was smiling. He pulled a sheepskin over their bodies, and used the fleece again, moving it lightly back and forth over her nipples, coaxing her to delirium. She opened her lustrous eyes and held his, and there was a sadness in them.

She said softly: "I dreamed, my love, that you had left me, and I woke in fear and found that you were no longer by my side. I was frightened."

He was smiling down at her as his manhood probed. "What foolishness!" he said. "I left the tent to relieve myself."

"Ah . . . Then all is well?"

"It is more than well. When I feel the touch of your body, as I do now . . ." He was strong again; so very strong, she thought, shuddering at the close contact! "I am in heaven with the gods!" He lowered his head and feasted on her breasts. "I, too, dreamed," he said, "I dreamed that you were our great Astarte, a goddess who is one with Baal of the Canaanites and Dagon of the Philistines. In the time of our forebears, she was known as Ishtar of the Babylonians, and ever since our world began she has been the goddess of love and fertility, depicted always naked as you are now, a woman of rare beauty whom no man or god could resist. The center of all pleasure was between her thighs, as for me it is between yours . . . And in my dream, I was prostrate at your feet, worshiping you and begging for your favors."

"Beginning? No, Beladus! They are yours for ever, to take as you wish, when you wish, how you wish . . . !"

"My dearest! Your flesh is so warm . . ."

"I want this night never to end . . ."

"It is not only by night that I will love you, my gazelle. But when the dawn comes—and it will be soon now—we must go to the guests."

"They are still here? I had forgotten them."

"As I had. Yes, still here. It will soon be over. But at sunup, we will go to them and eat a little meat and cheese, and drink with them for a while before I go about my duties. I will come for you in the afternoon, and we will return to this corner of paradise and love each other again."

"Oh yes . . ." She was holding him tightly in a long-fingered hand; much aroused by Seria's ministrations, he was very strong. She whispered, "Lie still. Sleep. Close your eyes and remember only that I am your Astarte, the naked goddess of love and fertility."

She raised herself up and placed her knees carefully on either side of his hips. She held him firmly, and as he reached up to fondle those smooth round breasts she lowered herself onto him, catching her breath as the hard containment filled her entirely. Very slowly and tenderly, she eased her body up and down in the search for her own ecstasy till the delirium came and passed; and then she gently moved herself from him and lay beside him, a slender arm across his chest. She waited until his fervent kisses assured her of his complete happiness; and then she slept, knowing that there was nothing ahead for both of them but a lifetime of the most exquisite happiness together.

A trumpet sounded, calling the men to the early morning parade, but Debrah did not hear it in the sleep of her utter contentment. Beladus awoke, by habit, stole quietly from her side, and let Seria dress him silently.

He whispered, "Let her sleep, Seria. When she awakes, bathe her, perfume her, and dress her, then take her to the wedding guests and tell them that I will come to them myself when my duties permit it. And that meanwhile, I am with them in spirit."

Fastening the armor on, she said quietly, "I will do so, Lord. And your night? It was good?"

"Yes, it was very good."

"I did not sleep, in case I might be required again. I counted the times you loved her. I am glad for you, Lord."

"And I thank you. Seria. There are many things yet that she must learn. Her mother will have instructed her, but insufficiently. You will teach her for me."

"Of course. An Israelite virgin knows very little of the arts of love. But she will learn quickly, as I did from the other women. I will teach her, Lord. Count on it."

"All the artifices that you yourself know so well, Seria."

"I will do so, Lord. She is a woman of great passion. She will learn very quickly."

185

He went out to face the day, and Seria sat on the ground by the bed, resting her head against the sheepskins, to sleep till her mistress should awake and require her attentions.

During the day, Beladus twice visited the wedding guests, so drunk and exhausted now that the feast was drawing to its close that they were scarcely conscious of his presence. He went also to the little tent that had been set aside for the three virgins who were Uzzi's dowry, and ceremonially deflowered them one after the other, as was his duty and their expectation.

Only one of them pleased him, a fragile child of some fourteen years whose name was Shulah.

10

Strangely, there also was an unexpected access of a great love this night in the gorge that housed the Philistine camp.

Akish was a crude and brutal man, but his seizure of the young girl he thought to be Debrah had not only elated him to a peak of triumph he had rarely known before; it had also left him confused and uncertain.

She will serve you, Beladus had said, *as you serve her.* And: *Treat her with gentleness, and see the advantages that accrue to you also.* The admonition angered him, because he felt that Beladus was right. And should he learn from a damned Phoenician?

And yet . . . It was well known that among the arts of the Phoenicians, not the least of them was the art of love that had been taught them by the goddess Dagan, whom in their foolishness they called Astarte. He caught himself, wondering at his own instinctive thought, the *art* of love? Surely, physical love could not be called an *art!* It was a matter of command, no more, that could be expressed very simply indeed: *Bend your body, woman, I have need of you.* Or: *Lie down, woman, and spread your thighs and service me.* Or: *Drop to your knees, woman, and take me, drink the honey of my loins.* There was no room in this ancient relationship for . . . in god's name, for *gentleness?* As well be gentle with a donkey!

He said aloud, mocking his own thoughts, "Will it please you, Master Donkey, to carry this heavy load?" He laughed, and Helah looked up at him, startled.

She lay naked on the pegged hide stretched out on the ground that served as his bed—not even oiled or softened, she had noticed—and stared up at him. His bare foot was at her loins, the great coarse toes probing idly. "I do not understand, Lord Akish," she whispered.

"An idle thought, Debrah, no more."

He had divested himself of his armor and undershirt, and the kilt with the strips of beaten iron running down its sides, and he was removing the final garment, the loincloth. There were only two lamps in the cave, and poorly made ones at that, with no artistry at all in the pottery jars that held the spluttering wicks. The feeble light they gave shone on his immensely powerful body, the pale-skinned barrel chest crisscrossed with long-healed but still livid battlescars. He threw his loincloth aside and stood with his legs, pillars of bronze and corded with bulging muscles, wide-spread. He dropped to his knees beside her and touched her breasts, twin mounds of alabaster, very lightly. And when one of those hands started to her stomach and her thighs, she closed her legs and waited for his reaction which came at once: "No. Do not close your legs, Debrah. Open them."

"As you say, Lord, your servant."

She did as she was bid, and as he explored her innermost secrets, he said, laughing, "Forget, Debrah, that till recently you were a virgin."

"Yes, Lord," Helah whispered. "It is hard to accept the touch of a man. But I do so willingly."

"Yes, willingly . . ." It was a word the Phoenician had used. He rolled over atop her, scarcely able to control himself, and began the clumsy, inexpert probing with his strong manhood, biting his lip till the blood came in an effort to contain his excitation until he was deeply inside her.

He thrust himself into her, and took great pleasure in

188

her gasps of pain. He held both her wrists above her head with one hand and mauled at her breasts with the other, dropping his head down to bite fiercely at a nipple. He exploded almost at once but continued the fervent pounding till he was quite drained. He dropped heavily on her at last, a giant on a slight and fragile body, and said very quietly (remembering his lesson), "I am heavy on you, my dove?"

"No, Lord Akish. There is great comfort in your strength."

"I do not hurt you?"

"Only pleasurably, Lord. If a man is not strong, he is not a man."

"You know all that is expected of you, as the bride of a strong man?"

She would not meet his eyes, but turned her face away in pretended shame. "Not all, perhaps, Lord," she whispered. "But my mother Micah, the wife of Uzzi ben Ezra, has told me what is expected of me. And she told me to accept, which I will do."

"A wise woman, then, your mother. And tell me, Debrah . . . My spies have informed me that Beladus took you to wife. He himself says you are merely a concubine. The truth! I must know the truth, Debrah!"

Helah was no fool. She knew that it was a question that answered wrongly, might betray her. She said carefully, "In the custom of the Israelites, Lord, there is little distinction between wife and concubine, save for matters of inheritance. A man buys the one as he does the other. Though the one is a freed woman, the other . . . a slave."

"And you, Debrah, are no slave."

"A freedwoman, Lord. But nonetheless . . . your servant, to please in all things."

"Turn over onto your stomach, Debrah."

"Yes, Lord."

She did as she was told, and he reached out and took her hips in an iron grip and pulled her up onto her knees. "Perhaps Beladus was right," he said. "We will

189

spend long weeks, perhaps months, together, you and I. Remember only that I am your master."

It was not new for her, but she screamed as she thought she should, and he drove into her and shouted again, "Your master!" He thundered into her, and fell back at last, exhausted. In a while he muttered, "Find yourself a corner to sleep in, Debrah. If I need you again I will call you."

"Your servant, Lord Akish."

She crawled to a darkened shadow among the darker boulders, and found some soft sand to lie in and curled herself up, shivering against the night cold, and thought of Beladus. She whispered to herself, "It is for you, my noble captain. For you."

Akish did not call her again. She awoke with the first rays of the sun at the cave's entrance, slipped into her torn robe, and went to the narrow ledge to watch the activity below her. Akish was there in full uniform, using his chariot whip to strike out occasionally at a long and very untidy line of men who were moving into the camp, more than a hundred of them, dressed in the bright skirts and flat caps of Gath and Ashkelon.

These were some of the recruits whose services had been bought with gold provided by Akish's father, Sinrusa the son of Goliath, and for several days now they had been trickling into the camp. Akish lashed out at them: "You will be *soldiers* before long, I promise you!" He thought he had never seen a more miserable-looking string of ruffians.

Further down the line, there was a commotion, the savage barking of dogs and a fearful screaming, and in a little while Tarson came to him and said, laughing, "A young man from Gath, Akish, a youth with no sense at all! He kicked out at one of the dogs that were snarling at him." He shrugged. "A man cannot kick a watchdog that has been trained as ours have."

"See that these new scum are equally well trained. And quickly, Tarson. How many in all?"

"Up to this day, a hundred and thirty. There are others on the way, they will be here soon."

But it was to be longer than Tarson thought, and the time slipped by. And now, there was more news. Tarson found his captain drinking beer in the shade of a stubby thorn tree, and he squatted down beside him, a sly smile on his face. He said, "Something you should know, Akish. Three deserters from a force of regular troops from Ekron have been brought into the camp."

"Deserters?" Akish frowned; there was no room in his philosophy for the idea of desertion. "Yes, deserters," Tarson said. "And from the regular army! One of our patrols found them wandering on foot a few thousand double-paces to the north of us and drove them in. They had lost their horses, their weapons . . . One of them had even thrown away his armor to make the speed of his cowardly flight more effective."

Akish said harshly, "They have been killed already?"

"Not yet. The officer of the day questioned them and reported to me. You may wish to hear what they have to say before they die. It seems they were attacked by two hundred men or more, close by Aijalon. They were led by Lieutenant Hasorar, who is known to us, an officer from the Phoenician camp above the pools."

Akish stared. "Two hundred of Beladus's men as far north as Aijalon? He told me, on that day, that he had four hundred and seventy men in his camp! It was a lie, then!"

"You know the reason now, why Beladus gave you his wife so easily. He was afraid to fight us."

"A coward, as all Phoenicians are! Take me to these deserters. We will find out how much truth there may be in their story."

He strode with Tarson to where they were pegged out on the hard sand. One of them had died, one was unconscious, and the third was staring up with pain-filled eyes. His naked body was covered with ants, feasting on the honey that had been poured on him. Akish kicked him. "Your name, pig."

191

The voice was almost inaudible. "Adula, Lord, from Ekron."

"A soldier of the regular army?"

"Yes, Lord."

"And you ran away?"

"To my shame."

"From Phoenicians?" He spat the word out.

"There were very many of them, Lord, far outnumbering us."

"Under whose command?"

"One Lieutenant Hasorar, Lord."

"And how do you know this, pig?"

"Our captain told us, Lord."

"He was sure?"

The deserter nodded painfully. "He was sure, Lord. He had fought with Hasorar before."

Akish grunted. "And where is he now with his two hundred men?"

"I do not know, Lord."

"How many of his men did you kill?"

"Lord, I do not know."

Akish looked at the guard standing stolidly over the bodies, and said coldly, "Kill them."

He turned on his heel and stalked away. He did not look back when he heard the sound of the sword. Tarson hurried after him, and they went to the cave together, where Helah was crouched in a corner talking quietly with the slave. The boy sprang to his feet as they entered, and Akish said brusquely, "Pour beer, and bring food, for the woman, too—she is not a slave to fend for herself."

"Yes, Lord, at once."

As they sat at the plank table and drank beer together, Akish muttered, "It seems that Beladus might have more men under arms than we thought. Unless, on that day, Hasorar was perhaps still with him . . . Would a soldier lie about the strength of his army, Tarson?"

192

Tarson shrugged. "Beladus is not a soldier. He is a Phoenician, and skilled in subterfuge. Our information is that he commands two hundred and fifty men, no more."

"But is it correct information? I would dearly like to know. I do not like so strong a threat on my flank."

Tarson spread his arms wide. "How can we know? We cannot send one of our spies to find out! A Philistine in their midst would be recognized immediately— we do not look like them!" Staring at Helah, he said softly: "Perhaps the woman knows."

Akish turned to her. "Well?" he asked. "How many men does your husband command, Debrah?"

"I cannot know, Lord," Helah answered swiftly. "Since he took me to his tent, I have not left it."

"No . . ." Akish turned his attention back to Tarson. "I am sure of that. And what would she know? She is a woman." He rose to his feet and stood looking down on Helah. "For the moment," he said, "I will content myself with the knowledge that his woman is mine, to use as I wish." Not taking his eyes from her he said, "Leave us, Tarson, the slave, too. I will take her again now. I find great pleasure in her."

"Your servant, as always."

When they had gone, Akish began stripping off his clothes. Mechanically, submissive and quite unafraid, Helah moved to the dusty skin that was the bed, pulling off the torn Phoenician dress. She was stoical and quite philosophic about her trial, not really regarding it as much of an ordeal, knowing that she was saving so many good lives—her beloved captain among them!— at very little cost to herself. She lay down and awaited him, even admiring the great power of the robust and sturdy body that would have brought pleasure to almost any woman.

He dropped to his knees beside her and she reached out to touch him, whispering "So fine a man, Lord Akish . . ." She clutched at his powerful shoulders as he entered her abruptly, running her slim fingers over the tight musculature, tracing the lines of old sword cuts that ran across it.

He was more gentle with her now, and he thrust at her quite slowly, lingering over the pleasurable sensations and remembering with some amusement the lessons the Phoenician had given him. Helah found to her surprise that there was delight in them for her, too, and she was gasping with her emotion. She could see his belt close by where he had dropped it, the ivory handle of his sharp dagger only a span's length away from her hand. She wondered what would happen were she able to grasp it and drive it into the bull neck, or slash it across his throat in a lightening, lethal movement.

Would she, then, be able to escape from the camp? No, it would not be so simple—there were guards everywhere, they would quickly kill her, without a doubt. Even so, her own life was a small price to pay if she could slay her captain's mortal enemy . . . And then, her own fire burst out in sudden ferment, and she writhed under him; the thought and the moment of opportunity were gone as he rolled from her, exhausted.

He lay still for a while, and then raised himself up and looked at her, deeply moved by her beauty. There was no other woman in the camp like this lovely child! "The fairest among women," he said. "I think that I will never leave this bed."

"A lion, Lord," she said softly. "You are a lion that searches out the springs in the desert, prowling over the gentle hills, taking what you will. A lion!"

"A hungry lion," he answered. "Your skin is on fire, like burning straw . . ."

"The fire will not so easily be extinguished, nor so quickly."

"Your breasts are mounds of ivory burned by the sun, and soft as the feathers on a dove. And there is more delight in your thighs than I have ever known in my life. Your perfume is like the scent of the figs that

194

grow in Socoh and Azeka . . . There is great pleasure in your body, Debrah."

"If it pleases you, Lord, I am content."

He lay on his back again and stared up at the crude drawings on the roof of the cave, a formal depiction of a hunter hurling a spear at a gazelle, a wounded lion rearing up with a javelin in its neck. At some time, many generations ago, these caves had been the home of a tribe of hunting nomads, and he wondered idly about them.

"And your Beladus," he asked. "Have you forgotten him, Debrah?"

"Not yet, Lord," Helah answered. "In time, no doubt, I will. I have found a stronger master now."

He fell silent. An intrusive thought was nagging at his brain, and he could not bring it to clarity, a thought that had come to him and quickly gone before he could place it in focus. There was only a sense of discord at the back of his mind, something that he himself had said; and it worried him.

Was it about Beladus? No. The perfume of figs? Not that, either. What was it then? Mounds of ivory, he had said, praising her breasts, burned by the sun and soft as the feathers on a dove . . .

Why were her breasts sunburned?

Satisfied with her love for the moment, he was more reflective now, less bound by his urgent passions, and he began to think. He knew that the Israelite women who were free wore gowns that covered the head, the shoulders, the body, all the way down to the ankles. He knew that they were jealous of their modesty and seldom removed the gown save only to wash their bodies, and that rarely.

Why, then, was her upper body lightly copper-colored? Why was there a quite discernible division at the waist, where a slave's kilt would be fastened to cover her whiter loins? He stole a look at her long legs, and yes, that unobtrusive darkening began again just below her knees, where a slave's skirt would end.

195

He did not stir, nor did her soft murmuring reach him now. He lay still, and remembered Beladus's words: *"If you want her, Akish, then I give her to you freely!"* He had even been scornful about it! Shrugging his shoulders elegantly as though the whole matter were of no importance at all!

"I give her to you freely, that we may live in peace together . . ."

So this, then, was the reason! Not Phoenician cowardice, but Tyrian trickery! He was trembling with suppressed rage as it dawned on him that he had been given a slave girl, perfumed and dressed in fine clothes and bejeweled, but a slave nonetheless! He had been tricked!

But he still did not move. He thought about it for a long, long time, and only when he was sure that he was right did he get slowly to his feet.

He looked down on the girl he had known as Debrah, and raised his knee and stomped a heavy heel into the pit of her stomach as though he were squashing a scorpion. She gasped and tried to catch her breath and could not, and rolled off the skin in her pain and tried to reach the darkness in the corner of the cave, doubled up in her agony and trying in vain to suck air into her lungs. Akish strode to the entrance and screamed at the top of his voice: "Slave! Slave! At once!"

The painted young boy was seated on a rock close by, and he came running, stumbling in his haste and falling to the ground. He picked himself up, very frightened by the evident rage; and he stammered: "Your . . . y-your servant . . . L-Lord."

"Dogs!" Akish said furiously. "Summon the dog master at once! Have him bring me three dogs on their iron chains! Now!"

"Y-yes, Lord, at once. . . ."

The boy ran off along the ledge and down into the gorge, and Akish went back inside and slowly put on his clothes, not deigning to look at Helah but taking delight in her moaning.

He was lacing on his sandals when the dog master came, a thin, wiry man with only one hand; the other had been bitten off long ago by one of his charges. His name was Kreskil, and there was a cast in one of his eyes. Three dogs were straining at the chains that held them, huge and monstrous beasts with long yellow teeth, closely matted and stinking hair, and eyes that seemed to reflect Hell itself. They were growling ferociously, the hair on their short necks bristling; the confines of the cave were strange to them and therefore hostile.

Akish went to them, and Kreskil pulled back on the chains and said: "Careful, master! They have not been fed and they do not like the cave. It is not theirs. There are smells here they do not know."

"I am not afraid of them! Give me the chains."

Fearfully, not daring to argue, the dog master held out the iron ring to which the leashes were fastened. He pulled a short spiked stick from his belt and said, "The prod, master. If they should even turn and look at you—a sharp jab toward their eyes—they understand it well."

"Why should they look at me? They have already found something else to interest them."

It was the truth. The gasping, sobbing shadow that was Helah was a sound and a shape and a movement in the darkest recess of the cave that had aroused their snarling fury. Akish took the iron ring, scorning the prod, and felt the great power of them tugging at his muscles. He held the chains firmly, and gave them a little headway as they sought to free themselves. They were snarling atrociously at Helah, crouched there and trying to suck air into her bruised body. He said, "And the word, dog master?"

"The word, Lord," Kreskil said quietly, "is *brah*."

Hearing the command to attack, the dogs threw their weight onto the leashes, and Akish felt that his strong

197

right arm was almost torn from its socket. They reared up and pawed at the air, their great teeth snapping, their eyes flashing, and they were barking now like demons. Akish hauled back savagely. "Not yet, not yet . . . !" Helah tried to scream as they bore down on her slowly, and could not. She stared at them in horror, so close to her now that she could smell the evil stink of their breath.

Holding them firmly, Akish said harsly, "So, woman. Now you tell me who you really are. You will tell me of the real Debrah, that I may find her. And you will tell me quickly."

For the first time in her young life, Helah knew the meaning of terror.

Down in the camp below the cave, there was much activity at this time of the day.

Over small fires of thorn twigs, superheated by leather bellows worked by slaves, soldiers were hammering out iron arrowheads for the smiths to work on, bolts of soft iron a hand's span in length roughly shaped before being handed over to the experts who would finish them with the skills that only they had. Others were carefully scraping slender rods of river birch to make into arrow shafts; this wood was very valuable here since it could not be found in Philistia and had to be imported at considerable cost from Egypt. Some of the recruits were drawn up at the butts for archery practice under the hard eyes of the master archers; others were being given their first introduction at the stable compound to the suspicious tempers of the horses. Slave women were washing the heavy saddle blankets at the stream and hanging them out to dry.

High on the cliff above them, Zimri was lying on his belly in a tiny crevice, motionless, silent, and watching. He turned his head carefully at a slight sound behind him, tensing himself and ready to spring if need be; his knife, honed to perfection, was ready. But it was Nemuel, worming his way toward him. Squeezing his slight body into the crevice, he whispered, "The cave where Akish is, something is happening there. I do not know what, but he appeared at the entrance, quite naked, and shouted for a slave to bring dogs."

Zimri frowned. "Why would he need dogs in his cave?"

Nemuel gestured broadly. "How would I know why? Can I read the mind of a naked Philistine?"

"And Helah? Have you seen any sign of Helah?"

Nemuel shook his head. "Nothing, nothing of her at all."

"Go back, then, and continue watching. If anything happens there, throw a small pebble. And when it is dark, I want you to ride to the pools again. I will have a message for the captain."

"Oh? Anything I should know of?"

Zimri sighed. "Another message that there is no message. Go now, quietly."

"What do you mean, quietly? You think I will sing and dance so that they may all know we are here?"

"Wait . . . Go first to the horses and make sure they have not been discovered."

"How should they be discovered? They are well hidden, as you know."

"Do as I say, Nemuel," Zimri said patiently. "I am a sergeant of scouts now."

"And still a slave, as I am. No one gave you your freedom yet." He shrugged. "But I will do as you ask so that we may always be friends." He added slyly, "Even though I am a Phoenician and you are merely an Israelite, we can always remain friends if you watch your manners carefully." He began to move away again, and a small shower of pebbles trickled down on them from above. He felt Zimri's restraining hand on his arm and glanced up. There, on the skyline above them, a bear was prowling, digging into the sand with its snout; it looked down on them and growled softly, then wandered off. Zimri had already turned his attention away from it and was peering down into the approaching darkness of the gorge to see if any of the soldiers might be staring up at the bear, exposing their hiding place to possible discovery.

But it seemed that none had. More fires were being lit down there, with slaves running from one to another of them with flares of thorn twigs.

"Go," Zimri said. "A stone to the rocks above if you see anything of note."

"What shall I see? In a few moments it will be dark, you think I am an owl? But I am going, you can see that I am going."

He slithered away in utter silence, and Zimri turned his attention again to the depths of the gorge, where there was little to see. The night was approaching fast, and men were moving in and out of the pools of yellow light cast by the fires. The sound of their voices drifted up to him now as the evening breeze caught broken snatches of conversation and bore them away again:

"It is said there is more gold . . . if they do so . . ."
"No, my friend, not unless . . . within three days . . ."
"A shekel, then, if you have it . . ."
"Yes, she loved me . . . after it was over . . ."
(The sound of laughter now.)

A word here, a phrase there; the wind was playing its tricks, and nothing of note was heard or perhaps even said. Zimri unwrapped the rag from a piece of meat and chewed on it morosely, and when it was quite dark he stood up to stretch his cramped limbs. A warm and gentle rain was beginning to fall, and low on the horizon the moon was obscured by heavy thunder clouds, laden with a storm on its way. He chewed on his meat and wondered if he could perhaps sleep for a while; he had not slept for a very long time.

And then, he was suddenly wide awake; a trumpet down in the gorge was sounding a strange three-note call. One by one, the pinpricks of the fires were going out. What was it then, an alarm? The wind was carrying the sound of the trumpet away and bringing it back again. Nemuel was beside him suddenly. "What is it,

Zimri? Is this what we have been waiting for so long?

Now there was only blackness down there, with disembodied and ghostly voices floating up to them.

"Archers, to me . . . !"

"Second, third, and fourth platoon of horsemen to the stables!"

"The new recruits! Lieutenant Tarson, on the commander's orders, to parade the new recruits, fully armed. . . . !"

"A light catapult, to be drawn by a single horse . . . ! Sergeant Lasminar! A catapult, to the stables at the double!"

"All horses to be readied immediately . . . And word . . . stables . . . full armor and weapons . . . word from your Commander!"

Zimri said, raising his voice over the sound of the now-heavy rain, "Nemuel, *all* of their horses! They are moving out!"

"But where to?"

"We will find out. A convoy was due to leave Jerusalem this morning carrying gold from my king Solomon to your Hiram of Tyre. It is my guess that through their spies they have found this out.

"Captain Beladus must be told at once."

"I will ride to him instantly . . ."

"No, wait, we must know more! Have you the courage, Nemuel, to climb down the mountain with me to within better earshot?"

"In the *darkness?* You are mad!"

"If you are afraid, I will go alone and you will wait for me here."

"Afraid? Why should I be afraid? No, I will go with you, of course!"

Zimri said fiercely, "We *must* know more! This is the word that our commander has been waiting to hear, and we will not fail him now, you and I. *All* their horses, Nemuel, you know what that means?"

"Yes, it means all their horses . . ."

"It means that by tomorrow there will be only a token guard here. With twenty or thirty men, Captain Beladus can ride in here and rescue Helah, a mission very dear to his heart."

"Then let us begin the descent at once. You talk too much, Zimri. For a man of action, it is not good."

They slithered over the edge together, moving by instinct in the pitch darkness, from handholds on twisted roots to precarious footholds which they groped for. A fire was being rekindled immediately below them, and they could clearly see Akish himself there, with many of his soldiers around him, lit by the flickering flames, and shadows beyond them, which were more and still more men. Once in a while, the firelight caught the reflections of their armor, little shafts of red-gold light that glittered in the darkness.

The wind was whining now; soon, it would be howling. The rain was heavier, a torrent pouring down on them.

The snatches of the shouted orders were louder as they descended, still broken up by the wind: *"And behind us . . . carrying no less than . . . to each man . . . slaves to guard the horses as we . . ."*

The two of them were closer now, but they were still too high, and neither their reaching hands nor feet could find firm holds; they were at the edge of the granite overhang, smooth as the flesh of a pampered concubine. Zimri was desperate now, and wondered if he could drop the remaining distance. How far was it? He could not guess, nor could he risk a broken leg and capture at this crucial time.

The wind was still carrying the words away, even though they were shouted now over the howling of the storm: *"The slaves with the empty jars . . . no less than a hundred double . . . break them into fragments . . . on the south and . . . but there, only dark . . . catapult, shielded by ten . . . cords at maximum strength . . ."*

And then, by the grace of the one God Yahweh, the wind changed, and the words of the Commander Akish came to them with startling clarity: "And the man who brings me the still-living Captain Beladus will be rewarded with an end to his service and a purse of one hundred shekels of silver! Two minas of silver, one thirtieth part of a whole talent! Enough silver to buy himself a harem of concubines!"

Zimri said, startled, "Up, Nemuel, up! We have learned enough! They plan to attack our camp!

Scutting like the hyrax rodents that infested the cliff, they clambered back up to the top and raced in the darkness to where the two wiry ponies were hidden. They threw themselves into the saddles, and whipped their mounts along the southern hills of the valley of Sorek, flogging them into a frenzy. They forced them at murderous speed up the goat track to the top of the bluff, and a sentry's arrow sped past Zimri's head. He shouted furiously, "I am Sergeant Zimri, you fool! Get the commander! Awaken him! Tell him that Zimri is here with news he must hear at once!

The sentry did not dare. Instead, he raised his horn to his lips and blew the single piercing note that would summon the guard commander. Rekam came running, and Zimri saluted. "News from the Philistine camp, Lieutenant. Akish is preparing to mount an attack on us here. I heard only part of what he was saying but . . ."

"Wait," Rekam said urgently. "The commander himself must hear what you have to say. I will fetch him."

But Captain Beladus, cradled in the arms of his bride, had awakened at the sound of the horn and was striding to them, a long white cloth around his waist and thrown over one shoulder. "Well, Zimri?" he asked, his eyes on the horses' steaming flanks. "What news is it that brings you here in such haste?" He was deeply worried; more than a week had passed since he had handed Helah over to Akish, and still his reinforcements had not arrived.

"An attack," Zimri said, "with all of their horses,

which presupposes most of their men. They are, I think, preparing to ride out now."

"And how many, Zimri, is 'most of their men'?"

"Of those I saw, Lord, my estimation is perhaps three hundred."

"And all of their horses, you say?"

"Such was the order I heard, Lord."

Frowning, Beladus turned to Rekam. "But he cannot hope to attack us here with cavalry! Horses must climb the cliff in single file. And slowly, at that. Why should he need horses?"

"To bring his army here faster, perhaps? The horsemen to become infantry once they are in position?"

"Yes, it may be. But so many horses suggests an attack in open country. Perhaps it is Hasorar he wishes to attack, somewhere between here and Beth Horon. They must be warned."

"They will be, instantly."

Beladus looked at Zimri, gauging the worth of this devoted young man. "Are you sure that he wants to attack us here, Zimri?"

"No, Lord, I am not. I heard him demand your blood. Since you are here, it seems a logical deduction that this is where his attack will be mounted."

"As it is indeed, Zimri. Though perhaps he has learned of our Beth Horon force, now in open country where they are vulnerable to cavalry, and believes that I am with them."

Zimri said hesitantly, "He also has slaves with him, Lord, who carry water jars, but empty . . ."

"Carrying *what?*"

"Empty jars, Lord, to be broken into fragments, though I cannot imagine why. And a single catapult."

"A catapult too?" He said to Rekam, "What can he hope to gain with a single catapult against . . . against an olive grove? And empty water jars?" He said, sarcastically, "Does he hope to fill them with our blood?" He turned to Zimri, his brow creased with worry. "And Helah, Zimri. Is she still safe?" He was very anxious about Helah. *Two days*, he had told her, *no more . . .*

"In truth, Lord," Zimri said honestly, "I do not know. In all this time I have not seen her. I know nothing of her. Akish has a cave high on the mountain. I think she will be there. And when the time comes, Lord, I hope that I may perhaps be honored to lead you to her."

"You will be, Zimri, you have my promise." He smiled. "And as a freedwoman, wealthy with the riches I will give her for what she has done, she would make you a very worthy wife."

"Oh, Lord . . ." Pleasure was suffusing his young cheeks. "If I could have your blessing, Lord!"

"She will be yours, Zimri. If honeyed words are needed, she will hear them from me. Though I suspect they will not be required at all. Well. To more important matters. Rekam, send a runner at once to Lieutenant Hasorar. Inform him that he may soon be under attack by a strong force of Philistines. And in case we are wrong, let us see to our own defenses. Arm those of the slaves who are willing to fight for us, those who are willing and not others, allow them the right of refusal." He laughed shortly. "It is good," he said, "that the wedding guests have gone at last. It would not be courteous to inflict upon them what may, perhaps, be ahead of us."

He hesitated, and said at last, "And give some thought, Rekam, to a problem that vexes me sorely— why should Akish need a single catapult to attack us here, or to attack an army in the field such as Hasorar's? It perplexes me, and I do not like what I do not understand."

"Yes, it is perplexing indeed. I will give it great thought, Beladus."

"Our complement now?"

"Seventy-six men. Forty-one came in a few hours ago. They are exhausted, but they can still fight."

"Let them sleep, but with their armor and their weapons close at hand."

205

Rekam said drily, "They are sleeping, Beladus. And the arms of *all* our few troops are close beside them. You have trained us well."

"Good. You will keep me informed."

"I will. Good night, Beladus. There are many hours of the night left to be enjoyed."

"Yes. And you too, Zimri and Nemuel. I am grateful to you; we are all grateful to you."

"Your servants, Lord, whose only desire is to serve you."

"Sleep while you can. A man who is tired is not a good fighting man."

He returned to his tent and found Debrah and Seria awake and wide-eyed, waiting for him to speak, knowing—with the Israelites' strange understanding of impending calamity—that all was not well.

He said gently, forcing a smile of pure amusement, "Our old enemy Akish is up to his tricks again. It may be—as it may well *not* be—that he is on his way here to attack us. But do not be alarmed. We are strong enough to fight him off, as we will."

"I am not alarmed," Debrah said calmly. "Only a little while ago, when Akish rode down on us, yes, I was afraid to die so young. But now . . . I have been loved by a man I dearly love too, and it is enough for a lifetime. If that life must be cut short now . . . It is no longer an empty life. I have lived well, and I will die happy."

"You will not die," Beladus said quietly. "None of us will die. Akish is no new enemy. I have triumphed over him before, and I will do so again."

Seria whispered fearfully, a catch in her voice, "With thirty-five men, Lord?"

His eyes were very cold and hard now. "It is none of your affair, Seria; but men have come in during the night, and we are strong enough, now."

He feigned a yawn, and put aside the cloth that was around his wasit. Seria's anguish pained him, and he touched her breasts gently. "There is nothing to fear,

Seria. I would comfort you in your distress, save that my wife requires my services now. And my duties are to her."

"Your duties only, Lord?" She bit her lip, wishing that she had not spoken so impetuously. But Beladus was still smiling. "And my desires, Seria. Go to your corner now, and sleep. Perhaps in a few days I will take you to my bed, but not now."

"As you say, Lord. Should you require me to strengthen you, as only I know how . . . I am here."

"I know it. Go to sleep, Seria."

"My hands, my breasts, my hair, my lips, to harden you, Lord."

"I am hard. Sleep, Seria."

"Your servant, as ever . . ."

Seria slunk away and crouched down on her haunches out of the reach of the candle's yellow flame, then brought her knees up to her chin and rolled over onto her side. She watched them, bathed in tallow light as they made love together.

In a very little while, she heard Debrah groaning and gasping out her passion under the noble captain's loins. Thinking of their passion together, she let her hand stray to her inner thighs to ease the tension that was on her. As the crescendo of their excitation arose, so hers arose too, and she tried to imagine that her own slender finger within her was the captain's pulsating manhood, strong and erect and constantly throbbing as she knew it to be; in her imaginings, she was kissing the broad muscles of his powerful chest, the taut, flat stomach, working her way down to the pleasures he delighted in so much.

The sound of their flooding together came at the precise moment of her own, and she could not hold back the sound of her gasping, and she wondered if Beladus would hear it, though occupied with his own strong passions. For a while, she wondered, too, if she should perhaps creep to their bed and join them, adding her expertise to their innocent fullness, arousing him again and again as she knew she could for more and still more assaults on the woman whom he so clearly loved beyond the limits of temperance, exciting him again and again with her proven skills.

Teach her, he had said. *There are many things yet that she must learn. You will teach her.*

Was this, then, the time?

With a fervent longing for him, she thought that perhaps it was not, and exhausted by her own emotions, fell into a deep and troubled sleep.

Amid the deep fleeces of the bed, Beladus was crouched below Debrah. He had lifted up her legs and had placed her slender thighs on his shoulders, his hands under her buttocks, and he was feasting on her, as she screamed out in her delirium. He lowered her back onto the bed and positioned himself just so, then plunged into her. She moaned, exhausted, still welcoming more of his love. She whispered, "Beladus, my love . . . There is no part of you that is not dear to me . . ."

"Be silent, my dove," he said, "and let me love you."

He began the slow, rhythmic, pleasurable pounding.

11

The moon had set early this night, and in its place were dark and threatening clouds lying heavily from horizon to horizon.

The night's habitual aspect had changed completely. Normally there would be an ice-blue glow over the hills, and when the moon was full it was almost as clear as day. But now, the low black clouds covered the earth, and the darkness was absolute, an uncanny pitch-black. A man could hold his hand only inches from his face and not see it; he could hear a fellow creature beside him, only a pace away, and could see not even a blur.

And three hundred men were moving from the gorge in the valley of Sorek to the plain where Solomon's pools lay.

The Philistines, who were plainsmen, did not like the mountains. But a few of them had accustomed themselves through long years of guerrilla warfare, to think, move, and even feel like animals. Akish was one of these few. Tarson, close beside him and not even knowing exactly where his commander was, said irritably, "We do not even know if we move north, or east, or south . . ."

The strong, confident voice came to him out of pitch-black limbo. "We move southeast, Tarson, my friend. Trust me."

"You cannot be sure, Akish! There are no stars to guide us, no moon, no distant silhouettes of mountains to fix our eyes on!"

"Does a wolf need the stars to guide him, Tarson? No. And I am a wolf in the darkness. Place your hand on my shoulder, as the men do."

The long column of horses (more frightened than the soldiers in this terrifying obscurity) were tethered by short nose-ropes that ran from each bridle to the saddle ahead. The infantry had been ordered: *hold onto the man ahead of you, each in turn* . . . And so they marched, the left arm outstretched and firmly clasping the leather strap of a backplate, each man knowing that if he lost his grip the column could be broken and half of it, inevitably, would walk to the edge of some dreadful precipice.

There were 123 mounted archers and lancers, 155 infantry armed with swords, bows, or javelins, and 27 slaves carrying pottery water jars in which small fires of thorn twigs were smouldering. The jars were filled with sticks, but the insufficiency of air through the narrow necks did not permit the bulk of the wood to burst into flame. At the rear of the column, a horse pulled the catapult on its light-weight carriage. It was one of the smaller models, capable of hurling a stone weighing as much as seven pounds for a distance of more than eight hundred yards, its power being derived from two skeins of tightly twisted ox sinews. A hammer-blow on the trigger would allow them to untwist with explosive rapidity, sending the missile in its wooden trough at great speed toward its target.

The rain was pounding down now, drenching them all and worrying the horses; but as suddenly as it had come, it stopped, and the dark clouds were broken up, opening great vistas in the heavens of that eerie blue moonlight. Akish stared at the faint silhouette of the bluff ahead of them, no more than half an hour's march away, and he said, his voice harsh with triumph, "There! You see, Tarson? There is our target! We will

210

call a halt soon, and you will send the slaves with their fire jars to the south, the west, and the north of the bluff. All horsemen and foot soldiers will move to the east, one thousand double-paces above Shemah. And when they are in position—there will be *silence*, Tarson."

"You may count on it, Akish."

"If a man makes a noise, his neighbor is to strike off his head. They will hide themselves among the boulders on both sides of the ravine. The horsemen may dismount, but they will stand by their horses and keep them quiet. The infantry may sleep, one man in ten to remain on guard and await the signal."

Soon, the column halted, and Akish called the senior slave to him. "Hehfasel," he said, "you understand your orders?"

The slave nodded. "I understand them, Lord."

"Every five hundred paces, one man."

"My men have their orders, Lord. They will obey them."

"Good. Move out now."

Hehfasel ran off to attend to his important duties, and Akish said quietly, "Now, Tarson, the catapult to the south, ten men to guard it. The rest of you—to the ravine above Shemah."

"And you, Akish?"

"I will be with the catapult. When the time comes, I will join you. We have four hours of darkness left. It is good."

Seria, once more, had awakened her master with the whispered words: "Rekam, Lord . . ."

Beladus left his comforting bed and went outside, then walked with his lieutenant a little distance from the tent. The dark clouds were scudding across the night sky, their huge shadows drifting like monstrous ghouls over the plain below, a moving patchwork of black and gray.

Rekam said tightly, "The Philistines, Beladus. They

are gathering all around us, very many of them indeed. I have counted sixteen camp fires, which indicates perhaps as many as five hundred men or more. Seven fires to the south of us, and nine to the west, where they seem to be their strongest."

Beladus frowned. "To the west? But he cannot hope to attack us there! And if he steals up on us in the night, why should he announce his presence with fires, and so lose the value of surprise?"

"I, too, find it strange. The patrol on the plain has sent up a runner. The catapult Zimri spoke of is on the south, well guarded."

"It is to send fire into the camp."

"Yes, I myself came to the same conclusion—there can be no other reason for it. Though why he should think a single machine is enough to burn us out, I do not know. I would have expected six, at least."

"Order the men to strike the tents then. They burn easily, and can do us unnecessary damage."

Rekam smiled thinly. "It is being done now, Beladus."

"Good." The captain laid a hand on his lieutenant's shoulder. "You read my mind, Rekam."

"No. But I, too, am a soldier, and think like one. Let Akish send us his fire; it will not harm us. But I am puzzled by the large forces on the sides we have always believed to be impregnable."

"Perhaps wrongly so," Beladus said, worried. "Certainly, the mountain cannot be scaled save on the south. But with so many troops . . . If a large number of them are archers—have you thought, Rekam, of what would happen if they were to approach the bluff closely and send massed flights of arrows high into the air to rain down on us from the heavens? A hundred archers or more, with forty or fifty shafts each, even fired at random in this fashion . . . ?"

Rekam scowled. "Yes, while he sends his men up the goat paths in a never-ending stream. He would lose many of his soldiers in the effort, but perhaps he can afford to."

A sergeant hurried up to them and saluted. "Camp-fires to the north of us now, Captain. I counted six of them, and more are being lit now."

"Then they are moving to surround us," Beladus said. "We must expect them to the east as well. And I will confess that I do not like it. It may well be that our bluff is untenable after all. Let us walk to the northern edge, Rekam, and see what may be seen of good or bad."

They moved off together, and Rekam said slowly, "I have been trying to insinuate myself into the mind of this Philistine, to think as he thinks. And even though he greatly outnumbers us, he cannot know how weak we truly are now . . ."

"Not so," Beladus said swiftly. "Among our recent wedding guests there may be some who spoke, when they reached their homes, of our slight numbers. There are many Philistine slaves in Bethlehem. It may be that there are spies among them. Indeed, I would be sur-prised if there were not."

"Ah, yes . . ." They had reached the perimeter and were watching the fires springing up. Staring to his right, Rekam murmured: "On the east, nothing. And if our position here is truly undefendable by so few men under a hail of arrows from the skies . . . perhaps we should force a way out to the east while we still can."

"No," Beladus said firmly. "Not till I know, with certainty, a great deal more than I know now."

"By then . . . it may be too late."

"But I will not act without thinking; it is the quickest way to sure disaster." He said lightly, "And it is not fitting that I patrol my camp under threat of attack dressed only in a length of cotton. Come with me to my tent, Rekam."

It was still some hours before the dawn, but Debrah, conscious that all was not well, had put on her robe and was waiting with her new-found friend Seria beside her.

213

He saw that the slave girl was alarmed, but Debrah seemed calm and very composed. He threw his arms around her and said quietly, "The attack we spoke of, my dove. It is not, after all, against Hasorar and his Beth Horon force, wherever they may be. It is against us. It is my belief that when the dawn comes, Akish will send his men up the cliff to do battle."

He heard Seria's frightened gasp, and he turned to her, half-smiling. "Do not be afraid, Seria," he said gently. "You will not be here when those vile Philistines begin their assault. Neither you, nor my bride."

He felt Debrah's arms tightening around his stalwart body, and he said to her abruptly, "I am sending you to Bethlehem, my dearest, where you will be safe, until the battle is over. Then I will immediately come for you."

"No, Lord!" Debrah said sharply. "I will not leave your side!"

He was smiling broadly at her. "What, you will wear a sword, and fight? No, you will return to your father's house till I come for you."

She said stubbornly, "I will not go, Beladus."

"You will, because of the great love I have for you."

"And by the token of that love, I dare to refuse you."

"You may not. You cannot."

"Beladus! I will not leave your side while you are in danger!"

He was holding her tightly now, touched by her spirit. "That danger is very considerable. I will not hide it from you. To overcome it, I will need all my wits, all of my concentration on that one objective. Would you have me fight only for the woman I love, when I should be fighting also for my men? I think not. In such times, a commander cannot divide his attentions, and fight with only half a mind."

She fell silent, knowing he was right, and he pushed home his advantage, "I *must* know that you are safe," he said, "so that I can devote all of my thoughts and my energy to overcoming this monster Akish. As I will.

Therefore, you go to Bethlehem with Zimri, who has my confidence, and with Seria, who will serve you."

Debrah said quietly, "May I speak at length, Beladus?"

Her composure surprised him. "Of course," he said gravely. "You are my wife, whom I love dearly." He turned to Seria. "Dress me, child," he said.

As Seria removed his cotton robe, brought his clothes, and began dressing him, Debrah, standing very straight and proud, said, "I must tell you about my father, Beladus."

He was surprised. "But my love, I know all that needs to be known about the good Uzzi ben Ezra . . ."

"Not Uzzi, but my true father, who was killed when I was a few years old, also by the Philistines."

"Ah yes, your true father . . ."

"When he died, Beladus, he was a potter, a master of his craft. But as a younger man he had served King David as a soldier, an officer. He was renowned for his bravery, loyalty, and strength. I was only a child when he was killed, but the strong memory of him is still there. And many times, both Uzzi and Micah have told me of his exploits. He was a champion warrior, who fought in personal challenge against champions of the Philistines no less than nine times, and slew all of them. He was not a man to be scorned, Beladus! And my blood is his blood! Yet you say, *'hide yourself, Debrah, that you may not be hurt . . .'* I was hidden *then*, Beladus, and the man I loved dearly was killed. I will not hide a second time, and find myself a widow even before I bear a child by the man I love so dearly now."

He was deeply moved by the strength of her passion, and he enfolded her in his arms again and said, very gently, "Listen to me, Debrah. There is a great love between us that passes all understanding; it must not pass the bounds of reason, nor distort wisdom. I must be a good soldier now, and a good soldier is not one who must run to his tent in the heat of battle—as I would do!—to assure himself that the woman he loves is safe. It cannot be, Debrah."

He stroked her perfumed hair and whispered, "You will not be a widow. Unhampered by the distraction of your presence, I will defeat this Akish. You go to Bethlehem, my love, not because I order it—and I will not be swayed—but to leave me in full control of all my wits, which are needed now."

Debrah sighed, and her heart was heavy. "Very well," she whispered. "I will do as you say, though reluctantly, so that your mind will be at rest."

He laughed. "And if it is danger you seek, you will have your fill of it. We are being surrounded, and the way to Bethlehem will not be easy. This is why I send Zimri with you—he will find a way through their lines. You must move in absolute silence, hiding when he hides, moving only when he moves." He turned to Rekam, standing in the half-light. "Send the guard, Rekam, to fetch Zimri."

Rekam went out, and Debrah took the heavy armor from Seria. "No, I will do that . . . " She slipped the plates over Beladus's head and fastened the straps that bound them together. "It will be hard to leave you, Beladus," she whispered.

He was laughing quietly: "Had you not agreed, I would have had you carried there by force. My father, too, was a warrior. Come, we will go outside. They will be striking the tent soon."

Seria stared. "Striking your tent, Lord?" It was a symbol for her, the collapse of a home in which she found great comfort. They went out into the new-bright moonlight, and Beladus sighed, "Yes, they must strike all of the tents. Akish has brought catapults to send us fire, and the tents burn like straw in the wind . . ." He frowned. "No, a *single* catapult. I do not understand it. What can he hope to accomplish with a single machine? Well, perhaps he had no more at his disposal."

Zimri hurried up to them and saluted. "Your servant, Lord, awaiting your orders."

216

"You will take the Lady Debrah to Bethlehem. There are Philistines all around us, so you will find a way through their lines, moving like a jackal that must hide from predatory lions. Another sleepless night for you, I fear, after so many sleepless nights."

"If it may serve you, Lord . . ."

"What is the word from the guards? Have the Philistines moved to the east of us yet?"

"There are no fires on the east, Lord. None at all."

Beladus frowned. "It is strange. He has so many troops, and yet he does not surround us . . ."

"A way out, Beladus," Rekam said, urging, "we should take it before it is too late!"

"No." Beladus shook his head. "There is too much in this endeavor that I find perplexing. Partial encirclement only. All of the horses, which cannot easily climb the bluff. A single catapult instead of many. Twenty or thirty slaves carrying empty clay jars, and for what possible purpose? I am bewildered, and it is not a state of mind that—"

He broke off, conscious of Debrah's gasp; her eyes, huge and wide, were on him. "Did you say . . . *clay jars*, Beladus?" she whispered. "Empty jars carried by slaves?"

"Yes." He stared at her. "It means something to you?"

"Yes, oh, yes, it does!"

He said abruptly, his interest keen now, "Tell her, Zimri, what you reported to me."

Zimri, too, had caught the sudden excitement, though he did not understand how it had come about. He said eagerly, "We heard Akish himself, Lady Debrah, giving orders to his troops, though the wind carried away most of his words. We heard something about empty jars, to be shattered into fragments . . ."

Seria said excitedly, "Yes, yes, of course, to be broken . . . !" Debrah hissed, "Sshhh . . . Go on, Zimri."

"At a hundred double-paces apart, I think," Zimri

said. "I did not understand what it meant. I still do not."

Debrah said, a note of triumph in her voice, "*Gideon*!" and Seria echoed her with equal triumph: "Yes! Gideon!"

Beladus was bemused. There was something that both these two young women understood very clearly and that he did not. His eyebrows were raised in a question as he looked at Debrah, and she said, "Eight or nine generations ago, Beladus . . ."

Seria interrupted her: "No, more. Nine or ten."

"Yes, nine or ten." She went on: "There was a great military commander named Gideon . . ."

"He was a judge, too . . ."

"Yes, he was a judge."

"He was the fifth of the judges . . ."

"Yes, perhaps . . ."

"Not *perhaps!* He *was* the fifth!"

"All right," Debrah said impatiently. "Let me speak!"

"Of course." Seria was abashed, but only momentarily. "Your pardon, Lady."

Debrah spoke very quickly now, sure that what she had to say was of the greatest possible importance. "Gideon was one of our great warrior-heroes. And some two hundred years before Solomon came to the throne, he defeated a great horde of Assyrians by the same kind of ruse . . ."

"Not Assyrians," Seria said flatly. "They were Midianites."

"Ah yes, Midianites . . ."

"But what ruse," Beladus asked impatiently, "what ruse are you talking of?"

Seria opened her mouth to speak, but Debrah silenced her with an imperious look and said, "During the night, Gideon came to the mountain and found—"

"Mount Gilboa."

"He came to Mount Gilboa and found that in the plain below there were thousands of Assyrians, no, Midianites camped. And he himself had only five hundred men—"

"Not five hundred, only three. Three hundred men, on Mount Gilboa."

"Seria!" Debrah threw up her hands. "What am I to do with you?"

Seria bit her lip, resolving to say no more, and Beladus said urgently, "It does not matter who tells me! The ruse! I must know about the ruse!"

"Well," Debrah said, "knowing that he could not defeat so large a force, Gideon sent slaves all over the surrounding mountains, each man carrying a clay jar in which small fires were burning, fires that could not be seen, you understand. And at a given signal—"

Seria said, "A blast on a ram's horn."

"At a given signal, the slaves took heavy stones and shattered the jars. Now, the fires sprang to life, and were quickly fed with whatever sticks they could find lying there. And in a very short time it seemed to the Midianites that they were surrounded by a vast force far larger than their own. They fell into a panic, and fled on their horses . . ."

"Not horses," Seria said. "The Midianites rode camels, not horses." She turned to Beladus and said earnestly, "It was the first time, Lord, that camels had been seen in the land of the Israelites."

Beladus was wrapped in deep thought. "So," he said. "It would seem that Akish, like the competent fighting man he is, has studied his military history. It means that he seeks to panic us, to drive us out of our secure stronghold into open country where he can cut us down with a superior force both of cavalry and infantry. But we will not blindly walk into the trap he sets for us. We will wait, and let him attack us here, which will cost him dearly." He turned to his lieutenant. "Our effectives now, Rekam?"

"Seventy-four men. Two of the patrol that came in from Baalah have died of their wounds. All are standing to arms and waiting. As we all are."

219

"And that is what we will do. Wait."

A heavy cloud passed over the moon, casting a dark blanket over the grove. "Zimri," Beladus said, "go now with your charge. Her life is in your hands. Move to the east till dawn, and then you can turn north for Bethlehem. Seria will go with you. It is fitting that even in times of stress the Lady Debrah should have an attendant. Deliver them to the house of Uzzi ben Ezra, and tell him it is for a short while only. Stay with them yourself until I come."

"It will be so, Lord."

"Move like wolves in the night, Zimri, in silence."

"I am not unskilled, Lord."

"I know it." He threw his arms around Debrah, masking the heaviness that was on him. Was this to be their last embrace? He did not dare let her feel his great anxiety. Gideon's ruse or not, Akish was out there in the darkness somewhere with overwhelming odds on his side, seeking battle as he had promised at their last encounter. He clutched Debrah tightly to the inhibiting breastplate and whispered, "My love . . . My blessings go with you."

"If you do not come for me, Beladus . . . If they send me word instead that you have been killed, then I will kill myself and join you in death. Be sure of this."

"I will not die, Debrah. Your great love gives me greater strength, to defeat all of my enemies. And if fate should turn against us, why then, we will meet under the friendly wings of our licentious goddess Astarte, and continue our life together in the hereafter." It was hard to tear himself away from her. "Go," he whispered. "Remember at all times to do as Zimri says. Your life is precious to me."

"And yours too, my husband."

"Do not waste it."

"Nor you."

"Till we meet again, then." Debrah reached up and kissed him lovingly, then broke away from him. He reached out and touched the slave girl on the cheek and said gently, "Serve me, Seria, by serving her. You will earn my gratitude."

"There is not one woman in the camp, Lord, who will not serve you as willingly as I do."

They were gone.

Not one woman in the camp . . . He thought of Helah, and wondered how she was faring in the Philistine camp, almost empty now as he had so long waited for it to be, for a swift, nighttime raid. He thought bitterly: *now, it is unprotected at last; I am hemmed in by my enemies, and powerless.*

He said to Rekam, "Let us look to our defenses now. And then—we will wait and see."

It was a very Phoenician philosophy.

To the east of the bluff, the ground was harsh and uninviting. There were very few tracks among the broken boulders that lay scattered on the hillsides, and the hills themselves were cut with deep gullies where, in the rains, brief rivers ran till their waters were soaked up by the sand. Some of them now, after the storm, were deep and tumbling furiously, but in an hour or two they would all be dry again.

Akish himself, on the south, would not leave the catapult. It seemed to exercise a strange obsession for him that caused his eyes to gleam in the darkness. He touched the twin columns of tightly twisted sinews, bound together to the thickness of a man's forearm and then turned with the bow rods till the tension was like a groaning, living thing. They were wound back with a heavy wooden ratchet, the pouch for the missile resting in a groove three cubits long that could be raised or lowered for correct trajectory.

He said, grumbling, "The springs are wet."

The engineer who handled the machine was a surly youth named Sloskari, who had once been a sailor in Ashkelon. "They are wet on the outside only," he said, "it has been raining. Inside, they are still dry. Even were they soaked through, it would matter little. I can still reach the bluff, and a hundred double-paces beyond it if you wish."

"Not beyond it. To the center of the camp as you were instructed. Show me the flare."

The young man unwrapped it from its protective rag and handed it to him in silence. It was a small bundle of reeds, heavy with wax and tied at their thicker ends with a leather thong that would be attached to the missile; it looked like a broom that a woman might use to sweep away goat droppings. He grunted his satisfaction and handed it back. "And the fire for it?"

"A tinder in my pouch," Sloskari said, "and dry grass enough in the box. When the time comes, I can make fire very quickly.

Akish began to inspect the weapons of the men who were guarding the engine, testing the edges of their swords and javelins, even their daggers, as he waited impatiently for signs of activity at the top of the bluff— a shout, the clash of armor, the drumming of soldiers' feet as they formed up into lines for their escape, anything that would tell him what he was expecting to learn. Surely it could not be long now! And yet, there was nothing but silence up there . . . He could see the distant fires glowing, pinpoints of light in the dark hills, well spaced as he had ordered. He grunted again and said, seeking a kind of comfort, "Would you say that a whole army was camped out there, Sloskari?"

The engineer nodded. "Yes, a very large army, Commander."

"And would you say the Phoenicians will see it, and run?"

"They will see it; they are not blind. Whether they will run or not . . ." He shrugged. "I am an engineer of war machines, and my work is with them only. I cannot see into Phoenician minds." He sat down on the limber of the carriage and said no more. He did not like talking with the officers, particularly not with his captain, whom he hated. Akish moved away and strained his ears for any sounds on the night air. He could not even hear his own men, moving now with Tarson along the ravine and being posted as the lieutenant had been ordered:

"Ten men here, and not a sound from them . . ."

"Twenty of you, among the rocks there, in silence . . ."

"Forty horsemen on each side of the gully, well hidden, to ride on the signal to the north of the Phoenicians and keep them away from the hills. We do not want them in the hills, on the plain only . . ."

"Remember always, we need no prisoners, save only Beladus and his woman. They are to be brought, still living, to Akish, and all others are to be slain . . ."

The junior officers and the sergeants were nodding their understanding. It was well known that for Akish, whom they all feared, this was no ordinary battle; it was, instead, a personal vendetta of great importance to him, a battle between several hundred men for the sake of one woman. It was known, too, that in defense of his female, a man—any man, even a Phoenician—would fight like a lion, and that many of them, therefore, would die. The gain would not be theirs; but they were trained to obey their orders.

The diminishing column moved on, dropping men off here and there, and at last, with little more than an hour left to the dawn, the whole of the Philistine force was hidden. The trap had been set; all that was required now was the waiting, for the enemy to walk into it.

A young Philistine scout named Esobrulin, who had been a soldier for three of his sixteen years, was Tarson's lover, a slight and effeminate boy with the delicate movements of a dancer and a strong streak of cruelty. In a score of battles, he claimed to have slain twenty-seven Israelites and Phoenicians, though they were not his own legitimate kills; they were enemy soldiers who had been wounded by his fellows, and he had merely hacked off their heads. He was soldier-servant to Tarson, and there was an affinity between the two of them

223

that overcame the differences in their rank. His great ambition in life was to become an officer.

The last of the army had been hidden, and the two of them sat down together in a little cluster of boulders, their duty done. Tarson said quietly, "I have wine in my flask. Will you have some, Esobrulin?"

"Yes, I will have wine. And I have dates in my pouch if you are hungry."

"Ah . . . good. I have cheese and some bread, but no dates. We will share a meal together."

He sighed. "Three hundred men hidden, and waiting—for what? I do not believe, dear Esobrulin, that Beladus will fall into our trap. He is not a fool, as Akish seems to think. But perhaps he will, who can tell?"

"I, too, think that he will not. And if we are right? What then?" He was slipping the skins off the dates and popping them into his mouth, enjoying their succulence. Tarson shuddered. "If they do not panic and run, as Akish believes they will and you and I know they will not . . . then there is another plan, a frontal assault on the bluff. It will not be easy. Three goat tracks only, and very narrow ones too, as sketched so expertly by the late Grenik. A handful of men could hold them against an army twice the strength of ours."

Esobrulin, not wise enough to understand the terrible danger of such a project, said, laughing, "And all this for a woman!"

Tarson sighed. "Akish himself," he said, "will no doubt be in the forefront of his troops in his anxiety to get his hands on this girl. And perhaps . . . perhaps that means that he will be quickly killed. If so, Esobrulin, you and I can return to the gorge, and I will be the new commander. If so, I will make you an officer."

"Ah . . ." Tarson reached out and laid a hand on the boy's slender thigh, caressing him. "That will please you, I think."

"Greatly."

"Only . . . as an officer, you must promise that you will not leave me."

The boy's eyes were gleaming. "I will never leave you!" he said fiercely. "Never!"

"And meanwhile, there is time on our hands, perhaps a great deal of time." He touched his friend on the cheek and whispered, "You are so beautiful, Esobrulin."

Esobrulin took the hand and kissed it. He murmured, "Time on our hands . . . If you wish me to service you now?"

"Yes, the night is soft and gentle; it is a night for love."

Esobrulin unfastened his kilt and slipped out of it, and lay down in the sand to rest his head in his master's lap.

12

The night was slow in passing, a long night full of danger and frustration. It seemed to Debrah that they had crept down the bluff very many hours ago, and yet, there was no sign of the red streaks in the sky that would herald the dawn. The clouds loomed over the hills, moving darkly along, and every time they covered the moon a pall seemed to fall over the land.

The thought was gnawing at Debrah's mind that she should have been more adamant in her refusal. She whispered urgently to the young scout, "We should not be doing this, Zimri! I allowed myself to be persuaded too easily!"

He was smiling, amused by her assumption of an authority that was not really hers. In the time of her stay at the camp he had come to adore her, almost to worship the ground she trod on; but under all the adulation there was the thought: *she is one of us, and a sweet young girl not yet accustomed to the power of her position* . . . "Persuaded?" he echoed. "The captain does not *persuade*, Lady Debrah. He orders. And we must obey him without question. I, because I am his servant, and you—because you are his wife."

"Yes, it is true. But still . . ." He could hear the pain in her voice, and sought to comfort her. He said gently, "Your presence in the camp would have troubled him beyond measure. He was right, it would have lessened his competence severely. Before this night is out, he will need all of his abilities, unrestricted by fears for your safety."

"Of course!" Seria said, a great deal of certainty in her voice. "He loves you dearly, Debrah, and there is a great load off his shoulders now. It makes a fine commander even stronger! He can turn all his attention to defeating Akish, as he will, you will see! Tomorrow, your captain will come riding triumphantly into Bethlehem . . ." she corrected herself. "*Our* captain. He will come to bring us home, and the whole village will turn out to welcome him again, you will see!"

"And now," Zimri said, "we will rest awhile."

Debrah shook her head. "No," she said, "I am not tired . . ."

"And neither is Seria, nor am I. But we will still rest. Somewhere ahead of us, there will be Philistines waiting, I am sure of it, if only a few patrols. When we pass among them, we will need all of our energy and our strength. And so . . . we will rest for a few minutes."

Remember at all times, her beloved husband had said, *to do as Zimri says* . . .

She followed him obediently to a cluster of dark gray boulders, and they crouched down among them. "Less than an hour to dawn," Zimri whispered. "At the first sign of light, we turn north, and if we pass among their patrols, it will be a time of great danger. You must both move like . . ." He broke off sharply and took Debrah's wrist in a firm, hard grasp, a warning. Seria had heard the slight sound too, and in the moonlight her eyes were wide and frightened. Zimri's finger was at his lips, urging silence.

Had the faint sound been a voice? Or a vagary of the breeze in the gullies? They waited, and then the wind changed and it came to them clearly, from very close by—voices indeed, very low and somehow casual, "*There is wine still in the flask, Esobrulin. Drink with me . . .*" And the answer: "*Yes, wine is good between friends.*"

227

It came from beyond their hiding place, only a few paces on the other side of the boulders. Zimri glanced up at the clouds and saw that the moon would soon be covered. He waited, and as the shadow sped across them he signaled the two women to follow. They crawled away very cautiously, like ghouls in the night. And in a little while Zimri tapped Debrah on her shoulder and whispered, "A cave here, follow me carefully."

They crept together under a low overhang of sandstone, and found a bore hole, long and narrow and snaking down into the depths of the hill before it widened. The darkness here was absolute, but Debrah followed Zimri, a hand at his ankle, and felt Seria's hand at her own.

They stopped soon. Zimri's hand was on her shoulder, his other reaching out to find Seria, touching a naked breast, an arm, a hand . . . He said, his voice low, "We are well hidden here, I know this cave. Once my people hid here when the Ammonites came raiding. It is very large, and a man can hide here for all eternity and not be found, or even heard. And now, you will both stay here while I explore, to find out if the voices we heard are two alone, or two among many. Do not move, and in a very little while I will be back."

He was gone, and the two women were left alone in the fearful darkness. Seria clutched at Debrah's hand to find comfort there, and she whispered: "We must not move now. And yet, I am frightened to stay in this dreadful place."

"We are safe," Debrah said, "and I am with you."

"Yes, I am glad of it . . ."

"Beladus is in greater danger than we are, and our thoughts must be for him."

"For our captain, yes . . ."

Zimri paused at the cave's entrance, listening, then slithered back to the boulders, even closer now to the two voices.

"And shall we return now, to where Akish is standing beside his beloved catapult?"

"The catapult!" There was a laugh, and a lisping young voice said, *"As you know, Tarson, I have no great love for Akish. But this gesture of his, it amuses me greatly."*

"Then let us go. The time for battle is approaching."

They moved away, and Zimri crawled to the top of the rise and looked down on forty or fifty horsemen there, standing by their mounts; the moonlight glistened on the armor of half a hundred archers waiting. He moved quickly and quietly in a wide semi-circle; in every ravine, soldiers were waiting, and the number of them alarmed him. On his way back to the cave he heard the whinneying of horses, a whispered joking among soldiers, the sound of dice on a board that someone had brought to while away the time. The alien sounds disturbed him deeply. His dagger never once left his hand, and he had taken off his sandals and had strung them around his neck; bare feet moved more quietly even than well-chewed leather. In the tunnel, his keen nostrils could discern the scents of the two women even over the powerful stench of the bats—both the womanly smells of the slave girl Seria and the almond and lavender oils that Debrah used on her body. Those perfumes, while pleasing, could be carried on the wind and betray them.

He made no sound till he was halfway down the narrow passage where, he knew, the cave broadened out, and then he called softly, "It is I, Zimri! I see nothing. Tell me where you are."

He slithered over and reached out to touch Seria's naked torso and Debrah's elaborately coiffed locks to reassure himself of their presence. He twisted his lithe body around and crouched on his haunches between them. "We have little of darkness left, and we must leave here at once. But the Philistines are all around us, in very great strength, there are horses and infantry everywhere." He hesitated. "Perhaps I should return to the camp and tell Captain Beladus how very strong they are. I do not know . . ."

229

Seria said quickly, "But he knows this, Zimri! And you have other orders! They are to take us to Bethlehem!"

"Yes, my orders . . ." He was very confused now, a good soldier but a very young man who had spent all of his life in obedience. Seria said clearly, "What, return to the camp and tell him that the Philistines are ready to attack him? He knows this! We will tell him that they are stronger than he is? He knows this, too!"

Debrah said quietly, "It is not your own craving, Seria, for the safety of Bethlehem that makes you say this?" And Seria answered emphatically. "No, Debrah! I will confess that I am frightened. But I, too, am in love with Captain Beladus, and will do whatever must be done to save him. Every time he has taken me to his bed, I have felt that there can be no greater delight anywhere on earth! If we must return to the camp and be killed with him . . . then so be it. There will be death there for all of us, and I will welcome it if I can die in his shadow!"

Debrah whispered, "For all of us? Are you so sure, Seria, of the outcome of this battle?"

"Yes! I am sure of it! There are only seventy-four officers and men to defend the bluff, and against more than three hundred of the enemy? He cannot fight them off!"

"And so," Debrah said calmly, "shall we return to the camp and tell him that there is no hope? There is little else that we can tell him that he does not already know."

"The choice is yours, Debrah," Seria said, and it seemed that her great fear had quite gone now. "If I die with you by his side, I will be content."

"And my choice," Debrah said clearly, "is that he *not* die. No. We will not return to the camp on a foolish errand. But neither will we go to Bethlehem and hide like frightened hares. We will go, instead, to Jerusalem."

"Jerusalem!"

"In Jerusalem," Debrah said, "King Solomon has a vast and powerful army. And within a mere five thousand double-paces of the City of David, our Philistine enemies dare to attack his Phoenician allies? The king will never permit it!"

Zimri said drily, "And who will persuade the great Solomon that the need for military action is immediate?"

"*I* will," Debrah said. "I am sure that if he learns, and quickly, that Beladus is in grave danger now, he will send help. Beladus is an ally, and a friend!"

Zimri shook his head sadly. "I think, Lady Debrah, that he will not be so easily approached. Yes, if the news could be brought to him, perhaps he would agree, though even this is not sure. But to see the great king *immediately?* No! It is true that any of his subjects may approach him on any matter. But without due notification? An audience will be granted, yes, but after days or weeks or months have gone by. The case of the two prostitutes that has aroused so much comment among our people . . . When they first approached him for his wise decision, the baby was but three days old. Yet when he ordered the sword to be raised to slice it in two to divide among them, it was three months old. Three months!"

"I will speak with him," Debrah said stubbornly, "and he will listen to me!"

Zimri said gently, "On the *Sabbath?*"

She was momentarily startled; she had forgotten. But she recovered quickly and said, "Sabbath or no, a holy day can not be allowed to interfere with matters of life and death. Come. We will go to Jerusalem."

He was still not convinced. "There is the matter also," Zimri said, "of my orders, which are to take you to Bethlehem. I dare not disobey my lord and commander . . ."

"Then as the wife of your commander, I give you new orders, Zimri! And you will obey me! We go to Jerusalem!"

"And we are in the midst of the Philistines! If we turn north now . . ." He turned to Seria, anguished, and wailed, "Help me, Seria! I am a simple man, not accustomed to making decisions! Tell me what I must do now!"

Seria said calmly, "Can you hesitate, Zimri, when the life of our beloved captain is at stake? You will find a way for us through the Philistine lines and take us to Jerusalem! The Lady Debrah will seek immediate audience with the king, and she will find it! He will send soldiers! Truly, it is all very simple. I cannot understand your reluctance, Zimri. It does not speak well for you."

"So be it, then."

He was indeed a simple man. And two women—one of them very strong-minded indeed—were arguing against what he was sure must be right; one of them was only a slave, but a woman of great determination nonetheless, and the other was a lady who surprised him with her air of authority.

"So be it," he said again, "we go to Jerusalem. But to do so, we must find our way out of these hills that are thick with Philistines. And there is little time—we cannot circle far to the south as we should and we must be out of their lines before the day comes."

Debrah was deeply conscious of his anxiety, and she knew its cause. It was not the great danger that lay ahead of them (she had no doubt of his courage) but simply that now, for the first time in his young life, he was disobeying orders, a terrible experience for him. She reached out in the Stygian dark and found his arm. "It is well," she whispered. "We go to save the life of a man we all love, and of men he loves almost as dearly."

Greatly comforted by her assurance, he led them out of the cave into the fresh, cold air, alarmed to see how much of the gray early-morning light had stolen up on them. Slowly, they moved on. Slipping from cover to cover, they heard the stomping of horses' hooves in the sand, and then a whinny . . . They saw three men ex-

232

posed on a skyline, squatting on the ground with their lances propped up between their knees, and a score of them moving to deeper cover . . . They moved erratically in silence, seeking out every shadow of every rock, pressing themselves closely to every cliff face that might offer them shelter. They were three frightened children scurrying to elude great danger in hills that they had all known since they were old enough to walk, hills that were now filled with the soldiers of an enemy bent on their destruction.

They were half-running now, knowing that precious time was slipping away, that daylight would soon be upon them and find them, perhaps, still surrounded. The gray streaks in the east turned to red and then gold, and the City of David was a brightening silhouette on the far Hill of Zion, an elusive refuge for them, too far away for comfort. Here, in the vale below, the half-light could bode nothing but ill for them.

And then, as they rounded a high and rugged bluff, three horses suddenly reared up in panic at their sudden appearance, and the three men resting on the sand beside them leaped to their feet. The encounter was too close for escape, and Zimri drew his dagger and hurled himself fearlessly on them. One of them, faster than the others, was already drawing back his bow string when Zimri's knife entered his heart, skillfully finding the chink where the two plates of armor overlapped. He swung round and saw an iron sword raised high over his head, and he dropped to the ground and rolled away as it thudded into the earth beside him. In a continuation of the same movement, he drove his dagger up under his assailant's kilt, sinking it deeply into the groin and drawing it quickly out again for the sudden thrust to the throat as the wounded man fell. He shouted, "Debrah! Seria! Run! Up, always up . . . !"

The third man, conscious of a formidable adversary, had backed away, his heavy sword weaving from side to side. He was crouched and ready to spring, awaiting the onslaught of a man armed only with a dagger. He

swung the blade savagely round, slicing at air as Zimri
leaped back; and as he raised the weapon in two strong
hands, Zimri slipped in under his guard, threw up his
left arm to ward off the blow, and drove his knife into
the unprotected throat.

He turned and ran . . .

The two women, in obedience to his shouted order,
were clambering over the rocks, seeking the broken
ground where the horses could not follow. Zimri ran
fast, sheathing his weapon as he ran and reaching out
for their fragile hands as he caught up with them, dragging them on and urging them to greater effort. For
now, there was an uproar behind him. The sounds of
the skirmish had been heard, and there was much confused shouting and the clink of armor . . . How many
of them there were, Zimri could not even guess. He
held tightly to the women's hands and ran between
them, pulling them along with him, as they came to
level ground and raced along it.

They heard the furious pounding of horses' hooves at
the gallop, but they were below them. They ran on toward yet another bluff to climb. A javelin clattered
against the granite beside them as they crested the rise,
then another; but they were over the top now and running fast among great heaps of rocks and boulders that
littered the landscape.

But one man was close behind them. He was one of
the new recruits from Ashkelon who had just recently
come to join with Akish's forces. His name was Kriter,
and he was an archer of great repute in his coastal city.
It was his boast that he could split a pomegranate with
a single shaft at one hundred and twenty double-paces,
each and every time. He stood now on the top of the
cliff, panting from the exertion of the climb, taking his
time because the targets were still temptingly close.
Quite leisurely, he pulled three arrows from the quiver
at his back and flipped two of them sharply into the
sand at his feet, ready for instant access. (He was very

234

proud of his speed, too.) The third, he fitted to his sinew bow string, and drew it back to his cheek . . .

And at that moment, Seria looked back and saw him aiming. She screamed, "Down . . . !" and threw herself at Debrah, her slender arms outthrust to hurl her to the ground. She heard the deadly sibilance of the iron-headed shaft as it sped on its murderous course; she did not feel it as it entered her body, quite high under her left arm, nor as it went completely out just above her right hip. There was only a numbness on her as she lay atop her mistress.

Debrah screamed, and she saw that Zimri, inexplicably, was racing at quite unbelievable speed toward the archer, seeking to diminish the distance between them. Kriter, too, saw the young scout hurtling toward him, and he plucked the second arrow from the ground and let fly. He saw Zimri drop and roll over and find his feet again as the shaft whistled over his head. He saw the upraised arm with the knife held by its point for the throw; he did not see the swift movement that sent it flying toward his throat, nor feel the heavy blow of it that knocked him off his feet and killed him.

Zimri was on his fallen body then, dragging out the dagger and sliding it quickly, for good measure, between the joints of the armor into the heart. And then, he was racing as fast back to the two women, and scooping Seria up in his arms like a baby and shrieking, quite beside himself now, "Run, Debrah . . . ! Run, with me . . . !"

As though he were carrying a wisp of straw in his strong arms, he ran toward the light of the dawn, knowing that Debrah, sobbing her heart out for her friend, was close behind him.

They ran till the tip of the sun was over the distant mountain that had once been called Urusalim, the "place of safety" of the ancient Jebusites, a highland township between the desert and the sea that had already, in this fifteenth year of Solomon's reign, four

235

hundred years behind it of suffering at the hands of nature and of man. For all of that time, the City of David had endured through earthquake, siege, invasion, and depredation; and now, for these three young people, it was indeed a place of safety.

They found a small gully through which a stream ran, and sank down beside it, exhausted. The pursuit was over now, and Zimri laid Seria down and carefully straightened her tortured limbs. Debrah was staring in horror at the wound in her side; she placed a hand on the slave girl's breast and found that the heart was still beating weakly. She whispered, "Seria? Seria, can you speak to me?"

There was no answer. Mercifully, Seria was unconscious.

They bathed her forehead in the cold waters of the stream, and Debrah could not hold back the tears. She whispered: "Had she not thrown herself at me like that . . ."

"Yes, I know it."

"Will she live, Zimri?" Her voice was hoarse with fear.

Zimri held a hand to Seria's breast. For a brief moment, he felt the tiny, irregular pounding; then it stopped.

For a long while, he did not speak. And then he said, very quietly, "No, Lady Debrah. Seria is dead."

He scraped out a shallow grave in the sand with his hands, then placed the body in it and covered it up as Debrah wept. He rolled heavy stones into place to keep out the predatory animals, then took Debrah's arm. "Come," he said. "We have little time now."

They hurried toward Mount Zion.

Akish was waiting by the catapult.

Tarson had returned, in a very good mood, and he said amiably, "So, Akish, the Phoenicians will not run."

Akish scowled. "No. It seems that they will not." He

236

shrugged and said tightly, "We take them by frontal assault. We are strong enough. When the sun is high . . ."

"It will not be easy, Akish."

"I can afford to lose a hundred men if need be. If twenty or thirty of them can reach the top—the battle is ours!"

"A hundred men? It may well be more . . ."

Akish seemed not to have heard him. "The day will be ours, and that woman of his will be mine! To do with as I please! I will not count the cost!"

"It is a very high price to pay," Tarson murmured, "for the love of a woman."

Akish said coldly, "I would send a thousand men to their deaths, just to lie with her! More, if I had them!"

"Of course, at your command. We would all lay down our lives for you, be assured of it."

"As, indeed, it must be. I am your captain." He looked to the red-gold streak in the east. "Now, then, the missile. It was to have been a parting gift for them as they moved out. But since they have decided to stay, it will be instead a portent of things to come. Perhaps it is even better so." He turned to the engineer. "We are ready, Sloskari. The flare, so that it will readily be seen and immediately found."

Sloskari crouched on his heels and struck his flint over the dry grasses from the box, and in a very short time they caught fire. He took the heavily waxed bundle of reeds and held it to the flames, and when it was alight he swung it back and forth in the air to make it burn even more fiercely, then tied it by its leather thong to the missile. He laid the dual charge in the wooden trough, and pulled on the ratchet for a few more pounds of pressure. He adjusted the height alignment a trifle and stood back. "It is ready, Commander."

"The flare," Akish said, worried, "it is spluttering."

"As it must, now. In flight, it will burn with greater heat."

"And greater brightness?"

"Of course."

"Then give me the hammer."

Sloskari handed it to him in silence. *A fine machine,* he was thinking, *and it is used for such foolish games at the whim of a maniac . . .*

Akish shouted, "For you, Beladus!"

He raised the wooden hammer high and brought it down with such force that Sloskari thought the trigger mechanism would surely be shattered. He heard the short sharp screech of the untwisting sinews as the tension arms snapped into their stops. The missile, with its trailing flare of waxed reeds, left its leather pouch and went hurtling through the air in a wide arc, seeming to hang immobile in the sky before dropping down in the camp.

Sloskari said drily, "Within a span, Commander, of the very center of the grove."

Akish took a long, deep breath. "You have done well," he said, "I am pleased." He turned to Tarson. "Ten shekels of silver to this man," he ordered. "He has given me great comfort."

Tarson raised his eyebrows. *"Ten?"* he echoed. "A single shekel would be reward enough for a man who has done no more than his duty." Akish screamed. *"Ten!* You hear me?"

The missile and its flare had indeed landed in the center of the Phoenician camp. It lay there, sputtering, until a soldier ran to extinguish it. Trained in matters of warfare, he crouched on his haunches and piled sand over it to put out the flames.

Then he saw the missile itself. He stared at it for a moment in shock.

At last, he tore the thong from it, and ran with it to the edge of the southern cliff where Beladus waited with his friend and lieutenant, Rekam. He dropped to his knee and held it out with both hands, sure that in an excess of sudden fury the captain would strike off his head. But he was a soldier, and he had a soldier's duty

238

to perform. He stammered "The missile, Lord, that . . . that was attached to the flare. I bring it to you in sorrow, and in shame . . ."

Beladus looked at it, and his heart stopped breathing for a moment. He took it from the soldier, and held it up in his hands high into the morning sky above him.

The missile was the severed head of the slave girl Helah.

A soldier, even a Phoenicain soldier to whom love was more important than war, could not easily weep. But the tears were streaming down Beladus's face as he looked at those sunken dead eyes, at the long, streaming hair, at the ragged cut at the neck . . . For a moment, there was absolute silence; then he screamed, "Helah . . . !"

The sound was repeated over and over again, a long drawn-out wail of anguish that reverberated among the olive trees and far beyond them till it could have been heard over the whole of the land. (Indeed, Akish heard its echo, and took great delight in it.) Beladus sank to his knees on the sand, the frightful head still tightly held, and began swaying back and forth in his agony.

Rekam said, startled and alarmed, "Beladus . . . You must contain yourself!" Never had he seen such an open expression of grief. Beladus laid the head gently on the sand in front of him, and he whispered, "Helah . . . You will be avenged. With my own death, I will avenge yours. You have my word . . ."

A broken man, he looked up at his friend. "I gave her my word once before," he said. "A few days with that monster, no more! I betrayed her, Rekam! And she went with him willingly, because I asked her to! Willingly! To her death! And who can know what indignities he inflicted on her before he killed her?" He stared at the awful symbol. "I am told that I loved her on occasion, and I scarcely remember . . ." He moaned.

He staggered to his feet and walked away from them

to hide his deep emotion. The soldier looked hesitantly at Rekam and said, "I could do no less, Lieutenant, than bring it to him . . ."

"Of course. No blame attaches to you."

"No blame?"

"None."

"Then . . . am I free to go?"

"Yes. Return to your post."

The soldier scurried away, and in a moment Beladus turned back and said, very calmly, "The patrols, no doubt, have sent word of the Philistines' strength?"

"More than three hundred. Perhaps much more than that."

"And our own?"

"Seventy-four soldiers. Twenty-two of the slaves have been armed, but . . . they are not skilled in warfare."

"And the enemy is where now?"

"Massing on the south of us. It seems that they were all on the east, hoping that we would leave our strong refuge and try to reach the safety of Jerusalem. But when they learned that we would not so easily fall into the trap they had set for us . . . They are now gathering on the south. It means a frontal attack in force. It also means . . . the end of us. I will die by your side, Beladus, content in the knowledge that we all die honorably. And so will all of your men. They have always loved you, and they are with you now. There is not one among them who will not willingly sacrifice his life for you."

"And I will not allow it," Beladus said clearly. "They will not die for me. I will meet this evil man in personal challenge. I have good cause now. And I will defeat him."

Rekam was shocked. "In personal challenge?" he echoed. "No, Beladus, no! How can you defeat this man? He is a monster, the grandson of the great Goliath himself! And you expect to defeat him in personal combat? Impossible!"

It was as though Beladus had not heard him. He stared at the head of the lovely young girl he had promised in marriage to Zimri. "I will avenge her," he said stubbornly. "But if I fail, will you do me a service, Rekam?"

"Anything, Beladus . . ."

"Take care of my affairs for me, then. All of my wealth, save a few jewels you may wish for yourself, will go to the Lady Debrah. Go to her in Bethlehem and tell her that I died with her name on my lips. Tell her that one day we will meet under the wings of Astarte, a goddess who loves those who have given their hearts to each other, as she and I have." He hesitated, half-ashamed even in this moment of anguish to bare his soul to his friend. "I have found such contentment in her," he whispered. "And in her veins there is the blood of her father, who was a warrior himself—she told me of him, with great pride in her voice. We must never forget the importance of bloodlines, Rekam. As Akish has in him the seed of his arrogant grandfather Goliath, so in Debrah there is a stream of courage and strength as yet untapped. This is no ordinary peasant girl, Rekam. And if I must die now, my only regret will be that I can no longer enjoy her company."

"A volunteer from among the troops," Rekam said urgently. "There are many who will be honored to engage him . . ."

"No. The fault is mine, the vengeance will be mine . . ."

"But this is madness! Let us await him here and take our chances! You are asking us instead to sacrifice to him a captain whom we all love dearly! And you forget, your death will be followed by ours, since we will have no one to lead us in defense!"

"No. That is not true, Rekam. Under the laws of personal challenge, if I am killed, then the field indeed goes to the forces of the man who kills me. But by those same laws, my men are allowed to lay down their arms and return to their homeland as defeated soldiers—but as free men." He added wryly, "And our homeland of Tyre, Rekam, is a better place even than the heavens where Astarte would welcome us."

"No . . . !" Rekam wailed. "There is not one among us who will journey back to Tyre in the knowledge that his freedom was purchased with your death! Even if Akish were to honor those unwritten laws you speak of—"

Beladus interrupted him curtly. "My decision is made." He was staring at Helah's ashen head, the eyes open and staring; he fancied he could see the horror in them, and he said hoarsely, "Two women . . . one whom I greatly love, and is still living, the other, who loved me, and is dead." He looked at Rekam, a distant expression on his face. "I must fight, my good friend. In this fashion Debrah will be safe, your life will be spared, the men will live."

"In dishonor for the rest of our lives!"

"There is no dishonor in choosing to live to fight again, to serve our king elsewhere. No, it shall be as I have said. When the men return from Beth Horon, then Hasorar will take my place here and continue the work that we have started."

"And the Lady Debrah?"

Beladus hesitated. He could not hide the vision of her, a tormenting vision of love and beauty, an overpowering memory that would follow him, he knew, into the grave and beyond. He said at last, "Take her with you to Tyre, Rekam . . ."

"Akish will seek her out!" Rekam said desperately, "even in the streets of Bethlehem!" Beladus answered, "That is why you must take her with you. She will be happy in Tyre. Tell my half-brother Juntus that I charge him with her care. He is a good man, and will carry out my wishes to the letter. Come, help me buckle on my breastplate. I will use no other armor."

"No other armor?" Rekam was aghast.

"None. No helmet, no backplate, no body chains, no kneeguards, no shoulder straps. A breastplate only, to

242

turn his first charge. I will carry sword and lance, and a dagger in my belt."

"Madness!"

"Akish is a very powerful man, Rekam, as we both know. There are two weapons I can use against him to lessen the advantage of his great strength. My wits, which are sharper than his sword, and a speed that I will gain from not being weighted down with iron and bronze, as he will be."

"Madness," Rekam said again, but Beladus shook his head gravely. "No. A fox cannot hope to escape the jaws of a lion save by his cunning, his agility, and his speed. I will need all of these things if I am to have any hope at all for victory. And my hopes are high, Rekam. I will ride the little mare named Minoh, the fastest horse we have—you know her?"

"Yes, I have ridden her." He was in the depths of depression now, knowing that nothing he could find to say would shake that strong determination.

"Let her be unarmored too, so that once I leave the saddle she may speedily leave the scene of the battle. Minoh will have served me well, and her body should not drain its blood into the sand to reproach me."

Rekam shook his head. "No," he said, "you must not leave the saddle. If you let him unhorse you . . . you are lost. Minoh's speed is as important as your own . . ."

"He will not unhorse me. When the moment comes, I will dismount of my own volition."

Rekam sighed. Finding his captain's armor hanging on a tree, he unfastened the buckles and took off the breastplate to improvise new straps for it. Beladus stared at the lightening sky and murmured, "The sun, I think, should be a quarter of its way up into the heavens when we fight. I need a pattern of light, there must be shadows where I can put them to use."

"A shadow is of little use against a strong man with a good sword."

"Every slight advantage is of use, Rekam. There is a

243

small gorge down there, and if I can lead him into it . . . Minoh is mountain-bred, but the horses of the Philistines come from the coastal plains and need smooth sand under their feet. In such a gorge, where the ground is heavily strewn with rocks and boulders, there are broken rises that we can climb, Minoh and I, which Akish and his horse cannot. Every slight advantage, Rekam!"

"At his first charge, he will kill you!"

"No. I will elude his lance, because without armor I can move easily and quickly."

"And on his second, he will strike off your head with his sword."

"I will not be where he expects to find me."

"It is not a conventional way to fight in personal combat, Beladus!"

"By conventional means, I could survive perhaps three charges, no more. It is not my intention to die so easily."

"And your own charges? His heavy armor will turn your blades, even if his shield does not."

"I will not charge him. I will goad him into a fury. And in a fury, a man of his violent character will rely on his great strength, the only advantage he has. He has no wits, as I have. He is a Palaestine. And now, if you would leave me alone for a while, friend? There are thoughts I must pursue."

"Thoughts of the battle?"

"Yes."

It was a lie. He was thinking of Debrah, safe now in her Bethlehem home. Rekam withdrew, and Beladus sat with his broad back against the gnarled trunk of an olive tree and thought of her. He remembered the last time he had loved her (and would there be no more of her love?) crouching first on the ground beside her bed, on his knees like a slave at the altar of her ivory body, naked and receptive under his caresses. The image of her was very clear to him now, an image of slender, unblemished limbs, of gently swelling breasts that were small and smooth and very firm, tipped with tiny rose-pink nipples that hardened under his touch. His hands were exploring, molding those soft breasts and parting her expectant thighs for his love. He was lying above her, and she was grasping his firm manhood in ecstasy, guiding it into her as he thrust his hips toward her. Their limbs were pressed to each other, hand to hand and foot to foot, his dark and glistening, hers sleek and ivory-white and silken as they loved each other passionately.

Beladus closed his eyes and dreamed of her, as he waited for the dangers ahead of him.

13

The Zion gate to Jerusalem, called David's Gate, was a center of bustling activity.

In and around Jerusalem lived the huge labor force that was building Solomon's palace—thirty thousand woodcutters, eighty thousand stone masons, and seventy thousand porters, all forced laborers, a state only slightly higher than that of a slave. Many of them still lived in their nomadic tents outside the walls, but for all of them the city gate was the center of their social activities. Here, too, the thousands of craftsmen and traders who serviced this great endeavor gathered—the weavers, potters, dyers, and merchants who had become part of a great metropolis. It was their meeting place, for gossip and the exchange of news as well as for trade.

The crowds here were thick as Debrah and Zimri hurried past them. There were countless donkeys, dwarfed by the huge loads they carried—sacks of wheat for the millers, piles of firewood brought in from the hills, crates of fresh fruit; oxcarts forced their way over the hard-packed earth, carrying jars of oil, honey, wax; merchants were setting up their stalls for the day's bartering, already shouting out their wares. Many of them stopped their incessant chatter to stare at the young girl, so beautiful in her Phoenician robe and yet distracted, a wild and angry look in her eyes as she ran with the young man who was leading her along the city wall toward the palace.

The street was narrow and deeply rutted, the stones and burnt-clay bricks of the houses hemming them in. There was a great commotion ahead of them as they ran, the people there yelling a warning and pressing themselves against the buildings to make way for a chariot that was bearing down on them. It was drawn by two spirited horses, and there was a single officer at the reins, in the uniform of Solomon's Guard.

Zimri clutched at Debrah and dragged her to a half-open doorway as the chariot swept furiously past them, and there was just time to see a quick look of puzzlement in the eyes of the driver, a big and powerfully built man in his twenties, with a carefully curled beard and a mass of black hair under his tall helmet.

They heard him yell an oath at his horses as he threw his weight back on the reins, so that they rose up and flailed at the air with their forelegs. A screaming woman hurled herself under their hooves and grabbed away a child who had fallen there, and the officer, laughing now, was looking back at them and calling out imperiously: "You there! Woman! To me!"

Debrah held Zimri's hand tightly and ran to him. She knew who he was, and it was means of a quick entry, perhaps, past the guards at the palace. Before she could speak, he said, wondering, "By all of your new gods, I know you! Your new Phoenician aspect disguises nothing! You are Debrah, I think, the peasant daughter of a merchant whose name I do not care to remember, but who now supplies our noble king with household requirements. Do you remember me?"

It was a confrontation. Forcing a calm upon herself, Debrah said quietly, "Yes, I know you, Lord. You are Captain Libni of King Solomon's Palace Guard. My husband, the Lord Beladus, once drew his sword against you, in a good cause, in the presence of your king and mine, the wise and good Solomon."

247

"Yes. And he should have had his head struck off for his arrogance! Tell me where I may find him now, so that I can fight with him and avenge my honor!"

"My memory serves me well, Lord," Debrah said. "And it was not the king's wish that he be killed. Indeed, I have come to Jerusalem to seek the king's help in saving his life."

"Ah . . . Then my next question is already answered. I was about to ask you what a painted Phoenician whore would be doing on the streets of Jerusalem."

"Not a whore," Debrah said calmly, "but an Israelite woman of known honesty who married, with due regard to the king's wishes, a noble man who is now in his service, as I take you to be, too. And I ask you to take me to him, at once."

"At once? Ha! Do you know what day it is, Debrah? Or have you already forgotten your religion? Do you already worship the Phoenician's Melqarth? Or their Astarte, perhaps, that licentious goddess whose only delight is in copulation?"

"I have not forgotten, Lord. I am an Israelite, and I know that today is the Sabbath. Still, I must see the king, on a matter of the greatest urgency. And I remind you that Solomon does not have the contempt for foreign gods that you seem to have. The hills around the city are filled with shrines to the gods of the Moabites and Ammonites, and yes, to Astarte, whom he calls Ashtaroth!"

"A sop to his foreign wives, no more than that . . ."

"And an indication of a wisdom that is greater than your own."

"And can an Israelite woman wedded to a Phoenician so quickly assume that Phoenician insolence? I find it strange."

"You will find it stranger still," Debrah said tartly, "when Solomon strikes off your head for letting his friend Beladus die so easily!"

"A viper!" He was laughing again now. "Very well, you shall see him. I will send word to the scribe that you

248

request an audience. In a week or two, perhaps, it will be granted. Meanwhile, I offer you the shelter of my own quarters, where you may wait in comfort. It is a humble place, but the bed is good, and wide enough for two."

"Sabbath or not," Debrah said urgently, "I must see him now!"

"Then tell me the reason. I am a reasonable man, I think. I will not take you to him on matters of womanly foolishness. I have too high a regard for my well-being."

The time was slipping by, and time was so important now! Debrah said quickly, "The Philistine commander Akish has surrounded my husband's camp with more than three hundred men, perhaps very many more than that. The main Phoenician force is on its way back from Beth Horon, where there has been a great and successful battle, and in the camp there are hardly three-score men. Akish has seized the opportunity to attack them. If he is successful, it will not only mean the death of my husband and all of his men. It will mean, also, no more protection for King Solomon's convoys, on which he depends."

Libni's excitement was rising, but he would not permit it to show. He said languidly, "Three hundred Philistines or more, so close to Jerusalem?"

"Yes, Lord, a very strong force gathered at Solomon's pools."

"Then perhaps I should ride there myself, unaccompanied, and take fifty of their heads. It would add greatly to my reputation, which is already considerable . . ."

"Captain Libni! Please, I beg of you! Take me to the king now!"

"And the battle, then, has already begun? If so, I fear we would be too late."

Zimri spoke at last. "The battle, Lord, will not begin for some hours yet. And still, haste is imperative."

Libni turned very hard and cold eyes on him. He

249

looked at the sash that proclaimed his rank and said icily, "A sergeant, I believe?"

"Yes, Lord, of scouts."

"And a mere sergeant can say, with such authority: 'the battle will not begin for some hours yet'? I find that very intriguing. Tell me why, *Sergeant*."

Zimri said, smiling gently, "Because, Lord, the objective of the attack is a camp on top of a very steep bluff. There are only three narrow tracks that lead to it, and they can only be climbed with great difficulty. It has rained very heavily this night, and the mud . . . May I suggest, Lord, one step forward and two back? Even a man as impetuous as Akish will know that he must climb those paths very quickly indeed. He will wait till the sun has dried them."

Libni was very angry. He did not like to be lectured on tactics by his inferiors. He turned to Debrah and said, masking his annoyance, "And it is still the Sabbath. It is true that Solomon has set up shrines for his foreign wives and permitted them to worship there. But this does not sit well with the elders of our own true faith, and so, the king is determined always to observe the Sabbath, so that his people may know he is still a true *Hebrew*." He spat the word out.

The Jews did not call themselves Hebrews. It was a term of the vilest odium. Many years ago, at the time of the Great Captivity in Egypt, the slave masters had called their captives *Eperu*, an Egyptian word meaning the lowest form of human life. In the harder accent of the Israelites, the word had become *Ebrew*. They did not like the term, preferring the Aramaic word *yehudi*. But some of them wore it as a badge of honor, a reminder of the Exodus.

Debrah said quietly, "You call your king *Hebrew*? Yes, indeed he is, as I am and as you are, Libni. As my companion Zimri is, too. And we come in a Hebrew cause against the Philistines. Sabbath or no, we go to the king *now!*"

A very volatile man, Libni quickly recovered his

good humor. "Then we go to him, child! We will see if he will receive us! It is more likely he will have us all exiled to the great desert of the Negeb!"

He leaned down and took Debrah's arm and yanked her aboard the chariot, and he shouted to Zimri: "But not you, slave!"

Zimri shouted back furiously, "Not a slave, a sergeant of scouts!"

"Then show us your mettle, Sergeant of Scouts! Run behind us!"

The horses were racing forward, and the carriage was bouncing like a mad thing with a mind of its own on its unsprung wheels. Libni's arm was tight around Debrah, profiting by the moment to clutch at a young and tender breast, finding its way under her gown with practiced efficiency. He yelled, "The strap, you foolish child! Take the strap from the bar and buckle it about your waist! Or I will never reach the palace with my precious cargo!"

Thrown from side to side, Debrah found the broad leather belt and fastened it tightly about her body, and that offensive hand was gone now, at work on the reins and the whip, driving the horses to a frenzy. On a single wheel, the chariot rounded a sharp corner and bounced into the clay-brick wall and back again. And in moments, Libni was pulling back on the reins once more at the entrance to the palace court.

A guard, with raised javelin, stood in front of them and shouted mechanically: "Identify yourself . . . !" Libni struck at him with his whip and yelled, "Your commander, fool!" (But had the guard not so challenged them, he would have been thoroughly flogged for his carelessness.)

The man fell back, saluting, and they raced onto the broad polished floor of the courtyard. The horses fought the reins, slipping over the polished surface, and one of them fell and screamed angrily, struggling savagely to right itself again. Libni leaped down and began to stride away, but remembered himself and turned

251

back to help Debrah with the confining strap. A slave came running, and the captain said, "There is a young slave who is not a slave hard behind us, a sergeant of Phoenician scouts, pumping the life out of his chest as he runs behind a racing chariot. Allow him entrance, to wait here. His name . . ." He turned to Debrah, his fierce eyebrows raised, and she said quickly, "Zimri, Lord, a loyal servant and a good warrior."

"His name is Zimri," Libni said to the guard, "and you have heard that he is both a loyal servant and supposedly a good warrior, though he has ideas above his station. He will wait here till he is sent for. Meanwhile, give him water to drink." He laughed shortly. "No, give him wine, it may be that he is a young man of merit."

He turned back to Debrah and sighed. "On the Sabbath," he said, "the king will not enter the Judgment Hall. I will take you then, to his harem, where he will be now."

His hard face was softened by his amusement. "It is not proper for Hebrews to work on the Sabbath, as you well know. Fortunately, by our laws, copulation is not regarded as work, though it may sometimes be a very considerable labor, even for a man of the noble king's undoubted virility."

He strode with her down the long marble corridor, a passage of great beauty built with finely polished limestone blocks and fragrant cedarwood from Lebanon, with bands of red and blue on its pillars, and beaten gold everywhere. At the end of it stood a eunuch, a tall, fat black man who had been a present, on her visit here, from the Queen of Sheba. His naked sword in his hand, he said in a soft, melodious voice, "There is no entry, Lord, even for you."

"I know it," Libni answered. "But you will take a message for me to the king."

"I will not, Lord. It is his Sabbath. He may not be disturbed."

"You will," Libni said amiably, "or I will have your black skin for a wine flask. Tell the great king that Captain Libni is here, conscious of the day, but that the safety of the king's convoys is at stake. Tell him the matter is of importance, and also urgent. Tell him that if I must pay for this intrusion with my life—I will do so willingly. Now go."

The eunuch hesitated. There were orders to be observed and yet . . . Libni said tightly, "You have my word on it, fellow. If the king does not quickly learn of an impending calamity, your life may well be forfeit. Tell him!"

"My life is as nothing, Lord. But I will tell him. He is abed with two Midianite women and an Egyptian. I will wait outside his chamber, and when he calls, not before, I will go to him. Meanwhile, you will wait here. And your Phoenician woman will come with me."

"No. She will wait here."

"She will come with me! You think, Lord, that because of your rank you can come and go as you please? No, you may not! This place is under *my* protection. I will not have it violated! The woman will come with me, a hostage should there be mischief in your mind."

"Eunuch," Libni said wearily, "there is no mischief in me at all . . ." and the African answered him, "Not eunuch, but master of eunuchs."

The captain sighed. "Take your hostage, Master of Eunuchs. She is the Lady Debrah, wife to King Solomon's friend and ally Captain Beladus of the Phoenician armies. I will wait here, as you suggest, for your return."

"Not as I suggest, as I order."

"As you order."

Miraculously, without any overt command, three other Africans unobtrusively appeared with drawn scimitars in their hands, and the master of eunuchs said to them, "The exalted Captain Libni of the guard will wait here for my return." Towering over Debrah, he held out his hand and said, "Lady Debrah, you will come with me."

She went with him into the inner complex of the

sanctum, and he sat her down in an antechamber and left her. This was within the confines of the harem itself, and Debrah could only stare around in wonderment . . .

It was a small room, floored with highly polished granite slabs that shone with the rays of the early-morning sun that came through the heavily barred window. There were three divans covered in woven silk in brilliant colors, and on each of them was a young and quite naked girl; one of them was fast asleep, and the others were staring at her with only very mild interest; they were all Edomites, she realized, from below the Dead Sea. A single pillar of carved cedar supported the ceiling of polished wood, also carved with an astonishing intricacy. In one corner, a small but very ornate gilded fountain was trickling water out of a lion's mouth into a copper bowl that was bordered with tiny bronze lions inlaid with ivory. In another corner, a huge copper cauldron was mounted over a tiny fire of thorn twigs, and a fourth young girl was crouched in it, luxuriating as a young African boy bathed her; he was hardly more than twelve years old, and he was scooping up the film of lavender oil that floated on the surface of the steaming water and rubbing it into her full breasts.

The child looked at her, unmoved, as she sat on the divan, and said casually, "Take off your robe, woman. I must look at you before I bathe and perfume you."

Debrah stared at him. "No," she said. "I have not come here to lie with the king. I have come for matters beyond your understanding."

"Not to lie with him?"

"No."

The boy sighed. "Indeed, how could you? He has taken seven women this night. Seven! And four of them virgins! There is neither seed nor strength left in him! And yet, he still calls for more, so perhaps, after this one here . . ." He rose and went to a shelf where a row of beautiful bottles of Phoenician glass stood, selected one, and took it back to the cauldron, then said

254

to the young girl, "Stand now, and part your legs. For your thighs, and for the secret places between them, we need spikenard."

Obediently, she stood up in the cauldron, and she whispered, "The water . . . it is too hot."

"No. It is hot because it must be, because I wish it. More, open your thighs more." She did as she was told, and he poured some of the oil into the palm of his hand and cupped her, massaging her carefully. "Spikenard," he said, "my lord likes the touch of it on his lips."

Rubbing her methodically and even mechanically, he turned his attention back to Debrah. "You are not here to love him?" he asked.

"No, I am not one of his women."

"A great pity. You are very beautiful, and almond oil would work wonders with you."

"Almond oil? I have used it, on occasion."

"Yes, it is very good for you." The young girl had thrown her head back, and she was gasping, her eyes glazed. "More," she whispered, "more . . . ! You drive me to distraction, boy . . ."

"Not 'boy.' My name is Hanal." He chuckled. "Think only of the delights that await you with the great Solomon. For my part . . ." He sighed. "They cut out my testicles a year ago, when I reached puberty."

"Then more, Hanal, I beg of you . . ."

Putting his fingers to skillful work, he turned back to Debrah and said earnestly, "The oils, Lady, they are of the utmost importance. My honorable work is to bathe the king's women and perfume them for him, and I am very skilled at this. I use cinnamon for those whose skin is dark, and lavender when they are of your own color, that creamy white that the king likes so much. For the black girls of Africa, the scent of myrrh, which complements their color admirably. And for the Edomites, nothing but frankincense."

He was laughing softly, a very happy child. The girl he was ministering to so offhandedly was beginning to move her body back and forth in cadence with his motions, and he took his hand away and slapped her lightly on her slender thigh. "No," he said, not unkindly. "Save youself for the king. Step out now, take a cloth and dry yourself, and await your call."

She wrapped herself in a long white sheet and began patting herself dry. Hanal looked at Debrah again, squatting on his haunches and drying his hands on his tousled hair. "Oh, yes," he said, "I am indeed expert in my work. Once, not long ago, King Solomon came to me in the early hours of the morning because he could not sleep, he came to me *himself*, you understand what I am saying? Here, in this very chamber, he kicked me awake and said to me—the king himself! 'Hanal,' he said—he even knows my name—'the master of eunuchs sent me a woman who is as cold as a watermelon, but the scent of her . . . ! Find me an Egyptian, but bathe her first in the same perfume, it arouses me greatly.' "

He sighed. "It was a very great honor. It so happens that I have learned to read and write a little and so I keep a tally. I found that the woman he spoke of was a Moabite, and I had used on her an essence of myrrh from the Land of Ophir, crushed with my pestle and mortar with a few drops of a very rich wine. I called a young Egyptian girl to me, and rubbed the same distillation into her body . . . And can you believe it? Through all of that long night, the king called for no other women!" He was nodding wisely, smiling at Debrah. "It is true that you have not come here for the king's pleasures?"

Debrah did not answer. Her thoughts were far away, and time was slipping by so fast! She could not control her impatience, wondering whether the dreadful enemy was already attempting an assault on her husband's ill-defended camp. *Not till the sun has dried the mud,* Zimri had said, but was it true? In her vision, Beladus was standing there at the head of his men, flailing his

256

sword in fury, tall and strong and imposing, and perhaps . . . very close to death.

She turned at the sound of the opening door, and
Solomon himself was there, regal and authoritative even
with the air of weariness on him. He was dressed in a
length of simple cotton around his waist and thrown
over one powerful shoulder. The master of eunuchs,
glowering, was with him. He stood in the open doorway
and said brusquely, "Even on the Sabbath, I am to be
denied the rest that a man must have."

Debrah dropped to her knees at once. "I would not
have dared to seek this audience, Most High, had I not
known that the urgency of the moment transcends all
custom."

The king grunted. "Preskon here, my master of eunuchs, spoke of an impending calamity. I wish to know
what that calamity might be."

"The imminent destruction, Most High, of the force
that protects your convoys."

"You speak of Beladus. I am informed that his
forces are strong enough for what he has to do."

"Most of his men are fighting with your enemies
near Beth Horon, Most High. Beladus himself has only
seventy men at his camp to fight off four, five, or even
more times that number."

"And therefore," Solomon said sourly, "I am expected to go to his rescue."

"It seems necessary, Great King."

"The Phoenicians," Solomon said clearly, "are in my
employ to protect *me*. It is no part of my contract with
King Hiram to protect *them*. And in all conscience, it is
an expensive enough contract! My coffers are being
drained, and the Sidonians are fattening themselves on
my gold!" (To the king, all Phoenicians were 'Sidonians', whether or not they came from Sidon.) "No, let
Beladus attend to his own problems. I see no profit in
helping him, where he is paid to help me."

"What, no profit?" Debrah said swiftly. Her desperation was bringing with it a dangerous rashness. "Since

257

when has it been unprofitable for Israel to allow Israel's enemies on our very doorstep?"

He was angry now with her presumption, but before he could speak, she rose from her knees, uninvited, and said clearly, "It is said, Most High and Mighty, that you are a master of riddles?"

"Of riddles?" The unexpectedness of the question both startled and intrigued him. He sat down on the edge of a divan, while the dark-skinned girl there curled up her legs to make room for him. "Yes, I am a master of riddles, it is well known. My good friend Hiram sends them to me from time to time, and I send them to him. We gamble on them." He sighed. "By the last reckoning, I owe him more than three talents of gold. It is a childish pastime, and a very expensive one. But I will confess that it consumes me utterly."

"Then will you answer me a riddle of my own making, Lord?"

He stared at her. "And for what stakes, child?"

"If you do not answer it correctly, then you send troops to help my husband."

He was almost laughing now. "And if I do?"

"You once honored me, Great Lord, with an invitation to join your harem."

"Ah . . ." He was delighted with the game. "Then pose your riddle, girl."

Debrah said clearly, "A devoted servant bows to the ground. A jackal bites off his head. The loss is to the master of that servant, for the jackal grows the black mane of the desert lion. Who, then, are the servant, the jackal, and the lion? Answer me this, Most High, and I will say no more."

It was a game that the king enjoyed above all others, and he thought about it for a while, nodding his head as he puzzled it out, and he said at last: "The devoted servant is you yourself . . . But no! Bites off *his* head, was it not? Then the servant is Captain Libni, who brought you here on the Sabbath and so incites my wrath. It is fitting indeed that I bite off his head for his

258

imprudence. Good. The jackal then . . ." A terrible
light in his eyes, he said coldly, "Even in a riddle, girl, I
do not like to be called a jackal, merely because I will
not grant your foolish wishes. But so be it. I am the
desert lion, too, and the black mane is the mantle of my
authority, a fitting parallel. And the master who suffers
the loss . . . ? Ha! It is your Beladus, it can be no
other! There, I have answered your riddle."

"No, Great Lord," Debrah said clearly, "you have
not answered it."

She raised her voice. "The devoted servant who bows
his head is my beloved husband Beladus who serves
you with such loyalty. The jackal who bites off his head
as he offers you his life is Akish the Philistine, the most
deadly of your enemies. And the loss, Most High, is to
yourself, the loss of your rich convoys. And with that
loss, it is the jackal Akish who becomes, in these hills,
as strong as the black-maned lion to prey on us all.
That, Great King, is the answer to my riddle."

For a long time, Solomon searched for flaws and
could find none. He was a fair and just man, and he
said at last, nodding his approval, "Very well, a good
riddle, and though I have lost again, I am satisfied."

He turned to the eunuch and said: "Preskon, bring
Captain Libni before me."

"Here, Lord?" Preskon stammered. "Into the
kharam?"

"Into the *antechamber* to the harem. Bring him."

"Your servant, Lord." Deeply distressed by this
flouting of all rules of civilized behavior, Preskon went
out and returned at once with the captain, equally surprised; it was the first time he had ever passed the in-
violate doors. He dropped to one knee, and the king
rose to his feet and said casually, "Troops, Libni, to do
battle with the Philistines. It is in your hands now." Not
even looking back at them, he swept out.

In the courtyard, Debrah muttered: "We have
wasted so much time . . . !"

Libni nodded, hurrying to his chariot. "Will you stay here and await my news?"

"No. I will come with you."

He was laughing. "You will ride in the lead chariot?"

"Yes, with your permission, by your side."

"You can use a recurved bow with its arrows?"

"No."

"Or hurl a javelin, perhaps?"

"If you give me a javelin, I am sure that I can throw it."

"*Throwing* it is not enough." He was still mocking her, openly. "And can you wield a sword?"

"I have never done so, of course not! Though with two hands I think I could lift one if need be."

"And lifting it is not enough, either. But so be it, I like your spirit." He shouted out, "Sergeant of the Guard! At once!"

The sergeant came running, and the captain said, "To the barracks, Sergeant, to alert the men. Fourth and Seventh Cavalry, Second, Third, and Fifth of infantry, and the Twelfth charioteers. We ride with all speed to Solomon's pools!"

The sergeant hurried off, and Libni helped her aboard his chariot, strapping her in carefully. "Keep your legs bent at all times," he said. "Over rough ground we soar like an eagle and plummet to the earth again like a hawk that dies in mid-flight."

He took the reins in his right hand, and his left was around her as they raced to the barracks, finding its way to cup her breast again. She pushed it away, but it was soon slipping under her gown once more, molding her naked flesh as she held onto the front rail desperately. She felt a finger and thumb gently fondling a nipple, and saw that he was laughing.

The men were already turning out when they reached the great square, and the smith was running to bolt the scythelike wheel-knives into position. In a few moments, they were moving out through the fortified gates, and at the bottom of the hill they took up their battle positions.

Fifty paces ahead of them all was their own chariot, and the captain was staring back to watch the men taking their places. The infantry were running into three phalanxes, the archers among them stringing their bows as they ran. The chariots were in a broad half-circle behind them, with the cavalry further out still in two long columns. There were four hundred and sixty men in all.

"It will be a good battle," Libni said, watching them form up. "But before it begins, I will put you under guard at a place far from it. So do not be frightened."

"There will be no battle at all," Debrah said tartly, "if we do not get there soon! It will be over! Our only task will be to bury the dead . . ."

"We will not move," Libni said calmly, "til we are in battle formation. It will not be long now."

"And I am not frightened. My veins flow with the blood of a great warrior, my father."

Libni laughcd. "Your father, a warrior? You forget, child, that I met the venal Uzzi ben Ezra . . ."

"Uzzi is not venal, he is a good man. But I speak now of my true father, who was a champion with King David. His name was Maaseiah, a warrior of great repute. He gave me enough of his courage . . ."

She broke off. Libni was staring at her in astonishment. He said, startled, "Your father was the great Maaseiah, the commander of Judah?"

"Yes, the same. You have heard of him?"

"My own father fought beside him! My father was Jehozabad, an army captain under the great Jehoshaphat! He fought side by side with Maaseiah in countless battles! And moreover, his youngest sister was Hamutal, who was one of your father's wives, his second, I think . . ."

Her eyes were on fire with unexpected delight, and all her fears had inexplicably gone. She was no longer a

261

stranger pleading for help, but a clanswoman rousing her family; and the family was always the strongest force in the land of the Israelites. She said, "Libni! Then we are cousins!"

"Cousins indeed!" His exploratory hand had left her breast now and was resting more discreetly around her waist. He shouted happily, "Cousins, family! And we go to the rescue of your Phoenician husband, whom I once nearly killed . . ."

He turned away from her and swept the field with excited, burning eyes. "We are ready! Trumpeter! Sound the advance!"

Debrah took great comfort in the thin, wailing note of the ram's horn. It was a sound that had been heard for generations over this land and the lands of Israel's enemies, as far north as the River Euphrates, as far south as the Red Sea. It was a sound greatly to be feared.

Like a great lumbering army blanketing the hill, the Israelite army began its march forward. Holding onto the horses' saddlestraps, the foot soldiers ran with the cantering cavalry. On the flanks, the chariots were bouncing furiously over the uneven ground.

And after the storm, the ground was drying out.

14

The time for the encounter was almost upon them.
On the bluff above Solomon's pools, all of the tents
had been struck, tightly bundled, and covered over with
a layer of sand. The sentries were lying on their bellies
at the edge of the cliff, hidden from sight, and the rest
of the men—so very few of them now!—were scattered
under the trees, out of sight, as they awaited the outcome of their commander's decisions.

Beladus looked up at the sky, a new day being born.
He said morosely, "If I die, Rekam, will you remember
your first duty?"

"If I live, Beladus," Rekam said quietly, "Yes, I will
remember it. It is to the Lady Debrah."

"Yes, to her. In the short time of our great happiness
together, she has consumed my soul and made it part
of hers. I can no longer imagine what my life was like
before we met. An unloving heart, to a woman, is like a
ghost, did you know that, Rekam? And Debrah knows
that my heart is filled with love for her, as hers is for
me. And now, without a doubt, she is safe in Bethlehem. It was a wise decision I made . . . Can you
imagine the heartbreak if she were here now?"

"And if you die, Beladus, she will kill herself."

"You must dissuade her."

"If Akish does not find her first! He is consumed
with a passion for her. All this show of great force is for
her, as it was before! He will search her out to the ends

263

of the earth! If I live, yes, I will reach her in Bethlehem before he finds a way to do so. But I am not convinced that so vile a man will honor the rules of personal challenge. Even if he does, my movements, after your death, will be greatly inhibited. It may not be easy for me to go to Bethlehem as a free man with a free man's choice and duty. It is more probable, in my estimation, that I may not even be alive to serve her as I would."

Beladus sighed. "I have given this matter some consideration, dear friend," he said slowly. "And I have found an answer to a problem that I know to be considerable. When I meet with Akish, I will find a way to persuade him that she is dead, that she has taken her own life out of fear of the coming battle. By this means, she need no longer be in fear of him."

"Ah, yes . . ."

"And so, you will contrive a way to go to her. You will take her with you to Tyre, perhaps disguised as a slave girl, perhaps your own slave girl. It is your right to take your personal slaves with you."

Rekam said, not convinced, "And I will hand her over to the care of your half-brother Juntus."

"Tell him it is my wish that he treat her with great gentleness."

"I will do so."

"He is a good man; he will understand."

"Yes, I am sure of it."

"And tell my wife . . . that her name was on my lips when I died. This is very important to me."

"Be assured of it."

Beladus studied the shortening shadows on the plain below. "If the field goes to Akish," he said, "you must ride out with no weapons, you know that?"

"Yes. I know the unwritten laws of personal challenge."

"Tell the men there is no shame in the loss of their swords."

"I cannot do that. The shame for all of us will be unbearable."

264

"And the women in the camp . . ." The thought of their fate troubled him deeply. "They have served us well. I am concerned that many of them will be taken to the Philistine camp, where they will be treated like animals. Perhaps Hasorar, who will take my place, can one day mount an attack on their camp and bring them all home." He added bitterly, "As I promised Helah."

"Do not blame yourself for Helah, Beladus."

"I must, and I will!"

"It could not have been foreseen . . ."

"I should have foreseen it . . ."

"No, you could not have done so."

"A woman is a human being too, Rekam."

"Yes, perhaps you are right."

"She is not an *animal*, to be slaughtered for a man's satisfaction!"

"Yes, I am sure of it. I will not argue with you."

"At the moment of her death, what was she thinking? That I had betrayed her? As I truly did?"

"No, I think not," Rekam said swiftly. "She would be thinking only that her death served you, whom she loved."

"It must not be so!" Beladus said passionately. "Would she have died swiftly and painlessly? No, I think not. And I will avenge her, Rekam. It is the thought of Helah, as much as the thoughts of my own dear wife, that give me strength to fight this monster."

He turned his attention back to the plain.

Akish and Tarson, tiny figures at five hundred double-paces, were striding up and down together impatiently, stopping now and then to stare up at a silent bluff that puzzled them both sorely.

Akish said, muttering, "No sign of life up there at all, Tarson! Where are they? What are they doing? A camp devoid of any life at all! And yet, we know that they are still there!"

Tarson shrugged. "I cannot read a Phoenician mind, Akish. No man can."

"And the tracks? Are they dry yet, or not? Can we climb them quickly?"

Tarson looked up at the sun, still low on the horizon. "Not yet, I think. We must wait."

"Waiting has never been part of my philosophy. Send three men, good archers all of them, to see if we can climb as speedily as we must, or if we will slither around like donkeys mired down in the slimy mud of these hills. I must know!"

"Very well." As he moved off to obey the order, Akish said casually, "Let one of them be Esobrulin, Tarson."

The lieutenant turned; he felt his blood running cold. "Esobrulin?" he echoed.

"Yes. A young man I have never liked."

Tarson's heart was pounding. "But with respect, Akish," he said, "Esobrulin's skill with the bow is minimal. Good archers, you said, which means men who can loose off three shafts while the enemy is still unsheathing his sword. Esobrulin is very young; he cannot do this."

"He is unskilled because he is not battle-hardened. His only proficiency lies in cutting off the heads of wounded soldiers and claiming them as his own, soldiers who have already been felled by his betters."

"A sortie such as this needs stronger men, Akish."

"A sortie such as this might make a man of him."

Was there a sly comment there? An acerbic contempt in the insistence? Akish had his own male lover, a painted boy of very fragile years, with carmine on his lips and cheeks and antimony at his eyes, lovingly applied by Akish himself. With a sudden shock, Tarson realized that the commander wanted the beautiful Esobrulin for himself, and that not having him he was prepared to send him to a certain death. Trembling, he said carefully, "To save his young life, Lord Akish, which is precious to me, I will surrender him, if need be. He is very skilled in the ways that he has chosen."

Akish said coldy, "Esobrulin, and two others. Send

them now to test the paths to the top of the bluff." He said, mocking now, "But do not be distressed, Tarson! If he should die, I will give you the choicest women in the Phoenician camp to take his place in your bed."

Tarson was seething with stifled rage and grief; he did not dare to answer.

He found Esobrulin, and, feigning a smile, said gently, "A great honor for you, dear friend. On the direct command of Lord Akish himself, you are one of three men selected to climb the bluff and explore an empty camp, empty of all save a few slaves, perhaps, and the women, a very great honor indeed."

Esobrulin stared. "Empty? So, after all, they left . . ."

"Yes, they left." Lying brazenly, Tarson said, "Word was brought to us during the night, they escaped. But not to the east, where we were waiting for them, but to the west, where we had nothing but a few patrols. Soon, we will pursue them and cut them all to pieces, and meanwhile, Akish wishes to know who might be left in the camp. There will be no soldiers; but one or two of the slaves, in their great fear of us, may have armed themselves. So have your bow and your sword ready, Esobrulin." His heart breaking, he whispered, "So great an honor for you . . ."

"And on the word of Akish himself?"

"Yes, Akish himself."

The young boy laughed softly. "The great commander," he whispered. "I have seen him, on occasion, looking at me with . . ." He dropped his eyes. "With a glance that I can only describe as lascivious, though I would never betray you with him. It is indeed a great honor, yes, very great! And if there are slaves there who dare oppose us, I will slay them all! The women too!"

"Yes . . . Kill them all, Esobrulin." He kissed the young man on the lips and turned quickly away to hide the tears that were welling up into his eyes. He moved off and found two more men, both of whom he personally disliked. He gave them their orders, telling them

267

the same lies. In a few minutes he returned to Akish and said quietly, "It is done. I have sent three men to their deaths."

"We will see," Akish said stolidly.

They watched the trio running over the intervening space, over the flat and still-wet ground that finished at the steep cliff. Esobrulin was behind the others, circumspect as always, carrying his bow in his left hand, a shaft ready in his right with thirteen more in the quiver at his back. Tarson watched him and wept openly, unable to control himself as the beautiful youth ran to his own extinction. Akish was laughing, mocking as they watched.

The three of them reached the base of the cliff, half a thousand double-paces away. Their leader, an aged veteran named Lastoranu, called a halt as he studied the ascent; the watchers could clearly see his head, turning back and forth as he sought out the best approach.

He pointed: this way. He took the lead as they clambered up the widest of the three goat tracks. He was slipping as his feet broke through the top coating of sun-dried mud and found the viscous slime underneath it. Halfway up, they stopped again, and once more Lastoranu pointed. Esobrulin, on his command, eased his slight body along a narrow ledge on the cliff face, very high up now, and pressed tightly into the rock as he moved along. The third man moved quickly and expertly to the other side, and then the three of them were climbing again. They were distant cyphers, climbing like mountain goats up a quite unclimbable cliff and hating everything about it; the Philistines were coastal plainsmen, and very unhappy in mountains. The bright red plumes of their helmets, Minoan-style, were pinpoints of fire against the granite and sandstone, picking up the rays of the sun and sending them back to the watchers in little bursts of yellow fire.

They were within fifty feet of the top now, slowly working their way upward, and Akish said furiously,

"By all the gods, Tarson, they are not there! They have escaped us!"

"No," Tarson answered. "It cannot be! Can they spirit themselves away in the night like ghosts? No! They must be there, and waiting still . . ."

At this distance, they could not hear the sounds that every soldier knew, and feared—the sharp twang of ox-gut bow strings and the sibilant hiss that followed, the incisive and mortal sound of arrows in flight. They saw only that almost at the same instant, the three men on the cliff face threw up their arms and seemed to hang there for an instant before toppling, with infinite slowness, from their precarious perches and falling, falling, falling, bouncing off jagged rocks, til they hit the bottom and lay still.

The penetrating power of a well-made arrow from a 220-lb. bow was a fearsome thing; two of the shafts had gone through the breastplates, the chest, and the backplates of two of the men, killing them instantly. The third—the shaft that had killed Esobrulin—had continued on its forceful flight and had left his body completely.

Tarson screamed, "Esobrulin . . . !" He fell to the ground on his knees and beat at the sand with his fists, sobbing. Akish stood above him with a sneer on his face, and put out a foot to send his lieutenant reeling.

He said harshly, "Get to your feet, Tarson! You are an officer in the Philistine army, not a faint-hearted woman!" He stared at the bluff, and said, musing, "They found false footholds, and they slipped too much. We will still wait. Go now, bring the army into battle formation for a frontal assault when the time comes. Go!"

Tarson stumbled off, and Akish waited.

And on the bluff above them, Beladus was watching as the long lines of Philistine horsemen and foot soldiers left their hidden rocks and rode along the crest of the hill, their long morning shadows dancing on the ground.

269

Rekam said softly, "One hundred of cavalry, at least. Infantry without number, and still they come." The seemingly unending line of mounted troops caught the sun now as they moved in column. Beladus watched, his heart heavy; behind him, with no order given but knowing the course of their duties, the seventy men were rising up from the ground and taking their positions along the edge of the cliff.

The Philistines halted.

On the crest of the hill, 120 horsemen were in line, each man ten paces from his neighbor, sitting his impatient, prancing horse and awaiting his orders. Below them, on the sandy slopes, the foot soldiers were taking up their positions in three groups; *one for each path,* Beladus was thinking. He looked up at the sun. "And the hour is good. I will go now. Send up Minoh."

Rekam raised his voice and shouted, "The commander's horse!" He turned back to his dear friend. "I will come with you. I have already ordered nearly one half of our force as your escort, thirty good men."

"No. Neither you, nor them. I will take one man with me only, to show my contempt for him, another small advantage. Your first duty is to stay alive, whatever humiliations may be forced upon you, if only for the sake of the Lady Debrah, whose protector you now are. Let your friendship be as dear to her as it has always been to me."

"One man only . . ." Rekam shook his head sadly.

"Yes, only one. I will take the young brevet-lieutenent from Sidon. Till the combat begins, he may carry my lance. It is well honed?"

"I have inspected it myself. A soldier named Mirhapi has been working on it, and every inch of its blade will slice a floating hair in two."

"And its point?"

"Its point will draw blood if a man even looks at it."

Soon, he was slipping fast and expertly down the steep path, the little mare Minoh sure-footed even in the slime. At the bottom, he waited for his escort, the young Sidonian; his name was Osludi, a thin and wiry man with a look on his face of perpetual astonishment. He carried the long lance upright at his side, the sun gleaming on its blade, unbarbed so that it could be used for stabbing and quickly withdrawn again. "You ride behind me, Ostreka," Beladus said, "at fifty paces."

"An honor to serve you, Lord. But my name is Osludi."

"Ah yes, of course. And the lance is in brave hands."

"Those of the champion are braver. And may it slay all of your enemies." It was all part of a ritual exchange laid down by military scribes centuries ago. "Only in a cause that is just," Beladus said mechanically.

"If it serves the gods of the Phoenicians," Osludi answered, "the cause is just."

"I bless you, Ostreka."

"And I bless you, Lord." Under his breath, he muttered, "Osludi, Osludi . . ."

"And if we die this day, Melqarth will welcome us."

"In the shadow of the great god, there is comfort for a warrior who dies in honorable battle."

"Enough. We will ride out now."

He stared for a moment at the long lines of Philistines, the emotion welling up inside him and ready to burst out in a deadly fury that he knew he had to control. His sword was sheathed. In his left hand, he held the reins lightly; his right dropped to his side and touched the sacred emblem there, almost lovingly . . .

The emblem, to give him strength and courage in this battle, was the head of the slave girl Helah, hanging now by its long dead hair from his leather belt.

He marched his horse to the brink of the little stream. Akish, with seven men around him, was riding down to meet him. He halted, twenty paces from the stream. And now, the whole rigmarole began again.

Akish called out, scornfully. "The gods have betrayed me! I dreamed this night that I would fight a worthy enemy, and they have sent me instead the child

271

of a Phoenician whore who sells her services for scraps of food on the dung hills of Tyre."

"Your insults, pig," Beladus said, "mean nothing to me. Should I listen to the wild screams of a hyena? No, I will not. I have come to challenge you to personal combat."

For a moment, Akish stared at him, his hard eyes wide with astonishment. And then he burst out laughing, and he shouted, quite incredulous: "*You,* challenge *me?* As well send a mangy dog on the point of death to attack a pride of angry lions!"

"A challenge!" Beladus said. "If you have not the courage to accept . . ."

"I accept, I accept! Though I do not believe that even a Phoenician can so far take leave of his senses!"

"I have come to kill you, pig," Beladus said, "because my heart is heavy and my life now means nothing to me." With a sudden, dramatic gesture, he slipped the long hair from under his belt and held up Helah's head for Akish to see, a token to bolster his hatred. He shouted, "When my wife, the Lady Debrah, saw this . . . she took poison, and died. And I come, Akish, to revenge the loss of her life, a woman I dearly loved and who is no more."

The raucous laughter had gone, and Akish himself was not unmoved. "And she is dead?"

"She is dead and beyond your reach. Gone to her ancestors."

"Then we will fight, in personal combat. On your ground, or mine?"

"I am the challenger," Beladus answered. "The choice is yours, I believe."

"Then you die on your own ground, which will soon be ours. I will so inform my aide."

He rode back to Tarson, and said, gloating, "You heard? It is to be personal combat! When I have killed him, we will take the bluff and put every man, woman, and child there to the sword."

Tarson frowned. He said hesitantly, "But under the

272

rules, Akish, the rules of combat—" Akish interrupted him furiously, "I care nothing for the rules! We kill them! We kill them all! What, shall I send his men away in honorable peace? No! I will not! There will be a slaughter that will not soon be forgotten . . ."

He swung his horse around and returned to the stream. He shouted, "I am ready, offal!"

Beladus said quietly, "My lance, Osludi." The young man cantered up and handed it to him, and whispered, "The gods go with you, Lord." Beladus tucked the haft under his right arm and lowered its point almost to the ground; he carried no shield, nor did he draw his sword; his only protection was the light breastplate. Akish, monstrously armored in iron and bronze, as was his heavy charger, carried his huge round shield strapped to his left arm, his lance held leveled in his right hand; he too had not yet drawn his sword. He drove his heels into the horse's flanks to canter along the bank before crossing over; he would require a very long run to reach the speed he needed for his charge. The sound of his approach was the sound of thunder; the heavy hooves pounded the hard-packed sand, the iron leg straps and the bronze skirt guard were clanking as he raced forward.

Now, by all accepted standards, it was the moment for Beladus to gallop forward and meet the onrush half-way. But he chose not to. Instead, his steely eyes were on the tip of his opponent's lance, and he waited til it was scarcely an arm's length away from him. Then he swung up his bare left hand and knocked the shaft away as he side-stepped the little pony to his right, a quick, dancing movement. The deadly blade hurtled harmlessly over his shoulder, and he swung lightly round to watch his retreating enemy. It was not easy for Akish to rein in, and when at last he did so and turned, breathing heavily, he saw that Beladus had not even raised his own weapon, its point still almost on the ground. He shouted furiously, "The next time, camel dung! The next time you will not be so lucky!"

273

He thundered into the charge again, and Beladus waited till he was no more than ten paces away and swung the little mare round, spurring her to one side, turning again to watch a furious Akish, unable to stop, go hurtling past him. Four times the maneuver was repeated, and now, the huge horse under its heavy weight of armor, was tiring. It was the moment Beladus had been waiting for . . .

At the end of the fifth charge, he side-stepped quickly and pulled the little mare around, then galloped fast after his opponent, his lance at last leveled and aimed at the broad and muscular back. His speed now was the speed of the wind, and he was already pulling the weapon back for the final drive home. But Akish was a skilled fighter, and had met with this tactic before. He turned in the saddle and swung his iron shield up, driving it forward to meet the tip of the lance. The point battered its way through it and sliced deeply into his forearm; he shouted, not in pain but in triumph as he twisted the shield back and snapped the blade off the lance as though it had been made of the most fragile reed.

Beladus still did not draw his sword. Instead, as they rode side by side very close together, he seized Akish's lance in both his strong hands and tried to wrest it from him. Akish shouted, "Ha! You dare try to disarm me, weakling, with your bare hands?"

But this was not what Beladus had in mind. He was cool and very calm now, quite sure of what he had to do next. He waited till they had slowed to a reasonable speed, then slipped from the saddle. He threw himself across the rump of Akish's lumbering horse and slipped down quickly over its haunches, and as he hit the ground he threw his arms around the fetlocks and hugged them strongly to his chest. For a moment, it seemed he could not hold them, but the great horse was tired now, and screaming out its anger, it stumbled, and fell.

Beladus was on his feet again in an instant, and drew

his sword. He saw Akish, a look of ungovernable fury on his face, lying on his back and beginning to rise . . . He drove the point of the sword up under the armored skirt, and found with its tip the base of the pelvic bone. He threw all of his weight on it and drove it home, and heard the frightful scream and withdrew it quickly. Standing above his fallen enemy on wide-spaced feet, he slipped the extremity of the long, sharp blade into the space between the breast and backplates of the heavy armor. With all of his strength, he thrust it through the body till he felt the point meet iron again.

Akish was dead. But Beladus was still not satisfied. He raised the sword high in both hands, and with a shriek of fury brought it down to chop off the head. He stooped and caught it up by the luxuriant red hair, and holding it high for the Philistines to see, he screamed in a kind of delirium, "Look on the head of your leader Akish, and know that the field is mine!" He could not control his trembling. He heard the cheers of his own troops lined up on the bluff, the loud wail that came from the enemy, and he shouted, "Go back to the hovels you came from! Your champion in personal combat is dead! The battle is mine!" He drew back his arm and hurled the severed head toward them. In mid-flight, incongruously, the elaborate Minoan helmet fell to the ground.

Beladus fell to his knees, quite overcome with his emotions, and crouched there for a moment, shuddering. He thought, "Debrah, my love, it is all over now . . ."

He looked toward the bluff and saw a solitary horseman, in Phoenician armor, forcing his mount in reckless haste to the top and wondered where he had come from. Osludi, who also was staring at the unexpected sight, *and he* turned back to Beladus and said, astonished, "It is Hofran, I think, Lord, a runner with Lieutenant Hasorar . . ."

He was right. Hofran forced his mount over the top, ignoring completely the drama being played out below him. He was hurt, and weak from loss of blood. He reined in beside Rekam, saluted, and said hoarsely, "I come from Lieutenant Hasorar . . . We are in the gorge below . . ."

Rekam stared. "*What?* How many of you, soldier?"

"No more than fifty-five men fit to fight, Lieutenant." He was swaying in the saddle, trying to hold himself upright, and Rekam shouted, "Medic! To me, at once!" He reached up to help the man dismount, but Hofran pulled away. "No," he said, "by your leave I will not dismount. I must return . . . return soon to my commander . . ."

"Wine, then," Rekam said, and signaled one of the troops. "Wine to drink, it will give you strength. And you must tell me what Hasorar is planning . . ."

Hofran took the proffered wineskin and drank deeply. "As the scouts came from the gorge," he said, "they saw that our commander was in personal combat . . . that the Philistines lined the hillside in very great number. He called a halt, and he awaits his orders now."

"Fifty-five men, you say?"

"No more than that, and very many of them wounded. We defeated the enemy at Beth Horon, but it cost us very heavily. We have a score of men on litters, being carried by their fellows, many of whom can hardly walk."

"And without orders, he will not move from the gorge, I hope?"

"I am sure of it. A slow-moving convoy of men barely able to raise their swords? Under the very eyes of so many of the enemy? It would mean annihiliation, the end to all our work . . . !"

"Good." Rekam looked down on the plain below. In the near distance, Beladus was crouched at the edge of the stream, scraping wet sand away in the shallow water and burying the slave girl Helah's head there. Osludi, mounted still, was close beside him, and beyond them both, the Philistines were drawing closer together; he could hear their wailing still.

He saw that Surgeon Felada was waddling up with his physics to treat the wounded runner, and that Brevet-Lieutenant Remposar was with him. He called the aide to him, pointed to the enemy, and asked, "What do you think, Remposar? By all the rules, they must leave the field to us now, their champion has been killed. But it looks to me . . . Are they forming into battle order?"

Remposar nodded grimly. "I see no preparations for flight, Rekam. Cavalry do not dismount to leave a field of battle, only to fight as foot soldiers."

"And yet not all are dismounting. I do not like it, Remposar."

At the stream, the little mare Minoh was cantering to Beladus, as though aware that the time had come for quick withdrawal. Beladus stared up at the enemy on the hill. He saw that half of the cavalry had left their horses in a group, tended by slaves, and were taking up new positions with the infantry, the other half of them moving out to the flanks. He said quietly, "They are moving to attack us, Osludi. We return at all speed to the bluff to fight as best we can . . ."

But as he swung himself into the saddle, he saw in sudden alarm and shock that Rekam, with Remposar hard on his heels, was forcing his mount at breakneck speed down the bluff, and that behind him, all of his meagre force was pouring over the edge. He raised his voice and shouted furiously, "Back, back . . . ! Rekam, get back . . . !"

Rekam's answer was blown away on the wind, and Beladus spurred his mare toward them. The officers came together and reined in hard, the horses prancing wildly, and Beladus shouted, "Are you mad? We try and hold the bluff. They are preparing to attack us . . ."

"I know it! But Hasorar is here . . . !"

"What?"

"With a weaker force than our own, in the gorge! He cannot join us, we must join him . . . !"

"Then we shall do it . . . !" Rekam was right, an officer trained to make his own decisions, well and carefully taught by Beladus himself. "The trumpeter, then, to sound the assembly. We will let Hasorar know that we are coming to help him."

"They will know it," Rekam said drily. "Hasorar's scouts will not be sleeping." But he gave the order, and the trumpet sounded its thin, reedy note. The column, taking more orderly form now, moved at an easier pace toward the sheltering gorge that perhaps might give them a few hours of precarious safety.

Scarcely more than seven hundred double-paces behind them, the Philistines were changing their formation; their scouts were not sleeping, either, and one of them was with Tarson now, pointing to the gorge where Beladus was heading with his men. He said, trying to control his impatient horse, "A small force of Phoenicians there, Lieutenant, under Lieutenant Hasorar, but no threat to us at all."

"Not Lieutenant Tarson," Tarson said coldly. "But *Captain*. Akish is dead. I am the commander now."

"Your servant, Captain."

"And my scouts will give me information, uncluttered with their opinions. Why do you say they are no threat to us?"

"Hardly more than two-score men strong enough to wield their swords, Captain. Many of them lying on litters in the shade, many others trying to walk on olive branches they have cut for themselves. Only a handful of them still have horses."

"And they are in the gorge where Beladus rides now?"

"They are, Captain."

"A death trap for them. Call up Lieutenant Daskon."

The runner rode off, and returned at once with Daskon, a wild-eyed and volatile man in his thirties; his bow was in his hand, and there were three full quivers at his back. His anger was always very acute, and he said harshly, "If we attack them now, Tarson, ready or not, we can cut them to pieces before they reach the gorge, which they can hold for a few hours."

"A death trap for them," Tarson said again. "Hasorar is in there, too, a convoy of wounded and only a few score in strength."

"Ha! A frontal attack, then! We have five times their number!"

"No." Tarson smiled thinly. "This, no doubt, is what Akish would have done. I myself prefer to put my intelligence to better use. The dismounted cavalry will remount and take two columns, one to ride onto the hills at each side of the ravine. See that they are well supplied with full quivers. Half of the infantry to join them, the other half to seal each end of the gorge, so that they may not escape. From the heights above, the archers will rain down their arrows upon them, until not one of them is left alive. By this means, we need not lose a single man." It was a concept very dear to him, because it was an easy way to win the approbation of his followers. Akish had been rash and impetuous, a commander who threw lives away with reckless abandon; but he, Tarson, was a shrewder man.

He was already framing in his mind the report he would send to his superiors in Ashkelon: *The Phoenician force under Beladus has been exterminated, and this at no cost in lives to ourselves . . .* The approbation of his seniors was much to be desired; they would quickly confirm him, no doubt, in his new, self-assumed rank of captain. "That is all, Daskon," he said. "See to it."

When the lieutenant rode off, Tarson turned his attention back to the scout; he was very young and slight, with almost no beard and a very girlish mouth, full and soft. He said quietly, "Your name, I believe, is Frihada?"

"Frihada, Captain."

"You are very young to lead the hazardous life of a scout."

"I am sixteen, Captain, and a soldier for two years now."

"And in those two years, have you learned to obey your officers implicitly?"

Frihada did not hesitate. "In all things, Lord," he answered.

"And the duties of a soldier-servant would come hard to you?"

"Most easily, Lord." He said softly, "I knew Esobrulin well, Lord, and always envied him the great honor of his position."

For a long time, Tarson did not speak. Esobrulin's death was still hard on him. He looked the young man up and down, and said at last, "You will finish, today, the duties that have been assigned to you. When the battle is over and we return to the camp, you will report to me and begin new duties as my soldier-servant."

"And I will serve you well, Lord," Frihada said, "in all things, as a servant should."

"Go now."

The young boy's eyes were gleaming as he rode off, and Tarson watched him, admiring the way he rode and taking pleasure in the smooth articulation of his limbs. He watched for a while as his troops began taking up their new positions under Lieutenant Daskon's orders.

More than five hundred men, he was thinking, and the day will soon be ours, with no losses at all—save the reckless and uncouth Akish, for whom no one will mourn.

15

The shock-haired Captain Libni had learned his trade well.

Though only twenty-three years old, he had served Solomon as a soldier for seven years, four of them as an officer. He had only recently been promoted captain, as a reward for a particularly daring mission against a rebel force of Prince Haddad's Edomites, who had raided Ezion-Geber and tried to fire the ships under construction there. He had driven them out, trapped them at the copper mines of the Timna Valley, and there had destroyed them utterly.

He was a very flamboyant young man. He liked to strut and posture, and was seldom happier than when he was fighting. Tall, well-built, and physically the equal of any champion in the Israelite armies, he was an expert alike with the sword or the recurved bow. For a wager, he had once challenged the king's best archer to a long-range contest, in which he had sent an iron-tipped reed arrow of his own making for the incredible distance of 187 double-paces, or 312 yards, winning thereby not only sudden fame, but also the wager itself—a purse of two hundred shekels of silver, a fine black stallion, and two of his opponent's best-trained concubines.

In spite of his exaggerated bravado, he was nonetheless a competent, sensible commander. When his strong force came at length to the last of the low hills that lay between Jerusalem and Solomon's pools, he called a halt and he gave a quiet order to his chief aide, Lieutenant Molid, "Send out the runners in silence now. There will be no trumpet calls yet. Tell the officers the cavalry may dismount and stand to their horses, the infantry may rest. I need three scouts now."

Molid, a gaunt and grizzled old man in his fifties, nodded silently and rode off, and Libni turned to Debrah and laughed. "And you, cousin," he said. "Unfasten your belt and lie on the ground for a while to rest your limbs. I am sure they have been severely punished in this ride, and there is worse—far worse—to come. When we drive at speed, as we soon must, you will feel that every bone in your body is being broken to pieces. So now, you must regather your strength."

Debrah was in despair. "But must we *wait?*" she asked. "Time is our enemy, and who knows what desperate straits Beladus is in at this very moment?"

Libni nodded. "Yes, we have little of time now, perhaps," he said. "But we have a deadlier enemy, and that is . . . impatience, the deadliest of all a soldier's enemies. I will not attack until I know precisely where he is, what his dispositions are, and the strength and mobility of his forces."

The scouts were cantering up; one of them was Zimri. Libni raised his eyebrows. "What?" he said, "you are now an Israelite again?"

"I was never anything more, or less, Lord," Zimri answered easily. "And with your permission, I have taken command of these two men, whose competence seems adequate, though less than my own."

"Ha! I do not recall having given you that permission, but so be it, then."

"I know these hills, Lord, as I know the palm of my own hand. I can be of great help in the service of my Lady Debrah and her protector."

"Very well. Ride out unseen and at speed. Find out where the Philistines are, how many they have of horses, men, chariots." He sighed. "Find out if they are indeed still here—they may have won this battle and gone home. But if not, there are a hundred gullies where they can be hidden, so search well."

"Every one of those gullies is known to me, Lord. I was born in Adullam, hard by, and as a child I herded goats between Sorek and Elah. There is not a rock, not a fold in the ground that I do not know." He hesitated. "And if I may ask, Lord, after the welfare of my Lady Debrah?"

"She is well, as you see her," Libni said, and Debrah wailed, "I am well, Zimri! But ride out fast, I implore you!"

The three scouts galloped off, and Libni turned to Debrah, smiling. "Now, cousin," he said, "your impatience, like mine, must give way to more practical demands. The infantry must have time now to catch their breath. You saw how they ran behind us, each man at the stirrup of a horse. Would you have them fight with no breath in their bodies? While the scouts learn what we must know, they will rest. As you must too. Lie on the ground as I say, and rest your poor body for the difficult trials ahead of us. When the news I need is brought to me, we will begin a very violent race, and a chariot is no place for a frail woman. At the top of the hill, I will leave you in the care of three good men . . ."

"No. I will ride with you, Libni."

"What, into battle? Foolishness, child!"

"Nonetheless, if I would be an encumbrance at your side, then I beg of you, give me a horse. I am sure that I can ride it fast enough to keep up with you."

"You are mad!" Libni said, but he was laughing, and Debrah answered gravely, "We go to help my husband, cousin Libni. I cannot sit safely by at the top of the hill and watch his suffering. I must be with him."

"With sword in hand? Is that what you want? Foolishness!"

"Not a sword. But a dagger, to turn on myself if he is dead."

The humor had quite gone from his florid face. "Do not talk of killing yourself," he said quietly. "I know Beladus is a soldier of great reputation, as I am, too. We do not die so easily, whatever the odds against us." The smile returned, broader now. "I have always admired the Phoenicians," he said, "for their skill in the ancient art of survival. Beladus is like the desert lion that lies dead, with a spear through its throat pinning it to the ground, a lion that, when its killer approaches, miraculously leaps to its feet and bites off the fellow's head. Rest now. We wait for the return of the scouts."

Debrah dutifully did as she was told, and was grateful for her decision to humor this stubborn man. And indeed, every bone in her body seemed to have been displaced by the chariot's fearful pounding. She lay on her back, her limbs thrown out, and tried to compose her thoughts, forcing her impatience away in the knowledge that Libni was right. An army could not just be thrown into battle rashly and impetuously; land had to be spied out, enemy positions studied, the various intermingling units carefully placed to support each other . . . And all this slow process was mandatory, while time slipped by regardless. She forced her mind to dwell on the man she loved so dearly, remembering the day he had come to Bethlehem to claim her, so noble and splendid and yet so fearful, too, of the ordeal ahead of him! She thought of his muscular body towering naked over her as his eyes, and then his hands and his lips, feasted on her slim body, bringing her the kind of delight that drove her to the point of bursting. She thought of the great love that was between them, and she prayed silently for him as she waited.

The sun was high in the sky when Zimri returned, alone. He was sweating profusely, his boyish face covered with the fine red dust of the plain, and the flanks of his horse were steaming. She leaped to her feet at once, and Zimri saluted her gravely before he even looked at Libni. He said, very quickly and softly, "He is alive, Lady. I saw him . . ." She caught her breath, but Zimri had turned to Libni, aware of his first duties and determined to follow them.

But before he could speak, Libni said darkly, "Well? Where are my other two scouts?"

"It needs only one man, Lord," Zimri said easily, "to make one man's report. I have sent one of the other two men to the south and one to the north, each a thousand double-paces or so from here and ready to ride to me at once should any change take place in the disposition of the enemy. As we rode together, I instructed them in the demands of their specialized duties, and I believe that their competence may have increased by a very little . . ."

"Enough!" Libni roared. "You found the enemy, then?"

"I was sent to find them, Lord. Would I do otherwise?"

He swung round in the saddle and pointed. "There, beyond the headland, there is a small plain. Beyond it, the wide entrance to a gorge that soon narrows to a very close defile. At the far end of the gorge there are thirty-two Philistine archers, closing it like the plug in the neck of a wineskin. At this end, there are three groups of infantry, about seventy men each. Climbing the hills on both sides, there are perhaps a hundred more mounted archers, and each of them carries four, five, or more quivers of arrows. A Philistine quiver holds fourteen shafts, Lord, and this means that they are well supplied with munitions, some seven thousand shafts in all, and from the cliffs above the gorge . . ."

"Silence!" Libni roared. "I know what can be done with a hailstorm of arrows! In the gorge itself, what did you see?"

Zimri's eyes now were holding Debrah's, though he was still talking to Libni. "I saw my Lord Beladus," he said softly, "and he was alive and well. He was conferring with our Lieutenant Hasorar. There are perhaps a hundred of our troops there, but . . ." His voice was very grave now. "They are in a sorry state, Lord Libni.

Many of them on crutches cut from olive trees, many of them heavily bandaged and bloodied. It is not a force of great potential against such odds."

Libni turned and raised his voice, "Lieutenant Molid!"

Molid was there at once, and Captain Libni said carefully, "They have separated their cavalry and their infantry, Molid, and now they will pay for that tactical error. But their archers are in a position of terrifying potential. We will take the army, therefore, over the brow of the hill, leaving all of the chariots, save my own, hidden still. In two phalanxes, Molid, with enough room between for a chariot charge to break through when the time comes. Let them see us form up slowly, to entice their archers from their position of advantage. But we take the army in two sections. Hold back the Seventh Cavalry and perhaps half of the Fourth, together with both the Third and the Fifth Infantry, let them remain hidden, too. A show of half our numbers, or perhaps a little less, will entice them to break off their incipient attack on the Phoenicians and drive to their rear instead. His tactics lead me to believe that Akish is seeking a painless victory over Beladus. Let us disappoint him."

Zimri's eyes were on fire. "Not Akish, Lord," he said. "There were only three officers in their command-post, and the senior of them was Lieutenant Tarson, who is known to us. And close by the stream a single dead body lay. It was the body of Akish, decapitated."

Debrah gasped, and Libni frowned and said, "You are sure? A body with no head so easily recognizable?"

"Even at a distance, Lord. I could clearly see the gold beaten into the iron of his armor. It is only Akish among them who affects the gold-decorated armor such as the Egyptian nobles use. Yes, it was Akish, there is no doubt."

Debrah whispered, "Akish . . . dead?"

He was a spectre to her. She felt his coarse hands tearing her simple *aba* open, down to her virginal

286

thighs, the cruel crushing of her breasts and then, the ultimate indignity, slipping down to clench her fiercely, a finger already probing, a triumphal assurance that she was still intact and to be enjoyed.

"And Beladus is still alive," Libni said.

"My beloved husband . . ." She threw herself at Libni and embraced him, and he said quietly, "I told you, did I not? The Phoenician art of survival."

"Then can we ride out now?"

He turned to look at the men. Molid was riding from one group to another, giving out his orders, and they were regrouping into their assigned positions, splitting up into the two forces. "Yes," he said, "in a moment now."

"And will you give me, after all, a sword?"

He stared. "A sword?"

"To carry, if only as an emblem."

For a moment, he did not speak. And then he said slowly: "Not my own, for I will need it. But . . ." He raised his voice and shouted, "A sword, for the Lady Debrah to carry!"

And then an astonishing thing happened. The echo of his cry had scarcely died out when there were four men there at once, holding out their weapons, and all around them others were slipping from their horses, some dropping to their knees as they held out their swords up to her, hilt foremost. In moments, there were twenty men or more gathered around her, and their cries were fierce with pride:

"Mine, Lady, take mine . . ."

And: *"A sword of great honor, Lady . . ."*

And: *"Mine Lady, by all the gods of our enemies..."*

One young soldier who could not yet have celebrated his seventeenth birthday was on his knees close beside her. He was clutching his naked blade so fiercely in his emotion that the blood, unheeded, was pumping out of his hand and down over his forearm.

Debrah could not know it, but ever since they had

left the barracks the word had circulated among the troops: *a new heroine has come among us*—. . .

There were murmurings of Jael, and Ruth, and Bath-sheba, and of the great Deborah herself who, two hundred years ago had cried: *March on, my soul, with might!* as she led her army with legendary vigor against the nine hundred chariots, bogged down in the mud, of King Jabin's General Sisera.

She looked at the eager face of the young boy, his blood seeping into the sand now, and said softly, "Your name, soldier?"

"I am Mered, Lady, a son of Pallu of the tribe of Reuben, and I beg of you, take no sword but mine!"

She reached out and took it from him, and the tears were streaming down her cheeks. "Then I take it, Mered ben Pallu, a son of my own tribe." She raised it high above her head and looked around at the assembled army, and she shouted: "For the honor of the tribe of Reuben . . . !"

A great cheer went up from the troops, and Libni shouted, "To horse! We ride now . . . ! For . . . ward!"

The chariot rumbled forward, quite slowly now, as a little less than half the army took up their positions; the rest of them, the surprise element, waited for the signal that would bring their decisive strength into the battle.

The gorge was indeed a death trap.

It was part of the route back from Beth Horon, and as the stubborn Hasorar, dying in his saddle but refusing to accept death, had led his men through it, the scouts had come back, alarmed, with the calamitous news that a horde of Philistines, stood between them and the bluff . . .

Hasorar had halted his pathetic column, and was waiting. Zimri had speculated, watching from under cover, that the wounded comprised about half of his force, but he was wrong. Of the men who had ridden to the Beth Horon battle—so long ago now!—less than a quarter had returned in any state to fight. On the long haul home, forty-two had been carried on litters borne by men who could hardly walk themselves. Very many of them were limping on the crude olive-branch crutches. Now, some could no longer walk at all, and had positioned themselves, seated or lying among the rocks and boulders with their bows at the ready. One man who had lost an arm was lying on the ground at the entrance to the gorge with his bow at his feet, painfully telling his neighbors, "Like this, I can send an arrow to the ends of the earth. Let them come . . ."

Hasorar was galloping up, a rash and impetuous man. He reined in hard by Beladus and shouted, "I am engaging their men at the far end of the gorge, Beladus! They have few men there, but we are in a trap! And my men are battle-weary!"

Beladus shouted back, "This is no time for weariness, friend Hasorar! Are they trying to force an entry?"

"No! Not yet, at least. They are trying to prevent our egress! And I will very soon need more arrows!"

"Make every one count, Hasorar! But I will send the sergeant-armorer to you. Hold the defile; do not let them enter. And above us, you have seen?"

"I have seen," Hasorar answered. "More than a hundred men moving into position up. Archers, all of them, to drop arrows on us: a coward's way to fight!"

"Ha! Do you think about military matters, friend?"

"Of course! Always!"

"Then think on this. The bow is a long-range weapon. A coward can kill a brave man at a hundred paces and more, much more, when a sword at close quarters would kill him immediately!"

"I know it! Can you spare me twenty horsemen?"

"For what purpose?"

"There is a cork in the neck of the bottle. I want to clear it. If they attack us from the front, as they will, we cannot hold them. We *must* have a way out! Twenty mounted archers with full quivers!"

"I will give you ten."

"Then it will have to suffice. I will have my own walking wounded in support of them with their bows, while your men cut a way through. We *must* keep that defile open!"

"Keep your support under cover from above, every overhang of rock they can find, or we are all dead! And let them use their bows to good advantage!"

Hasorar said furiously, "Then give me more arrows! Some of my men have no more than four or five shafts left!"

"Four or five shafts," Beladus said, mocking him, "will kill four or five Philistines if well used!"

"A hundred more, I beg of you. I *must* have them!"

"Very well. Tell the armorer-sergeant you have my orders. A hundred, no more."

This was to be a battle of numbers, of arrows against arrows, swords against swords, men against men. And in each case, the odds against the Phoenicians were calamitous.

Each side was waiting for the inevitable collision.

And now, the arrows began to fall. The archers at the tops of the cliffs were loosing their shafts quite casually, many of them not even bothering to aim but knowing that one arrow in five or ten would surely find a mark. Some of them, more daring than the others, were crouched on the very edge of the rocks and aiming carefully; but when one of their number died, a shaft from Beladus's bow through his throat, the others drew back and began firing from under sure cover again.

On the plain, Tarson was watching, the angry Daskon beside him. He said languidly, "A little more time, I think, for the archers to wreak what havoc they may. And then . . . a frontal assault, Daskon . . ."

A thin and piercing note sounded on the air . . .

It was the sound of the ram's horn shattering the midday silence, rebounding back and forth from the hills, a sound that had been heard for centuries and had

290

brought great fear to Israel's enemies, who were great in number.

In sudden alarm, Tarson swung round in his saddle and stared in shock at the hill behind him.

The red sandstone, spotted here and there with gray-green shrub, was dark with an army moving down, 200 men and more, led by a single chariot well in front of them with two people aboard, one of whom, at this great distance, seemed to be a woman, and a Phoenician woman at that, dressed in the royal purple. There were lines of cavalry at the canter, with foot soldiers running at their stirrup straps . . .

Tarson screamed in sudden panic, "All units face to the rear!" The trumpet sounded, and he watched the infantry turning around; but the mounted archers were still up on the cliffs, and he shouted, "Cavalry to break off engagement! Cavalry to the front . . . !"

The trumpet sounded again, the two calls, and he saw the first of them riding fast down the steep slopes. He stared at the advancing enemy, and Daskon said urgently, "The advance, Lord Tarson, now . . . !"

Tarson was calmer now. A single chariot, three-score horsemen or so and no more of infantry . . . His own forces still outnumbered them. He shouted, forcing a calm upon himself, "All units will advance into battle!"

He heard the comforting sound of the trumpet call, and saw his infantry trotting forward, the cavalry coming down from the hills and fanning out into their positions on the flanks . . .

In the gorge, Beladus had heard the shouts, too. In the confusion, one had sunk into his consciousness more than all the others: *all units face to the rear!* It was the call to an army that had been outflanked, and it meant only one thing to him; there was a new threat out there somewhere to the Philistine army, and he could not guess what it could be, nor what might be its strength. He knew only that it was an advantage that had to be seized on at once. He screamed, "Hasorar! Reakm! Remposar! to me . . . ! All units, forward!"

291

No trumpet call answered him. The lone trumpeter, running to drag his horse under cover, had heard that dreaded sibilance and had looked up; an arrow from above had penetrated his eye, killing him. But his officers were answering his call, and their men were following them, in a most unmilitary medley, some on horseback, some running, some hobbling on improvised crutches.

And then, a single horseman was galloping at great speed and commendable ease down the hill toward him, swinging his mount around as they came together so that they were moving fast side by side.

Beladus shouted, "Zimri! In the name of all the Gods, where did *you* spring from?"

"From Jerusalem, Lord," Zimri shouted. "To the help of our great allies, the Phoenicians!"

"And the threat out there, what is it, do you know?"

"The Israelite army, Lord! In great strength!"

The horses were racing neck to neck. "And they come in good time, our salvation . . . !" Only half-consciously, he was spurring the little mare Minoh to greater endeavor, but this brash young man was still riding neck and neck with him. "And your charge, Zimri, the Lady Debrah . . . She is safe in Bethlehem, I trust?"

The rhythm of their horses' hooves, moving together at great speed now, had taken on a mutual cadence as they left the confines of the gorge. Behind them, Rekam, Remposar and Hasorar were whipping their mounts furiously in an endeavor to catch up, followed by their own horsemen and—far behind—the foot soldiers, with the pathetic wounded far, far in the rear and hoping that the battle would not be over before they got there. It was an army of desperately wounded men who, out of love for their commander, would not lie down and die.

Zimri shouted back, "Not in Bethlehem, Lord. But here on the field of battle with us! When last I saw her, she was riding in the foremost chariot with a sword raised above her head, so heavy she could hardly lift it, and she was shouting, *'Beladus!'* "

Swearing, Beladus spurred the little mare on. Falling behind now, Zimri shouted, "And several hundred Israelite horsemen, hard on her heels, were screaming out her name, Lord Beladus!"

None of them could keep up with him now. Swinging his sword like a madman, he drove through what was now the rear of the Philistine lines, and rode on, and saw his beloved Debrah, unbelievably, in the single chariot, with a shock-haired man he recognized at once as the unlovable Captain Libni of King Solomon's Palace Guard . . .

And all of the soldiers, charging down to do battle, were chanting over and over the one word: "Deb*rah*, Deb*rah*, Deb*rah*, Deb*rah*."

Debrah had seen him, too. She screamed: "Beladus . . . !" a long, drawn-out cry. She tore at the strap that held her in place and slipped the buckle open, and Libni shouted, "No, Debrah, no!"

His warning was too late. The chariot was bucking over the rough ground like a mad thing, first on one wheel and then on the other; and once free of the constricting belt she felt herself being thrown very forcibly up. She held on to the rail with both hands, and for a brief moment she felt that she was almost upended. Then the rail was torn from her hands and she fell to the ground. A wheel passed over her waist, and she scarcely felt the pain of it.

Libni was swinging the chariot furiously around as a brace of arrows thudded into the front shield and embedded themselves there. He shouted, "Trumpeter! Second unit into battle!"

The piercing note of the ram's horn sounded . . .

And now, the cavalry and then the infantry came over the crest of the hill, and a moment later, the thundering chariots; they bore down into the battle, and the cry was on their lips too: "Deb*rah*, Deb*rah*, Deb*rah*, Deb*rah* . . . !" a monotone of excited fury.

Beladus reined in Minoh and slipped from the saddle as the chariot came to an impatient halt beside them. He threw his arms around her and held her tightly, lovingly, and he whispered, "My love, my love, my dear wife . . . And what can I do with you in the heat of battle?" Libni had wrested the chariot to a halt and had leapt down to stand by them, his hard face transformed by a look of pure good humor.

Less than a hundred yards away from the three of them, the two armies had collided, and the air was filled with the clash of swords, the heavy clang of javelins on shields, the deadly hiss of fast-loosed arrows in such thick mass that they seemed to darken the sky. And still the chant went on: "De*brah*, De*brah*, De*brah* . . . !"

The great chaos of battle was very close to them, but now there was to be a *personal* confrontation.

Beladus glared at Libni, and he remembered only those strong hands at Debrah's young breasts, mauling, and his own anguished cry: *Give me your permission, Great Lord, and I will kill this man!*

Now, there was no King Solomon to order him to put up his sword, and the need for vengeance was heavy, strengthened by the fury all around him. He shouted, snarling now, "Libni! The so-called champion of the Israelites! In the heat of a great battle, draw your sword if you have the courage!"

He unsheathed his own, and Debrah screamed, "Beladus, no! He is my cousin . . . !"

Shocked, Beladus stared. He saw that Libni was laughing, a harsh soldier's face transformed by his pleasure. "Your cousin?" he echoed, and before Debrah could answer him Libni shouted happily, "My cousin, Lord Beladus, yes! We discovered it but a short while ago, and therefore . . . therefore, I embrace you as my family, too, all enmity behind us and forgotten!" He threw out his arms, and Beladus, bewildered, accepted the embrace.

Debrah was reaching out for both of them, and she

294

whispered, "My beloved husband, so dear to me . . . And my new-found cousin."

Beladus slipped his sword back into its scabbard and held her tightly. "My love," he whispered, "I am a soldier, and yet I find myself trembling, in fear of what might have been . . ."

The battle below them was drawing to a close. The chariots of the Twelfth Company had wrought havoc in the lines of the Philistines, and the very few left alive were fleeing the field. A young Israelite soldier was approaching them, shoving before him a bloodied and disarmed Tarson. He saluted Libni and said, "Their commander, Captain. If it is your wish that I kill him now . . . ?"

Libni smiled thinly. He turned to Beladus and said lightly, "Your prisoner, cousin. Shall we strike off his head?"

Beladus saw the look in Debrah's eyes. He turned to the young man. "Your name, soldier?"

"I am Mered, Lord, the son of Pallu of the tribe of Reuben."

"Then take his armor, Mered, strip him down to his loincloth. Turn him in the direction of Gaza and send him on his way, to report to his superiors that the forces of Akish have been destroyed. Let them no longer think to harass our convoys. For this will always be the inevitable result. Always."

"Your servant, Lord."

Debrah said, "And I return your sword to you, Mered." She reached into the chariot and handed it to him, and he dropped to one knee and said, "If it has served you well, Lady . . ."

"It has served me well, Mered, and I am grateful. It was a token. And it is with tokens that battles are won. I thank you."

The young boy took his sword and marched his prisoner off.

Libni turned to Beladus, smiling broadly. "It is well done," he said. "And you and I . . . once, we were enemies, and saved from mortal combat only by the wisdom of the great Solomon whom we both serve. But now, we are dear friends, and more—we are family. The battle is over, so will you then invite me to your camp? I have heard that it is a place of great luxury, a tent city that compares with Solomon's marble halls."

"Yes," Beladus said, "and you will be an honored guest . . ."

As he looked over the diminishing field of battle, his arm was tight around Debrah's waist, gripping her as though transfixed by a determination that she would never leave him again. In the far distance, the fine dust that hung in the air signified the Israelite chariots in pursuit of the last fleeing Philistines. "My camp, then, where the slaves will already be setting up the tents once more. It is a good day for all of us. My love is in my arms again . . ."

"My Beladus . . ." She wanted to rest her cheek against his chest, by the light breastplate that was burning in the heat of the sun.

"We will have a feast," Beladus said, "to celebrate this great victory. Zimri, and Nemuel, and Seria will prepare it for us . . ."

Debrah could not meet his eyes. "Seria," she whispered, "is dead."

His fierce eyes were wide with shock. "Seria, dead?"

She told him what had happened, and his eyes were moist. "Seria," he said, "and Helah. Two of our most devoted servants."

She gasped. "Helah, too?" The tears were streaming down her cheeks.

"Yes, and Helah, too," Beladus said somberly. "And though I avenged her by killing Akish . . . it is very small consolation for the loss of so young and lovely a life."

"You slew the great Akish?" She gripped him fiercely, trembling. "When they brought us news that he was lying there dead, I was sure that it was you . . ."

296

"Yes. I cut off his head and hurled it into their lines to show my contempt for them."

She was silent, remembering her great fear of him, the look in his greedy, demanding eyes when he had mauled her so brutally. And now . . . Akish was dead. And Helah was dead, and Seria was dead. She cried out in anguish, "Must there always be so much of hatred in this world of ours?"

The battlefield was empty. There were shells of bodies everywhere, their blood draining into the thirsty sand. Wherever they bled, vincas and wild poppies would grow, the seeds long dormant in the hot earth and only awaiting nourishment to flower bravely, if only for a very short time, as though to show that life, in one form or another, went on.

Libni, staring at the bluff, murmured, "I fear that my chariot will not climb those tracks. A horse then . . ." He called Molid to him and gave him orders, and Beladus summoned Rekam and said to him: "I leave you in charge here, good friend, and I thank you for the good work you have done. The wounded in litters, carried with the greatest care . . ."

"Of course. It is being done now."

"The Philistine armor and weapons to be divided between our forces and those of the Israelites, in a ration of five to them, and one to us." He looked at Libni. "Agreed, friend?"

Libni was laughing and shaking his head. "We were indeed five times your number, but let the division be equal, to signify the equality of our esteem for each other."

"A generous offer, and I thank you for it." He turned back to Rekam. "Take good care of Hasorar, he is badly hurt . . ."

"And a very stubborn man. He refuses a litter."

"When all has been done that must be done, join us with the rest of the officers."

"We will do so."

Beladus mounted his mare, and placed his beloved Debrah on the saddle ahead of him. He looked at his new-found friend Libni and said, "Come. Let us return to the bluff that is our home."

16

The slaves had indeed already reerected most of the tents.

From their secure bluff, they had watched—very fearfully at first—the great panorama of the fighting below them. And when the Israelite army had arrived over the brow of the hill there had been a wild, wild cheering from them; they, too, were Israelites, save the five Phoenician women whom Remposar had brought from Tyre. They had broken out the wineskins, ostensibly in readiness for the returning victors but doing a great deal of tasting themselves to make sure that it was good. The seniors among them had called for some sort of order to the delirium, and they had gone to work with great gusto setting the camp to rights again.

Now, the elements of the Phoenician army were struggling painfully up the tracks, the slaves and the women above them lining the cliff and applauding them in great excitement.

Some of the troops, laughing with relief from certain death, were even feigning a mock anger because they had not defeated the hated Philistines unaided, and all of them were boasting of their achievements, shouting from one to another along the paths:

"A great shame, is it not, that those damned Israelites did not arrive just a few hours later? They would have found us victorious on a field of dead savages . . ."

"Ah, but they were led by the great Lady Debrah . . ."

"And she is one of us now, a Phoenician lady . . ."

"I slew seven of them myself, and as I charged toward another seven, a foreign chariot drove in and robbed me of my satisfaction . . ."

"The stench of their corpses is like that of camel dung. Why is it that a Philistine smells almost as bad dead as he does when he's alive . . . ?"

"Mirhapi . . . ! There is blood at your thighs, did they cut off your balls . . . ?"

"Who saw me strike off two heads with one blow of my sword, who saw it . . . ?"

A happy group of weary warriors staggered over the lip of the cliff, and the women were all there to greet them, showering them with kisses and promising their favors. Even those on stretchers seemed to have their spirits lifted by the show of affection, though sometimes the smiles were on faces that were wet with women's tears; some of the wounded were in a shocking state.

But it was a time, nonetheless, for great rejoicing. Libni said, "Beladus, by your leave, a suggestion?"

Beladus turned to him, smiling. He was beginning to like this impetuous young man. "Of course, friend Libni. *Cousin* and friend!"

"The matter of your sentries . . ."

"We remain well guarded, as always."

"No! Permit me to say that your men have earned a respite from their labors and their anxieties. My army, below us, will return to Jerusalem when their work is done and the division of spoils is completed, save only my own bodyguard, which numbers fifty good men. Awaiting my return, they will patrol the base of the bluff. You have no need of sentries." Libni was laughing; it was not a very military concept, and he knew it.

Beladus hesitated; but many of the soldiers had heard Libni's words, and their expectant eyes were on him. He shouted, "Officers and soldiers, hear me! It seems that for the space of . . . of some hours, we are

300

protected by the Israelites whom we came here to protect! So be it, then! For the rest of the day . . . All sentries, guards, and patrols are relieved of their duties. First, the wounded will be cared for and made as comfortable as possible. There will be a period of rest till the sun goes down. And then . . . a night of feasting, of wine and women! It is to be a night of celebration of a great victory for us, a splendid victory in which, it must be said . . ." He paused, his eyes dancing with amusement, and went on, "It must be admitted that our allies the Israelites were of some slight assistance to us."

A great cheer went up from the men, and Beladus held up his hands for silence. When the noise died down, he shouted, "And if there be one man among you so sorely wounded that he cannot fill his belly with good wine and cannot accept the ministrations of a young girl, then he is not . . . he is not a *Phoenician!*"

The cheering was deafening.

His arm tight about his love, Beladus walked to his tent. He stood aside courteously for Libni to enter, and the young Israelite captain looked around him in wonder, marveling at the hanging drapes, the splendid furnishings, the beautiful carpet covering almost all of the floor. He said amiably, "So this is how the Phoenicians live . . ."

"Nothing in the world," Beladus said equably, "is more readily available to a demanding man than a degree of comfort . . ." He raised the tent flap again and shouted, "A slave to help us with our armor! And let her bring wine!"

He turned back and said, "We will drink together now, Libni, to cement our friendship. And when the sun goes down, we will feast. Till then, I will have a tent prepared for you to sleep in after the efforts of the day. And you will, of course, stay with us for as long as you can, an honored guest to share our happiness."

"You are most kind. I welcome the hospitality of a man I once would have killed."

"Or been killed by . . . But now, we will be friends for ever more." Beladus embraced him and said gravely, "I have much to thank you for, Libni. Only a few hours ago, when I saw the great odds that we faced, I was sure that the end had come. I was angry with our gods because I thought they had deserted me in my time of need. Had I died, I was determined to challenge the god Melqarth himself to personal combat, to punish him for ending our great love after so short a time. I was prepared to say to him: die, great god, because you took my Debrah from me."

"I would have joined you," Debrah whispered, "at my own hand."

"Yes, I know it . . ."

The tent flap opened, and a young girl stood there with a wineskin in her hand. She let the goats' hair drop behind her, and said very softly, "I am Orpah, Lord, come to serve you in whatever fashion I may."

Beladus stared at her. She was quite short and stubby, with very full breasts and rounded hips and a quite incredibly narrow waist, almost the shape of the hourglass that the Assyrians used. Her smooth skin was the color of freshly picked almonds that had not yet turned to their natural light brown. She had a sweet round face with rather small but very dark bright eyes, and unbelievably long black hair that hung down her back almost to her waist, a great shining mass of it. Altogether, she was a very dramatic little creature, her breasts upstanding and firm, and set very wide apart. A wisp of that long black hair had fallen in front of her shoulder, caressing a dark nipple.

Beladus said, "Orpah? I do not think I have seen you before. And by the color of your skin, you are what, an Edomite?"

She laughed, showing strong white teeth that were not in the least decayed, though she must have been at least fourteen or fifteen years old. "An Edomite?" she echoed. "No, Lord, not one of those dreadful people!

302

But a daughter of Moab, a Moabite from the desert beyond the Dead Sea!"

"Ah yes, I should have known. And have you been long with us, child?"

"Ten days only, Great Lord." Her voice was melodious and very sweet to listen to. "I came here from Zoar, where the Brook of Zered meets the Salt Sea. My father sold me to a trader to pay off a debt, twelve cubits of cloth he could not pay for."

"And your age, Orpah, if you know it? Some fourteen years, I would say?"

She laughed again, a very happy young girl. "Fourteen? But no, Lord! I know my age, my father told me, and he was a very learned man. I have always known my age. I am eleven now, and I have been a woman for two years. A neighbor sat me on his knees when I was nine years old, my thighs spread about his, and made a woman of me."

"And you are happy here, Orpah?"

She nodded eagerly. "How could I not be happy here, Great Lord? And shall I pour wine now?"

"Yes, we will have wine now, Orpah. And then, you will help Captain Libni here with his armor."

"Your slave, Great Lord . . ."

She filled their beakers and set down the wineskin, and began unfastening the straps of Libni's armor; and she was chatting away, just like Seria. "You know, Great Lord, about our forefather Moab? After the destruction of Sodom and Gomorrah, the two daughters of Lot seduced their father when he was drunk, and one of them gave birth to Moab, who was to become a great leader and the head of his tribe. Lot himself was the nephew of Abraham, who came from Ur of the Chaldeans in the Valley of the Euphrates . . ."

Beladus said wearily, "Orpah! If you are to serve me well, it is necessary that you know . . . I will listen to your idle chatter, the persiflage of women is sometimes comforting. But use restraint, child!"

"Yes, Lord." Libni's armor was removed and hung on a copper nail in a tent pole, and she moved lithely to take off Beladus's breastplate. "It was Saul," she said, "who first conquered my people of Moab, and then his son David, who was the father of Solomon. It is necessary that you know these things. Shall I remove your robe and loincloth, Great Lord?"

"No. Go to the slave's corner now."

Rekam had arrived with Remposar, standing by the raised flap of the tent. And as they entered, Rekam held out, with both hands, a heavy Philistine sword, held horizontally across his body in its scabbard.

He said quietly, "From the battlefield, Beladus. The sword of the evil Akish."

In a moment of acute silence, Baladus took it from him and drew it from its sheath. For a moment, he stared at it, held horizontally, and he whispered, "For Helah, and for Seria, and for my wife Debrah." He brought up his knee and smashed the blade down across his strong thigh, breaking it in two.

He strode to the entrance and lifted the flap, and hurled the pieces far out. When he returned, he smiled, as though ashamed of his sudden emotion, and said quietly, "Remposar, the victory feast . . . Is it in hand?"

"In hand indeed, Beladus. We have lamb meat cooked on swords over flaming coals in great quantity, with lentils, beans, onions, leeks, cucumbers . . . And pomegranates and figs, and wine flowing like water."

"And the bread, Rekam, who will bake the bread? It should be Keturah, hers is the best."

Rekam smiled drily, "Unhappily, Keturah is a very beautiful woman, and much in demand tonight. She is also deeply moved by the suffering of the wounded, and she moves from one to another of them, taking their seed by whatever means she can contrive into her receptive body. I spoke with her, about the bread, you understand, and she said to me fiercely, 'I will not bake bread! I have other talents, too! And this day, I have

304

taken more than forty of your wounded! Before the sun sets, I will take forty more! And before it rises again, another hundred, if need be! When my lips close over theirs, they forget their agony for a few brief moments. *This* is my duty now! Not bread!' These were her words. And so, other women, who can find the time, will bake the bread."

"So be it, then. And the men?"

"The men have chosen not to wait for sundown. They have begun their feast already."

"Good. I will join them soon, perhaps, and give them the thanks they deserve."

Orpah, well taught, was already filling and refilling his beaker, and Beladus, already a little drunk, shouted, "This shall be a night we will all remember!" He turned to Libni. "And for you, dear friend, you shall have your pick of the Tyrian ladies. There is one among them I recommend to you strongly, her name is Adri . . . Adru . . ."

"Adruphet," Remposar said, beaming. "She is my sister, Lord Libni, a lady of great quality and beauty."

"And her breasts," Beladus said. "They are the shape of small pears, almost as hard and yet soft to the touch, quite exquisite."

"Ah . . ." Libni raised his beaker. "Then I drink to your health, Beladus, to the health of the ladies of Tyre, and to the health of all the Phoenicians, who are our friends!"

"And to you," Beladus responded, "and to all the Israelites, who are our friends too. Let this day live forever in our memories!"

They drank together, boisterously, and Beladus said at last, "A tent, then, Remposar, for our friend and cousin Libni, so that he may rest awhile after his endeavors and store up his energies for the feast, or lose them in the arms of beautiful women, as he desires. See that he has a foot bath of hot, scented water, see that he has Adruphet to serve him, with a slave girl, too, in

305

case he should need her services. And when the sun goes down, we will feast together."

In a very short time, Debrah was left alone with Beladus.

There was only the slave girl Orpah, only recently assigned to her new duties and a little unsure of them. She was crouched in the slave's corner of the huge tent, watching carefully and ready to move should she be wanted, as Debrah slipped off Beladus's robe and kilt. And when he was naked, the sweat of battle still glistening on his rippling torso, he in his turn removed her long gown and held her tightly to him, crushing her breasts against his manly chest, a hand at the back of her head as she looked up lovingly into his handsome eyes. The hand moved down over her shoulders and the small of her back, and on to her buttocks, pressing them into him so that she could feel his throbbing.

"My love," he whispered. "I was so close to losing you for ever."

"I would have joined you, at once, in the afterlife. We would have been together again."

"Yes. But the pleasures we know of now are better than those of heaven."

"I am sure of it."

Her hands were stroking his back, and the fingernails began to rake him now as the emotion built up inside her; that strong muscularity, pulsating against the soft flesh of her stomach, was more than she could bear. She sank down on the soft sheepskins and reached for him, but he dropped to his knees on the carpet and whispered, "Other pleasures first . . . Lie still, close your eyes, imagine that we are indeed in heaven."

He covered her body with little kisses, and his fingertips were moving over her like little breaths of air, brittle touches that brought her to the edge of hysteria. His lips were feasting on her, and she moaned, very softly, writhing under his skilled caresses. At last, he called out quietly, "Orpah . . . ?"

The young slave girl rose quickly to her feet in her

dark corner. This, she was sure, was the moment she had been told to wait for. She unfastened her loincloth and dropped it to the ground, and went to them, naked, to crouch beside Beladus on her knees. She saw that he was very strong, and she touched him lightly and whispered, "Whatever is your desire, Lord. I am very young, but I have been well taught."

Beladus said gently, "Not now, Orpah. Later, without a doubt, I will enjoy you, but not now. In the box by the table there, you will find flasks of perfumed oil. Bring me the myrrh oil."

"At once, Great Lord."

He had not taken his eyes from his beloved Debrah. As he stroked her long limbs, he heard the heavy chest being opened, and the tinkling sound of the bottles as Orpah searched. He could smell the strong perfumes as she opened one little stoppered glass bottle after another. She brought it to him at last, a small amphora made of exquisitely striated Phoenician glass, filled with a dark and heavy oil, reddish in color, that gave off the sweet scent of cedarwood. "Cup your hand," he said quietly, "and pour a little into your palm. It is for me."

Orpah knelt beside him and filled the hollow of her child's hand with it. She set aside the amphora carefully, and rubbed her hands together, and began to massage him with it slowly, trembling with her own desire as she felt the great strength of him. She whispered, "It does not burn, Lord?"

"A little. The burning is good."

Her hands were very small and soft around him, and in a little while he said softly, "Enough. Return to your corner now."

"Yes, Great Lord." She moved silently away, and Beladus stretched himself out beside Debrah; her breath was coming fast as she waited. He rolled over and lay between her white thighs, and took her wrists and held them above her head as he entered her, slowly and tenderly, then with increasing force. She gasped at

307

the unexpected heat, and thrust herself up to meet him, seeking desperately to contain more and more of him. She cried out, "My love, my love, my love . . ."

He buried his face at her breast and whispered, "All that I can ever desire, in this world or the next, is here in my arms."

Their bodies were joined, fused together as one; and when at last the explosions came for them, he collapsed on her and they lay still together, wrapped in each other's arms and knowing there could be no greater happiness anywhere than in this close embrace.

There was a great and very satisfying surprise in store for Captain Beladus.

Shortly before the sun went down, he was sleeping in Debrah's arms as, wide awake and craving his love, she toyed with him, sweeping her perfumed hair across his loins to arouse him yet again. In his sleep, he was murmuring soft words of endearment to her, only half-conscious of the warmth and the moisture, when Remposar burst impulsively into the tent.

Covered in confusion, he pulled up short, and Debrah drew a sheepskin over their naked bodies. He stammered, "Your pardon, Lady, it seems that my visit is untimely. But there is no sentry to forbid entry, and so . . . Will you forgive me?"

"Of course." She reached for her gown and slipped it over her head, and Beladus awoke as Orpah hurried to him with a robe. He rubbed the sleep from his eyes and took in the fading light. "What, already? The feast is upon us, and I have hardly slept for a minute."

He could hear the sounds of the slaves outside, setting up the table and the benches, clattering the dishes as they made their preparations. "And Libni?" he asked. "We have not, I trust, neglected the welfare of our honored guest?"

"Captain Libni," Remposar said happily, "is asleep in the avid clutches of my sister Adruphet, with a slave woman named Nehushta beside them. But there is greater news for you, Captain. Juntus is here from Tyre!"

"What, *Juntus?*" He was instantly on his feet and wide awake, as Orpah eased the robe around him, tying the sash and dropping to her knees to fasten the gold-embroidered sandals. He said happily, "Good news indeed . . ."

"He is waiting outside, Beladus. If I may bring him in?"

"Of course, and at once! My half-brother, a man who is very dear to me, bring him!"

He was a tall, slender, and distinguished-looking man, much older than Beladus, gray-haired, gray-bearded, with a deep, booming voice. Everything he said was *shouted*, as though it was of the greatest possible importance and had to be heard (which was not always so). He stood by the entrance with his arms outstretched, and shouted, "Beladus!"

"Juntus! A happy day for both of us!"

The two men embraced and kissed each other, and Beladus said, "In the name of Melquarth, what brings you here? What momentous events have caused you to leave the comfort of your Tyrian villa for the arid hills they call mountains here?"

"Why, to see my young half-brother, of course, before the Gods call him to account for all of his impiety, what else?"

"And I am glad of it . . ."

"And to bring you great news. But first . . ."

He turned to Debrah, and boomed, "Word was brought to me that you had taken an Israelite woman to wife. This, no doubt, is she?"

"My beloved wife Debrah," Beladus said, "whom I love with more passion than I can find for life itself. And this . . . my half-brother Juntus, who is very dear to me."

Juntus took both her hands and said slyly, "A woman of rare beauty, Beladus! If she brings you only half the pleasure I derive from looking at her . . ." He would not let go of her hands. "A dove! And you are happy with her?"

"Beyond imagining."

"Remember always to whip her when she does not satisfy you."

"You are wise, as always."

"And the concubines I sent you, they please you, too?"

"Er . . . yes, they please me too, and I am grateful."

"Good. And I see a well-filled wine flask there, being put to no use. Have you forgotten the graces I taught you, Beladus?"

"They are not forgotten," Beladus said, laughing. "Orpah! Wine, at once!"

She hurried forward. "Yes, Lord. Your servant." Beladus turned back to his half-brother as she poured. "And your journey here, it was comfortable, I trust?"

"The ship to Joppa was tolerable, no more than that. From Joppa here . . . I do not like horses. And close by, I passed through the field of a recent battle, which Remposar here tells me took place this very day. More than a thousand Philistines, he said."

"A slight exaggeration of their numbers, but they were indeed Philistines."

"Dreadful people. I like them even less than I like horses. And I learn too that you slew the notorious Akish in personal combat. I am proud of you, Beladus."

Beladus shrugged. "Others will come, unhappily," he said, "the fight will go on for all eternity. But you spoke of great news . . ."

"Ah, yes . . . Well, when word came of your marriage, I was with King Hiram, whom the gods preserve and so forth . . ."

"And he was angry?"

"Angry? Ha! He was delighted!"

Juntus sat down on a sheepskin chair and took the beaker of wine that Orpah offered him. He patted her bare breast and said happily, "Ah, such splendid rotundity, delicious!" He drank deeply and said, "Where was I?"

Beladus sighed. "At Hiram's court."

"Ah yes. The king said, and these were his very words: 'So Beladus has taken an Israelite to wife, and thereby shown a wisdom worthy of Solomon himself, a great sacrifice to cement still further an alliance which is very profitable for me. I am pleased.' Those were his words."

" 'A wisdom worthy of Solomon?' " Beladus echoed, awed, and Juntus shrugged. "A trifling compliment," he said. "Hiram knows, as we all do, that Solomon is a fool."

"No! Not a fool, brother Juntus . . ."

"But he is! Can he build a palace? No, he cannot even build a miserable hovel with anything but clay bricks. Can he construct a ship? No, if he built it, it would sink at once! Can he carve cedarwood or work with beaten gold? Of course not! No, for all of these things he has to hire Phoenicians, and it costs him dearly. Every time King Hiram says so many shekels for this, so many talents for that, Solomon eagerly agrees, not even haggling, and this is not the attitude of a wise man. He has beggared himself and his country with his extravagances! He has kept his realm safe by bedding the daughters of his enemies and thus making them his friends. Yes, I suppose there is a kind of limited wisdom there . . . But wisdom, dear Beladus, is in a man's head, not between his legs."

"There will be a guest at our feast tonight," Beladus said dryly, "one Captain Libni. I beg of you, do not voice these sentiments in his presence, or he will strike off your head and I will be obliged to kill him."

"Discretion," Juntus shouted, "was always one of my greater virtues! But the rest of the news . . ." He held out his beaker for more wine, and as Orpah poured it for him he slipped a hand under her kilt to feel her thighs. "Ah . . ." he said. He drank deeply and turned his attention back to Beladus.

311

"It is the king's command," he said clearly, "that you return with me to Tyre. In your absence, the commander-in-chief of the Palace Guard has died, of the Egyptian sickness, and you are to take his place."

Beladus could only stare. "To Tyre?" he whispered. "As *commander-in-chief*?"

"The king said to me, 'Juntus, I have misjudged your brother sorely, and I wish to make amends. Bring him home, together with his Israelite wife, so that I may enjoy both his protection and his good company.' Great honor awaits you, Beladus, and honor, too, for all of our house, the House of Tirgan."

"To return home . . ." Beladus breathed. He took Debrah's hands fervently and said, "And you, my love? Could you be happy in Tyre? It is a splendid city."

She threw her arms around him passionately. "Oh, my love . . . To be wherever you are, it is all that I desire . . ."

"Moreover," Juntus said, "King Hiram wishes me to express to you his great satisfaction with the work you have done. And this, mark you, before he has heard that Akish, who has been a dreadful trial to him, is dead! When *this* news reaches him . . . ! You can be assured of a hero's welcome, Beladus! King Hiram suggests that before you leave, you might care to promote Hasorar to captain to take your place here."

"Yes, of course. He is a brave and capable soldier."

"Though I heard he had been badly wounded. Will he live?"

"Hasorar," Beladus said drily, "is too stubborn a man to die before his time. And when he hears of his promotion, he will be on his feet in an instant."

"And how long will it take you to hand over your command to him?"

"Two days, no more."

"Excellent. Tomorrow, I must pay a courtesy call on King Solomon, if I am sober, which I hope not to be." He sighed. "The king has ordered me to remind him of certain debts that remain unpaid, three months of wagers on unsolved riddles. So perhaps we should admit that Solomon is a wise man after all, since he prefers not to discharge his obligations too eagerly . . . So in three days, can we leave for a homeland I already pine for?"

"Three days it shall be."

Beladus could not contain the sense of elation that was sweeping over him. He looked at Debrah's shining eyes and saw her excitement, and he took her in his arms and whispered, "My cup of happiness has never been so full, not since the day you decided to become my wife."

"Oh, Beladus . . ."

Juntus coughed loudly, as though more important things were on his mind. "There is a feast, you said," he boomed, "a victory feast. Shall I have time to refresh myself? To scrape the dust of travel from my weary limbs? Or are your courtesies truly forgotten in this savage land?"

Beladus broke away from Debrah and laughed. "Not forgotten," he said. "The feast, Remposar?"

Remposar leaped to his feet. "The sun is down on a momentous day," he said, "and soon, they will light the flares. In an hour or so, it will be ready. There will be six officers, including our two guests, and out of deference to the Lord Juntus, I have taken the liberty of asking the Phoenician ladies to join us."

"Good. Then you have time, Juntus, for what you wish to do."

"Then you will, of course, take care of my creature comforts, too?" Juntus said happily. "I have not lain with a woman for a week—there were none at all on that damned ship—and for the rest of the journey . . ." He sighed. "At my age, copulation on horseback is a pleasure long since denied me."

"Then you shall have your pick of the women in the camp. Perhaps from among the Phoenician women you sent me? A breath of our homeland to refresh you?"

Juntus shook his head, frowning over this weighty

matter. "No," he said, "what use is travel if a man is to drink only the wines of his own country?" His avid eyes were on the young Orpah, and he said, "An Israelite girl, I think?"

"A Moabite," Beladus said, "from beyond the Dead Sea."

"Ah! Even more exotic!"

"My own personal slave, Juntus, though she is new and I have not yet savored her. And she is yours. Remposar! A tent for my honorable brother!"

"At once." Remposar put aside his beaker. "Lord Juntus, if you will come with me?"

Orpah was already moving to them, and her eyes were alight with pleasurable expectancy. She had been listening and watching, and she liked this handsome and boisterous old man; she was already thinking of the ways she could devise to please him.

Beladus said to her gently, "Go with him, Orpah. Bathe his feet in water that has been heated, soothe his body with oils, for he has traveled very far. Comfort him as you would comfort me."

"An honor, Great Lord," Orpah whispered. "I will serve him well, in all things."

"And when the feast is ready," Juntus said, "should I still be lost in the abyss of those lovely thighs, I beg of you . . . Send for me and drag me, screaming, from her embrace. I will be hungry for good food and drink, too."

Orpah said to him brightly, "One of my ancestors was named Juntu, which is the same as Juntus, is it not? As a young man of eighteen years, he slew the champion Sasu of the Midianites."

Juntus held a contented arm around her, his hand cupping a bronzed and resilient and very rounded breast as they went out with Remposar, and she was saying happily, "Juntu, too, was a very handsome man, by all repute. He was not rich, but he had five wives, and it was a matter of honor for him to satisfy each one

314

of them every night. He died very young, but he was well remembered in his tribe . . ."

The tent flap dropped behind them, and they were alone again.

He put his strong arms around her slender waist and crushed her to him. "It will be a more tranquil life for you," he whispered, "with no fears of battle, a richer, fuller life."

"With you beside me . . . And is it truly so beautiful in your country?"

He said, smiling, "More beautiful than you can imagine. Tyre is a small island, very close to the shore and quite ancient, an island fortress of great and stimulating vitality. It is a city of stone buildings with wide porticoes that look out over a calm sea the color of beaten, polished iron. From the verandahs of my house you can see the sailing vessels floating silently by, laden with ivory, sandalwood, peacocks, and spices from Ophir and the land of Sheba. A man can dream his life away watching those peaceful ships, transported in his mind to shores so remote that they cannot be imagined! There are flowers and good fruit everywhere, and the trees are tall and green, not gray and struggling for survival as they are in this harsh and arid land, but nourished by deep rivers and streams that come down from distant, snow-capped mountains that are dotted with great cedars . . . Our arts and crafts are highly developed, our sculptures, glassware, engraved bronzes and gems the finest in the world, and we spin a cloth there, sometimes dyed purple with the heads of sea snails and fashioned into stuff so fragile that it clings to the body of a beautiful woman and makes her, fully clothed, appear naked in all of her glory! Yes, you will be happy there . . ."

"I desire only your love, it is enough . . ."

As he was speaking, he was slowly removing her robe and his, and he whispered, "We have a little time for the pleasures that, I am sure, are already driving Juntus to distraction."

315

They lay together on the deep bed and loved each other, and when the shouting and the laughter outside told them that the guests were making their appearance, they dressed each other and went out to join them.

Debrah looked around at the excited faces, flushed with fervor, and knew that their happiness was for her—Libni, Juntus, Rekam, Remposar, the new captain-to-be Hasorar, and the five Phoenician concubines in their finest dresses . . . There was a little break in her heart at the thought of leaving them; but Beladus's hand was holding hers tightly, and all was well.

Two days, she was thinking, and we go to a distant land of dreams, far from this desert I have always called my home; with the man I love so dearly and who returns my love . . . for a new and wondrous life, together.